THE STRAIT

A NOVEL

DOM STASI

WILDBLUE
PRESS

WildBluePress.com

THE STRAIT published by:

WILDBLUE PRESS
P.O. Box 102440
Denver, Colorado 80250

WILDBLUE PRESS is registered at the U.S. Patent and Trademark Offices.

ISBN 978-1-948239-13-4   Trade Paperback
ISBN 978-1-948239-12-7   eBook

Interior Formatting by Elijah Toten
www.totencreative.com

THE STRAIT

For Gloria: my muse, my joy, my wife

"Unable to make what is just strong, we made what is strong just." - Blaise Pascal

-PROLOGUE-

Something was wrong.

But the airplane was old. She'd grown tired. Wrong was her prerogative.

Tonight, though, as she roared her way northward above a coal black sea, something was *deadly* wrong, and her pilot, Swede Bergstrom knew it. What Swede didn't know was *why* he knew it.

So, caressing the controls, he flew on, clinging to his knowledge of the old plane's virtues, knowing too that those less enlightened, need only look to the polished metal of her perfect nose. For there, in paint baked brown by 70 summers, once-golden words still whispered her glorious name: Queen of the Southern Sky.

But nostalgia could not temper Bergstrom's growing unease and he began to feel imprisoned by the old plane's musty cockpit, constrained as well by his clothing: the threadbare flying suit, the GI jacket, its collar stained dark by the oily blonde hair that brushed his broad shoulders.

Seemingly of its own accord, Swede's hand moved to the jacket's right breast where a solitary splash of color—an embroidered crest—depicted a winged sword soaring above the gilded words TACTICAL AIR COMMAND. The crest, like the soiled garment to which it clung, was a vestige of better days, horrible days to be sure, yet better somehow than these.

But, Swede found small solace in gilded words and titles. There was just the wind now, that and the starless sky. It was an angry sky, whose mournful wail pierced the Queen's weathered seams driving Bergstrom to the brink of an ever-lurking madness.

Confused, angry, growing desperate, he knew the time had come.

Reaching into the knapsack beside his seat, Swede retrieved the bag of white powder. Tucking the bag into his jacket, he pulled the zipper tight across his barrel chest.

Returning to the knapsack, he found the razor-knife and carefully worked its point between the fingertip and nail of his left hand's middle finger. His breathing coarse, his every muscle tensed, he clenched his eyes and pushed, sinking the little blade to its hilt.

Extracting the knife, he dropped it back into the knapsack, finding now the glassine envelope. Ripping its seal, he removed the contents: a tiny black and gold monolith.

Gripping the object between his teeth, he raised the ravaged finger to his mouth and carefully slid the centimeter-long monolith into the incision, forcing it downward, into the gash until it disappeared beneath the finger's cold skin.

His promise kept, he jammed the throttles forward and climbed.

Upward through the darkness, man and machine finally burst free. Brilliant moonlight blazed across a sea of white as the clouds fell away beneath the airplane's wings, and Swede Bergstrom tumbled and burned and died in those clouds as his Queen exploded around him.

PART ONE

- CHAPTER 1 -

Jake Silver inched his way across the dimly lit bedroom of his Manhattan apartment.

Stopping by the bed, his eyes were drawn to the woman's prone form, and beyond to the far nightstand where a pair of champagne flutes—one on its side, the other upright, its silhouette clear through the tiny garment flung over its mouth–recalled visions of an evening well spent.

And, though the night had been special, it had not yet occurred to Jake that it was the first during which his sleep, however brief, had not suffered the nightmare and its aftermath. That this gutsy woman had chosen to remain by his side, would serve as adequate good fortune for the moment. Though they'd known one another a mere 36 hours, Jake felt an uncommon affinity for Sandy McRea.

The bedroom was comfortably warm against the crisp autumn dawn, so *Cassandra*—as the decidedly unaffected Ms. McRea would soon become known—had let the bedclothes slip below her waist. Jake made no move to raise them, but instead allowed his eyes to wash slowly over his new lover's sculpted upper back, indulge the ivory sweep of torso, the narrow waist, the sensual, summoning breadth of hips laid bare by the retreating folds of linen.

He wanted to wake her, lift her to him. But he knew she'd need her rest if only to survive the upcoming day of job interviews at what seemed every ad agency in town. So Jake ever-so-gently moved an amber curl away from her face and bent to softly kiss her cheek.

Opening one eye, Sandy smiled sleepily. "Is it morning already?"

"Not for you. Not yet." He adjusted her blankets.

Reaching up to touch his face, she said, "You slept well, peacefully."

"I was tired. Can't imagine why," he teased.

"Well, you think about it," she countered, suppressing a mischievous grin, hoping he'd find himself able to think of little else.

Both eyes open now, she girded her courage and asked, "Will I see you again?"

"We both know that answer," he whispered, pleased as much by her candor as her interest. "I'm flying back tomorrow night. We'll put on our big-boy pants and celebrate your success."

"Success?" she laughed. "I haven't landed anything yet."

"You will," Jake said. "You're beautiful, brilliant, *and* talented."

"Right," she yawned, a hint of cynicism aimed less at the choice than the order of his words. "Maybe the last two qualities will carry the day for once."

Their faces nearly touching, Jake understood the distraction such a face as Sandy's might impose upon a hapless interviewer of either gender, especially those unable to see the aspiring artist as anything other than an "aging" ingénue. He smiled. "I've seen your renderings, kiddo. Those drawings are gonna knock 'em dead."

With that bit of encouragement, they shared one long and lingering last kiss before Jake playfully pushed Sandy's distracting face into the overstuffed pillow, teasing, "Now, stop pointing that thing at me, or I'll never get out of here. I'll see you tomorrow night... and remember, big boy pants."

They exchanged a smile, she closed her eyes, and Jake turned to leave.

Suddenly, in wrenching contrast to the moment, he recalled the horror and the visions that had overwhelmed him two nights past. As he stood in the doorway, his back to the bedroom, vivid images of the recurring dream shattered his idyllic morning.

Once again the specter emerged and walked toward him. Once again he saw its wet garments, its shredded hand beckoning, looming, horribly cold as it drew near. But this time, like no other time, the hand had touched his face. With no little embarrassment, Jake recalled how he'd awakened then to pitch his sweaty, shaking, combat-veteran's fit, all of it playing out before the wide-eyed and terrified Sandy.

Now, a full day and night later, Jake tried to shake the memory as he turned back to have one last, bittersweet look at the extraordinary person still sharing his bed, and despite himself, despite the nightmares and learned caution, despite Sandy's earlier terror, despite all of it, he allowed himself to feel the rush of new romance.

Stepping back into the bedroom, Jake picked up a pen from the nightstand, and scribbled a few words of endearment, along with an admonition—his second—that Sandy use the apartment for her remaining few days in New York. He closed with a promise to call when he got to LA.

Tucking the note under his alarm clock, he also left a key.

It meant taking things another step, leaving that key. But, he clearly cared for this woman, eight years his junior. He wanted her to feel at home at his place, safe, comfortable, naked, but most of all *here* when he returned.

Setting the key atop the note, he checked the night table drawer. His pistol was there. Sandy, who liked to call herself a country girl, should have found that New York made her nervous. Since it didn't, that made Jake nervous. So, and since this Iowan knew how to handle a weapon, he'd decided to leave the gun out of its locker for her quick access.

With slight apprehension, he slid the drawer closed, and left the apartment.

It was slightly past 6:00 a.m. when Jake stepped from the building's lobby and into a fast-building rain shower.

A few cabs drifted by. None were available.

Then, just as he turned back for the shelter of the lobby and was about to ping Uber, a medallion taxi pulled up to the curb, discharging a man.

His hat pulled down against the weather, the guy left the cab's door ajar while gesturing for Jake to do the same with the apartment building's door. On impulse, Jake obliged, but regretted his rote courtesy the moment the stranger disappeared into the building. Uttering a muffled, "Dammit," Jake ran for the cab.

"Airport this morning?" the cabbie asked, recognizing Jake's uniform.

"Yeah, JFK," Jake responded, absent mindedly while looking back and making a mental note to find a new place, one with a doorman.

As the cab wove its way east through an awakening Central Park, Jake peered from the window, impressed by the number of people out jogging so early on so dismal a morning.

He recalled having once shown similar discipline as a light heavyweight boxer in New York's Golden Gloves.

Always disdainful of bullies and bullying, young Jake had found amateur boxing a sensible outlet for his adolescent-male aggressiveness. What began as an outlet grew to an avocation he'd later carry into intercollegiate competition. But despite his emerging pugilistic promise, everything changed when, in the final second of the final round of an otherwise unexceptional bout, a blow to the head caused Jake's vision to flood white.

And though he'd neither gone down, nor lost consciousness his clearest recollection was of a doctor shining a light into his eyes as he sat on his stool in a corner of the ring while the referee raised his opponent's hand in triumph.

Given that the study of head trauma to athletes was in its infancy, Jake was simply declared fit, sent on his way and no medical record established. Only later did he learn that following the blow, he'd continued throwing punches despite that the bell had rung and his opponent had returned to his own corner as the crowd roared with laughter. The revelation so disturbed and embarrassed Jake that he'd never climbed into a ring again.

So, these days, Jake Silver liked to boast that he kept his fitness regimen limited to the rigor of chewing an occasional airline steak.

To the annoyance of some male colleagues, Jake's cynicism was not entirely without motive. A darkly handsome six-footer, he was among those fortunate few who need put forth little more than a shave (and what his airline considered a too-infrequent haircut) to maintain his masculine good looks. In fact, the only thing at which Jake seemed to toil was the public projection of himself as the carefree New York bachelor: a less-than-accurate image, yet one he did little to assuage.

Because, to Jake's mind, despite his entreaties that Sandy stay on at the apartment, and despite her clear desire to do so, once the woman now asleep in his bed stirred to wakefulness, he suspected she would come to her senses and take flight as had so many before her, wisely choosing to disappear before anything akin to real feelings for Jake could develop. Yes, Jake Silver had long ago convinced himself that as long as his nightmares and nocturnal ravings continued, each new liaison, however promising it might first appear, was likely to end with a frightened woman beating a hasty, often pre-dawn exit, leaving Jake's ostensibly precious bachelorhood securely, if not preferably, intact.

So, on this fateful morning, he would do that which he'd done on so many mornings; he would steel himself against what he'd come to consider inevitable. He'd endeavor to deny his feelings for the alluring, but ultimately sensible woman of the moment, and prepare to face the day, his singular expectation being that Sandy McRea remember to leave his key as she left his apartment, his life, and in time, his thoughts.

The latter, he'd learn, was not to be.

As the taxi pulled up to his airline's curbside entrance, Jake over-tipped the driver and made a dash for the crew room.

The brightly lit room was empty but for the lanky form of Ed James, a first officer with whom Jake had trained a few years back.

A compulsive talker, Ed was the kind of roommate Jake knew awaited him in hell.

Without looking up from his newspaper, and before Jake could bolt, the rangy Southerner drawled a hearty, "Jake-boy!"

"Mornin' Ed. What brings you to the frozen north? I thought you were living out your golden years on the Miami milk run."

"I'm deadheading to La La Land with you and Cap'n Willie today." Ed spoke the words with a wink and a smirk. "I got some important bidness out there, if you catch my drift."

"Would that *bidness* be of the blonde or brunette variety?"

"Oh, my Yankee friend," Ed admonished, "a Southern gentleman does not kiss and tell."

In contrast to his own romantic reticence, Jake suspected that Ed did a great deal more telling than he did kissing.

"So you won't be regaling us with details of your little peccadillo?" Jake said.

"My little *what*?"

Leaving the answer to Ed's question dangling, Jake decided to forego his coffee, and as he turned back for the door, he fibbed. "It'll be nice to have some company up front this trip."

Jake was pleased to see Captain Bill Gance already seated in the cockpit when he arrived. Gance was talking to Operations on the company channel. Jake, who had a special affinity for his boss, had given up a regional captain's spot so that he might spend a year or so flying the big iron beside this universally revered chief pilot. To the younger man's mind, knowledge gained at the knee of Captain Gance would prove more meaningful than a seniority-based promotion. A pilot to the core, Jake placed profession before career.

"Mornin', Number One," Gance said warmly, welcoming his copilot as Jake took the right hand seat. "She's holding thirty-four tons," meaning fuel, "and three-hundred souls." Turning then to their hitchhiking colleague, who'd entered behind Jake, Gance added jovially, "Top-o-the mornin' to you, Edwin."

As Ed wiggled into the small jump seat, Jake's brow furrowed at the clutter of planes on the JFK ramp. Though the rain had subsided to a mist, he was eager to climb into the sunlit upper air.

"Get me the current ATIS, please," Gance directed Jake, ATIS being the airport's automated terminal information system for flight crews.

While Jake and his captain worked as one, the radio crackled with the ground controller's instructions: "NorthAm Two-four heavy, Kennedy Ground, taxi runway Three-One Left at the Kilo-Echo intersection, via left on Bravo, hold short of Lima. Holding short of taxiway Lima, monitor tower, one, two, three point niner. They'll have your sequence. Good day."

As the big jet pushed back, Ed said, "Looks like we'll get out on time this mornin'."

"Clear on the left." Gance announced.

"Clear right," Jake responded in the opening movement of a cybernetic ballet that would ensure safe carriage of this crew and its charges across a continent.

Again, the radio crackled to life. "North Am Two-four heavy, Kennedy Tower. Wait for and follow the second heavy Boeing 767 from your left at Lima. They'll be your sequence. You'll be number eleven for departure."

Groans from the two younger men.

As the plane slowly moved up in line, Jake felt a tap on his shoulder and turned to see Ed holding up a rumpled copy of the New York tabloid he'd been reading in the lounge. "Seen this yet, Jake-o?"

Looking over his shoulder, Jake read the headline whose font size would overstate Armageddon: IRAQ WAR HERO KILLED IN DRUG CRASH.

"Yeah, right," Jake said, his voice dripping with cynicism as he turned to Gance, whom the younger pilot knew would disapprove of Ed's cockpit discipline breach. "Everybody's a hero now. Some drunk drives into a tree and it's news because he's a vet."

"Not a car crash, y'all," Ed corrected, shaking the paper, demanding attention. "This boy flew an old Charlie-four-six, Commando into the ocean. Thing was full of drugs. So was the guy, I reckon."

Annoyed by both the breach and Ed's penchant for military nomenclature, Jake grabbed the newspaper from Ed's outstretched hand, aware, as was Gance, that acquiescing to their dead header's compulsion would be less distracting than ignoring or upbraiding him.

Reading the article, Jake became visibly upset, frantically leafing through the paper, looking for the continuation of the story, tearing pages in his frenzied search.

"Knock it off," Captain Gance barked, tired of the whole affair.

Rather than comply, Jake crumpled a page in his fist and said, to his colleagues' surprise, "We gotta go back to the gate."

Incredulous at his normally disciplined first officer's behavior, Gance looked askance at Jake over the half-lenses of his wire-rimmed reading glasses. They'd already advanced, and were now fourth in line. "Go back to the gate?" Gance asked. "Is this your hobby now?"

Not responding, his breathing coarse, his expression somber, Jake stared straight ahead.

Gance realized his copilot was serious. "This's a helluva time..." The captain paused, took a breath. "What is it, Jake? You sick? Got a pain?"

Jake could see his captain's patience dissipating. "It's personal," he said.

"Nothing's personal on my flight deck. Spill it."

Two airplanes were released in rapid succession.

Gance picked up the microphone as if to abort, but Jake raised a hand to stop him.

"Talk to me, Number One," Gance commanded, inching toward the runway. "We're runnin' out'a yellow lines, here. What's this about, son?"

"I'm sorry, sir," Jake said, embarrassed, forcing calm against the gravity of his outburst. "It's...it's this story. It's about Swede Bergstrom."

"Bergstrom?" Gance replied. "Oh, sure. Bergstrom," the captain recalled, keeping his gaze straight ahead. "Your flight leader in the sandbox." Sandbox being GI slang for the Middle East. "He got hit on your first sortie. Right?"

"Right," Jake said, reigning in his emotions, "after saving *my* sorry ass."

Unlike Ed James shifting uncomfortably in the jump seat behind him, Bill Gance had not seen the newspaper article. "What's it say?"

"Says Bergstrom was killed yesterday flying dope out of South America. Claims he got lost and went down off Cuba, a hundred miles west of his flight planned route."

"Really?" Gance asked, surprised. "He was flying an old Curtiss Commando?"

"This's bullshit, Skip," Jake affirmed, "Pilots like Bergstrom don't get lost, and c'mon, what drug runner would be dumb enough to file a goddam flight plan? I gotta find out what's behind this."

"North American Two-Four-Heavy, I say again, this is Kennedy tower," said the irritated voice of the overworked controller, indicating the crew had ignored his initial call.

"North Am Two-four," Gance responded. "Go ahead, tower."

"I repeat. North Am Two-four is cleared for immediate takeoff, Three-One-Left, Kilo-Echo. No delay on the runway. Take off or get off, sir."

"Roger," Jake responded to the tower in a reactive protocol breach that preempted his captain. Turning to Gance, he then said, "I'm good to go, Skipper."

Knowing his first officer as well as a mentor could, and ever conscious of both the CVR and sterile cockpit rule, Gance found himself committed to act.

His eyes burning into those of his errant copilot, he pressed his transmit button. "Two-four is rolling," he growled at the mic.

"Are you…?" Jake began.

"Harness," the captain barked, cutting off the younger man, and asserting his authority.

"Harness secure," Jake responded, relief evident in his voice.

"Flaps."

"Fifteen and fifteen. Two green…" and so on the pair went through the takeoff checklist.

When Gance eased forward on the thrust levers he felt Jake's hand come down gently atop his own. "No sweat, Cap," the younger man said, his voice calm yet well aware that he'd not only abused his authority but compromised his captain and would be called to the carpet—or worse—for his actions.

Equally aware that the CVR was recording the crew's every word, Jake said nothing more.

Gance nodded and both men applied power exactly as they had hundreds of times before and the big jet accelerated.

"Vee-one," Jake called.

"Rotate," Gance replied, and they were flying.

As the airplane rolled into a climbing departure turn, Manhattan's sun-draped spires glistened vermillion through the mist. And, though disappointed by his copilot's brief but serious transgression, Captain Gance took confidence in Jake's recovery and in doing so allowed himself to be awed by the beauty so unique to their vantage. Knowing, too, that he needed to ease the residual tension on his flight deck, the captain waxed poetic, saying, "Red sky at morning..."

No one heard Ed James respond, "...sailor take warning."

- CHAPTER 2 -

Once at altitude, and not content to endure the uneasy silence that permeated the cockpit, Ed spoke first. "Sorry, Jake. It was a dumb thing I said about your friend being on dope and all. You know how I do."

"It's okay, Ed," Jake said. "Don't dwell on it."

But Ed did dwell on it, and Gance, knowing the CVR would record over itself in two hours, allowed it while collecting his own thoughts. "I, well...I just didn't know," Ed said. "The paper called him *Leif* Bergstrom. But you just called him Swede. Ain't that right, Cap?"

"Swede's a nickname," Jake corrected, "a call sign."

Gance, forcing calm, gestured toward the newspaper crumbled on Jake's lap. "Okay, Number-One," he said. "It's time to come clean about Bergstrom." A pause. "I know you don't like to talk about your time in Iraq," he went on, "I get that. But, if something disrupts procedure, I have to know why. So, spill it or we do this by the book."

"I flew one recon mission with Swede," Jake finally groused. "I hardly knew the guy"

"Do not push me, Jake!" Gance admonished. Having himself flown F-4s in the first Gulf War the captain was not about to put up with patronage from a fellow combat pilot. "You learn more about a man after five minutes of war fighting than you can in a lifetime at anything else. If that man risked his life to save *your* ass, he's your brother for life. So start talking."

Embarrassed, realizing how far his captain had stretched the rules on his behalf, Jake relented. "Look. I just can't believe where a pilot like Swede ended up, that's all. Learning a thing like that, it's like a punch in the gut."

"At least he was flying again," Ed James noted, referring to the news article. "I thought he'd been badly wounded."

"You thought right," Jake affirmed. "But that doesn't make him a drug runner."

Observing the younger man's performance, his deft touch and movements, the captain knew Jake was back in control of both his emotions and the aircraft. So, and with a qualified man in the jump seat, he pressed. "Was Iraq the last time you saw him?"

"Yes. When Swede disappeared, my fighter was really shot up, but I circled the area until my last drop of fuel reserve was gone, so were half my systems. I never saw his chute or any wreckage, never heard a beacon. He just disappeared." Jake shifted in his seat, uneasy with the memory "I know he got picked up alive. But that's all I was told. Of course, Command and Control knew exactly what happened in that sky, but Swede and I had engaged against orders and it was the day after the president had made his Mission Accomplished speech from that carrier deck, so nobody said shit."

"I thought no F-16s were lost to enemy action since like the Nineties," Ed pondered aloud. "Hell, didn't one of 'em just shot down a MiG-21 in India or someplace?"

"I never said..." Jake began to explain, only to have the captain cut him off.

"...and the other side claims it was their MiG that took out the F-16. That's the fog of war, Ed," Gance declared, satisfied with Jake's explanation, the hard-earned wisdom and quiet comprehension of a combat warrior relieving the younger man of further painful recollection.

"Ever reach out," Gance went on, "call Swede's folks?"

"Absolutely," Jake answered, relief at the unexpected tolerance apparent in his captain's tone. "Even visited his parents out in California first time I deployed back stateside. Lemme tell you, it was, uh…interesting. But it's how I learned what became of him."

"Sounds like he fell on hard times," Gance said.

"A man's gotta eat, y'all," Ed offered.

"There's more to the story," Jake added. "Swede's father, Truls Bergstrom, told me what he knew." Both men listened intently as Jake began. "Whoever got hold of Swede, worked him over good. But he didn't talk—he couldn't, none of us knew shit. You were Navy in the first go, Skipper. You get it. We were tip 'a the spear, period–but they pumped the poor bastard full of pentothal anyway and God knows what else. Between that and the beatings, he came back, well, different, y'know, according to his father."

"But whoever had him, released him, right?" Gance asked.

"Right. Swede spent a year in Walter Reed. After that some desk-jockey dropped his discharge papers and a couple of campaign ribbons into his B-4 bag and sent him home. But what he went home to was also different. He had a kid sister, talked about her all the time." With that, Jake paused, pensive, thinking. "For the life of me, I can't recall her name. I only know she thought Swede hung the moon, and he doted on her like a mother hen. After the family learned he was MIA she, well, she was at that age, maybe thirteen or so when you still think you can change the world. She got bitter, started going to protest rallies." Pensive, Jake shook his head as if rejecting the image. "Anyway, Swede had always said she was a good-looking kid, not that you could prove it by me. The kid I saw was a mess. But, anyway, it wasn't long before one of the rally leaders got his hands on her. Prick's name was Philippe… probably bullshit. He was just a grifter with a tie-dyed shirt, working his con on the kids. Pretty soon, she's living with him, strung out on his heroin, hooking for him. Apparently Swede found her that way when he got out of Walter Reed. Truls had been told of his son's release, but Swede never went home. He just swept in and out of town like a ghost."

"But his sister made it back home?" Gance asked.

"Affirmative," Jake continued, his gaze distant as he struggled with the memory. "Kid was in bad shape when I saw her. Looked like a zombie, but I guess she was trying. I dunno. Old Truls Bergstrom dragged her into the room when I visited. She kept her head down, trying to hide her face. She didn't look like the other Bergstroms. She was a scrawny little thing with black hair. The rest of them were big, round-faced blondes. She was different...trying to be different, too, I guess. Huge eyes, skin white as a sheet, just stuck on her bones like wet paper. But what really turned my crank was she had needle marks up and down her skinny arms. Man, I never seen that before. But Truls made sure I got a good look, pushing her in front of me like he expected me to scold her or something, and all the time she's trying to hide herself as if she were a leper. She didn't say a word the whole time I was there, which wasn't long, believe me."

The other men listened in silence as Jake mused. "But, y'know what sticks out in my mind the most?" he said. "Despite the way old man Bergstrom pushed that strange, skinny kid around, I was dead certain she scared the shit out of him. She had a menace about her, and it filled the room like the stink of the place."

"What happened to the drug dealer, Philippe?" Ed asked.

"Disappeared."

"Swede's doing?"

"I'd bet on it," Jake said, handing the crumpled newspaper back to Ed. "So, like I said, knowing what I know about Swede, about his family, and especially about the kid sister he adored, I know Swede Bergstrom didn't smuggle drugs or knowingly fly airplanes for the scumbags who do."

The cockpit went quiet and Jake sensed his crewmates' discomfort. "Okay, gents, now you know all, so let's drop it?"

"Roger that," Gance said while Ed searched for the puzzle page.

- CHAPTER 3 -

It was early afternoon when North Am-24 touched down at LAX. Jake was pleased to be in California with much of the day still ahead of him. He thought he might stay over and look up the Bergstrom family in Stockton.

However, as the day wound toward evening, Jake sat in his airport hotel room, staring at the phone, frustrated.

Unable to find a listing for Truls Bergstrom in Stockton, he'd tried several other California towns and come up empty; while the name Truls was unique, the surname Bergstrom was not. Nonetheless Jake ran down every iteration in the state, calling any and every Bergstrom, leaving detailed voicemail messages, his name, number, and his reason for calling. His old flight leader's family had moved on.

Jake was stymied. What to do next? As he contemplated the phone, it rang.

"Jake?" It was Gance's gravelly voice. "Had any luck running down Bergstrom's family?"

"Nothing," Jake said, then added, "and, Bill, thanks for cutting me a whole lot of slack today. I know it wasn't easy."

"Easy? Hell, I'm not sure it was even regulation. Breakfast?"

"Affirmative, Skipper. What time?"

"I'll see you downstairs at six."

Jake looked at the clock. It was only 7:00 p.m. but that would be 10:00 p.m. New York time and last night's joyful romp with Sandy McRea, had left him tired.

Within an hour, Jake was in bed. Sleep, however, eluded him. Swede Bergstrom's abrupt re-emergence had frazzled his nerves and he lay silent, letting his troubled mind wander back to an earlier time, a younger time, when life was filled with wonder and the lure of adventure.

To young Jake, adventure meant but one thing: flight.

Unable to afford civilian pilot training, he took another somewhat riskier path. The country was at peace, so within a week of his college graduation, he chose the Air Force. As expected he scored high on the entrance aptitude tests. His mental acuity, physical condition, and spanking new degree in aerospace engineering qualified the aspiring airman for a commission and undergraduate pilot training. There, too, he excelled, earning a place on Training Command's elite Fighter, Attack, Recon (FAR) track.

Everything was going according to plan until the morning of September 11th 2001, when Jake's plans along with those of countless other Americans, evaporated in a noxious cloud of ash and metal and blood and bone, leaving the Manhattanite incensed and seeking only retribution against whatever monsters had presumed to attack his home city.

When his chance finally came, the young lieutenant left the training grind of Luke AFB for his first duty station.

Tensions were high when Jake arrived at the coalition airbase in Saudi Arabia. The adrenal rush of combat permeated both the conversation and posturing of Jake's squadron mates: young men all. Jake, however, found himself increasingly unable to reconcile the events that had colored the two years between the World Trade Center attack and this, his first combat assignment. If this war was indeed a response to the events of September 11th, it seemed an irrational one. As Jake's frustrations had grown, so had his incredulity. Why, he'd wondered, was he finding himself based in the same country that had spawned the mastermind of those attacks and 15 of the 19 perpetrators? If that weren't confusing enough to the conflicted young officer, why was he here to fly against Iraq, none of whose people took part in the attacks?

Bound by love of country and a staunch determination to stand by his sworn oath, yet finding it ever more difficult to suffer his dissonance in silence, Jake tossed in his bunk. Unable to sleep, he rose and quietly dressed, deciding to take a pre-dawn run in the hope of clearing his head.

Donning his flight jacket above a t-shirt and shorts, he stepped into the cold desert night.

His path took him in the direction of the flightline where the unmistakable sound of departing F-16s drew him closer. Stopping at the foot of the tarmac he jogged in place and watched as the magnificent little warplanes streaked past, each lifting off to soar above the desert floor, its engine trailing a bright cone of flame against a black and moonless sky. But to young Jake, the terrible beauty of such spectacle served only to reinforce the sense of privilege he felt at having been granted command of so awesome an instrument of dominion and the almost unbearable responsibility contingent upon its use.

Unwilling to voice such ambivalence to those he assumed were his unsympathetic squadron mates, and not a man who'd seek comfort from his chaplain, Jake did the only thing he thought he could; against the roar of jet engines he shouted a catharsis into the beautiful uncaring Arabian night.

Mesmerized by the spectacle unfolding on the runway, he hadn't noticed the young captain quietly standing a few feet to his rear. At first showing no reaction to Jake's outburst, the aloof officer seemed to be ignoring the rookie until, finally, rather than upbraid the young malcontent, the veteran stepped closer and tempered his derision with advice. Without turning away from the sound and fury of the departing jets, the reticent officer raised his voice above the roar, saying, "I hear you're a boxer."

"*Was* a boxer," Jake corrected, as startled by the man's presence as he was surprised by his insight.

"I know a thing or two about boxing, myself—and boxers."

"Is that right?" Jake replied, hiding his embarrassment behind a macho fighter-jock demeanor. Then, noticing the guy's collar bars he added an obligatory, "...*Sir.*"

"That's right, shavetail," the slightly older flier said, now turning to speak directly to the young lieutenant "And the first thing I know is that every boxer has a plan."

"Affirmative," Jake said, lowering his voice as the last warplane climbed away.

"Yeah," the stranger concluded with a nod, "you all have a plan...until the bell rings."

Despite his mood, Jake had smiled in silent agreement.

"That's how I also know," the captain added, "that once it gets real, guys like you stop giving a shit if the man comin' at you is big or small or loves his mother or has a friggin' puppy. You just wanna kick his ass before he kicks yours. Everything else is suddenly bullshit." With that he paused, making certain the metaphor was not lost on this naïve lieutenant. Satisfied, he went on. "So be advised, pal. The same thing applies here...in spades. Now I'm gonna try to forget that pile of crap you just spouted, and remind you that you're not a politician, and you're sure as hell not a philosopher. What you are," he said while stepping closer that he might poke the pilot's wings printed into the leather nametag affixed to the breast of Jake's MA-1 jacket, "is an American airman. So unless you want to spend the rest of your tour pulling my size thirteen boot out of your worthless new guy ass, you will think and act and fight like the exquisitely trained US goddam fighter pilot those wings represent."

With that, the young captain leaned close to Jake's ear, and concluded with, "By the way, hot shot, I have it on good authority—my own—that your bell's just about to ring and when it does, your rationale *will* KO your half-assed rationality."

As the officer turned to leave, Jake followed him into the Base Ops shack. "Captain," he called out. "You seem to know a lot about me, and I don't even know your name."

"You will, Lieutenant," the stranger barked before disappearing into the night.

Without looking up, the sergeant behind the operations desk said, "Most call him Swede."

The ensuing weeks found the squadron's new pilots each assigned to a *flight*: a small subset of their squadron wherein they'd be engaged in seemingly endless local area orientation drills and systems training exercises. During these drills, Jake did get to know Captain Leif Bergstrom's name quite well. Bergstrom was the young pilot's Flight Commander. And, over the course of these increasingly arduous dry runs, Lieutenant Silver's flying impressed Bergstrom. From that common bond and anticipation of impending combat, the two young lions drew close. Then, when Bergstrom not only declared Jake Silver mission-ready, he also assigned the young pilot to fly his wing on what would be Jake's first combat sortie.

Theirs would be an NTISR, or Night Time Intelligence Surveillance and Reconnaissance mission—clandestine, defensive, and among the most dangerous assignments in all of aerial warfare. With Swede Bergstrom's, *"until the bell rings,"* admonition top of mind, the junior officer hung on every word of the pre-mission briefing.

Satellite surveillance and JSTARS airborne battlefield management systems had been encountering unusually high surface vehicle traffic in an area around Baghdad, an area that had been largely neutralized by the previous two months' of massive SEAD air defense suppression operations, but could confirm little beyond that. Theirs, then, was to be an armed recon mission, old-school, daring, and exactly how fiercely independent Swede Bergstrom liked it. And though the pair expected to be tracked, there would be no directions from Command and Control. Officially, they were alone and unknown.

Before first light, Jake's and Bergstrom's F16s—Vipers, as their crews called them—were streaking toward "The Line," a name given the 32nd Parallel gateway to Baghdad.

Their mission objective was to fly within detection range of the city's defenses and evaluate empirically what remained of Iraqi antiaircraft missile systems.

As they approached the city, Jake flew the number two airplane, with Bergstrom a mile ahead. Swede had named their two-flight Bolo.

Though it was known that the IrAF—the Iraqi Air Force—posed little if any threat from the air, it was suspected that both Russian and Iranian tactical aircraft were operating in the area.

The two American pilots were under orders to avoid engagement unless attacked.

The primary threat would come from Iraqi ground batteries. The mission objective was to find out just how formidable those batteries were by luring the Iraqis into activating their defensive radars and thus exposing their remaining SAM locations.

These recon missions were the aerial equivalent of strolling into a dark alley in the hope of provoking the bad guys you knew were hiding in the shadows to shoot at you, and by doing so allowing you to report the location of their muzzle flashes. So, as the pair approached the heavily defended airspace, Jake was tense and adrenal.

They were at altitude, and fifteen miles out when a SAM site's aiming system detected them, thereby exposing itself to the Vipers' RWR, or radar warning receivers.

"Tally-ho, Bolo Two," Swede declared. "Sam in the air!"

"Bolo Two is tally," Jake responded with false calm, his heart pounding.

His warning systems began beeping and lighting up like Times Square and Jake was suddenly in the fight of his life and caught himself white-knuckling his fighter's side-mounted stick as the dark space ahead filled with flash after flash, trail after trail.

When one missile's fiery exhaust trail morphed into a halo encircling its warhead, Jake knew that the thing had a lock on his jet.

He threw his fighter into a violent, rolling evasive turn streaming chaff and perhaps causing the SAM to acquire a false target. He did not see or detect his wingman's fighter closing the distance between them and doing the same. Perhaps their combined efforts confused the SAM and it missed them both, but its proximity fuse caused it to explode sending a shock wave and fragments slamming into Jake's fighter. The force—which would have destroyed a lesser aircraft—knocked Jake nearly unconscious as his head was whiplashed with such violence it nearly snapped his spine. His vision flooded white.

Struggling to recover while frantically attempting to assess the damage to his fighter, his warning and weapons-systems in disarray, his data link and IFF transponder out, his radios were now the only reliable link to Swede.

As Bergstrom joined up, their course took the fighters out of range of the ground batteries and into broken clouds.

Once clear, Jake could see his lead's jet drifting out from underneath his own straining to assess the damage to Jake's airplane through the dim light and obscuring clouds.

"You're pretty chopped up," Swede reported. "Your avionics hatch is gone, so's a chunk of your radome and you're streaming fuel. Okay Wing, we're RTB. Acknowledge."

"Jake zippered his microphone, its two transmitted clicks barely acknowledging the order to *return to base,* but concealing his condition.

"Heading two-one-zero," Swede directed. "And keep a swivel. Saddam or his buddies might still have flyable assets up here,"

Thus forewarned, Jake, brought up his stores and punched air-to-air just as the gleaming MiG appeared out of nowhere running for the wall of cloud a mile distant and Jake "pickled" a Sidewinder air-to-air missile.

Realizing it was a desperate reflexive act, he was momentarily relieved when the rocket misfired and the MiG disappeared into the clouds. Swede Bergstrom's F-16 took chase, and the errant rocket fired and screamed off Jake's wing.

Swede's fighter chased the MiG into the clouds while Jake's missile chased them both and despite his state, he knew that without a radar lock the rocket's own sensor could lock on Swede's fighter as easily as it could the MiG and he sat galvanized, silent, as the audible whine in his helmet confirmed his fears; the little rocket had found its mark—*its* mark—and the cloud flashed orange as fuel and ordnance thundered in serial conflagrations behind its opaque wall.

Trembling, heart pounding, Jake pulled his airplane into a tight six-G loop, waiting, watching to see what would emerge, a MiG-25, an F-16. Or both. Or neither.

After a second that seemed an eternity, one sleek fighter streaked away dead ahead of his jet and Jake took chase. "Bolo One." No response. "Bolo One, acknowledge."

As the distance between the fighters closed and Jake's eyes regained clarity, there could be no mistaking what he saw. Dancing a mile off his fighter's nose were the distinctive twin-tails of the MiG-25 as it streaked for the north country, running for its life, and rather than pursue, Lieutenant Jake Silver choked back the vomit rising in his throat as the heads up display began flashing FUEL, FUEL…

Jake sat bolt upright as the dawn light and the LAX hotel room slowly refilled his tortured consciousness.

The sweat-soaked sheets at his waist, his eyes were drawn to the newspaper lying on the floor at his bedside. Its headline seemed to mock him: IRAQ WAR HERO...

- CHAPTER 4 -

At 6:00 a.m. Jake headed down to join Gance for breakfast.

The captain called out with a wave as his copilot entered the hotel restaurant.

Jake took a chair opposite him, ordered coffee.

Gance spoke. "I've made a decision, Jake. You're grounded."

"What! C'mon, Cap. Yesterday was…"

"Forget it, Jake. You want to come with us, you ride in the back. Smile at the ladies."

"Bullshit, Skipper, I…"

"I'm serious, Jake. Don't fight me on this."

Before Jake could react further, Gance stood. "I'm speaking as your friend *and* as your boss. Either you deadhead back to New York with us, or you grab a couple of days off, get your head right."

"*Us?*" Jake queried.

"Yeah. Ed has offered to fly right seat on the backhaul."

"Ed? Really?" Jake said, surprise evident in his tone as he added absently, "I guess *his* bidness took *her* bidness elsewhere."

"I don't know what that means," Gance said, "but Ed's a good guy when it counts. He's current on our bird, and knows this is serious for you."

"It's *more* serious for the CVR," Jake quipped, a reference to Ed's loquaciousness.

Ignoring his copilot's jab, Gance held firm. "Do whatever you gotta do, Jake. Report back in when you've worked things out. I told the front office you have a family emergency."

"What kind of emer…?"

"Hell, I don't know. It's *your* family."

With that, Gance turned and was gone.

Finishing his breakfast, Jake found himself strangely relieved. His crewmates had helped him appreciate his wealth of good and caring friends. Swede Bergstrom was gone, and needed to be relegated to the past, a casualty of war. Perhaps Jake's enduring guilt and nightmares would depart with him.

Decision made, Jake picked up his cell phone and dialed his captain's number.

Gance's phone went straight to voicemail. Rather than leave a message, Jake hung up. He'd try again in a few minutes.

As Jake stood to retrieve his wallet, he patted his side pocket to feel for his keys, a habit he'd developed when traveling. With a rush he realized he'd left them behind at the apartment. "Dammit!" he said, knowing he could always call a neighbor to buzz him into the front door, but his locked apartment was another thing. He checked his watch. It was 6:30 a.m. He'd have to call Sandy, knowing it was 9:30 in the morning in New York, he only half expected her answer. But, nonetheless, he'd take a shot and leave her detailed instructions for when she next left the apartment. She should first find his key ring, remove the door key and drop it into the flower pot across from the elevator. Sitting back down, he dialed Sandy's cell.

Though the restaurant wasn't crowded, Jake was too annoyed and distracted to notice a woman enter. Perhaps thirty, she wore a green sweater which hung loosely from her slim body, and fashionably-tattered skinny jeans. As she crossed the room with purpose, a subtle trace of heather trailed in her wake. Coming up just behind Jake's table, she waited politely, within earshot, but just out of his view while he spoke his instructions into Sandy McRea's voicemail.

Instructions left, Jake rang off and gathered his things to leave.

But as he turned, the woman stepped up and they nearly collided.

Standing close before him as her fragrance rode the breeze, she spoke. "Mr. Silver?"

Jake found himself looking directly into a pair of pale-gray, almond-shaped eyes. They were clear, wide-set and large, regarding him from an oval face made small by a crop of short onyx hair that curved downward from a center part. The glistening mane set off pale but alluring features, unaided by makeup. He stepped back. Smiled tentatively.

"You *are* Jake Silver?" she asked, the voice throaty, the big eyes sizing him up.

"Guilty," Jake answered. "I'm sorry, do I know...?"

Without answering his question or returning his smile, she instead extended a manicured hand. "Good morning, Mr. Silver. I'm Christina Bergstrom."

Jake struggled to find his voice. "Please, sit down Miss... *Ms.* Bergstrom," he finally managed, pulling out a chair before being seated himself, banging his knee on the table's edge as he did so. "I... I'm sorry for what must have seemed a strange phone call but...."

Waving his concerns away, rather than take the chair opposite Jake, she sat to his right, leaning toward him as she spoke. She seemed bold, confident. "Your voice, the message, it was like a godsend, not at all strange," she said, stopping short of touching her fingertips to the back of his hand while making it apparent that she'd intended to. "I was in San Francisco and on the shuttle within an hour. Impulsive, I know, but I've been out of my mind. Leif is my brother and I love him, and...."

Seeing her choke up, Jake searched for the handkerchief he didn't have and instead asked, "Have you been here all night?"

"Yes, wandering the lobby. The desk clerks must have thought..." She waved a hand, dismissing the desk clerks and their thoughts. "Anyway, I picked up the house phone a thousand times, trying to get up the courage to call your room but I just couldn't. I was about to leave when I saw you come in here.

"Hearing from you was fateful," she went on, never taking her big eyes from his face. "You might be the one person who'd understand."

Jake's brow furrowed. "Why didn't you just call me back?"

"I didn't want to scare you off."

"I don't frighten *that* easily," he said, still trying to reconcile this striking and forthright woman before him with the emaciated, shadowy creature he'd encountered years ago.

Again, her words set him at ease. "I just had to be with someone who'd sympathize."

"Of course, Ms. Bergstrom. I..."

"Please. It's Tina," she stated, adding, "Look. You know my brother was no angel..."

"...but not a drug runner," Jake said, risking a finish to her sentence.

She looked away. "Like you," she explained, "Leif saw what drugs had done to me."

Hearing Swede's proper name spoken with such familiarity was at first disconcerting.

Letting Tina's words hang in the air for a moment, Jake looked down at her hands. There were no rings. "Your parents, Tina," he finally asked, "are they still...?"

"Both gone," she said, her gaze distant . "I think between Leif's troubles and the mess I'd made of my own life, we broke our mother's heart and it killed her."

"And your father?"

Her face contorted. "When our mother died, my father, well... he just drank himself to some other place." Jake moved to speak, but unhearing, Tina kept venting, a catharsis. "By the time I got my own empty head straight, my parents were beyond reach."

Seeing her discomfort, Jake changed the subject. "Who has your brother's remains?"

Remains! He was making things worse!

"Well, that depends."

"Excuse me?"

"He's going to be remanded to the Dade County medical examiner's office." She looked up, chin forward, subtly defiant. "But right now, the Haitian authorities are holding him—or a body they contend is his—at Port au Prince."

"How were you notified of that?"

"I wasn't. I made a million phone calls when I heard about the crash. I finally hit pay dirt."

"But *they*—Dade County—they don't have the body yet," Jake surmised. "Do they?"

"They do not. The ME's office in Miami told me the Haitian authorities are preparing it for release to the States tomorrow. They'll take custody then."

"So," Jake asked, "what's the problem?"

Tina's jaw tightened in an expression of resolve. "The ME's office also told me I won't get to see the body itself, just a photograph. It's the coroner's policy in criminal cases."

Jake understood the desire for closure, but that sounded like concern or a rush to judgment. Knowing Swede had died in a violent crash, he knew too that his old comrade's body would already be horribly disfigured, broken and fish-bitten, exposed flesh burned. Either way, the Dade County coroner's policy seemed prudent.

Anticipating Jake's reaction, Tina spoke first. "I want to see him, Jake. I need to *see* my brother, not some damned polaroid picture, and see him before they cut him to pieces."

Realizing a picture, however gruesome, could be sent anywhere, Jake asked, "Did they request that you do an ID on site?"

"No. And that's where it gets weird."

Jake shuddered to think what might constitute *weird* to a Bergstrom. "How?" he ventured.

"Well, my brother had a connection in the government, a guy whose helped him out from time to time. The guy was wounded in some bullshit war or another, too. He was Leif's VA counselor. Leif once told me to call the guy if anything bad ever happened to him."

"So, you called him."

"He called *me!*"

"You mean a VA guy knew what was going on?"

"Well, not exactly. This guy's name is William Peterson, and he's not in the Veterans Administration anymore. Peterson's now a big shot in the Department of Homeland Security."

Homeland Security, Jake mused: the catch-all for government meddling.

"Was he offering condolences?"

"That's the weird part, Jake. Peterson was pissed that I'd contacted the medical examiner. He said my brother's body was evidence in a *federal* terrorism investigation with *national security* implications, and I was to stay out of it."

National security: how many times had Jake heard that hackneyed phrase since *9/11*?

"Baloney," was as much as he could muster.

Nodding agreement, Tina added, "To hear Peterson tell it, he and Leif were old pals. Claims he was stepping in to make it easier on the family of a friend. His words, the tone, they were hardly those of a friend. He was clearly trying to discourage me. "

"Something tells me he couldn't."

"He pissed me off."

"Are you absolutely sure you're not reading something into this, Tina?" Jake asked, playing devil's advocate. "Could it be he's just an officious bureaucrat?"

"He's a jerk who expects me to sit by and let them cut Leif to pieces, then pin this drug runner thing on him. My brother is not some piece of evidence. It's a cover-up and I'm going to expose it. If that means throwing my own body across Leif's, I will. I just..." She choked up, turned away. "I have no right to drag you..."

"Look, Tina, I'm alive because of Leif. C'mon. How'd you leave off with Peterson?"

"He said," *sniff*, "he'd meet me at the Dade County Medical Examiner's offices day after tomorrow."

"I'm going with you," Jake said. Then, seeing her incredulous expression, he quickly added, "You had me at *Good morning.*"

She sniffed again and squeezed his hand. "If we leave right away," she gushed, "we can still be in Port au Prince tomorrow. I might still get there in time."

"Wait. What?" Jake said, taking her shoulders and holding her at arm's length surprised and a little miffed at what appeared a subtle deception. "Port au Prince?"

"Yes. I'm not going all the way to Florida to look at a polaroid."

"You're distraught, Tina. You're not thinking rationally."

"Of course not," she said with a frustrated sigh. "I'm just an emotional female to you. You disappoint me." Before he could protest, Tina moved on. "Look, Jake. There's something I haven't told you."

He was beginning to suspect there were a few things she hadn't told him. But discretion will out and he simply said, "What, that I'm being a chauvinist jerk?"

"Well, yes. But that's not it." She paused then, gauging his demeanor. Satisfied she went on. "My brother has something I want. He has it on him. It's valuable and it's personal and yes, it might seem silly to you, but it's important to me and I don't trust some Haitian stranger to turn it in, or…or to even look at it. It's mine."

"Okay," he said, reluctance yielding to empathy. "I won't ask, but I will go with you."

Before he could change his mind, she stretched forward and kissed his cheek, "Thank you, Jake. Thank you, thank you. I even have the location," she said, speaking in rapid-fire bursts. "We have to hurry. I only hope…"

"Take a breath, Tina," he cautioned. "You need to prepare yourself for what you'll see. Your brother died in a violent crash. His face…"

"If it's him, I'll know." Her eyes went to the floor. "I know all my brother's secrets."

Though he'd always found such absolutes absurd, the comment sent a chill along Jake's spine. *What dark secrets did these strange siblings share?* Again he flashed back to his nightmare in the Baghdad sky. In his mind's eye, he saw the errant missile fly. Again he saw the clouds before him glow orange as the missile finds its mark, and the blood drained from his face. How could she know what he'd done to her brother? Jake thought. Could Swede have known? Jake had never sent a brevity code or voiced a warning. No! Whatever happened in that long ago Iraq sky, was forever lost in the fog of war and to Jake's punctuated recollection, leaving not one, but two casualties, and a secret Jake had vowed he'd carry to his grave.

Forcing himself back to the moment, Jake saw Tina's eyes on him, penetrating.

He made one last, futile plea for reason. "Look, Tina, if you think this fed has an agenda, maybe we can push back… and I mean really push back."

Her expression turned quizzical.

"My family is not without influence," Jake pressed.

Tina quickly withdrew. "Let's not drag anyone else into this, Jake. Please, do this for me."

Seeing the disappointment in Jake's eyes, Tina pressed her point. "Look," she said, placing a hand on his arm, "I don't know what will be waiting for me in some voodoo-land morgue. I only know I don't want to face it alone."

Not willing to aggravate an already sensitive situation, Jake acquiesced. "Okay," he said. "My airline doesn't fly to Port au Prince, but I can make arrangements to get us at least to Florida for free."

"Just us?" she asked.

"Just us."

Tina smiled, and again she kissed his cheek. "Please hurry."

Back at his room, Jake called the North Am crew desk to arrange a pair of seats on the next Florida flight, then texted Sandy that he'd be delayed. Tina, meanwhile sat on the bed busily rearranging her overnight bag. Despite the bag's carry-on size Jake couldn't help but notice the SFO/LAX baggage-check tag hanging from its handle. He also noticed her hurriedly closing it when he approached. "We're all set," he said. "Seems we're getting priority treatment."

What Jake called. *priority treatment* turned out to be a free ride on the personal Dassault Falcon bizjet belonging to one of the airline's major shareholders. The exec who ironically eschewed airline travel, liked to fly left seat on the sleek little machine himself and would be returning home to Palm Beach.

He agreed to jump off there, and let his personal pilot scoot the hitchhikers the 700 over-water miles to Port au Prince, Haiti.

Jake considered this stroke of luck to be either the influence of Bill Gance made manifest, or fate's aiding and abetting his own poor judgment when it came to all things Bergstrom. Nonetheless, a guilt-and-doubt ridden Jake

Silver found himself packing his already heavy chart case—
or "brain-bag" as pilots call them—for Port au Prince.

Once at Van Nuys Airport, the pair were quickly checked
in, boarded, and by mid-afternoon the speedy little machine
was off and eastward bound.

Tina looked down from her sofa-like seat and watched
the countless orange tile rooftops recede below the little biz
jet's swept wing. Jake sat beside her.

Her lips shining moist with red wine she'd been sipping,
Tina turned, catching Jake looking her way. "My brother
spoke of you. Did you know that?"

"Really?" Jake said. "From my vantage point, he just
dropped off the planet."

"Don't read into that," she said. "The Leif who came
home was not the same naïve kid who went off to save the
world for Exxon... or more to the point, to escape a life of
abuse."

"Well, all he got to save was me," Jake mused, leaning
back.

On the armrest, their hands touched. Jake withdrew his.

"I do remember seeing you at our house," Tina recalled,
changing the subject, "but I somehow couldn't remember
your face. Funny. It's a nice face. I guess I couldn't reconcile
something nice with that time in my life." Her expression
turned pensive. "I could use another vino," she said, and
made her way to the Falcon's galley. "How about you?"

"Beer. Thanks," he answered. "...and a glass."

He admired her fluid movement, the muscular yet delicate
curves of her legs as she walked to the galley.

When she returned to their seat, she was loaded down
with Jake's beer and another little bottle of Chardonnay for
herself. A chocolate bar and two bags of chips were wedged
in the crook of her elbow.

"Just the beer for me," Jake said.

"That's all I brought for you."

Jake smiled as Tina unwrapped the candy bar. "I need the calories," she explained, "or at least my muscles do. It comes with being a dancer." The wine apparently having lifted her spirits, she added a comic pirouette before falling into her seat, now quite close to Jake

"Well, then, here's to the arts," he said, pretending to pretend to leer, feeling the physical warmth of her as he opened the wine and leaned in to pour her another glass.

"If jumping around half naked in music videos has a place among *the arts*," she said with air quotes, "then hell yes. Here's to 'em!" Their glasses clinked, and Jake was pleased to see Tina letting go, less intense if only for the moment.

"Just to be clear," she said while looking at her wine glass, "I *was* a dancer. Now, at my age, I'm a has-been." Then, and without a trace of false modesty, Tina added, "I did use my looks to land the music video thing, though. That was my only currency back then, my looks and the hunger for a better life. Dancing gave me that life, and a direction, and the money to become independent. I met real dancers along the way, too, talented, artistic, brilliant dancers. For the first time in my life I was around extraordinary people. They inspired me. Up until then, my brother was the only one who ever gave a damn about me. I fell in with the wrong kind, I guess. Maybe that's all I thought I deserved." Snapping out of it, she blinked, shook her head and added, this time with purpose, "You saw what I was, Jake. I did unspeakable things to escape my family situation. Those stains don't wash off. But then I'd found myself surrounded by a very different kind of people...generous, supportive people. So I studied my ass off and saved every penny I could. By the time I got good, though, I was too old to make it. I'm a dance teacher now. I have a small school in the city. Mostly girls, kids. I love it...love the kids." With that she paused, contemplative. "I'm human again."

"And your personal life?" Jake dared ask.

"Are you asking if there's a special someone?" she mused, interpreting Jake's question before smiling and saying only, "I still have trust issues."

Knowing better than to push it, Jake asked, "What became of your father? I met your father. Remember? He was..." he searched for the right words, "a little rough around the edges but he seemed to care about you and..."

Before he could go on, Tina put a forefinger to his lips. Shaking her head slowly, she said, "I'm sure you love your parents, Jake. I tried to love mine. They wouldn't allow it."

Jake's mind flashed back to the troubling domestic scene he'd witnessed in California all those years ago. Meanwhile, Tina's voice was saying, "...my so-called father never accepted me as his. He never showed anything even remotely akin to giving a damn about me. To his mind, I wasn't his daughter." As she said the words, she avoided Jake's eyes, and for the first time, he could reconcile this determined woman with the emaciated, somehow menacing girl he'd encountered long ago.

"Did..." Jake paused, considering the sensitivity of what he was about to say, "Did you say you *weren't* Truls's daughter? You're speaking figuratively."

"Look at me," Tina prodded, which Jake had found himself doing far too willingly since she'd walked in on him.

She raised her eyes to him while mussing her onyx hair with both hands. "Tell me," she said. "Do I look Swedish to you?"

An image of this raven-haired beauty in a Viking helmet flashed before Jake's eyes.

"Okay," she said, suppressing a knowing smile. "Do I look anything like my brother, then?"

"Fortunately, no," Jake answered, feigning horror at such an image.

The smile faded, but she went on recalling, her expressive eyes showing neither discomfort nor anger, only distance. "My father knew," she said. "He treated me like garbage and he beat my mother senseless. Called her a godless whore whenever he came home drunk, and when he came home at all, he came home drunk. Leif and I were peripheral to their lives."

Jake started to reach out, but stopped short of touching Tina's arm. She needed to speak, and he let her. "Whenever mother was out of reach," she went on, "he'd assume the worst and come for me, his little black-haired reminder of his wife's infidelity. Somehow, Leif would always find a way to be nearby. He'd step in and take the punches meant for me. I could only watch the hatred building, and I knew that someday my father would kill my brother. The demented sonofabitch would kill his own son to get to his bastard."

Feeling clumsy, Jake measured his words. "So you left?"

"Yes. Once I was gone, really gone and not coming back, I remember hoping that Leif would follow."

"Did he?"

"He enlisted. I thought he'd abandoned me. But he just needed to escape, too."

After what seemed an eternity of quiet contemplation, Tina perked up, as if a weight had been lifted. "Alright," sipping her wine, she said with verve, "that's enough about moi. I'm gonna catch a nap. We have a long night ahead of us." In seconds, she was out.

Seeing Tina so peaceful, her face serene, she looked almost childlike, small and vulnerable, and Jake realized, though their circumstances could not have been more different, they'd arrived at the same self-inflicted emotional crossroads.

Retrieving a light blanket, he gently placed it over her. As he bent to raise the blanket to her shoulders, the little jet bounced, causing him to stumble, their faces to touch.

Pulling back ever so slightly, Jake felt Tina's breath soft on his skin, its aroma wine-sweet.

Her tough façade crushed beneath the catharsis, Tina's serenity in sleep did little to pacify Jake's growing sense of foreboding. As he admired the lovely enigma before him, the jet's owner/pilot spoke over the intercom informing his guests that they had just crossed the Mississippi. Jake wondered if it might be his Rubicon.

- CHAPTER 5 -

It was midnight in Palm Beach when Jake and Tina bid thanks and farewell to the little bizjet's generous owner. Then, with fresh fuel and a leg stretch, they were off again and southward bound, this time with Jake sharing the cockpit, while in the cabin Tina slept.

A short ninety-minutes later the pair stood alone on the tarmac at Port au Prince International. And, as the night sky consumed their little jet, an energized Tina Bergstrom turned for the terminal, declaring, "I need to see my brother."

"I understand," Jake answered.

"I mean now."

Exhausted, his patience waning, Jake followed, barking, "Dammit, Tina, we don't even know where he is."

"Of course we do," she claimed, while keeping up the pace, eyes on her phone, "He's at the Saint Sebastian hospital. How hard can *that* be to find?"

"It's going to be upsetting. You've never seen a crash victim."

"And I never will once the feds get him," she reminded Jake. "It's now or never for me." Then, realizing she was being harsh, she paused, and in a gentler voice said, "I'm sorry, Jake, but there are things you don't know about my brother. Things he told to me alone."

"What does that have to do with this... this sense of urgency? I don't understand."

Inhaling deeply, she explained. "When Leif ejected from his plane over Iraq, his left hand caught on something, the controls or something. Half of it—half his hand—was torn away. He lost fingers, bone, nerves, tendons. When he was found, he was already half-dead. Nonetheless, his captors beat him savagely. When he wouldn't talk, they beat him until he couldn't talk and left him to die in the desert."

"We were never told," Jake said.

"No one was," she affirmed. "When he was found by a band of Shia Arabs, he was delirious. But he was alive. That meant a reward. They fit him with a tourniquet and did what little they could to keep him breathing. Anyway, by the time they reached a hospital, some kind of desert bacteria had turned the wound gangrenous. The doctors in Basrah had no choice but to amputate what remained of my brother's left hand. That kept his body alive, and eventually some memory returned. But he drifted in and out of coherence."

"So did he remember what happened? Jake asked anxiously.

"He remembered the trauma," Tina said, her eyes lowered. "He recalled the beatings by his captors, or some of them. But he never could—or would—reveal what caused him to crash his plane. Anyway, he finally came back. Somehow he found me, but the brother I knew, had died on that desert floor. He'd died then and there just as surely as if his heart had stopped—and in a way I guess it had."

Jake was shaken. Fighting back an involuntary sense of relief. His mind and heart raced. "I... Tina... I didn't know."

"Nobody knew. Remember, Jake, this all happened at about the time Bush stood on that aircraft carrier and declared 'Mission accomplished.' With that, nobody wanted to know about the mighty F-16 going down, or why it went down, or acknowledge that it did go down, or anything about the American flying it. No wreckage was reported. It's like it never happened."

"I tried to find out, Tina. Believe me I did. But everywhere I turned I hit a brick wall."

Jake did not mention that he'd been immediately transferred and reminded that he and Swede Bergstrom had been on a recon mission and sworn to secrecy. He would either forget the incident or face the unnamed, but clearly dire consequences. *Alone and unknown*, mere words at the time he'd first uttered them, had suddenly defined his everything. So, with nearly eight years remaining on his enlistment, and finally accepting that he could do nothing for his lost comrade, Jake understandably chose prudence, persuading himself it was duty.

When Jake's attention returned to the present, Tina was explaining, "My brother was fitted with a prosthetic hand. It's an ugly Teflon-covered thing with straps. It looks like a rubber forearm and glove with fingernails. But Leif could make it open and close by moving his arm this way and that." She demonstrated.

Jake knew that she was describing a transradial prosthesis, and while such a device might allow Leif to handle the control yoke of an airplane, it would disqualify him from keeping an unrestricted American pilot's certificate, and the military or airline career that went with it. Small wonder then, that he'd been reduced to pushing an old Curtiss C-46 around these tropical backwaters.

"My brother is not capable of what they say he's done," Tina said with purpose. "Now someone's trying to keep me from seeing a body they claim is Leif's. I need to know why." She picked up her bag. "So, I'm going, Jake. I don't need a face to recognize my brother... or to prove it's not him."

Pushing through the airport's terminal's doors, Tina flashed her passport and made straight for the exit where a taxi waited at the curb.

His resistance defused by the revelation, his guilt-fed need to protect Tina from herself only amplified, Jake did the same.

"Centre de Sainte Sebastian," she told the driver in surprisingly comfortable French.

"Le language du ballet," she said, answering Jake's silent question.

The cab moved forward.

Within a mere 15 minutes they were approaching a quaint, gaily painted green and white one-story structure facing the harbor, its entrance a columned arch. Atop the arch sat a carved wooden caduceus, its entwined serpents the solitary indication that this was a medical facility. As the cab turned in, Tina's phone squawked: "You have reached your destination."

"See," she said. "We're here."

Tossing a wad of money onto the driver's seat, she leaped out waited for Jake to do the same. Then, as the cab drove out of sight, rather than push through the hospital's entrance doors, she trotted quickly around the smallish building toward its rear, stopping before an overhead door protected by a retractable gate.

Coming up behind her, Jake stared at Tina, his heavy chart case in one hand, his other palm upright, his posture demanding she explain.

While opening the zipper on her overnight bag, she said, "The morgue is somewhere behind those doors. I'm gonna get in there. I just need to figure out how."

Before they could argue, the solution to her problem arrived with the loud *woop, woop,* of an approaching vehicle. As the rig swung in, its strobe lights flashing, Jake could see what appeared an official-looking shield on its door. He stepped back as the driver gestured from its window, shouting something in undecipherable Creole.

The man had apparently mistaken Jake's pilot's uniform for that of an official of some sort. When Jake turned back around, the gate had swung wide and the overhead door was rising. Tina was nowhere to be seen.

"C'mon c'mon!" her voice called out with jubilant urgency. "Sonofabitch," Jake marveled.

Incredulous, her force of will having quelled yet another obstacle, Jake did the only thing he could: he followed.

A couple of green-garbed personnel trotted past them and toward the arriving rigs, leaving the pair's incursion unchallenged.

"What's your plan?" Jake asked, catching up.

"Flexibility."

"That's a noun, not a plan."

Ignoring his objections, she disappeared down a hall and around a corner. She stopped before an elevator. Next to its door an arrowed sign announced, CORONER'S BRANCH. "Aha!" she said, and quickly pressed the cracked plastic "Down" button.

Encased by metal walls, they rode a lurching, rattling oversized elevator down to the subterranean world of the little hospital's morgue.

The elevator doors opened onto a harshly lit hallway. It was deserted.

As they walked quickly, Tina reached in her bag and appeared to be fiddling with her phone again. "I'm turning off the ringer. You should do the same. Where's your phone?"

"Forget my goddam phone," Jake whispered. "I'm sure they'll have one at the prison." Then, "It's buried somewhere in this thing," he relented, meaning his overstuffed chart case.

Deciding not to push it, Tina jammed her own instrument into a pocket of her jeans.

Moving close against him, she held Jake's arm as they briskly walked the dismal subterranean hall, its bare bulbs casting a shadowy pallor. It seemed the minor emergency unfolding one level above was commanding everyone's attention.

Their search for the crypt was proving pointless when from behind a pair of doors came a squealing mechanical *whir.*

They froze. As Jake and Tina locked eyes, the whirring sound stopped, and someone gave forth with a stream of vile, un-doctor-like epithets.

She stopped and looked at Jake as if awaiting an explanation.

"Workmen," he said. "This is pointless. We need to get the hell out of here."

With surprising strength, Tina lunged through the double doors pulling Jake off balance and into what could've been the set from an old horror movie.

At the charnel room's center stood a long, flat sink, its white porcelain surface chipped and discolored in the dim light. On it lay a nude body, its toe tagged, its head a charred knob.

Standing next to the corpse, a man in a rubber apron faced the intruders. His unmasked brutish face tightened at the unwelcome sight of the pair. He'd been in the midst of opening the cadaver wide at the thorax with a surgical saw.

"Oh, shit! I..." Jake stammered, appalled that they'd violated an autopsy in progress. "Sorry, I didn't know," he said. Taking Tina's arm, he turned for the doors, when the man with the saw spoke, "Stay where you are!"

The accent was Australian, the tone menacing.

As the man spun to confront the pair, behind him the cadaver's left arm, still attached at the shoulder, flopped free and dangled from table. The naked appendage, bloodless gray and ulcerated, terminated in a perversely healthy-appearing pink hand.

Staggering backward in abject horror, Jake's pulse pounded hammer-like in his head, his every survival instinct screaming RUN!

"Who in bloody hell are you?" demanded the man. He appeared unshaven, wore jeans and brogans. This was no medical man.

Composure returning, Jake realized Tina had slipped from his grip and run forward.

"How'd you get in here?" he shouted.

"My God!" Tina gasped, her eyes fixed on the mangled cadaver. "That's Leif on that slab!"

The butcher glanced down at the body on the sink before coming around to confront them.

"Take it easy, pal," Jake said, yanking Tina back to him, his words unheard above her screaming.

"What are you doing to my brother?"

Brandishing the saw, the man moved forward.

"I said easy, pal," Jake growled in the most threatening tone he could muster, moving forward to place himself between Tina and the advancing butcher, he raised a hand to block the advance.

Then he saw it.

There, on the floor, where the room turned to the left, lay another body, its green scrubs blood-soaked at the chest.

When Jake looked up, the saw-wielding man was looking straight into his eyes. He knew Jake had seen the body of the *actual* morgue attendant.

Squealing saw in hand, the Australian pounced.

Jake swung his 15-pound chart case.

Propelled by its powerful upward arc, one of its metal corners smashed hard into the attacker's jaw, sending him reeling backward, spitting blood. He dropped the saw.

As the attacker's knees folded, he reached behind him and drew a gun.

Raising the weapon, the assailant struggled to his feet.

Unable to close the distance between them, Jake spun like a discus thrower, this time heaving his hard-sided chart case arcing through the air. The heavy missile struck the gunman square in the chest and sent him sprawling again, his pistol spinning across the tile floor. As the man scrambled to retrieve his weapon, Jake grabbed Tina's arm and shoved her backward, shielding her with his body while he pushed her toward the double doors shouting, "C'mon, move. Let's get out of here!"

Jake and Tina careened into the hall as shots were fired from behind the closing double doors.

As Jake pulled Tina by her wrist, she cried, "I saw him. Oh God, I saw Leif!"

"I know, I know! I did too." Jake tried to calm her as he searched the dismal halls for something to use as a weapon: a chair, fire bottle, anything. "Keep your voice down."

"But it…"

"Shut up and look for something I could club this bastard with!" he insisted as Tina pried her wrist free from his grip.

Unarmed against a gunman, Jake realized they had no choice but to run back down the hallway to the elevator. "Stay close and be quiet."

"Okay," her shaky voice replied, and he felt her small hand on his back as they moved.

The harsh hallway light made every shadow a gun-wielding maniac, but no one and nothing stirred. Stopping, Jake peered around the corner.

It was clear.

He forced himself onward, taking tentative steps forward until they once more approached the autopsy room. Turning to Tina, he put a finger to her lips. She nodded compliance.

His every sense heightened, the only sounds Jake heard were Tina's rapid breathing and the cannon reports of his own pulse.

In the hall, bloody footprints marked the floor as they approached the nightmare room. The footprints turned left and faded away. Jake and Tina had turned right.

Certain his heartbeat could be heard in the eerie quiet as they passed the double doors, Jake no longer felt Tina's hand on his back.

Turning quickly, he saw her push through the doors of the charnel room only to disappear inside.

For a long moment, Jake stood looking into the room, his breathing coarse, uncontrollable, his anger volcanic. His every rational impulse was to abandon the crazy woman to the crazier man stalking them, and save his own life. Instead, he stepped through the double doors.

Back inside the hideous room, his view was unobstructed. On the floor was the bloodied corpse of the hospital employee, killed for being in the wrong place at the wrong time.

Carnage and the stink of it pervaded the chamber. At its far end Tina had thrown herself across her brother's eviscerated corpse, her small body wracked with sobs.

Jake, stricken dumb, stared at his old comrade's charred, half-eaten face and head.

Fighting back panic, he reached out to pull Tina away from the mutilated thing that had once saved both his life and hers, but now threatened both.

Feeling Jake's hand on her back, Tina turned on him like a wild thing, teeth bared. "Leave me alone!" she screamed, her right hand gripping Swede's prosthetic left.

"Let him go, Tina. We gotta get out of here!"

She turned and swung her right hand at Jake's head, stumbling as she did so.

Brushing off her blow, Jake started for the doors, alternately lifting and dragging with him a struggling Tina Bergstrom.

Hearing a meaty thud, he turned. Tina had not released her grip on the prosthetic hand, causing her brother's body to fall from the table and land head first onto the floor, splashing blood and ash across the hard white surface.

"Let me go!" Tina yelled hysterically, punching Jake's arms and chest.

When he released her, *she* fell to the floor crawling frantically back toward her brother's charred and broken body. Finally, Jake grabbed her waist, lifted her bodily, and ran from the room.

Limp in Jake's powerful arms, her fighting subsided. "We have to find a way out of here, Tina, or *we're* gonna wind up on that table." He searched her eyes while lowering her to her feet. "Do you understand?"

She dropped her head to his chest, still sobbing, absent fear, wild with grief.

Placing an arm around Tina's waist, he turned her toward the elevator.

Standing exposed at the midpoint of a long corridor, Jake remembered his chart case.

The elevator doors stood closed before them, while a pair of steel doors remained shut at their backs. Scanning the corridor, Jake considered going back for the case, wishing he'd packed his pistol in it, as so many of his pilot colleagues had begun to do.

Abandoning the thought, he frantically punched the elevator's UP button. After what seemed an eternity the sound of rushing air indicated the elevator had started down toward them. At long last, the doors parted and he moved Tina to the elevator.

Stepping in first, she gasped, pointing to the convex mirror in the elevator's corner.

Looking up, Jake glimpsed the distorted reflection of a man cowering out of sight.

Instinctively, Jake reached in to pull Tina back, only to be pulled into the car himself by the waiting assailant.

As he spun to face the man, a fist slammed squarely into his right cheek.

Staggering backwards, Jake recovered, raised his own fists boxer-like, briefly pausing the man's approach before the assailant rushed him.

As the elevator's doors closed them in, the Aussie raised his gun to Jake's face. "Don't be a hero, Yank. You'll just die tired."

Suddenly Tina was on the assailant like a bobcat, her right hand pulling at his gun arm, scratching at his eyes with her left as she hung on his back.

In that microsecond, Jake's left jab sent the man reeling onto his heels, his nose shattered by the skilled and powerful blow. The movement slammed Tina against the opposite wall, causing her to let go and collapse to the floor in a breathless heap.

Choking on blood and cartilage, his ruined nose flattened, the Australian nonetheless managed to shake it off and propel himself from the car's opposite wall only to meet a powerful body blow from his trained target. A left uppercut sent the Aussie slamming against the far wall, dazed and spitting teeth.

Right fist poised before a coiled bicep Jake leapt at the attacker, but the wide-eyed, adrenaline-crazed Aussie managed to get off a sloppy gunshot, causing Jake to dodge the errant bullet, while giving the desperate, street-fighting savage the microsecond he needed to ram a shoulder into Jake's side, the bigger man's weight slamming his victim hard against the elevator's metal wall.

As Jake pounded his attacker's back with hammer-like blows, he was lifted bodily by the larger, adrenaline-crazed, heavily-muscled man and slammed onto the elevator's floor.

Fighting to remain conscious himself, Jake felt the elevator rise and the gun's butt come down hard.

Jake felt neither the second blow to his head nor the chemical-soaked rag denying him breath.

Jake's return to consciousness brought a catalogue of agonies. His mouth and nose were swollen. Breathing came in barely adequate gasps. His lungs burned. Once more, he tasted blood. His torso, ribs, and kidneys throbbed with a pain he'd not have thought possible. With the slow return of faculties, he realized he'd been stomped and pummeled even after he'd lost consciousness.

But he was alive. Was Tina?

He lay on his stomach. Attempts to move revealed that he was bound at the wrists, knees, and ankles. A coarse cloth bag encompassed his head, denying him sight, his every breath an incendiary torture.

Confused, nauseated, denied any tactile sense save pain, Jake attempted a shout but managed only a muffled, "*Tina...*"

He snorted to clear his blood-clogged airways. The action restored his olfactory senses but he could discern only musty odors and exhaust fumes.

The scent of heather was gone. Where was Tina Bergstrom?

Trying desperately to assess his situation, Jake sensed only velocity and rushing air. He quickly reconciled the low rumble and vibration engulfing him with the unique odor of spent aviation gas. He was in an airplane! The sound and rumble of radial engines told him he was in an old airplane.

The machine was aloft and moving at speed. The rear compartment where he lay was cold. The thin air engulfing Jake punished his battered ears with sound. With each turbulent bounce, his inflamed midsection experienced a new agony.

After how long he couldn't know, the engines throttled back, and the plane entered a steep left bank—so steep that Jake struggled against the G-force to avoid tumbling sideways across the deck. Suddenly the plane's nose lifted and Jake felt the sensation of falling. As the aircraft plummeted in a steep, nose high, wing-low, side-slipping descent, his ears felt new pain thanks to the swollen passages. The plane trembled at the edge of an aerodynamic stall.

From the sound of the slipstream, Jake knew the wing flaps were deploying as the machine rolled level at last. Jake sensed continued deceleration. The air around him grew warm. Hydraulic pumps squealed as the aircraft's wheels extended and locked into place with a bang. They were landing.

The wheels hit the ground hard. Brakes were applied harder still. Engines roared. As the machine shed speed, bouncing to a stop, Jake's bound body slid forward despite the restraints. His already battered head slammed against the bulkhead.

The pilot was heavy-handed, skilled but uncaring.

They were on the ground.

With a mechanical, sliding sound something, a cockpit window—no, a hatch—opened. The space around Jake filled with sodden, heavy air. He smelled rotting vegetation. No sooner had the hatch been opened than did a large insect crawl beneath Jake's hood. The unseen creature paused as if to think, then quickly scampered toward his eyes. Panicked, Jake rolled his head to the side, crushing the bug beneath his cheekbone. It died with a hideous crunch, its flattened carcass sticking to Jake's grimy, blood-caked skin.

As Jake lay bound, gagged, terrified, confused, and miserable on the floor of the airplane's rear cabin, he waited, helpless as well, his every sense heightened.

The starboard side engine fell silent. There was a rustling from the cockpit. As the pilot pulled himself from the left seat and strode into the rear cabin, the last of his heavy footfalls stopping inches from Jake's face.

"Awake now, are we, mate?" the pilot croaked, and Jake, unable to see his tormentor rubbing a sore jaw, nonetheless recognized the Australian accented voice from the morgue.

"Yeh hit like a mule, Yank. Dumb as one, too." He laughed and checked Jake's bindings. "Alright, playtime's over."

With that, the man reached across Jake's prone form to open the airplane's main door. In his haste, the Australian's leg brushed against Jake's hood, lifting it enough to admit a patch of light.

Jake tried to clear his vision. As he did, a mechanical click signaled that a ladder was being attached to the exit door. It locked into place.

Jake, still bound and unable to stand, tilted his head back trying to take in the scene unfolding around him. He caught a faint, too-quick glimpse of another oblong shape prone on the floor, poorly defined in the dim glow of approaching dawn. The figure was wrapped in a tarp.

Tina!

Before Jake could be certain, the doorway darkened as another form filled the opening; someone was coming aboard.

"Don't muck about, Cegato," the Australian's voice said. "The major will be wonderin' why I stopped so far from the hangars."

Perceiving very little from beneath his hood, Jake could hear more than see that the enwrapped figure he presumed was Tina Bergstrom was being dragged toward the doorway to the outside.

"Go," the Aussie said, speaking to the shadow figure just above a whisper. "Close the hatch and ditch that ladder. Be quick about it. I'll meet you tonight." Jake heard the man return to the cockpit and waited blindly for the hatch to close. It did not. Instead he heard, "What the... why you sodding little wog. I'll..."

Gunshots! Two, three, four shots rang out from the direction of the hatch. Jake heard the slugs striking something—the Australian, judging by his screams.

The airplane's port engine roared back to life and the machine began rolling as the ladder fell away with a clatter from the slowly accelerating plane.

Short bursts of gunfire were heard outside the cabin as the plane bounced across the aerodrome's unpaved field. Its pilot—the injured Aussie—seemed to be pushing the throttles forward in an uncontrolled effort to escape the attacker, who'd stopped firing.

As the plane gained speed by the second, its nose and starboard wing abruptly pitched down. It jerked to a sudden, violent stop. The port engine quit.

The eerie whine of the cockpit's gyros were the only sound, the only smell, the faint scent of spent powder.

Then, through the still-open hatch, footfalls could be heard approaching at a run.

"Damn! Bloody damn!" came a British-accented male voice from outside the airplane. The voice grew louder, closer with each profanity.

Leaping easily through the doorway, whose threshold was suspended just two feet above the ground thanks to the collapsed landing gear, the running man came aboard, shouting, "What in bloody hell happened here?"

No answer.

The Englishman's footsteps came closer, and he yanked the hood from Jake's head. The two men's faces now an inch apart, the Englishman shouted, "And who is *this*?"

Jake shook his head to clear the fog. Looking past the Englishman, he saw that the tarpaulin wrapped bundle he had thought was Tina was gone.

A groan came from the cockpit.

Turning from Jake, the Englishman made his way to the sound.

Looking toward the cockpit, Jake saw the Australian brute, prone, on the deck, half-in, half-out of the cockpit. As the Englishman yanked the man's head back, Jake saw that his left ear dangled by a single strip of crimson sinew.

Dried blood surrounded his flattened nose, while more still, covered an entire side of the Australian's face. His most serious wounds, not visible to Jake, were at the man's chest; he was alive, though barely so.

"What happened here?" the Englishman shouted an inch from the Aussie's dangling ear, teeth bared as he dragged his man into the rear cabin. "Where's the microchip?"

The Australian responded by flailing out wildly at the Englishman, his hands scratching his inquisitor's face.

"Aghh!" the Englishman screamed, throwing his head back, hands going to his eyes as fresh blood dripped down his cheek below the left eye.

Without opening the swollen orb, his balled fist came down hard against the Australian's cheek. "Look at me, Tretooey!" The Englishman roared, his literally blind rage overcoming the pain of a scratched cornea as he roughly pulled the Australian to him. "Did you find the Swede's body? Did you recover the chip?"

Barely conscious, the Australian, whose name apparently was Tretooey, tried to speak, but failed. The Englishman mercilessly and repeatedly shook and slapped him back to wakefulness, shouting the same questions over and over.

If only to stop the abuse, Tretooey finally mustered his fast-waning strength. "I... I'm sorry, Major, I never should'a trusted the little wog," he croaked. "I'm... I..."

"What are you saying, man?" demanded the Englishman, his uninjured right eye maniacally wide as he wiped blood from the other with a shirtsleeve. The injury to the Englishman's eye looked serious. Jerking a thumb toward Jake, his voice turned icy cold and he demanded of Tretooey, "Just tell me you found it! Tell me you found the chip."

"I cut Swede open, figurin' he swallered it." the dying man said, his voice coarse whisper. "But, then *this* bloke and the sheila..."

"Damn your eyes, man, talk sense!"

Jake knew that *sheila* was Aussie slang for woman, and again he thought of the tarpaulin-wrapped bundle that had lain next to him.

"Did you find the Swede's body?" the Englishman repeated. "Did you get the microchip?"

"Cegato took her," Tretooey babbled, fighting to hang on, his words barely audible. "It was Cegato," he said, pointing toward the open hatch. "The little wog just…he come outta the bush and took her… He waited for us and he come aboard… He shot me and took her."

"Cegato!" the Englishman raged. "No way that filthy savage could have known about this." With realization, the shocked look of a betrayal suddenly shone in the major's one pale blue eye and he placed his right hand on what Jake could not see was a slowly-bubbling wound at Tretooey's chest made by one of the attacker's bullets. "How could he know?" the major demanded, squeezing the dying man's wound. "Speak up, man! How could Cegato know?" Getting no response, his fingers curled into a claw. "Tell me or I'll rip your goddam lungs out, you bloody double-crossing bastard."

The Australian barely managed an answer. "Cegato, he didn't much like you, Major, and he fooled me into trustin' him." Tretooey struggled for a breath. "He come to me with a plan, and I fell for it. We was…" But Tretooey said no more. After one last, guttural exhale, he fell silent. His head fell forward. Ian Tretooey was dead.

From the deck of the rear compartment, Jake looked on in horrified disbelief. Then something pressed hard against his carotid artery and, again, blackness descended.

- CHAPTER 6 -

NYPD Detective Patrick Francis Garodnik, Manhattan North homicide, practically leapt down the three concrete steps leading from the front door of his Forest Hills two-flat.

Rubbing sleep from his eyes, he'd had just ten minutes to dress between the time the call had come in and the cruiser arrived to take him into the city. His shoes were untied. Under his arm he carried a holstered snub-nosed .38 and the balance of his clothing. His freckled face was a scowl as he stormed past the nervous young patrolman holding the door of the black-and-white that headquarters had dispatched to drive the lieutenant into the city.

It was 5:00 a.m.

Garodnik's enormous orange mustache twitched as he jumped in the patrol car, growling, "OIC," to the nervous young officer at the wheel.

"What do you see, sir?"

Garodnik glared at the young rookie. "What?"

"You said, *Oh, I see,*" the fledgling asked, checking his rookie's-crisp uniform for a flaw. "I… I'm sorry, sir, but what do you see?"

"What?! No! O I C! O I C!" Garodnik growled impatiently. "Who's the officer in charge of the scene? Jeezis."

"I don't know sir. They told us to get here on the double, wait for you, and drive you to that address."

The second rookie held out a card. "Sir?" he said, somehow a question.

Garodnik was not pleased that HQ thought it wise to send a couple of newbies in a patrol car, even if this was a simple chauffeuring errand. "Let's go," the lieutenant said, reading the card's Upper West Side address. "And take the Grand Central Parkway."

"But it's…"

"Grand. Central. Parkway." he growled slowly.

No sooner had the cruiser inched forward than Garodnik was on his cell phone, choosing it over the radio for privacy.

After three rings, desk Sergeant Robert Connelly picked up. "I'm tellin' you, Lieutenant, it's the son's place…yeah, ex-DA Silver's son's apartment. That's where we found the body. I figured I had to send a car. Had to get you there first. I ain't even called in forensics yet, and the scene's a friggin' bloodbath."

"You did right, Connie," the veteran cop said, recalling the elder Silver's tenure as Manhattan District Attorney with a respectful nod. "What's Silver's son's name?"

"Jacob. Jacob Silver."

With that, the veteran detective knew this would be a hyper-sensitive case. The elder Silver was a prosecutor who knew every defense attorney's trick, and was universally revered by the police, a cop's DA, so to speak.

"Who's OIC, Connie?" the detective asked.

"Anthony Grasso, Sergeant out of TPF. Couple units out'a 24th responded first, though."

Garodnik curled his brow, "Get hold of Grasso, Connie. Tell him to keep a tight lid on this thing until I get there."

"Already have, Lieutenant. Tony's old shoes. He knows the drill."

Garodnik thought for a moment. "On second thought, Connie," he said, "get the Old Man on the horn too. Phone him at home, wire-line telephone, no radio. The chief's gotta know about this before it breaks. Tell him I'm on the scene. Tell him… *ask* him not to do anything until we talk, me and him."

Garodnik turned to his young driver, ordering him to turn on the light bar but not the siren, "C'mon, son. Code-two." The rookie got it right.

Outside the door to Jake Silver's apartment, the dimly lit, usually quiet hallway of the stately old building was now awash with chattering voices, police radios and flashing camera strobes. Silver's neighbors milled about in robes and slippers, huddling together, frightened, feeling out of place in their own building. The police, strangers here, seemed the only ones with purpose, the only ones who belonged.

"Where's Sergeant Grasso?" Garodnik bellowed as he bullied his way through the hallway crowd, *waving tin* as he charged forward.

Seeing Garodnik's gold badge held above the heads of the gawkers, a uniformed officer called to him from behind the yellow-taped entrance doorway of Jake's apartment: "The sergeant's in here, sir." Stepping forward to raise the tape, the uniformed officer directed Garodnik into the apartment. "Can I get you to log in, sir?"

Garodnik scrawled his name and badge number without stopping.

"Sergeant!" the uni shouted into the open doorway realizing the lieutenant, who'd already brushed by him, had no intention of waiting for the OIC or anyone else. "Lieutenant's on the scene," he shouted. This announcement heralded a frenzy of camera flashes from the hallway.

"What a goddam zoo," Garodnik grumbled. "Sergeant!"

Gray at the temples, West Point straight and fit, Grasso stepped from the hallway leading to Jake's bedroom. He met the detective mid-stride in the living room.

"What is this, Sergeant, a goddam movie premiere?" Garodnik barked, jerking a thumb toward the hallway. "I called for a blackout on this."

"Sorry, Lieutenant. It's mostly neighbors. We *hadda* tape the door to keep 'em out. But, cell phones now, y'know. This thing will be all over the Internet."

Garodnik nodded, knowing the futility of his charge.

"It gets worse, Lieutenant."

"Worse?"

"Yeah." The sergeant pointed toward the taped doorway. "One of the ghouls out there is some kind of half-assed newspaperman." Grasso glanced at his notepad as he spoke. "Guy's name is Wendell Leitch. He's the one called this in. Lives upstairs. Sonofabitch was here before I was. The unis found him waiting outside the door when they responded. Prob'ly corrupted the hell out of the doorknob. His photog just got here too. I got a man on her already, on both of 'em. The rest are civilians, other tenants sniffing blood. It was a circus before we could secure. Sorry, Lieutenant."

"Jeezis," Garodnik groaned. "Awright. Keep everybody here. And, Sergeant, that means *everybody!* Have an officer get all their names and info. Nobody leaves the floor until we run a make on 'em." He looked down the long hallway leading to the bedroom, steeling himself for the carnage. "Okay, Anthony, what've we got?"

There are three organic smells a homicide cop recognizes when approaching the scene of a murder: decomposition, burned flesh, or the one that now assaulted Garodnik's nose as he approached the bedroom. Even before seeing it, the all too familiar odor of exposed entrails told the veteran detective this was a savage kill.

Grasso led Garodnik into the bedroom and here even the veteran lieutenant's well-conditioned reactions were tested by what he saw. "Sweet mother of God."

He stepped closer. The woman's nude body was half off the bed as she lay supine with her torso hanging over the edge of the mattress, her head just touching the floor. The back of her cranium was gone, blown off by a bullet to the forehead. Inconsistent with her position in death, bits of the her brain and fragments of parietal-bone–the back of her skull—were splattered across the wall adjacent to the bed's wooden headboard.

Garodnik knelt and, donning nitrile gloves, he carefully arranged the young victim's hair away from her face and neck to better reveal her wounds. There was a bullet hole just above her wide open, wide-set eyes.

Awful as the fatal head wound was, it was the bared teeth frozen in a scream of agony, and below that the more horrific wound at the victim's throat that held the seasoned homicide cop's attention. As he violated protocol and gently closed her green eyes he stared at her neck.

Below the neck wound, a blood pool had formed, from which a crimson stream traversed two feet of wooden floor to end near an old cast-iron radiator at the near wall. Most of the victim's blood had probably flowed from the gash at her throat. As his eyes followed the river of crimson, Garodnik saw that the blood ran to a hole some two or three inches across in the floor at the base of the steam radiator. The gap accommodated movement in the two-inch steam pipe passing through it from below. The oversized chrome ring normally covering such a hole was missing, allowing the blood to make its way into the bare hole as it would a drain.

Detective Garodnik stood again, and just looked at the victim for some time. He recognized the killer's grisly calling card. Finally, removing the bloodied gloves, he turned to Sergeant Grasso. "Recognize the MO?" he asked, the morning's bluster gone out of him.

"Yeah," Grasso replied. But rather than look at the victim, Grasso simply pointed across the bed to a small glassine bag of white powder, open and spilling its contents across the nightstand. "Goes along with that."

"What's it been, Anthony," Garodnik asked, "eight, maybe ten years since we seen one like this?"

"Just about," Grasso replied. "But, I don't know, Lieutenant, this vic don't fit the profile. Let's even say she *was* a mule–which I doubt—this ain't the 90s and even if it was, this is capo level shit."

"None of this fits," Garodnik mused. Despite their feigned indifference, both seasoned officers were upset and more than a little puzzled.

"No sign of forced entry," Grasso observed.

"Perhaps she knew her doer."

The veteran sergeant nodded. "Lividity looks fixed. What blood's left inside her pooled at her back. That splatter on the wall says the gunshot is what killed this girl. Looks like the bullet's lodged in there, or in the wall behind it." Grasso pointed to the bullet hole. "Trajectory and spatter don't jive with the position of the body."

"Exactly," Garodnik agreed. "She was shot while standing, then moved after she fell." Pausing, he pointed at the neck wound. "Then the killer took the time to do that."

"Looks like her body was placed on the bed, then set in this position to bleed out. Cool hand at work here, Lieutenant. Sonofabitch took his time. That open mouth was staged. Whoever did this hung around until rigor set in, forced open the vic's mouth so it looked like a scream. That and the tongue—pure theater."

"Find a weapon?"

"Forty caliber revolver," answered Grasso. "Been fired, still smells. Box of low velocity shells in the drawer." Grasso jerked a thumb toward the living room. "Gave it to the uni outside to bag."

"Isn't that what pilots carry now?" Garodnik asked. "Slow 40s?"

"Some do," Grasso affirmed, "ever since World Trade Center."

Instinctively, both men's eyes went to the bedroom clothes closet where Jake's spare NorthAm uniform hung, its three gold stripes plainly visible.

"Soon as you gimme the go sign," Grasso said, "I'll get the techs to dig the slug out of the wood and see if we get a ballistics match."

"No struggle," Garodnik observed, looking at the victim's hands, her knuckles in the blood above her head.

"What do we know about the flyboy lives here?" Grasso asked.

"That reporter see any of this?" Garodnik said, dodging Grasso's question, and by doing so answering it to the seasoned cop's satisfaction.

"Nope. The unis kept him outside when they arrived. Nobody else's been in here."

Garodnik pressed a point. "That deck on the nightstand," he was referring to the glassine bag of white powder. "Coke?"

"I got a buck says it ain't for jock itch."

"Planted."

"I don't figure the guy who lives here is the type to leave his dope lying around in a bag," Grasso said. "This scene is *not* rich with nuance."

"Keep talking, Anthony," the lieutenant urged. "What're you thinking?"

"Well, Lieutenant, somebody is leaving a message. Whole scene's been staged. We'll do a tox screen, but I got another buck says the resident and the vic both come up clean."

"Collateral damage," Garodnik mused.

"The girl, probably," Grasso mumbled. "Wrong place wrong time, maybe."

Garodnik didn't acknowledge but simply moved closer to the bed, being careful to avoid the blood pool on the old wooden floor, "Got a make on her?"

"Stuff in her purse makes her one Cassandra McRea. Cedar Rapids, Iowa address on the driver's license. Business cards say she was a free-lance artist." Grasso pointed toward a large, flat briefcase-like object leaning against the far wall, "Portfolio over there, pin shots and model-type stuff. Also there's a lot of art supplies, a resume, all spread out in the living room. She maybe picked up work as a model, lookin' for a break as an artist. Damned pretty little thing. Very middle-western looking."

"Yeah. Welcome to Fun City, kid. What else?"

"Fifty bucks still in her wallet. Address book says she had appointments yesterday and today around midtown. Had a key card for the Millennium Hotel over on 44th. We'll run it all down."

"Ok, Sergeant, I'm assigning you as CO." Garodnik handed Grasso his card. "Finish securing the scene. This case is priority-one, and we keep it in the family." He touched the sergeant's shoulder for emphasis. "Anybody gives you static, call me and I'll kick it upstairs fast." He paused, raised a finger. "I mean all the way upstairs."

"Got it," Grasso confirmed, adding in a lowered voice, "Sir, I'm gonna hafta call the ME, and get the place dusted and Luminoled, get the vic's phone to the techs."

"Yeah, go ahead, Sergeant. But tell everybody to keep it dark, at least until we handle the vic's family and get back to you," he said, a sadness in his tone, "and I'm gonna meet with the chief." The detective headed toward the living room. "Where's that scribe?"

"Detective," a voice called from behind the taped doorway.

The lieutenant turned to fix his withering gaze upon a civilian pressing against the crime scene tape blocking his entrance to the apartment. Unlike most of the gawkers, the smallish, tousle-haired man was in street clothes, wore a plaid jacket over jeans and sported wire-rimmed glasses. He held an electronic tablet and a reporter's long paper notepad that he was waving into the room for attention. He also clenched a pen in his teeth. "Detective," he slurred again to the lieutenant, "who do you fink is rishbonshible?"

Grasso jerked a thumb in the inquisitor's direction, saying, "Mumble-mouth here is our citizen," meaning this was the man who'd called in the situation: the reporter Wendell Leitch.

Garodnik sized the man up, then growled, "Take that goddam pen out of your mouth and speak English."

"Is this a drug hit?" Leitch shouted as he pressed against the yellow tape crisscrossing the doorway and denying him entry. "We lookin' at a botched robbery here, a lover's quarrel? Gimme something I can use." The smallish man sneered for the benefit of the audience of neighbors who now focused their attention on him, inspiring him to performance. "Did the flyboy maybe get caught boinkin' some dago wiseguy's *comare*?" He waved his press credential as he spoke.

Getting no response beyond nodding commiseration from his audience in the hall, which he acknowledged with a wink, Leitch pressed into the room, straining the tape.

Surprisingly, Garodnik gestured to the uniformed officer restraining him to let Leitch pass. "But keep the rest of those ghouls out of here and in the hall. You!" he jabbed a finger into the eagerly approaching newspaper man's chest, stopping him in his tracks. "What's your name again? Wendy something?"

"It's *Wendell!* Wendell Leitch," the reporter enunciated clearly, raising his iPad. "I already told that to…"

"I'll take that," Garodnik barked, grabbing the electronic tablet.

Glancing at its glowing screen which was in the camera mode, he saw only his moving selfie. "I know you wrote something on this thing, *Wen-dell*," Garodnik said, emphasizing each syllable unnecessarily. Where is it? And what are you, a blogger, local cable, what?"

The small tousle-haired man deigned to clarify while trying to peer beyond the big detective and into the hall leading to the bedroom. "I'm a *newspaper* man," he said, a boast.

"Really," Garodnik said. "The Times, Daily News, what *news*paper you on?"

"The New York Register."

Garodnik let a grunt of derision as Leitch settled down, adjusted his trendy wire-rims and watched Garodnik jot notes of his own with a pencil. "I don't have to tell you what I wrote," Leitch added, righteous indignation flaring. "I wanna know what *you* wrote, Detective. If it's about me, I have a right to know?"

Garodnik stared blankly at Leitch. "It *is* about you, Wendell. I wrote that you're a tabloid flak," he lied. "But now that you're in the room I'm upgrading it to material witness."

"Great," the reporter groaned. "How about my iPad?"

"You must be new at this," Garodnik said, holding the man's tablet just out of reach. "But here's how it goes. I ask you questions. You answer the questions."

"What? I…"

Garodnik raised a finger in warning. "*I* ask, *you* answer."

"But you can't just take my stuff…"

"Of course I can. I have a gun. See?"

"What gives you the right to harass the press? If…"

"Okay," Garodnik growled, "let's pretend the Register really *is* the press. In here you're a witness. Maybe you should have stayed in the hall." He held the iPad before the reporter's face. "You made notes on what you heard. Then you carried this thing into an active crime scene. That makes it relevant, material, inculpatory."

"C'mon, man," said the frantic reporter. "You coaxed me in here!"

Obscured beneath his mustache, a barely visible grin crossed the detective's mouth. "Listen to me, Wendell," he said, knowing the story would get out no matter what. In fact, given the array of smart phones flashing in the hallway, some nutso versions of it already had. Garodnik also knew that this was the biggest story Wendell Leitch had ever been close to. He also knew the type: too antsy to behave himself.

But, more than that, the detective knew that a *useful idiot* with a bullhorn might be just what this case needed.

"Leitch," Garodnik said, "you wanna be treated like a hostile witness or a journalist?"

The reporter settled down. "What are you talking about?"

"Simple," Garodnik said. "Keep a lid on this and you'll get your toys back... and maybe a little piece of this story, too... the real story." He handed the tablet to Grasso without taking his eyes from Leitch. "Tag it."

"Wait..." Leitch said, "an exclusive?"

"That gal in the hall, she your photog?" the detective asked, ignoring Leitch's question..

"What gal?"

"Stop sparring with me, dammit."

"C'mon, Detective. Let me do my..."

"Y'know, Wendell, I can't remember a time when you weren't talking."

Leitch nodded, resigned. "Sorry."

Garodnik turned to the nearest uniformed officer. "Have his photog—she's the one with the Marine Corps crewcut and the real camera—have her shoot the crowd outside. Then confiscate her SD card. Keep an officer on Mr. Leitch, here. Get his statement... and get some fresh tape on that damned door!" As Garodnik dialed his cell phone, he turned to his witness, "Cooperate, Wendell, and a few hours from now you'll be on CNN."

An hour later, Chief of Police Alton Portlock, along with his boss Commissioner William Yost, and Pat Garodnik sat in a circle at the 21st Precinct station house. Beyond the caged and painted windows of its ancient green and gray interrogation room dawn was breaking, while inside, a statement was being taken from the NYPD's only witness, Wendell Leitch.

"Give it to me again, Leitch," Garodnik demanded.

"I told you, Detective, I didn't call it in right away because I didn't think it was any of my concern. Couples fight." Leitch looked at the floor and added, "I'm not sayin' this babe asked for it or anything. I just mean chicks can piss a guy off, y'know?"

"You said that the upstairs apartment was usually quiet."

"Right, the guy lives up there is a pilot. He's away most the time. Seen some women come and go with him in the elevator, the lobby. But those babes all looked plenty alive."

"Had you ever seen the victim before?"

"No."

With that, Chief Portlock, who'd been facing the wall, turned toward the witness, the dark features of his Denzel-handsome face transformed into a scowl. "Lieutenant, you told me this witness didn't get into the bedroom!"

"He didn't, chief," Garodnik answered coolly. "Leitch, how the hell do you know you've never seen the victim if you don't know what she looked like?"

"Somebody said she's kind of a redhead. I never saw any redheads with the flyboy."

A look of incredulity crossed Garodnik's face.

"I'm a journalist, detective. I notice things. Sorry if that includes leggy female things."

Rolling his eyes, Garodnik pressed him. "So you thought you heard a scream and some running. But, being the observant journalist that you are, you mistook the sounds of mortal terror for foreplay. What time was this?"

"The screaming and running happened yesterday morning, early, a little after eight, nine, maybe. So, I figured the guy's having himself a kinky little aperitif. I'm a journalist, detective, not a pervert."

"Yeah, well, nobody's perfect."

"Ha, ha. Next question."

"So," Garodnik obliged, "after that, it was quiet?"

"Yeah. After the argument, it got quiet."

"That didn't seem strange to you?"

"No. I figured they were enjoying a little makeup cuddle. Besides, the guy's out of town all the time, so quiet is normal, like I already told you."

"Then what?"

"I ate breakfast, and left. Then, last night, I got back home around eight. Everything was quiet. I went to bed around eleven. Then later, I come back to bed after taking a leak. I lie back and reach over to turn out the light and there it was."

"The stain?"

"Right. Dark red stain spreading across my goddam ceiling. Thing like that gets your attention at three in the morning."

"And you figured it was blood right away, first thing?"

In a veiled critique of his inquisitors' police work, Leitch said, "In this city? Yeah. First thing."

With that, the interrogators left the room to discuss the situation, Leitch called out, "Your forensics techs are crawling all over my place now. My stuff better be there when I get back."

Deciding finally that they couldn't hold him any longer, a detective had Leitch sign his statement and cut him loose.

With Leitch gone, a uniformed sergeant stepped up and addressed the chief. "May I see you in the squad room, sir?"

Seeing the papers in the officer's hand, Portlock said, "Whatever it is can be said in front of the commissioner."

"Well, sir…sirs..," the sergeant began, "these just came in from the Federal District Office in Dade County, Florida." To the chief's surprise, the officer handed Portlock the papers, then abruptly turned and left the room.

Portlock, his brow furrowed, read what he was handed, breathed deeply and passed the papers to Commissioner Yost.

Yost read the words, looked up to meet Portlock's waiting gaze and asked the inevitable question, "What in bloody hell is going on here, Al?"

"I don't know, Will," the chief said, resignedly. "I only know what's next."

"I don't suppose I could persuade you…"

"Sorry, but I'd prefer to stay here with the killers and rapists." Turning serious, Portlock added, "It *would* be better coming from you."

"Of course," Yost agreed. "*I'll* make the call…" The commissioner then hesitated. "No, I'll do this in person. Besides, MJ probably knows where Jake actually *is*. Meantime, Al, get hold of Miami FDO. See what else they got and FAX it all to me in the car."

His jaw set for the task ahead, Commissioner Yost called for his driver and headed across town to the apartment of his dear friend: former colleague, and unsuspecting parent, MJ Silver.

- CHAPTER 7 -

The elder Silver was a legend in New York police circles. In cop parlance, that meant if an officer brought in a solid collar, Silver was a prosecutor who'd navigate the legal labyrinth with the cool precision of a surgeon to see an indictment returned. A brilliant attorney, who'd recently retired from public service, Myrna Juliette Silver, Jake's mother and New York County's first female DA, had been respected far and wide as a fair if determined jurist.

Known simply as *MJ* to her friends and colleagues, the statuesque advocate was a quick-witted and formidable presence able to command a room whatever that room's prefix or pretext. In fact, her forthright tell-it-like-it-is manner and tailored good looks, as much as a remarkable ability to reconcile an impressive record of convictions against her own controversial positions on mandatory minimum sentencing had made MJ Silver both a sought-after lecturer, and a less than reluctant celebrity in the media-crazed environment characteristic of her New York City domicile.

But first and foremost, MJ Silver had *made her bones* as a fearless prosecutor with whom a plaintiff, defendant, or arresting officer need speak the truth and the whole truth and nothing but the truth. To do otherwise was to be exposed for a liar; this ability she credited to her agile brain's *"bullshit detector."*

Sorely missed since having left public service and the judgeship that awaited her merest assent, she'd elected instead to turn her considerable talents to what she'd famously called the *just* in justice, by signing on as chief counsel for the advocacy group Common Sense; the decision earned MJ Silver far more enemies than allies.

Despite her colleagues' disappointment, the youthful 54 year old remained close with both Portlock and Yost.

Now, having been briefed by the former on the ride over, the latter stood in the kitchen of his dear friend's west side apartment where he faced the Silver family matriarch as she stood before him dressed in fuzzy slippers and a terry bathrobe. The strong, if finer facial features of her missing son were clearly evident on her troubled countenance as Yost recited the soundtrack of a parent's nightmare. "Your son's prints are on the murder weapon, MJ."

"Did he leave a video confession as well?" she countered, her cynicism betraying her distress as she began nervously pacing the room. "Jake is in Los Angeles."

"We don't know where he is, dear heart. His airline has him on personal leave."

"What of the girl, Will?" she asked, as her hand went to her mouth. "Who is she? Oh… oh my God. Does her family know?"

"Her name is Cassandra McRea. Her parents are being notified as we speak."

Traumatized, trembling, MJ walked aimlessly to the living room as if escaping, searching for words, for meaning. Speechless.

"I'm sorry Myrna," Yost pressed as he followed. "Forensics found nitrile powder on the gun's trigger. So whoever fired it wore gloves but was careful to leave Jake's prints on the stock and muzzle."

"Dammit, Will! It's clear then that Jake didn't do it," she said, hitting a clenched fist against her thigh. "This is *my* son we're talking about, my son and someone's daughter."

"Be that as it may," the commissioner said, struggling to reconcile the terrified parent standing before him with the stone-cold prosecutor he knew so well, "but there were two murders, MJ."

"Two?" she said, incredulous, what fight she had left dissipating.

"Yes, two," Yost affirmed. "The McRea woman in Jacob's apartment, another person killed in a small hospital in Port au Prince, Haiti."

"Haiti?!" she exclaimed. "What? Wait, I… No. Jake is in LA."

Again, Yost knew that to be false. "His prints are on another weapon. This one was recovered by Haiti's Police Nationale at the scene of a local homicide," he said. "It's a knife. It might've been used to kill a morgue attendant. Poor bastard was guarding the body of a dead drug runner. Knife was found in an elevator outside the morgue."

"When you say knife, you mean like a scalpel, right?"

"This was no scalpel. It was a six-inch dagger. Someone had a flair for the exotic. Thing was wiped clean except for blood on its blade and Jake's prints on the handle."

Incredulous, unable to process Yost's words and the horrors they portended, MJ turned away to hide the welling tears. She lifted a framed photo from the mantle. The picture depicted Jake in his high school graduation gown and mortarboard. In the photo her eyes were clenched in an expression of boundless love, as she hugged her handsome only child.

Placing the picture back down, she turned on Yost, and with false bravado betrayed by a slight tremble to her voice, she said, "Dammit, Will, go home and sober up. Jake is not capable of this. He's in LA. Assume what you will, but I know his schedule. Besides…"

Yost went to where MJ stood now facing the wall and the photograph. His hand on her shoulders, he felt her muscles tense in anticipation of more bad news.

Speaking softly, the commissioner did not disappoint. "The Haitian hospital's security video shows a female moving about outside the ambulance bay and interacting with a man fitting Jake's description."

"Listen to yourself," she said to the wall before turning on Yost again.

A mother lion now, defiant, in her old friend's face, she roared. "You're talking about my son, damn it, not Son of Sam. You sound certifiable."

Still holding the photo, she strode across the room purposefully yet without purpose. Again Yost followed, beseeching. "HSI was dispatched to the scene. They recovered Jake's chart case, his maps, his toothbrush, iPad, even his cell phone. All of it was in the autopsy room where the morgue attendant's and the drug runner's bodies were found."

"Homeland Security?" she shouted, knowing the initials only too well. "So Jake is a terrorist now, too? C'mon, Will. You've known my son from the day he was born. This is madness. You know that, too."

As Myrna Silver's voice trailed off, her friend's words refused to let go, and her lawyer's brain yielded before a mother's heart as she succumbed to a gut wrenching desperation.

"I'm telling you what was found, dear heart," Yost continued, gently at first, coming to her, embracing her as his words turned less tender. "We like the morgue female for the dead drug runner's sister. But, physical evidence clearly places Jake at both scenes, time and place."

"Who else shares this fantasy?" she asked the wall.

"We've kept it in the family... so far," Yost replied. "But, there was a reporter from the Register at Jake's apartment scene, a neighbor. We gagged him, but he'd already riled the scene. That part will hit the street any minute now. I wanted you to hear this from me first."

"What about motive?" she challenged. "We're both a long time out of Columbia Law, Will, but I'm pretty sure a double homicide charge, still requires motive. This is bullsh…"

"Okay, Counselor," Yost intervened, turning her to him. "Let's back up a little. No one's been charged with anything. But there *is* something else."

"Something else," she said, a statement not a question.

"A high placed fed is involved, too. A Homeland Security section chief named Peterson."

"And?"

"This whole thing seems to center around the dead drug runner I mentioned." Yost held up the two-day-old edition of the *NY Register* he'd had folded in his pocket. "This Peterson was working him."

"Wait," MJ said, grabbing the paper from Yost's hand. Reading the first few lines, she looked up, her expression one of surprise. "I know this name, Will. Leif Bergstrom is not some random drug runner."

She explained the Jake/Bergstrom connection, finally saying as she slapped the tabloid with the back of her hand. "If the female unsub *running around* with the figure you like for my Jake turns out to be Leif Bergstrom's sister, all they can pin on them is compassion. That might be passé these days, but I think it's still legal."

"Nonetheless," Yost continued, understanding MJ's rationale as that of a desperate parent's motivated denial rather than a lawyer's cold logic, "the body's on ice at the same scene where they found Jake's maps and phone. The body…this Leif Bergstrom, was scheduled for transfer to the Dade County coroner's lab in the morning. Peterson was supposed to meet the stiff's sister there that same morning. She told Peterson that Jake would be coming with her when she came to do a next-of-kin ID. Peterson recognized the name right off."

"He recognized Jake's name?"

"No. Yours. The infamous MJ Silver has been on the radar of every federal agency and private prison corporation that's sucking at the tit of the Drug War from the first moment you took up with Common Sense. Few share your legalization and sentencing philosophy, dear heart. There's money and emotion involved, and—as you're only too aware—that's garnered you a lot of enemies on both sides of the law. Now, they're gonna gang up on *you* by tying *Jake* up in these homicides."

"Morons," she said, and tossed the newspaper back to him. "I'll eat them alive first."

"Anyway," Yost went on, "the Bergstrom ID session was scheduled for yesterday. The morgue attendant's murder happened some time the night before, as did the McRea girl's killing."

"You're implying there's enough time between incidents to show prior intent."

"Yes. Somebody was after Bergstrom's corpse. Since the autopsy wasn't scheduled until after the body was ID'd, that body should have been on ice, and not on the autopsy table. And it sure as hell shouldn't have been all chopped up. Somebody took it out of the fridge and put it on the table and maybe Jake and the sister walked in on that. I don't think that was blind luck."

MJ's mind kept flashing back to Yost's mention of Common Sense. For despite Jake's warnings about his mother's involvement with the narcotics-legalization advocacy group, she'd insisted on pursuing that which her son had once called a *personal crusade*. Now the older, and ostensibly wiser woman felt a fool. To her, Jake's disappearance was a prophesy fulfilled. Thinking herself the cause of whatever had befallen her only child, MJ recalled the Sunday school teachings of her youth, ...*visit the sins of the father upon the children*. And the weight of guilt at her selfishness was crushing.

Yost pressed on. "Peterson said the event confirmed his suspicions about somebody wanting to get to the body of this drug runner. It's why he had a morgue attendant stationed in the room. Cost the poor bastard his life."

Fighting back the flood of conflicting emotions, she asked, "So why an attendant and not a cop or a security guard?"

"I don't know," Yost acknowledged. "But the point is this. Jake and the female are in the wind. No trace. There's a 50-state BOLO and a felony want issued."

"Local?"

"Federal. Peterson, the Homeland Security guy, claims jurisdiction. They're cutting us out, citing national security."

"Ah, the catch-all," Myrna Silver said, adding cynically, "Putin's our buddy, but my son is a threat. Maybe using Jake to get to me is not beyond those imbeciles, after all." She took several deep breaths before breaking the uneasy quiet that followed. Moving close to her old friend and taking his hand, the pair walked to the door. "Look, I'm sorry, Will. I'm upset, a little scared maybe—more than a little."

"You don't have to explain yourself to me, kiddo," Yost empathized, opening the door to the apartment building's hallway. "We've been around the block too many times."

"So tell me. Should I steel myself for the same message that Cassandra McRea's parents are hearing right now?"

"Let's not go there. If the feds find Jake," Yost answered, his voice low, "we can only hope the circumstances are calm, and cool heads prevail."

"He's done nothing. And that poor poor girl... Oh my God."

"We know that," Yost affirmed. "But we also know you've made powerful enemies."

"Do you know an honest prosecutor who hasn't?"

"I think Peterson is on a mission, and it starts with your fronting for Common Sense."

The detective was well aware that by having brought their argument to the House floor on three occasions, all of which had been carried on CSPAN, Common Sense had raised awareness of the country's simplistic drug laws to a level that rivaled the anger which led to the repeal of Prohibition. The specter of even a slight relaxation of current enforcement and mandatory minimum sentencing policies posed a clear and present threat to the bloated federal infrastructure and private prison industry that had grown up to enforce those policies.

MJ Silver was the all-too-apparent and increasingly influential face of that threat.

"It gives that sonofabitch plenty of firepower," Garodnik was saying. "If Jake really is being railroaded to get to you, there's an army of Feds and lobbyists who would be quick to get behind an effort to discredit Common Sense. They'll tie the department's hands to do it."

"If they think they can do that, the inbred bastards are dumber than even I make them."

"Maybe so, " Yost said, "but *that's* motive aplenty. So if I'm going to help you, and you know I will... I don't know how yet, but I'm going to, then you must level with me. Have you any idea where Jake could be?"

"I do not."

"I spoke with Chief Portlock this morning. He says he looks forward to hearing from you."

"I don't want to call him. It'll only put him on the spot when he can't do much. This thing will go federal before he can lift a finger."

"Rolling over a few bureaucrats is therapy for the old dog."

"This is different. It's my kid. I won't put Al Portlock in that position because a few careerists and profiteers think they can launch a vendetta against me. I'll find Jake myself if I have to. And God help the moralist hypocrite who tries to stop me."

A long hug and kiss on the cheek, and Yost took his leave.

With Yost gone, MJ's tough façade disappeared. The distraught, widowed mother felt impossibly alone.

She again strode to the ornate old fireplace that dominated the living room of the 19th century brownstone she'd once shared with Jake's father whom she now missed with a desperation she'd not imagined possible, and she allowed her thoughts to drift back to very different time.

It was the Eighties, and Myrna, a rebellious teen of sixteen, along with a group of her Buffalo, NY friends all bearing false ID, found their way to a Woodstock-like rock concert outside Toronto. As with pretty girls everywhere, she was invited backstage. There she'd become smitten with one of the stagehands. The boy, a 20 year old American, unaware this friendly girl was underage, felt the same. The pair spent the night together under the stars. With no expectations, and despite convention, they stayed in touch. As fate and fertile youth would have it, a few months later, in trembling voice she confided to the boy that she was pregnant.

Knowing he'd been her first, the young man pleaded that she keep their child.

Meanwhile, her devoutly religious parents, siding with pious strangers to publicly ostracize their own child, demanded their teenage daughter surrender her pending offspring for adoption. To do otherwise was to be disowned. Unrepentant, and faced with this choice, on the day Myrna Juliette Leblanc graduated high school, with only a bus ticket and $74 to her name, she packed what belongings she could carry, climbed from her bedroom window, and ran into the night, never to return, in effect disowning *them* before they could her. It was a young girl's act of will that would define the woman she'd resolved herself to be.

That same day, the young stagehand, Myron Silver, had hitchhiked up from New York City and was waiting for her at Niagara Falls. They married. Three months later, at Queens County Hospital, their beloved only child was born. They named him Jacob, for Myron's grandfather.

It was the age of MTV, and opportunity abounded. Young Myron's drive, talent, and concert experience would soon earn him success as a freelance TV producer in Manhattan.

Once Jacob was old enough to begin school, *MJ* as Myron had been the first to call Myrna, returned to school as well. Enrolling at Queens College and with strong support from her two "guys," MJ ultimately graduated cum laud from Columbia Law.

When it seemed their nearly idyllic existence would go on forever, the trio's lives were shattered. Jacob's adoring father, the love of MJ's life, was struck down on a New York street by a single errant bullet fired from a fleeing car during a late-night drug pursuit.

The incident nearly drove the young attorney and mother mad, and with Jake now in high school, his college tuition guaranteed, she made the tough decision to leave private practice for government work.

MJ descended on the Manhattan District Attorney's office with a single, burning desire: to prosecute those who might stoop to the commission of mindless violence. It was a goal she'd meet with a literal vengeance.

Now, all these years later, she was being told that tragedy had been visited upon the only other man she'd allowed herself to love unconditionally, her son, and for the first time in a very long time, she did not know what to do.

Sitting in the back of his city staff car, unable to help a dear and lifelong friend, Commissioner Will Yost felt that same unfamiliar paralysis.

As his driver inched through crosstown traffic, Yost, more by rote than intent, reached for his cell phone. After staring at it for a long moment, he set it back down. The powerbroker found himself with no one to call, no influence to impose. He knew only that MJ could not go this alone, nor was he was about to let her.

He leaned back in his seat and clasped his hands behind his head trying to think. But concentration eluded him amid the traffic and muted horns just beyond the bulletproof windows as the car made its tortuous way through the glass and limestone canyons of the bustling, self-absorbed city. So he allowed his own thoughts to wander back, back to a time before the corner office and chauffeured limo.

For him, too, it was the Eighties again. Yost and his Columbia Law gal pal who liked to be called "MJ" had just graduated and together they were building a law practice and a sterling reputation.

About that time Yost and *his* new bride, MJ's former CCNY sorority sister, Elizabeth Krause, took a small apartment in the Flatbush section of Brooklyn.

Four blocks away, MJ and her *guys*, as she called her husband and young son, had set up housekeeping.

Yost and MJ would often run into one another as the two young lions rode the subway into Manhattan every morning. Sometimes Elizabeth–or Lizzy, always Lizzy, to MJ—would accompany them part of the way, changing for the Wall Street train halfway through the trip. Pooling their modest earnings while paying back student loans had kept the quintet fed and sheltered during those lean and happy years.

Eventually, careers advanced bringing a measure of security to both families. It wasn't long, then, before Yost and Elizabeth were expecting their first child.

With that thought, as he sat in his limo, Yost's reverie took on a bitter sweetness the years had not erased. It was at about this time, impressed with both his newfound success and the social liberation characteristic of the age, that Will Yost started spending more and more time working or traveling and ever less with Elizabeth.

It was why he found himself in Washington, DC chasing a client and catching a skirt when his very pregnant young wife came due.

A snowstorm, a blustering poorly predicted nor'easter had blanketed the East Coast from Maine to Washington, leaving Yost stranded, but unlike Elizabeth, not alone.

On that same night, back in New York, MJ was fighting the rush hour trains and trying to get back to Flatbush from Manhattan. After a two hour struggle, she'd stumbled through the still falling foot-deep snow and into her walk-up where Myron and young Jake anxiously waited. It was 7:00 p.m. and her feet were frozen into her business pumps. She'd always been certain of those two things–the time and the frozen feet—when relating the story.

Thinking back, Yost knew full well that his partner would normally have simply spent such a night on the office sofa but—as MJ had put it at the time—she *just had a feeling*. She'd tried to call Lizzy but couldn't get through.

Myron, who'd been listening, and well aware that Lizzy was well into her third trimester, decided he'd endure the blizzard and walk the four blocks to the Yosts' apartment. He pulled on his jacket, and headed out.

When he arrived, he could see a light, but no response to his ringing. He ran up the stairs, hammered on the apartment door and finally used his key.

Lizzie was on the floor, unconscious. There was blood on her white bathrobe and nightgown. She was hemorrhaging, but still breathing. It was the baby. He cried out for a neighbor, but got no response. He picked up the phone and beat on its cradle to no avail. The lines were down. Finally, verging on panic, he simply wrapped Lizzy in a blanket, took her up in his arms and trudged *like a malamute,* as he'd explained later, through the driving snow toward Flatbush Hospital. After a few blocks, he was puffing and prevailing well beyond his normal endurance and near collapse. It was then that a cruising patrol car, its tire chains clinking, appeared out of the whiteness and the officers took over.

There had been considerable blood loss, but mother and baby daughter came through, knowing nothing of the ordeal beyond what Myron and the doctors would relate to the new parents in the days that followed.

The baby girl and the woman she'd grow into became the light of Yost's life. Such were William Yost's thoughts as he contemplated the conversation he'd just had with his dear friend and former partner. Now hers and Myron's own child, Jake, was in trouble, implicated in a murder, missing, maybe even fighting for *his* life as time ran out.

The cell phone in his lap brought Yost back to the moment and an idea struck him. He touched an icon on its screen, and a female voice said, "NYPD. Chief Portlock's line."

- CHAPTER 8 -

Three-thousand miles south of Manhattan's towers, a land of stark contrasts steams beneath a tropical sun. The broad Atlantic Ocean forms this French protectorate's futuristic north coast, while to the south, rivers cleave a jungle as primeval as anything on this earth.

If someone wanted to disappear from the prying eyes of so called civilized men, they would be hard pressed to find a refuge better suited than the trackless interior of French Guiana.

Here, at an abandoned airstrip carved from the primordial flora, the plane carrying Jake Silver had come to ground. Now, as the equatorial sun kissed the peaks of distant purple hills, he stirred to wakefulness, a prisoner in a small, windowless room.

The chamber's sole source of light was an eight-inch by two-inch slot cut into its stout wooden door. Through this opening, a shaft of sunlight assaulted Jake's dilated pupils.

Turning away with a start, he rubbed his pained eyes. No sooner did his vision clear then nausea set in. For unlike the flood of relief one might feel upon waking from a nightmare, Jake realized he'd awakened *to* a nightmare.

The room's concrete walls were thick with mold, yet the space appeared free of webs, dung, or any other sign of companionship. The room had apparently been recently cleaned, not scrubbed, but at least given a cursory once over—small solace as the space remained suffocating from the day's heat.

Jake's gaze fell upon his old Breitling chronograph. The watch's hands formed a blurry diagonal line from upper left to lower right. Turning his attention to the door, he saw that the dusty shaft of light that had burned his eyes now cast its spot a bit higher on the wall: the sun was setting.

He tried to determine where in the world he might be.

His watch like all pilot's watches, showed it to be 23:20 Greenwich Mean Time. Given that the sun was setting, it meant he must be somewhere between forty and fifty degrees longitude. That would put him in Greenland but this place was far too hot to be Greenland. He had to be on the South American continent, its eastern extreme, on the middle latitudes.

He checked his pockets. His wallet was gone. It had contained about $35. Why would someone take *that,* yet leave behind a wristwatch worth thousands?

Jake's mind turned to Tina Bergstrom.

Rising on unsteady legs, he stumbled, recovered and slowly made his way to the door.

He'd endured a savage beating, much of it after he'd lost consciousness. Every movement brought a new torment. Nonetheless he crossed the room only to fall against its locked door.

Panting as he peered through the door's small opening, he saw that the room in which he was imprisoned was itself within a much larger structure. He recognized the encompassing space as the cavernous interior of an old, wood-beamed airplane hangar, military by its look. He was being held in a storeroom within that hangar.

From his portal, Jake could see through one corner of the hangar's massive steel and glass main doors. They'd been swung wide.

Shielding his dilated eyes against what daylight remained, Jake could discern that the hangar looked out upon the scene of last evening's melee. Out on the field itself, beyond the single runway, Jake spotted the now derelict airplane that had carried him here.

As memory and reason flooded back into his drug-addled brain, Jake recalled the newspaper article that Ed James had insisted he read. The airplane lying shattered some 100 yards from his cell was a '40s-era Curtiss Commando— identical to the one that had carried Swede Bergstrom to his fiery death.

Struggling to process this implausibility, Jake looked out past the hangar doors and past the wrecked Curtiss. In the distance, thick vegetation bordered the open airfield. An infinity of trees soared above, while below a waist-deep carpet of tangled underbrush precluded escape or even trespass.

Stepping to the door once again, he shouted, "Hey! Anybody here?" Getting no response, he tried, "I know you're out there. Answer me!"

After a couple of minutes abusing his voice, Jake kicked at the door and gave up.

Feeling unsteady, he returned to his corner and sat down, preferring the concrete floor to a mattress of dubious provenance. His thoughts returned to Tina, recalling what she'd said back in Los Angeles: *"I know all my brother's secrets."*

Tantalizing in its subtlety, the remark haunted him. One recollection upon another flooded his sobering brain. He remembered how she'd looked at him with those mesmerizing eyes, the steely orbs boring into Jake's psyche, seeking, beseeching. Then, just as suddenly, she'd appeared satisfied, and to Jake's relief, had simply turned away.

Even in his drugged state, objective reasoning came easier to Jake when he stood beyond the range of Tina Bergstrom's wiles. The excitement he'd felt in her presence seemed foolish in hindsight. He'd behaved like a smitten schoolboy.

No, Jake decided, if Tina were still alive, she was in even greater danger than was he.

Jake was startled from his reverie by the sound of footsteps approaching across the hangar's concrete floor.

As he got to his feet, the last traces of dusk at the door's small opening flared white as the hangar's lights were switched on with a bang. The light streaming through the hole was as quickly dimmed, blocked by what appeared to be a head. As Jake's eyes adjusted, the head became a face, a face whose eyes were peering at him.

After a loud click, the heavy wooden door swung wide, filling the room with the hangar's incandescent light. Jake began to step back, but reconsidered and held his ground.

Difficult to recognize in the blinding backlight, the slender silhouette entered the room.

"I'm Sinjin Porter," said the silhouette.

His eyes and brain adjusting further, Jake could make out a slightly-built, light-skinned black man, his features fine, his accent Caribbean. He also recognized the pronunciation of the man's name, Sinjin, as being patois for the surname St. John.

Sinjin—St. John–flipped another light switch and Jake's prison cell brightened. In the bare bulb's harsh light, Jake saw that St. John Porter sported shoulder-length dreadlocks, wore a flowered shirt above knee-length khaki shorts and high-topped brogans that seemed large for any feet that might extend from so absurdly skinny a pair of legs.

Sporting a holstered handgun at his side, the man made no move to unsheathe it while he assessed his prisoner's physical condition.

Confident he could overpower the diminutive stranger even in his weakened state, Jake considered a move. He need only be quick enough to make his break.

But St. John Porter was nobody's fool. He read his prisoner's intentions in the man's eyes and accommodated those intentions by stepping aside, leaving Jake a clear path to the open door. Taking the bait, Jake lunged past St. John to the exit, only to slam chest-first into a girder-like forearm.

The collision dropped a still dazed Jake to the concrete floor as St. John's heretofore unseen companion stepped into the small room to tower above his victim.

Flat on his back, Jake looked up and into the eyes of the dark-complexioned giant.

Despite the man's size and shaved boulder of a head, Jake saw no malice in him, merely dominance.

Holding an old wooden-stocked assault rifle over his broad left shoulder, the man had been standing silent sentry just outside the door.

A knowing look crossed St. John's caramel face as he dropped to one knee and calmly returned to assessing his charge. The larger man stood silently by as Jake propped himself up, reluctantly accepting St. John's ministrations.

Escape would have to wait.

His mouth agape and dry, his eyes red, Jake assessed his captors. Despite the weapons, despite the silent titan's bulk, his visitors appeared less threatening than merely confident.

"Sorry 'bout dis," St. John said, holding a canteen to Jake's parched lips. "Be still now," he added, jerking a thumb toward the open door. "And stop your gawkin'. Is only jungle out there: jungle, flies, and every kind'a death."

As Jake drank voraciously, his head tilted back, St. John Porter observed his prisoner's neck, checking the puncture mark where his hypodermic had been jammed following the previous day's melee. "Knew I wouldn't be comin' back down here last night so I give you a dose of sweet dreams before I left for the evenin'." St. John smiled, pleased with himself.

He gently lowered the canteen to prevent Jake's gulping its entire contents. "Easy does it, mon. There's plenty more water 'round here." Rather than returning the canteen, St. John poured its contents over his charge's face, draining a layer of sweat and grime from Jake's broken and bruised flesh.

"What's this all about?" Jake coughed. "Why am I in Brazil?"

St. John considered his prisoner. "Brazil?" he said, puzzled. The man's slightly built body shook with laughter. "This is no Brazil, mon. This place is no place."

"What does that even mean?" Jake asked. "I know this is South America, and I know there's a runway out there. It must have a name. Gimme something."

"Okay, mon, okay. I'll tell you some more but don't go shoutin' about it."

Jake again fell back against the concrete wall. The simple effort of discourse proved taxing. He did, however, seem to be confronted by a civilized man, his first since entering the Haitian morgue.

The imposing giant stood silently in the background, the Russian automatic slung over his beefy shoulder. The big man repeatedly shifted his glance from Jake to the broad area beyond the doorway. He seemed less concerned with Jake than with whatever might be out there. He appeared anxious, hemmed-in by the room. These men's weapons were meant for whatever they feared lay in wait outside these walls.

St. John's voice brought Jake back to the moment. "Airplane runway is here because you in the middle of nowhere. No roads in. No roads out. Just an old runway. Maybe 50, 60 clicks to the next settlement. Welcome to French Guiana, mon."

"French Guiana?" Jake croaked, incredulous. "So I *am* in South America!"

"Oh yeah, you're in South America alright," St. John confirmed, suppressing a laugh, "the shitty part."

Jake had many more questions. "The woman. Where is she?"

"Woman?" St John said, curling his umber brow. "Didn't I just say this is the shitty part?"

The man was pretending to misunderstand. But, St. John was a better nurse than he was a liar. Realizing he'd been made, he relented. "Okay, okay. I'll tell you 'bout dis place."

Once the slightly built stranger opened up, he seemed happy to be talking. While wiping the blood and grime from Jake's neck and hands, St. John explained the old aerodrome's part in the big war of decades past. He spoke of bauxite mines that had provided the raw material needed to produce the then-rare alloy, aluminum, for that war's prosecution, first to the Germans through Vichy French collaboration and later, as the tide turned, for the Allies. He spoke of the English family that ran the place after that war, their now crumbling mansion that Sir Walter Chichester, an English patriarch had constructed against the odds deep in the jungle for his unhappy French wife. Sir Walter had also created and controlled the aerodrome and the mines, leaving behind a legacy of success and riches, failure and destitution, bequeathed in time to his son, and finally his grandson, Dwight Chichester, Major, RAF, retired, current lord of the manor and St. John's employer.

Jake was interested in more recent history. "Why am I here, St. John?" Jake asked as he took another drink from the canteen. "What are any of you doing…?"

Before Jake could finish his question, a somehow familiar male voice resonated into the room through the vast expanse of hangar. "You've said quite enough, St. John."

The large bodyguard moved behind Jake and restrained him by the arms as a third man strode into the now crowded space.

This was the Englishman who'd savagely interrogated the Australian, Tretooey, following last evening's assault. The man's left eye was covered by a large padded bandage.

"Feeling better, I see," the Englishman assessed, his voice calm. The screaming tirades of last evening's inquisition seemed almost implausible now in the soft glow of a tropical dusk.

As the Englishman moved closer to better assess his prisoner's condition, the giant tightened his grip on Jake's arms.

Jake could see that the Englishman's clothing and face were scrubbed, yet his boots were dusty. Like the others, he was armed, a pistol holstered at his hip. His breath hinted of gin.

Standing at about Jake's height, the man was slender, tanned, with the sort of sharp-featured Anglo face women might consider handsome. His full head of straight blonde hair had grayed at the temples with silver strands scattered throughout the side-parted rest. Below his pointed nose, a thin mustache set off equally thin, if determined lips.

He appeared to be perhaps 60 years old, and like his surroundings, at least that many years out of place and time. Despite the steam-bath atmosphere, his loose-fitting cotton clothing bore creases. Here stood an Englishman straight from central casting. The only breach of absolute cool was to be found in the man's one visible hazel-hued eye. Set deep in his sweat-free face, the bloodshot orb betrayed a troubled countenance.

Looking from the Englishman to St. John and back again, Jake ineffectually struggled to free himself from the silent giant's grip. The effort proved more symbolic than effective.

"We've not been properly introduced," the Englishman said. "I'm Dwight Chichester."

Before Jake could respond, Chichester's attention turned to a small card held in his right hand. Jake realized the card was his own pilot's license, and recalled his missing wallet. Reading Jake's license, Chichester said, "Jacob Alan Silver. Is this your name?"

Rather than answer, Jake looked askance to where he was being restrained by the silent giant. Chichester nodded, and the big man released Jake's arms.

"Are you going to tell me what in hell is going on?" Jake said, shaking himself off. "And what have you done with her?"

"*Her?*"

"Tina Bergstrom, your goons took her when they took me. Where is she?"

"I assure you, young sir, that I have no *goons.*" Chichester wasn't ready to answer Jake's questions, so turned to questions of his own. "What were you doing at the morgue in Haiti? Why did my man take you?"

Jake, struggled to accept what he was hearing. "Are you telling me your, uh, *man* was acting on his own, not under your orders?"

Again, the question went unanswered.

"Why were you there, Mr. Jacob Alan Silver?" Chichester repeated, a bark.

Jake acquiesced. "I was there to help identify the body of a friend, Leif Bergstrom."

"Swede," he heard St. John mumble under his breath.

Chichester turned, silencing his employee.

Slowly pacing the room, his hands clasped behind him, the Englishman pondered this stranger's words. "Tell me what you *do* know, Silver." It was less request than demand.

Jake described the altercation, and at Chichester's insistence, related every detail. Yet in the end, the man's single question betrayed his true concerns: "The body—did my man go back for Bergstrom's body?"

Jake emitted a sigh of frustration. "We fought. Your goon pistol whipped me, and I woke up here. That's all I know, and I'm not sure I know even that," he concluded truthfully. He nodded toward the field and the derelict Curtiss. "There was another body on that plane, if that's what you mean."

"Yes, it's moldering out there right now," Chichester parried.

"Stop dodging. I'm talking about Tina Bergstrom. What happened to her?"

Chichester stepped away from Jake. "Lads," he finally said. "Take our guest to the main house. Clean him up, feed him, and wait for me in the great room. Keep him in your sight."

As the others headed for the main house, Chichester left the hangar and crossed the cracked tarmac to the wreckage of his Curtiss. Approaching what was his last transport plane, he saw that its starboard main landing gear was collapsed, its wing bent against the hard earth. The sight only added to the remorse he'd felt since aligning himself with the man with whom he was about to speak: one Guillermo Filho, a madman he'd allowed into his life, a madman with a mad scheme.

Stepping onto the old airplane's fractured wing, Chichester strode toward the fuselage.

Stopping at the hatch, he heard the buzz of insects feasting on the corpse of Ian Tretooey. The mercenary sat dead and decomposing in the tropical heat where Chichester had left him.

Doing his best to ignore the carnage and stink of it, Chichester remained in the heavy outside air. Sitting on the wing's leading edge, he unhooked the satellite phone from his belt.

As he began to dial, he glanced upward, past the pair of old military hangars and above them to the decaying manse where it sat forlorn and brooding, its windows looking out upon his failed utopia. Chichester considered the chain of events that had brought him—and through him, his family's legacy—to ruin.

Deliberately stalling, postponing the call he was about to make, and with it the revelation he so desperately dreaded, the aging padron let his mind wander. With trepidation, he recalled other days, not least among them the day he'd arrived back here. Having studied engineering at London's Imperial

College, and following a brief career as a munitions officer in the RAF, young Major Dwight Chichester had returned to his ancestral home ready to assume the role expected of him, that of heir-apparent to the Chichester family's lucrative mining operation.

He remembered the pride that his father felt knowing he could one day turn over the reins of a proud family business to his son. The young sire's engineering education and military experience with explosives seemed the ideal background for success as a mining scion.

But Chichester's brief glow of nostalgia was–as always— crushed by the ever-present memory of his most deeply-held secret. The major's military training in munitions was but a fallback after he'd washed out of RAF flight school. He'd completed primary pilot training, but was unable to handle the more challenging aspects of tactical airmanship.

It was a secret Chichester held until his father's premature death of malaria, which death saw the family business pass to the returning prodigal.

But, in time, the bauxite ore began to peter out. So, Chichester, now lord of the manor, had turned to the mine's most stalwart employee: Dr. Gerhardt Franz. The German chemist, once a fuels expert at the rocket base on Guiana's north coast, and fired when his security clearance had been inexplicably revoked, had found gainful employment as an assayer and key asset to Chichester's father at the mine. The good doctor could be counted upon to maximize the yields as times took a turn. When the worst of those times descended upon the operation's third-generation proprietor, despite his suspicions that the scientist was a long forgotten Nazi fugitive, Dwight Chichester began delegating ever more of the mine's operations to the strange, impersonal doctor.

Pleased by Franz's otherwise off-putting aloofness, this abrogation of duties allowed young Dwight to turn his full attention to his first love: flying.

Ostensibly to augment the struggling mining business, Chichester started an air taxi and transport service.

In a flash of brilliance, he did this by refurbishing a pair of the dozen or so military transport planes–Curtiss Commandos in this case–that the US Army had abandoned along with their airfield three decades before.

In no time, Chichester was flying wealthy American sportsmen down from the coast to the fishing camp at Saul. Later, he flew passengers and cargo to and from the burgeoning new European Spaceport that had sprung up in Kourou on Guiana's distant north coast.

For a while, it went well. Chichester maintained a robust house staff, among them St. John and the former French Legionnaire, Montoya, the silent giant from the hangar. In time, however, the major's drinking and carousing in the oft-exciting locales to which he'd fly, when coupled with his lack of business acumen, took the same toll on the transport business that it had already taken on the family mine.

In desperate straits, young Chichester had turned once more to Dr. Franz, but by then the old man's health had gotten the better of him. As he neared 100, a stroke had left Franz debilitated and unable to handle any but the slightest physical tasks.

Still of reasonably sound mind, though, and sensing Chichester's panic, Dr. Franz was moved to commit a dubiously altruistic act, the second of his long, but fast-fading life. Summoning Chichester to his bedside, Franz held a key in his outstretched and trembling hand, urging Chichester to relieve him of it.

No sooner did the younger man comply, than did Gerhardt Franz close his eyes, breathe his last, and slip away.

Chichester had set the key aside then, thinking it an example of the frail doctor's ever more erratic behavior. However, one day weeks later, St. John had come to him with a request.

The Jamaican had been clearing out Franz's quarters, when he came upon a small, ornate wooden box at the rear of a closet. Finding it locked, he took the box to his boss.

Seeing it, Chichester recalled the comparably filigreed old key.

Bringing the box to his office to test the key in privacy, Chichester was at once delighted and apprehensive when discovering that it fit. Yet he could not bring himself to turn it. Returning the key to his desk drawer, Chichester had gone about his day.

That night, tossing in bed, unable to sleep, the box nagged at him.

He arose and made his way to the office and the box.

Opening it, he saw that it held a dog-eared and crumbling notebook. When he opened the book's leather cover, a small glassine envelope fluttered to the floor. Picking it up, Chichester saw that the envelope held a tiny microchip.

Putting the chip aside, he turned again to the notebook. He saw that many of its brittle pages were covered in molecular structure diagrams and mathematical formulae. Chemistry.

Why, he wondered, would Franz have considered this old box and its contents important enough to have handed Chichester its key as the old man's dying act?

He found his answer in Franz's narrative. Written in stilted English, the scientist's words were galvanizing. The notebook was a diary. It revealed Gerhardt Franz's past work at the infamous Dachau concentration camp.

Reading far into that night, Chichester was at once fascinated and reviled.

The brittle pages described how, early in the European war, the naively idealistic young chemist had signed on to work as a pharmacist under a surgeon of some renown, Dr. Eduard Klemple. It was a rare opportunity to simultaneously serve the Reich and tend to the prisoners' medical needs.

To his horror, however, young Franz would soon learn that his mentor's passions had little to do with prisoners' needs, but extended in fact to performing live surgical experiments on the dark eyes of his Jewish and Eastern European captives in a perverse effort to validate the Nazi eugenics hypothesis.

On the occasions such horrific butchery would be slated for performance under anesthesia, the topical of choice was organic cocaine. As might be expected, however, the camp's sadistic hierarchy had found more interesting personal uses for that narcotic. Thus the limited supply of the numbing agent found its way to a prisoner's eye with far less frequency then did a scalpel.

Franz's diary revealed that he was repulsed by his mentor's cruelty, and so he spent every spare moment in his pharmacy, determined to develop an analog of the cocaine molecule, an easily-replicable synthetic that would exhibit both the anesthetic qualities *and* the metered dopamine release of the real thing, yet never be in short supply. Though he remained powerless to stop the hideous surgical practices themselves, he might discover a way to at least limit the unspeakable suffering of his sadistic mentor's victims.

As Chichester dug deeper into Franz's notes, he struggled to recall what he could of the organic chemistry lessons fundamental to his long-ago munitions training. Slowly, the arcane words scrawled across the yellowed pages came back to him: tropane, atropine, fluorine and their like, each creating a clearer picture of the old doctor's work.

Chichester compared the crude diagrams accompanying Franz's narrative against the molecular structures illustrated in his own old chemistry textbooks. At last he was able to isolate the compounds fundamental to Dimethocaine, a cocaine analog and mild anesthetic contemporary to the era. But, as the pages advanced, Chichester saw differences emerging between the chemical structure of the old analog and the geometries illustrated in the notes. Albeit slight at first, the variations became more pronounced with each page, as did their author's enthusiasm. Franz was clearly onto something. But what?

Now, a decade having passed since Dwight Chichester had first opened the old Nazi's lockbox, he sat on the wing of his derelict Curtiss, the satellite phone in his lap, and he recalled the moment Dr. Franz's real objective leapt from the crumbling pages. Franz's words revealed that he'd finally succeeded in synthesizing a crude iteration of the elusive synthetic: a more powerful anesthetic than Dimethocaine, and one far more easily synthesized. But the war had ended before he could put his discovery to humane use. Instead he made his escape, as had so many of his compatriots, to South America, desperate to assume a new identity.

In time Dr. Franz found his way into the employ of Sir Walter Chichester, the major's grandfather, a man whose love of wealth and power assuaged ethical inhibitions.

Franz had settled into a life far from the eyes of Nazi hunters or the compliant French who'd tossed him out of their rocket base, and he never again mentioned his pursuit. But he did not abandon the quest for its perfection, and tested each subsequent iteration personally.

Modern science eventually synthesized any number of cocaine analogs for medical use, thus obviating the anesthetic potential of Franz's formulation.

Aging and pondering his mortality, Franz had at last attained what he'd sought: the perfect empirical analog to high-grade organic cocaine, and, if only to verify its ease of synthesis and support his now hopeless addiction, he'd formulated nearly a ton of the stuff.

Storing it in steel drums in one of the compound's outbuildings, he recorded his final results, but not in the notebook. The secrets of his final synthesis he burned onto the microchip, and there he'd encrypted it.

The diary also revealed that the old Nazi had fathered a son with an Indio woman of the house staff. But upon recognizing the woman's condition, Andrew Chichester, Dwight's patrician father, had banished her to the jungle, without knowing or asking after the child's paternity, leaving

Gerhardt Franz to live out his years without ever laying eyes upon his only progeny, a phantom he knew only as Emiliano.

Now, as Chichester lamented his own fate, he wished that he'd never opened that Pandora's box, letting its secrets die with their creator. Such were the major's thoughts as he finally, reluctantly dialed the satellite phone.

Halfway through the first ring, the call was picked up. "Are we secure?"

"Must you always ask?"

Satisfied that their conversation was safe from prying ears, Filho's voice dripped with more than its usual disdain. "What's the status, Chichester? I've been waiting all goddam day for your call. Have you prepared a replacement sample for transport?"

Chichester breathed deeply, easing into a conversation he knew only too well would end with a tirade. "Bergstrom was carrying the lion's share of Franz's supply when he blew up. But, as we stipulated, I kept another thousand kilos in reserve. But it's the last of the old Nazi's cache and it's ten years old."

"But you've sampled it yourself…"

"That I have," Chichester replied, "and will again, I assure you."

"Snort your miserable brains out. I do not care," Filho said. "This time bring the chip with you. If our clients are satisfied with the sample, if its retained its potency as you claim, I'll hand over the chip. They'll have their formula, and we'll have our payday." Filho, paused, always distrustful. "Is the sample on board and ready for immediate shipment to the States?" he added, more a demand than a query. "I've calmed our clients after your Bergstrom debacle, and I see a window of opportunity. But, Chichester, we have to move now. Right now.

The clients Filho spoke of were Bratva–the violent Russian mob in America–and they'd paid a great deal in advance for the precious synthetic. A great deal more–the lion's share–would be forthcoming upon the Russians' satisfaction with the sample, and subsequent receipt of its formula chip.

With this exchange, the major began what he knew would be a descent into the maelstrom of Filho's wrath. "We've had a setback," he confessed.

"You assured me that you had a replacement sample, and another airplane capable of making it to the States, so what's *this* goddam setback?" Filho growled.

"When Leif Bergstrom left for the States, he took more than our first sample of the product with him." Chichester girded his courage and spoke the dreaded words: "Bergstrom also took the old man's notebook."

"You fool!" Filho growled. Then, realizing his clients could still retrieve what they needed from the microchip, he asked, "...and the chip?"

Though a silence followed, both men knew the gravity of that which went unsaid.

"Tell me it's at the bottom of the ocean, Chichester. "Tell me that chip is so deep no one will ever find it. Tell me that!"

"I only know it's gone, and that Bergstrom somehow stole it."

"No one but you and I knew where that chip was hidden," Filho hissed. "You gave me your word on that."

Not willing to admit that he'd simply kept Franz's box on a shelf in his office, its key in his desk drawer, Chichester stonewalled. "Yes, I know. But Swede was a strange creature. He sensed things in a way no normal man could. But, but... hear me out," Chichester stammered. "It might *not* have gone under with the wreckage."

"Why you—Who has it?"

"I don't know if anyone has it, but there's more. The chip is but the half of it." As he spoke, Chichester could almost feel Filho's murderous rage across the miles. He forced himself on. "Apparently, Bergstrom also wiped out the hard drive of Franz's computer, as well. That leaves the missing chip as the only existing copy of the formulas."

"You mean there was no back up?"

"The chip is the back up. That was *your* demand, yours and your clients. No copies."

"And you abided?" Filho said, incredulous. "Who does that!? Your servile stupidity has killed us both."

"Perhaps not, Filho," Chichester pleaded. "Since you told me the authorities were holding Leif Bergstrom's body at that Port au Prince hospital, I figured that he'd perhaps secreted the chip somewhere on his person. So I exercised initiative."

"I dread your next words."

"I sent Ian Tretooey to retrieve it."

"Did he?" Filho said, momentarily encouraged.

"I don't know. When Tretooey landed back here, he was attacked and killed. The attacker got away. But Tretooey took hostages. One of them is Leif Bergstrom's sister. Our only hope is that she has the chip or knows where it is. Why else would he take her, bring her here?"

In the background Filho mumbled, "Why, that double crossing little whore."

"What?" Chichester asked. "Speak up. This phone…"

"Does she have it or doesn't she?" Filho interrupted.

"I don't know. The man who killed Tretooey took her."

Chichester could hear rapid breathing from Filho's end.

"You said *hostages*."

"Yes, Filho. There's another American. He doesn't know anything."

"Then dispose of him before he does."

"Yes, yes, of course. But for the moment," Chichester paused as he touched his bandaged eye, "for the moment he could prove useful."

"Fine, but I want no witnesses. What about the guy who took the Bergstrom bitch?"

"He calls himself Emiliano el Cegato. He's a local savage. If he has her and if she has the formula or knows where it is, he'll get it from her."

"Alright," Filho shifted. "How did this Emiliano el.., el whatever… How did he know all this? How'd he know where to meet the plane and when?"

"Tretooey. The mercenary bugger cut us out and made a pact with the devil," Chichester went on. "He made a deal with el Cegato. Those were the Aussie bastard's dying words. At that point, he had no further cause to lie. The double-crossing bastard was shot full of holes."

"Did you search *him* for the microchip?"

"Of course," Chichester said, frustration evident in his every word. "If he…"

In an outburst of implacable rage, Filho's forced composure imploded at the thought that all was lost. "If you're lying to me, I'll rip out your innards, or better yet, I'll watch as our clients do it for me you miserable limey fop!" With no response from Chichester, Filho regained some of his cool. "It's obvious, Chichester, that the woman, your double-crossing pilot's whore of a sister, has what we're looking for. Where did this Emiliano asshole take the thieving bitch?"

"I don't know."

"Find her, Chichester. Take back what is ours, or the Russians will find you, and when they do you'll die a thousand times."

After a thoughtful pause, Chichester said, "As I expect, my dear Filho, will you."

- CHAPTER 9 -

Back at the manor house, freshly showered and fed, his wounds treated by St. John, Jake felt his strength returning.

Donning a clean white shirt and pair of the major's khaki trousers, he followed St. John into what Chichester had called "…the great room." The tattered upholstery of the room's overstuffed chairs combined with the faded paint of its walls and water-stained high-ceiling bore witness to decades of neglect.

Montoya entered the room and moved within striking distance of Jake.

Chichester followed close on the big man's heels, a troubled look on his dusty face. Seeing Jake, he assumed a more benevolent mien. "I hope you'll accept my apologies for treating you as a prisoner, old boy, but when a white man appears here unannounced, he's usually running from something. So I checked you out." he lied. "I had a chum run your pilot's license against Interpol's database. It seems you're as pure as falling snow."

"So the authorities know I'm here," Jake said, pleased at the thought. "What about Tina Bergstrom? What has..?"

With a subtle nod of reassurance to Montoya, Chichester interrupted, "It's clear now that she's been abducted. Given the circumstances, it's best to leave her recovery to me. We need to keep this quiet for her safety."

Jake challenged, "What about the police?"

With a patronizing smile, Chichester explained, "Miss Bergstrom's been taken by a local reprobate named Emiliano Cegato. As for the *police*," Chichester said, his inflection inferring Jake's ignorance of the local culture, "the authorities here are corrupt, gun-crazy thugs, hardly more than savages themselves, and almost certainly in Cegato's pocket. If there's any possibility of finding Miss Bergstrom alive, and keeping her that way, it's up to us to do it."

"Why was she taken?" asked Jake.

"That's not clear," Chichester said. "But I'm certain now that her brother was involved in drug smuggling, along with Ian Tretooey."

"I'm not buying that," Jake retorted, getting to his feet, as did Montoya. There's…"

Chichester raised a reassuring palm for Montoya to let Jake alone. "The Swede flew for me and I trusted him. The night he crashed, he was on a routine flight bringing radial engines to the States for overhaul. But it's clear now that he was smuggling something else on that plane–my plane, mind you! Whatever it was, Tretooey was looking for it in that morgue," Chichester shook his head as if sad. "We're left with only Swede's sister. Cegato will beat and torture her until she tells him what it is he wants to know."

"If Swede had been duped, it's unlikely his sister would've known."

"All the worse," Chichester said. "If she doesn't talk, Cegato will beat her to death."

Jake wanted to grab the evasive Englishman by the shirtfront and shake him. "They can't have gotten far. Goddammit, Chichester, we have to do *something*!"

Chichester was having none of it, and pointed toward the encroaching jungle. "There's not a single road, Silver, not a trail. We don't know which direction he took. Nothing."

The satellite phone on Chichester's belt buzzed. Getting to his feet, the major's face assumed a look of utter disgust. "What now?" he mumbled as he walked to a far corner.

Turning his back to the large room, he placed the instrument to his ear. "I've been wracking my brain for a way out but we're fairly well screwed, Filho. So bugger you and your threats. Send your Russian henchman. I'll be waiting, and you can slink back to whatever hell spawned you. I rue the day I first heard your name."

Before Chichester could disconnect, the caller said calmly, "I've located the Bergstrom bitch. She's on Ile du Diable."

Chichester suppressed a laugh of derision. "You're as mad as a hatter, Filho. Do with me what you will, but I'm done with you and your ravings."

"She's being held in the ruins of the old French penal colony," Filho said to Chichester's surprise. "It's a mere eleven kilometers off your north coast."

"Assuming I did believe you, Filho, it wouldn't matter if that God-forsaken island were eleven *inches* off the coast. Getting there means crossing the Desirade Strait and there's a tropical storm building. Even a seaworthy small boat would be swamped if it tried to ply the straits in a storm. A larger craft would have risked detection by the authorities. How on earth would Cegato have reached such a place? There are only bleached bones and ghosts on that sodding rock. I'll take my chances with your Russian thugs."

"Cegato found a way. If he believes, as I do, that the Bergstrom woman has knowledge of our microchip, what better place to wring information from her than a deserted dungeon?"

"How do you know all this, Filho?"

"I know where she is, as surely as I know where you are, Chichester." Filho paused for dramatic effect. "We need the bitch alive. How quickly can you get her?"

Chichester knew Ile du Diable–commonly knowns as Devil's Island.

One of the world's dark places, its moss-covered stone ruins and abandoned dungeons once housed French political prisoners under the most brutal of conditions. The poor souls condemned to this horrific place suffered beneath the whips and jackboots of sadistic guards a broad ocean removed from the eyes of any overseer. Devil's Island was—and remains—a fog-shrouded, crumbling monument to the uniquely human trait our conceit calls inhumanity.

Having flown over it many times, Chichester knew the physical features of this small rugged chunk of jungle protruding from the shark-infested waters a few miles off the northern coast of his French Guiana.

Filho's voice brought Chichester back from his unpleasant reverie. "If the Bergstrom bitch knows our plans, Cegato *will* make her talk. You need to find her, and you need to deal with this Cretan, Cegato. That means kill him. Then find the woman, learn what she knows, and take back what is ours."

"There are no airports on Devil's Island, Filho. To get there on a boat, I'd have to navigate treacherous straits between the southern Salut Islands, and there's a storm surge building."

"If Cegato can do it, so can you. When you bring me that microchip, bring that second sample of analog along with it. I'll expect you in Miami in two days, or you can expect the Russians at your throat in three."

"The Florida Strait is crawling with DEA and US Customs assets."

"You do the flying and leave the authorities to me," Filho said and clicked off.

Chichester stood facing the wall, powerless, the silent phone at his side.

When he finally turned back toward the room, Jake Silver stood directly in front of him, blocking his way. They locked eyes, Jake's hand on the major's chest.

"Stand aside, Silver."

"Your friend likes to shout."

"What you heard are the ravings of a lunatic. Now step aside."

"Who is he?" Jake pressed, dropping his hand, while his feet remained planted.

"Forget him," said Chichester. "Even if he's right about Swede's sister being on Devil's Island–which I very much doubt—she's beyond our reach. Now stand aside!"

The major gestured to Montoya who, rather than approach, turned and headed down the outdoor stairway to the aerodrome and a waiting St. John.

Watching the big man take his leave, Jake stepped aside. "Maybe Tina's out of reach, and maybe she's not," he said as he followed the major across the room.

Stopping by the windows, Chichester observed his two men entering the big hangars through a side door.

Jake was persistent. "However implausible it might be, Major, we have a lead on Tina Bergstrom's whereabouts, and if running down that lead means I have to steal one of your goddam airplanes myself, that's what I'll do." The major laughed at Jake's bold assertion, yet the latter remained undeterred. "Suppose that caller is right."

"His name is Guillermo Filho." Chichester spat the name. "He claims to be a Portuguese expat living in the States but he's the devil incarnate."

With that phone call, something had changed in Chichester. He'd become pensive.

Jake tried another tact. "I know Leif's sister has something of yours, Major, something you need, if only to mollify that gasbag on the satellite phone."

"It's well beyond that, Silver, I assure you."

"If you do have another aircraft," Jake pressed, "we can get to the coast in minutes. There must be a boat we can rent there–or one we can *appropriate*."

"Am I supposed to fly with one eye, Silver?" Chichester said with a huff.

"I count three eyes. If your remaining aircraft has wings and propulsion, I can fly it."

Chichester walked to the center of the room. "This whole thing is bonkers, Silver. How could Filho have traced Cegato and the Bergstrom woman to Devil's Island, of all places?"

"You just admitted that you don't know who he is, who he *really* is." As Jake spoke, he considered the satellite phone in Chichester's hand. "Something like 800 satellites orbit this planet, Major. Eight hundred! At least one of those things knows where Tina Bergstrom's cell phone is. Suppose Filho, whoever he really is, has access to a satellite that can do that."

Jake's words rang true. The major had never questioned Filho's ties to the Russians, and in turn *their* ties to oligarchs with tentacles reaching into all the halls of power. In his desperation and greed, Chichester had never actually questioned anything about this man. "Very well," the major acquiesced as he turned toward the staircase leading outside. "Follow me. Let's explore our options."

Descending the stairs, Jake noted that the big glass and steel doors of the farthest of the two old hangars had been swung wide. Looking in, he spied an apparition, a ghost from a bygone era.

"Is that…? Yes!" Jake exclaimed. "That's a Douglas A-26 Invader!"

"She *was*," said Chichester, gesturing toward the gleaming silver machine. "This one was modified to be an executive transport decades ago. She's an On Mark Marksman now, and was the fastest people-hauler flying before jets came along. I found her deserted on a dirt strip supposedly used by drug runners back in the Eighties. They'd violated her, removed the stair-door and added a wider cargo hatch in order that they could dump their cargo quickly. They ripped out her seats and stripped her cabin bare, all in order to haul their dubious treasure."

"Why this old airplane?" Jake asked, realizing that criminals could have as easily stolen a modern airplane, a jet perhaps, for their nefarious enterprise.

"Because," Chichester explained with obvious pride, "she could lift any load, and with the right man in the left seat, outmaneuver whatever tried to stop her.

"I brought her back here," Chichester went on, "cleaned her up, fitted her with removable passenger seats, and never looked back. We use her to fly sportsman down from the coast for the fishing. We can also pull the seats out and run light cargo. She's configured that way now."

Jake ran his hand along the machine's slick belly. Its huge engine nacelles and long landing gear made the converted old warbird appear ready to pounce. This legendary twin-engine attack plane, introduced late in WW-II, was so advanced it was not retired until the US withdrawal from Vietnam.

Upon reaching the plane's empennage, through the modified entry door Jake could see St. John and Montoya wrestling with a large wooden box in the plane's now bare aft section. Seeing no seats, Jake asked, "What are they doing?"

"Securing cargo that had been scheduled for delivery to a client in the States," answered Chichester. "She's more thoroughbred, than dray horse, but we had an order to fill."

Jake looked the airplane over. What he saw impressed him. What he could not see was an auxiliary fuel bladder, installed amidships, just forward of the wooden crate.

"Even with the oversized cargo door," Chichester explained, "the engine nacelle protrudes well aft of the wing, making it impossible to load a crate that size in one piece. So the lads constructed that crate in place, and filled it onboard. To remove its contents, we'd first have to disassemble it or remove the nacelle, and you'll agree that at the moment we—or should I say, the Bergstrom lass—simply cannot afford us the time."

Jake assessed the crate which barely fit through the modified starboard hatch. Looking forward he saw the fuel bladder. "What's that for?"

"Range," Chichester answered. "This cargo was bound for the States. For as you know, my best pilot crashed my real transport airplane into the Windward Strait."

Seeing Jake's growing uncertainty, Chichester prodded. "A boat will be waiting for us at Kourou, Silver. Every minute we waste here, could be the last for Swede's sister."

Breathing deeply of the hot, dank air, Jake said with less logic than conviction, "Let's go."

- CHAPTER 10 -

MJ Silver sat in her Battery Park office. Her eyes were red and swollen from a sleepless, tear-filled night, and her every thought centered on her missing son.

Behind her a not-quite-full bottle of Pierre Ferrand cognac teetered on the edge of the credenza. In front of her lay a copy of the *New York Register*. Though she'd read the article three times, she picked it up yet again, wincing at the words above the headline: *MODEL BRUTALLY MURDERED ON WEST SIDE, A* Register *exclusive by Wendell Leitch.*

Feeling helpless, she crumbled the tabloid and tossed it into the wastepaper basket, poured herself another 100-dollar inch of cognac and breathed a sigh as the intercom buzzed.

"There's a Lieutenant Garodnik here to see you," her assistant, Darlene, informed her.

More friends than workmates, the women had been together since MJ's early municipal days. Jake knew her to this day, only as *Aunt* Darlene. "Shall I send him in?"

MJ paused a few seconds before answering with a resigned, "Sure."

The office door opened to reveal the slightly cherubic, mid-fiftyish detective.

MJ, being tall herself, put him at about five feet, ten or eleven. His orange hair was wild, his mustache vast, his necktie a spinnaker of paisley.

Standing to greet him, the lady lawyer in a blue wool Pendleton suit and smooth shoulder-length brown bob painted a sharp contrast to the chromatic-Columbo standing before her as she extended a hand. "Please, Detective, take a seat."

"May I offer you a cup of coffee, Lieutenant?" Darlene asked from behind him.

"No coffee, ma'am, thanks," he answered, glancing back to offer a courteous nod to the woman. Sensitive to the situation, the cop affected a pleasant voice and manner as he turned to face MJ. Handing her a business card, he said, "I'm Lieutenant Patrick Garodnik, Mrs. Silver, Manhattan North Homicide."

The H-word sent a chill up MJ's spine. "You don't look much like a cop, Lieutenant."

"A mixed blessing, ma'am." Again, the cop smiled: a signal intended to invoke relief. "I realize this is a difficult time, Mrs. Silver, but I need to ask you a few questions."

Knowing now the cop was not the bearer of tragic news, the former DA asked, "Do you have anything yet?"

"All leads are being followed. Look, ma'am… Counselor, I…"

"Call me MJ," she said. "So, what's an uptown murder cop doing way down here?"

"I'm here because my boss wants me here, and because the federal authorities don't."

Interest piqued, lifting the snifter between her fingers, MJ took a sip at her cognac. "So this is unofficial?"

"Speaking unofficially, yes."

"In that case…" She reached behind her and took a second snifter from the credenza, poured the detective two-fingers of Ferrand, and slid the glass across her desk. "Do go on."

Garodnik looked at the glass, then back at MJ. "Chief Portlock is out on a limb in this, Mrs. Silver."

"It's MJ."

"Right." Garodnik looked at the glass again, scratching a non-existent itch on his chin, a tough guy ill at ease. "The chief told me to be straight with you. We all know the motives the Feds are serving up are too convenient. Your son Jacob is innocent. But he's also missing. That's rarely a good combination."

"You think he's been set up."

Knowing she was seeking validation, the cop sidestepped. "Let's just say somebody has to look at all possibilities."

She nodded appreciatively. "So what've you got?"

"Well," Garodnik began as he stood and paced the room, "somehow it all goes back to that airplane that went down in the Gulf. The pilot and Jacob had a history."

"Yes," she observed. "Jake and Leif Bergstrom flew together in Iraq. They were together when the Bergstrom boy was shot down and captured. There was an inquiry. I remember Jake being very upset."

"That could explain why your son's LAX hotel room and cell phone records show that on Monday he made several calls to people named Bergstrom. One of them was to the dead pilot's sister," he glanced at his notes, "one *Christina* Bergstrom. We have her coming through airport security at San Francisco. The video matches the woman in the Port au Prince morgue incident. The Feds never told us about the phone calls or anything else. They're obliged to respond to our bulletins when they have information on a subject's whereabouts. They did not."

"Are you sure they knew?"

"They knew. We ran all that down in a single morning. The Feds' silence raised a red flag for the chief. He's suspicious, thinking maybe they have an agenda."

"An agenda."

"Yes, ma'am. By implicating Jake, they splash mud on their real nemesis, *you*."

"You realize, Lieutenant, that your boss is a paranoid." MJ said, remaining incredulous. Garodnik remained poker faced as she went on. "When you refer to *me*, what you really mean is my organization Common Sense, do you not?"

Garodnik nodded affirmation.

"Kind of hard to swallow," MJ mused. "Sure, what we advocate threatens a few bureaucrats' jobs, but that's hardly motive for murder."

"It threatens a billion dollar a day enterprise. That's motive for nuclear holocaust."

"I say this with love, Lieutenant, but right now you sound as crazy as your boss."

With that, the detective's tone and manner turned somber, and he held out the open newspaper for MJ's attention. "If it's crazy you want, have a look at this."

"Yes, I know," the lady lawyer said, jerking a thumb toward the wastepaper basket and her own crumpled copy of the *New York Register*. She'd been embarrassed to buy it, and had walked two blocks past her usual newsstand to do so. "That poor McRea girl was strangled and shot. My God, why?"

"We think it has something to do with what the Coast Guard found on Leif Bergstrom."

"Some new kind of narcotic, the paper said...."

"Yes, it's a new modality that we don't know much about yet. Not exactly news, but the stuff planted in Jake's apartment was a strange modality too. Maybe the same stuff. The preliminary labs make it a similar compound, not in any database."

"Another bullshit cathinone or opioid, no doubt. Dime a dozen now." Turning contemplative, MJ asked, "Tell me, Lieutenant, how was Cassandra McRea really killed?" Before Garodnik could dodge her question, she added, "I know what the paper said."

Garodnik cut her off, while confirming her suspicions. "That's privileged, Counselor."

"You're already pregnant, Lieutenant."

Garodnik paced, buying time. Turning away, he could feel her eyes boring into his back as he spoke to the wall. "She was shot, but for effect the doer finished the job with a Colombian Necktie."

"So she *was* strangled."

"Not a real necktie," Garodnik explained, turning to face MJ, approaching her desk. "A Colombian necktie is a rite used by the old Cali cartel. Goes back to the bad old days. The killer cuts his victim's throat real deep, ear-to-ear, right along here." Garodnik pulled a finger across his upper neck to demonstrate. "Goes in with a blade and saws a deep slash. Then he reaches into the cut and pulls the victim's tongue out through the gash. Leaves it hangin' there outta the victim's throat like a necktie. Get it? It's the stiff's tongue hanging there where a necktie…"

MJ held up a hand. "Please," she said, thinking that such a monster as would do this might have her son.

"Clearly, whoever's behind this is sowing outrage," Garodnik offered, reading a mother's anguish. We had an ear witness, though. Jake's upstairs neighbor." The detective pointed toward the wastebasket and crumpled newspaper. "He's the reporter who wrote that story."

"Had?" MJ asked.

"Yeah. It seems he's had an attack of amnesia."

MJ curled her brow, confused.

"He's retracted his statement. Said he's not sure of the time."

"Somebody got to him," MJ said, her gaze momentarily distant. "They're feeding the anti-drug panic the imbeciles in Washington are sowing." Looking back at Garodnik, she pointed. "That's why you're leading the press, faking the MO, isn't it?"

"That's one reason, yes," Garodnik said, admiring this, albeit distraught, woman's sharp mind–too sharp. "Like I said, Counselor, we don't need a public rush to judgment."

She sighed deeply. "Does the McRea family..?"

"Not all of it. But now the victim's sister has come forward."

"Oh?"

"Cassandra McRea had texted her sister about Jake. The sister told the Cedar Rapids PD that Cassandra was teasing in one of her texts, just *'joking around like she does*,' the sister reported. But she went on to say that Cassandra had confided to her in this text thread that Jake was having violent nightmares and fits, as she put it."

"Fits?"

"Yeah. Cassandra texted the sister that if she 'turned up dead, not to be surprised.' That's a direct quote from her statement." Garodnik shrugged his shoulders before adding, "Then Cassandra closed out the string of text messages with LOL and a smiley face. I have the transcript if you…"

"Dammit," MJ huffed, hands on hips, jaw clenched. "Dammit! Dammit!"

Garodnik turned and paced the room before asking his inevitable next question. "Counselor, you know as well as I do that we can't afford to be blindsided on this one. If Jake has a, well, a history. These fits.…"

"Patrick," she interrupted, "*fits* is one of those words like *tarmac*. It never inspires thoughts of butterflies and fairies. So, if you're dancing around the issue of Jake's emotional health, let's clear that up right now. He's never been to a shrink. He's a pilot. He'd sooner bail out without a parachute than create a psych record."

"That's not helpful. The Feds are gonna let this case play out in the media. The guy heading up their probe is a climber. So's this flak, Leitch." The cop gestured toward the wastebasket. "If the government guy is willing to pin at the very least an accessory rap on Jacob to get to you, well, that's the kind of bullshit that makes me nervous. So if you know something, I gotta know it too."

"I know something, alright,," she said. "I know that sooner or later whoever has Jake, will get what they want or dispose of the, uh, evidence, shall we say." The distraught mother made air quotes around the word evidence. "So, are the abductors going to contact me?"

"No. If your son's been taken, we're thinking it's a capture, not a kidnapping."

"So, whoever has Jake and the Bergstrom woman, does not want something *for* them, like ransom, but something *from* them, like information."

"From one of them, at least," Garodnik mused. "But whatever's going on here, Chief Portlock says you're family. So we're not gonna waste precious time waiting for the feds to find Jacob." She stood and extended a hand. "Thank you, Lieutenant."

Before turning to leave, Garodnik looked tentatively at the snifter. Picking it up, he downed the cognac in a single gulp, and blinked his eyes. "You're welcome, ma'am." He left his card and his cell phone number with Darlene, advising her that she or her boss should not hesitate to call him at either number, anytime, day or night. The curly-haired policeman tipped his non-existent hat and took his leave.

Alone now, MJ dropped her guard and, her eyes misting up, whispered, "Will I ever see my son again?"

As the day wore on, Myrna Silver tried to lose herself in work. Just as she thought she might be succeeding, she yielded to compulsion and checked the New York Register website for updates.

The lead story sent her into a rage.

"Darlene!"

The assistant stepped tentatively into MJ's office. "You roared?"

"Get that Lieutenant Garodnik for me."

In less than a minute, Garodnik was on speakerphone. "Good afternoon, Mrs. Silver."

"Lieutenant, I've been giving a lot of thought to what you said this morning—your theory about Homeland Security using these events as fodder to discredit Common Sense and at the same time keep the department at bay."

"Not Homeland Security exactly," Garodnik corrected. "My boss did a little sniffing around. He thinks it's just this one director, fed named William Peterson, lookin' to make a name for himself by discrediting you and by extension Common Sense. But, the guy has major pull and nobody's gonna get in his way to help you." His tone implied, least of all, you.

"So what do you know about Director Peterson?"

"I know he's a pain in my ass."

"You said he's a climber and he has pull."

"That's right," Garodnik mused. "He's new to what they call an SES position, a senior executive post. Next rung on the ladder takes a presidential appointment. Looks like he's bucking hard and early."

"Do you see his involvement in this investigation as standard practice?"

"Hell no. Peterson brought in Homeland Security. Raised the profile and framed it as a single national security case."

"Does that make sense?"

"It's Homeland Security. Making sense is optional. It's an attention-getter."

"Where did you say this Peterson is based?"

"I didn't, but he shuttles between DC and the New York FDO."

"So sometimes he's here in Manhattan?" MJ said, surprise edging her voice.

"Yeah, he keeps an office in the federal building down on Varick Street."

"You said Homeland Security *assumed* the case…"

"Well," Garodnik corrected, "more like they insinuated themselves by way of Director Peterson. From what Chief Portlock tells me, the guy got things rolling right away. Cut us out of the investigation too. Normally I'd say the Feds are welcome to it. But Chief Portlock won't let this one go, as if we don't have enough to do here in Mayberry."

MJ sensed the veteran cop's growing personal attachment to the case, and understood that to hide it, Garodnik was putting up his best jaded big-city-cop persona.

"Lieutenant," MJ asked, "have you checked the Register's website today?"

He palmed his smartphone. "What am I looking for?"

"You'll know when you see it."

The two rang off, but a half-hour later Garodnik appeared in MJ's outer office. "This stuff about the Analog drug," he was saying as he brushed past Darlene, waving his smartphone. "This did not come from me, or anyone else in the department, Mrs. Silver."

"MJ."

"Right." Garodnik's tone was contemplative. "Y'know" he said, pacing back and forth in front of MJ's desk like a caged leopard. "This is info we *do not have*. It's been leaked from somewhere else."

"That's what I suspected, Lieutenant," she said, giving forth with an unladylike snort of derision. "This jerk Leitch's unnamed source is claiming that the drugs in Jake's apartment and those the Coast Guard recovered from Leif Bergstrom's crash are not only the same, but they're... they're this Analog, a supposedly perfect synthetic cocaine."

"Yeah, but that part's baloney. Analog, fauxcaine, nocaine, call it what you will. There's been a hundred versions hit the streets over the years... a thousand more in medicine. Analog might sound all sciency on the street, but it's just another bag of bullshit. Designer cocaine is a pipe dream. Somebody's been watching too much Breaking Bad. Besides. There's no Certificate of Analysis on this stuff yet, so whoever leaked this is just trying to tie Leif Bergstrom to Jake, and by extension to you."

"You like Peterson for the leak?"

"I do," the detective admitted. "A little too on the nose to be random. But these government assholes are doing their best to keep us from finding out who *is* behind it. They're denying us access to evidence. If they're also leaking critical info to the press, they're blowing their own case! How does that work?"

"Easy," MJ asserted. "It lets the bad guys they're supposed to be chasing do their dirty work for them. Tell me, Lieutenant, how else is the department been denied evidence?"

"Well," Garodnik said, "in order to tie the Cassandra killing to anybody, it's important that we know what Bergstrom's real cargo was the night he crashed his plane. Homeland Security took custody of the cargo manifest but won't give us squat or even discuss the case. They're holding the manifest in evidence."

"Has it been deemed classified?"

"I don't think so. Not yet."

"Peterson again?"

"Good as any."

MJ curled her brow, but said nothing.

"What are you thinking?"

"Just this," she said with a huff. "If Leif Bergstrom is being looked at for smuggling, and the Feds are tying that in with Cassandra's murder, I'd like to see that cargo manifest."

"So would I, Counselor."

"Do you have Peterson's number, Patrick? …and it's MJ. MJ."

He gave it to her and she dialed it from her desk phone.

An officious sounding woman answered, "Director Peterson's line."

"Is the director in?"

"Whom may I say is calling?"

Click.

Remembering the pocket flask her late husband, Myron had often carried and she could not bear to discard, MJ pulled it from her desk drawer. Never much of a drinker, she'd found, the cognac she'd been sipping to be a comfort in this trying time. She wanted to be a partner to this cop, not a burden. That meant hanging tough. So she filled the flask from the Ferrand bottle, again offered a drink to Garodnik, who declined, and she placed the flask in her briefcase, asking, "I don't suppose you have a cop car thoughtlessly double parked downstairs by any chance?"

Within fifteen minutes Garodnik's unmarked was pulling up at the Varick Street address of the Federal Building. MJ took a drag at the flask, smiled warmly, thanked the burly redheaded cop, and made her way to the lobby while punching Peterson's office number into her cell phone.

The woman who answered the phone insisted that Mr. Peterson had a full agenda and was not taking appointments.

MJ assured her that she didn't have an appointment.

The woman seemed humorless, and so finally the well-seasoned lawyer asked to convey a message to the busy Mr. Peterson, giving him both hers and Bergstrom's names.

Peterson quickly picked up. "Good afternoon, Counselor."

"Hello, Agent Peterson. I'm…"

"I know who you are. How may I help you?"

"I need to meet with you."

"I'm on my way out. I'll have my assistant arrange it for when I return."

MJ knew a dodge when she heard one. "No, *sir*. I'm afraid we'll need to meet now."

"Hold on, there. What's the…"

"You're making baseless allegations against my son," she said, her tone stern. "Since those allegations cite a local homicide, I contend that absent presentation of evidence, NYPD–*not* Homeland Security–remains the appropriate adjudicating authority in the Cassandra McRea murder investigation."

"I'm not talkin' about a local homicide. Your son, Jacob, is an accessory after the fact in a federal investigation."

"An accessory?" she asked, incredulous. "What are you alleging now?"

"I'm stating a fact. He and Christina Bergstrom attempted to abduct evidence in an ongoing federal investigation."

"Well," MJ cut him off, "since you've already indicated that the cases are related... Thank you for that, by the way. Then, independent of adjudication, as an officer of the court I'm entitled to examine any and all pertinent additional evidence. See, we're making progress."

"What additional evidence?" Peterson said calmly, though the seasoned prosecutor she had him fuming at being outmaneuvered so early.

"Let's start with Bergstrom's cargo manifest. There's certainly a cargo manifest."

"Got a warrant?"

"I can have one here before you reach the lobby, along with a police chief to serve it with far more visibility than grace. So unless you want to miss your flight and give your colleagues a hearty laugh, you'll stop wasting your time, my time, and taxpayer money."

"You can't hold..."

"Do not presume what I can and cannot due, sir. And do not test me."

Peterson acquiesced. "You'll settle for a *copy* of the manifest. But you'll see it just renders Bergstrom doubly culpable. No amount of paperwork or theatrics can change that."

"What *was* he carrying?" MJ queried. "All they recovered from the crash was a kilogram of something that resembled cocaine. Everything else went down with the fuselage."

"Leif Bergstrom was smuggling dope, and operating an airplane while impaired. Those are both federal crimes. A million dollar loss adds a class one felony."

"Again," she insisted, "what was he carrying that was worth a million dollars?"

"He was, um…" Peterson paused as if reading. "He was carrying airplane engines. Radials, I believe."

"Radial engines," noted MJ, ever a pilot's mother. "Isn't that the old, propeller kind?"

"Yes."

"An old engine is worth a million dollars?"

"Apparently five of them are," Peterson said with a huff. "Can we move on?"

MJ did a quick calculation and wrote on a legal pad: *5 radial engines, $1 million.* "I need to see that cargo manifest—the original, and since I'll also need a copy for my use…"

"I'll have Gretchen messenger a copy to your office," Peterson huffed.

"You're not listening. No copies. Not until I put eyes on the original. I need you to show me that original, you, sir, not your assistant. You can show it to me, or you can show it to a judge." Knowing she had Peterson on the ropes, MJ then fabricated a ruse. "Those are the rules of evidence as mandated in Jencks…"

"Fine," Peterson huffed, not knowing what *Jencks* was any more than MJ did. "I can see you in my office in fifteen minutes. I'll show you the original manifest, personally, but we won't have time for a meeting."

"Agreed," MJ replied, making a celebratory fist but suppressing a victory whoop.

"I'll tell the officer at the security desk to give you a visitor's badge. Come to the eighth floor. Gretchen will meet you. Fifteen minutes, Counselor, not a minute sooner."

"Very well." MJ rang off, while under her breath she mumbled, "Weasel."

Stepping out of the building, MJ checked her watch. With time to kill, she called Will Yost's private line.

After three rings, the commissioner picked up. "This is Yost."

"Hello, Will. It's MJ. Sorry to wake you, but I need a favor." Aware that it was Yost who'd turned both Portlock and Garodnik loose on the case, she added, "Another one."

"Is it something I can have my assistant take care of? I'm behind the curve today."

"Yes, that's fine," MJ agreed, and she related the situation to the commissioner.

"You need it right away?" Yost said, then paused, before adding, "Why do I ask?"

"Thank you, Willy," she purred, animatedly. "Fax it to Darlene."

"I'll email it. And stop calling me Willy."

"No e-mail. Fax or bonded messenger."

"Got it." Yost rang off, pleased that his old friend was back in fighting form.

After fifteen minutes had passed, MJ stepped back into the lobby.

Her visitor's pass was waiting, but before being allowed to proceed, she had to agree to have her briefcase searched. Upon surrendering the leather-bound and already half-spent pocket flask, she was directed to the elevators.

As she stepped out onto Peterson's floor, she popped a breath mint and asked the receptionist to ring the great man.

Soon after, another woman—this one looking to be about MJ's age, officious, unpleasant, her too-long hair, that sort of dull blondish gray with bangs and no discernable part, that made the woman look older than she probably was—arrived and escorted MJ down the hall. Walking with her back to MJ, she knocked on Peterson's office door, opened it and wordlessly waved the unwelcome visitor through.

Peterson, his head balanced atop a thick, over-long neck, sported a short-cropped Marine-style haircut. He was tanned or naturally dark complexioned. His tapered white shirt accentuated a muscular build.

Interrupted in the act of tossing a few of what appeared to be last minute papers into an attaché case, Peterson stood to greet, and unabashedly check out the lady lawyer, her man-tailored business suit accentuating a trim figure.

Closing the briefcase, Peterson's gaze finally completed its slow climb to MJ's eyes and he reached across his wooden desk, which sported two little flags abeam his name and title, and offered his hand. "Please, have a seat. As you can see, I'm preparing to leave."

She watched Peterson watch her cross her legs. She was glad she'd worn slacks, since it seemed to annoy him.

"Thank you for seeing me on short notice," she offered.

"An unexpected pleasure, Counselor."

The bold inference caused MJ to recall an old and tasteless joke about the guy who was so full of shit his eyes had turned brown. She fought back the urge to point that out, but did, however, note that Peterson's leering eyes were indeed brown. She smiled, knowing her learned silence would eventually force him to find something to say while she held his gaze and coolly looked *him* over.

Peterson was bigger than Jake's six feet but to MJ's surprise, what distinguished him at first glance was what had befallen his face: it was heavily scarred. The man's upper lip was stretched taut. His nose was unnaturally narrow, the right side a plain of scar tissue. Peterson had been badly burned at one time, banged up as well. Car wreck, perhaps… or war injuries. MJ felt a twinge of empathy as she scanned the wall of plaques for a Purple Heart certificate. Amid the awards, she saw nothing so noble.

Feeling the chill, Peterson began, "Time is tight, Counselor, so how may I help you?"

"I'll see that cargo manifest, thank you."

Peterson nodded, "Spoken like a lawyer."

To MJ's ears that meant not like a mother.

"You'd be wise to keep that in mind," she said."

His expression blank, Peterson spoke his piece. "Here's what *you'd* do well to keep in mind, Counselor. Leif Bergstrom's employer trusted him. That trust cost his client over half-a-million dollars, because the cargo they were contracted to transport is now sitting on the ocean floor. In fact…"

While Peterson droned on, MJ had stopped listening after his second sentence. When she tuned back in, the G-man was saying, "…your people are smart, Counselor. So you should know better than to really believe Bergstrom is innocent."

The lawyer took note of, but did not react to the deliberately inflammatory 'Your people' crack. Though he was defaming what he associated with her married name, it did not distract her as it was doubtless intended. She remained focused on what Peterson had said in their phone conversation. He'd said Leif Bergstrom's cargo was worth fully a cool million dollars, not *over half-a-million*, as he'd just claimed. "What did you say he was carrying?"

"Airplane engines," Peterson drawled. "The cargo manifest says Bergstrom was carrying airplane radial engines. Three of them. We've been through this."

"Yes, but earlier you mentioned their value was a million dollars," MJ said, opening her briefcase on her lap, looking for her notebook. "I wrote it down. You said it on the phone. His cargo was worth a million dollars."

"You wrote that down?" Peterson probed. "On paper?"

"Of course, on paper," MJ retorted, not looking up from her search. "*My people* found stone tablets impossible to fold."

Peterson stretched to see if she indeed had such a note. Seeing nothing, he concluded, "Counselor, I have a plane to catch."

"Okay, forget the value," MJ said, abandoning her search for the note. "Show me the manifest and I'll be on my way."

Peterson stood and turned toward a row of filing cabinets behind his desk. She watched as the fed opened a top drawer, and shuffled through the rows, quickly coming to what he sought. Pulling out a folder, Peterson handed a her a single sheet of paper.

"This is Bergstrom's cargo manifest," he declared with righteous indignation.

"Is this the original?"

"It is."

"Um, hmm," was as much as MJ would convey as she looked over the manifest. Part of it was filled in by hand, other entries were typed. The typewritten portion showed Leif's cargo to consist of *Three (3) each, Wright R-3350, twin-row radial aircraft engines, individually crated...* so on and so forth.

"Careful with that."

Disappointed, MJ handed the form back to Peterson. "I'd like a copy."

As if on cue, Peterson's assistant, Gretchen, looked in, pointed to her wrist.

With a nod toward the woman, Peterson held up a hand. "Counselor, I really must skedaddle. I'm gonna call this meeting to a close. I hope I've been helpful."

When Peterson turned to leave, MJ pointed to the file folder in Gretchen's hand. And though she wanted desperately to inform Gretchen of the striking resemblance she bore to the farmer lady in the painting, American Gothic, MJ instead simply smiled the sickly sweetest smile she could muster and went with, "May I have a copy of that manifest?"

Gretchen looked at Peterson with a frown. He nodded his permission and she took the folder, placed the manifest on her desk scanner.

While MJ waited for her copy, a security guard approached. Speaking to MJ, he said, "I'll escort you out, ma'am."

MJ raised an index finger, and looking at Gretchen, pointed toward the scanner. Gretchen handed her the scanned copy of the cargo manifest and hurriedly returned the original to the file cabinet in Peterson's office. She closed the drawer and pushed the lock. As she brushed by MJ and the guard, returning to her desk, MJ again offended her, this time with a blinding smile she knew Peterson would be seen ogling.

Enjoying Gretchen's flared nostrils, MJ watched the woman place the keys back into her desk drawer, lock it, and after fidgeting in the hope that the interloper would leave, tuck that key under her desk calendar.

"If there's nothing else, sir, I'll be leaving now, too," Gretchen said to Peterson who was standing awkwardly nearby.

"If we're done here, Counselor," Peterson said, and without looking away from MJ, added, "Thank you, Gretchen... and have a pleasant evening."

"Good night, sir," she cooed like a big pigeon. "I've set the lock on your door. Don't forget to pull it closed... and have a good trip."

As Peterson ushered MJ out of his office and pulled the door closed, he turned to her, extending a hand. "I'm off, Counselor. Fred here will escort you out of the building."

Standing in the elevator bank with Fred the security guard, MJ felt the sting of disappointment. She had gained the evidence she sought, but it was useless. The numbers on the manifest accorded directly with what Peterson asserted. Had she misunderstood him the first time? Had she been grasping at straws?

As she stood on the sidewalk in the gathering dusk, feeling frustrated, MJ had little interest in returning to her empty office or emptier-still apartment. Spotting a tavern across from where she stood she crossed over to the old, oak-walled pub.

Inching her way toward the surprisingly crowded bar, MJ found that the joyful din of happy-hour revelers did not suit her present state of mind, either. But just as she turned to leave, a young gentleman, a guy just about Jake's age, dressed in a sharp business suit, stood to offer her his barstool.

MJ demurred, but the young man politely insisted.

She finally acquiesced, and found herself pleased to have done so. Besides, the ostensible bit of chivalry apparently accomplished the young man's true objective, that of earning a smile of approval from the lovely, equally young blonde sitting cross-legged at the adjoining barstool. The young swain wasted no time chatting her up.

The end justifies the means, MJ thought. And, though the little snippet of life-as-it-should-be seemed part of some alternate reality, it nearly caused MJ to smile. Instead, she ordered a brandy, downed it and ordered another. Finally, like a cowboy in an old western movie, she had the bartender leave the bottle.

Within an hour the lady was mercifully drunk—a condition she'd not experienced since college.

Noticing her cell phone ringing and vibrating against the bar's hardwood surface, she blinked her big hazel eyes before lifting the glowing device to her ear. "Hello, Patrick.," she slurred.

"Mrs. Silver?" asked Detective Garodnik, incredulous.

"It's MJ, Patrick. Call me MJ."

"Are you alright, ma'am?"

"Yep."

Hearing the chatter and din in the background, the detective quickly assessed MJ's circumstances. "Where are you, Mrs.... Tell me where you are. I'm coming to take you home."

MJ shot a wobbly look toward the bartender. "Where am I?"

The bartender gently took the phone from her hand, and described the situation to Garodnik. He also agreed to keep the slightly-tipsy lawyer from leaving. He needn't have bothered; MJ had no intention of going anywhere.

Upon hanging up, the bartender escorted MJ to a nearby booth. A group of friends graciously evacuated their little cocoon to accommodate. The bartender also brought the half-empty glass of brandy and the lawyer's briefcase.

"Thank you, dear," MJ said, as she sat quietly lost in thought.

Garodnik arrived a few minutes later, having parked his unmarked at a fire hydrant in front of the tavern.

Recognizing the visitor as a plain-clothes cop, the bartender pointed to MJ's location.

Garodnik nodded and worked his way through the crowd, which parted like the Red Sea before Charlton Hesston.

"Hello, Lieutenant," she said, while beginning to stand only to decide otherwise.

Her jacket lay on the seat beside her, her sleeveless white blouse revealing her toned arms. "I have a confession to make, Lieutenant," she said, then paused to address the gawking crowd. "I always wanted to say that to a detective."

"Is that right?" Garodnik said, sizing up his inebriated colleague while giving the crowd that cop look that said, *Okay, show's over.*

"Let me take you home, ma'am. I have a car right outside."

"Thank you, but, I'm fine right here. If you're thinking DUI, forget it. I own no car and I have cab fare to my apartment." MJ's eyes appeared to grow quite sober as she lifted the snifter to her lips. "I need this right now, Patrick."

Garodnik said nothing, understanding.

But the terrified mother wanted to talk. "Are you married, Patrick?"

"Divorced. Occupational hazard."

"Children?"

"I have a son. He's a sophomore at Fordham."

"Y'know," MJ offered with surprising lucidity, "a famous writer once said that we humans are the only creatures who can fully anticipate the implications of producing offspring, and yet we do it anyway. He said it proves that we're nuts."

The detective patiently forced a smile. "We should go now."

"I must tell you, Patrick," she went on, insisting to be heard, "I don't agree with that guy. No, I do not. We have kids long before we're old enough or smart enough to really grasp the implications. Having kids was just a thing we did, like going to school or marrying. We just did it. Y'know?"

Seeing that MJ was not about to stop babbling, Garodnik took a seat at the booth.

Face to face now, MJ continued, "But all those other things, Patrick, those other things we do when we're coming up, they have a beginning, and if you want them to, they have an end. You have control of those things. Had enough of school? Then quit or graduate. Had enough of being married? Get a divorce. Tired of working? Retire or become a homeless person. The decisions were ours to make.

"But having kids," she opined, "that's not something one can undo, now is it? It's not like they come with a rewind button." She covered her mouth to hide a dopey grin.

Garodnik reached out. "You've had enough, Counselor. Please let me take…"

"But, this is important." She paused. "What was I saying?"

"Kids."

"Yeah, kids. The worries don't end when they grow up, not if you're worth a shit. No, we didn't know we'd love them so damned much," she said with emphasis, her voice raised. "Then they grow up, your kids. They think they can take care of themselves, and just when you always expect your worries to be over and you can get on with your life, *your* life—you realize that those worries, hell, they never end. If you have anything like a heart, you worry about your kids every damned day until they put you in the ground, and even then, only if you're lucky enough to kick-off before one of them. No, Patrick, we're not nuts," she concluded. "Nuts is defensible.

"Okay," she said, getting to her feet, "we can go now."

"Don't forget this," Garodnik said, handing MJ her jacket.

A gentleman, the detective began to help her on with it, when she abruptly turned to him. Her face was moist with the tears that had been welling for hours. Her effort to hide them, served only to enhance the depth of emotion she'd been struggling to suppress. As another tear peeked out, paused a second as if uncertain, then rolled down her cheek, MJ let forth a moan so sorrowful it nearly broke Garodnik's heart. "Oh, God, what have I done?"

Garodnik—a father, a son, a tough guy, a cop—moved to comfort her, then pulled back.

"I don't know what to do," she pleaded through tears. "This is all my fault."

Aware that the noisy bar had gone silent, Garodnik saw through the corner of his eye that everyone in the room was looking their way. Taking MJ by her shoulders, he threw the crowd that fierce look cultivated by cops and lion tamers.

As the crowd self-consciously turned away and the din returned to the room, MJ pulled back and looked up at the big, uncomfortable cop. "I'm sorry," she sniffed.

She began rooting around in her jacket's pockets, seeking a tissue that wasn't there. When Garodnik produced a handkerchief, she sniffed, blew her nose with the toot of a foghorn, sniffed again, and forced a half smile and sat back down.

"What's that?" Garodnik asked, pointing to MJ's right hand.

Looking down, her brow furrowed. Apparently when she was rooting around in her pocket, rather than a tissue a little yellow Post It note had stuck itself to the back of her hand. She began to discard it, but it seemed familiar. Reading what was scribbled on it seemed to bring her back from the brink. "This!" she said, her expression stern, the fight returning.

"What is it?" Garodnik said.

"Look at it." She handed him the note. "Says a million bucks worth of airplane engines, right?'

Reading it, Garodnik nodded, watching her closely.

"That's what Leif Bergstrom thought he was carrying," she asserted, her voice growing steady, "airplane engines, not dope." She opened her briefcase and produced her copy of the cargo manifest, the copy she'd gotten from Peterson's assistant. She handed it to the detective. He compared the two documents.

"Look here" she said, still sniffing, struggling for lucidity. Again, she blew her nose, less nautically this time, as she pointed to a line on the manifest. "It says Leif Bergstrom was carrying airplane engines. But Peterson—Mister Federal Extra-Special Super-Executive Agent Peterson, the guy who's jerking your department around—he told me Bergstrom's cargo, these engines, had a value of a million bucks. He said there were five of them. That was the first time I talked with him." She reached across the table to touch the sticky-note. "When he said it, I wrote it down." She poked at the paper with a manicured finger. "It says *5 radial engines $1 million*. That's what Peterson first told me."

Garodnik looked up from the manifest. "Why is this important?"

"Because the schmuck originally told me over the phone that Bergstrom's cargo was worth a million. Then later, when I went to his office he told me it was over half-a-million. I keep thinking he'd originally said there were five engines, now he says there were three. I know what the manifest says, but my eyes tell me one thing, my ears quite another. I can't shake what I heard."

"Probably just a mistake. Besides, a million *is* over half-a-million."

"Right, and Sunrise Highway is over a half-a-million feet from Sunset Boulevard. But who says that? Nobody."

"Well," Garodnik maintained, scratching his ear while looking over the manifest, "if this is the original manifest, why the concern? It says three engines, end of story."

"Really?" MJ challenged. "Suppose there's an insurance fraud being covered up here?"

"Mrs. Silver, you're grasping at straws. People don't *lower* the value in an insurance fraud."

Chalking MJ's logic up to a mother's alcohol-enhanced desperation, Garodnik the detective also knew that Chief Portlock would have him walking a beat again if he blew this case because he overlooked something, especially something from an admired former prosecutor, albeit a temporarily compromised one.

He looked at the paper closely, searching for anything that might sate the lady lawyer's curiosity. "Did you just say that this was copied from the original manifest?" he asked.

"Yes," she verified, taking the document back.

"Did you see the original?"

"I did, and had Peterson confirm its provenance," she said with a tiny burp. "His assistant, *Cousin It*, made this copy from it. Why?"

"I'm guessing you mean Gretchen," Garodnik said. "Are you absolutely certain Gretchen copied this from the original?"

"Yes. I handed Peterson a baloney story. He pulled the original and handed it to *Gretchen*." MJ made a face. "I then watched *Gretchen* make this copy from it. Chain of custody, y'know."

The detective leaned forward, and pointed to something on the document. "See that?" he asked touching his fingertip to a little heart-shaped dot near the lower right corner of the scanned copy.

"What—the dot?" MJ struggled to focus. "Probably from the scanner machine."

"Right," Garodnik said. "It's probably a speck of dirt or White-Out that was on the scanner's glass. We've all seen these things before. Right?"

"Sure," MJ acquiesced, seeing dots of her own, blinking. "Who uses White Out anymore?"

"People who use typewriters."

"Who uses a typewr..." She paused, breathing deeply, struggling mightily to clear her mind, to focus. Something about this was important. "What are you getting at, Patrick?"

"Parts of this were typed." Garodnik pointed to the line that described the cargo as *Three (3) each, Wright R-3350, twin-row radial aircraft engines...* "Look here," the detective insisted, "right here."

MJ could see that Garodnik had a cat-that-ate-the-canary look on his round face.

The detective turned the photocopy 180 degrees and again held it under MJ's nose. He pointed to another, identical heart-shaped dot at the upper *left* hand corner of the page. "Now, look here. See that?"

"Another dot," she said with a shrug. "Are we playing connect the dots?"

"In a way," the detective said. "What I'm showing you here is the same dot. This time it's inverted and displaced. Both dots are identical, but inverted, and equidistant from center."

MJ blinked, still trying her best to focus. "And that means, what exactly?"

Garodnik held out his palms. "It means Peterson or his assistant didn't clean the scanner's glass between the time one of them made the first copy and Gretchen made this one for you. It left a speck of wet White Out on the scanner's glass. She never cleaned the glass."

"Probably thought it was beneath her exalted station,," MJ said.

Garodnik was unflustered. "Yeah, real funny, I'm sure. But you're missing the point. It's not just another dot. It's the same dot...same dot, same shape, just inverted and offset."

"I know there's a point to this, Patrick."

"There sure is," said Garodnik. "Two dots means Peterson was not being straight with you. This was not copied from an original."

MJ perked up. "How do you get to that?"

The detective heaved a sigh, frustrated by the normally brilliant prosecutor's state. "Because the same dot is in two places," he said to his compromised crony. He gathered his patience and pointed again. "One dot here, another one here. This is a copy of a copy. The first time it was copied, they probably used the original. Then they altered that copy in haste and a little wet White Out was left on it. Then, Gretchen, or maybe even Peterson himself put that copy in the machine the other way around when making this copy, *your* copy. Bingo, another dot, different location."

Somewhere in a sober part of MJ's brain, it clicked. "So this is a third-generation document—a copy of an altered copy of the original."

"Yes."

"Peterson was lying to me," MJ declared, perking up. "You gonna shoot them? Can I?"

A smug nod from Garodnik. "Without the real original, we're just speculating."

"Yes, but you're onto something here, Patrick. Peterson altered the manifest. I never saw the original, not the real original. I smell malicious intent!"

"Tough to prove, Counselor. Think he'd give you the real original?"

"No chance," MJ said, still looking at the tiny dots, squinting as she turned the copied manifest over and back. "That was very good, Patrick."

Garodnik smiled. "Can I get a copy of this?"

"That would be a copy of the copy of the copy of the original. No. Take this one. Stick it somewhere safe."

Garodnik said, "Are you certain I can't give you a ride home?"

A faraway look came into MJ's eyes. "Go home and get some rest, Lieutenant. I'll be fine... feeling better already. I'll have the barman call me a cab. Oh, and thank you Patrick, for, well... thank you." She leaned across the table and kissed the detective's cheek.

Turning redder than ever, Garodnik grinned, and reluctantly took his leave.

Certain the detective was gone, MJ paid the bill, leaving a generous tip for the patient bartender, who asked if he might call his elegant, if tipsy customer a taxi.

The lady declined. There'd be no taxis for MJ Silver, not yet.

Leaving her locked briefcase with the kindly bartender for safekeeping, she crossed the street.

Standing alone on the sidewalk outside the Federal building, she watched and waited, for just what, she did not yet know, trusting instead that an idea would come as one always had.

The evening rush hour crowd that had poured from the building's doors an hour or so earlier had diminished to a trickle as the hour approached seven.

With a willful clarity, MJ realized what she must do. How she might do it remained an unknown.

Looking through the glass doors of the office building, she could see the security desk. Instead of the professional Fred, a slick-as-an-eel security guard was holding sway over the building's lobby. Slick was casually checking ID badges: a burden he bore with little grace and less diligence. His central preoccupation instead being the purposeful assessment of the ankles, calves, knees and derrières of the young female employees as they stepped from the elevators.

Upon further observation, MJ determined that Slick's dereliction of duty varied in more or less inverse proportion to the length and fit of the women's skirts as they crossed his domain on their way to the street.

The only variation in this cycle came with the occasional appearance of a workman or delivery person, each of whom came and went with barely a nod from the guard: Slick had his priorities, security not being prominent among them.

During the hour or so she'd been here, MJ watched eight such service people enter the building. Of the eight, four had been making food deliveries—sandwiches and salads from a nearby deli whose name was emblazoned on the deliverymen's hats and aprons. Several federal office staffers, it seemed, were working late, eating take-out dinners at their desks.

The deliverymen's comings and goings gave MJ an idea.

A quick trip back to the tavern, she withdrew cash from its ATM, and trotted back across the street in time to stop one of the delivery boys as he passed with his cardboard tray of food and white paper hat.

"How much you want for the food?" she asked, breathless.

The deli kid, a slightly built, stringy-haired Midwestern white-trash-runaway type with an attitude, was taken aback. "Say what?" he answered in his best hackneyed street smart patios.

"I'll give you ten bucks for the food."

"Piss off, lady," the kid said, hardly turning as he brushed by MJ. "Crazy old bitch."

"Hey," MJ upped her game. "You kiss your mother with that mouth?"

"My mother's dead to me."

"Oh, sorry. I'll make it fifty if you'll throw in the hat."

She regretted the words almost as they left her treasonous mouth.

The kid stopped on a dime, turned around, fixed his gaze upon this weird old broad.

Meeting her gaze, he dropped his eyes. Two decades of analyzing jurors' faces told MJ that a decision had been made. Everybody has a tell.

The kid sauntered over, trying his best to look hard.

"Wha's up wit'choo, lady?" he said. "I really love this hat." He paused to let his cool steal the warmth from the surrounding air, confident now, ready to deal. "Make it a-hundrit."

MJ held the kid's gaze, realizing now how young was this waif. "Don't push it," she said as she counted out fifty dollars in front of the tough talking child's big soft eyes. "Throw in the sneakers and this is yours. She knew she could have achieved the same for less."

"Hardly worth it, lady," the kid said, looking at the money in MJ's hand, still trying for more, yet removing the paper hat as he spoke. "I could lose my job for this. Whaddaya figure I'm suppos'ta tell my boss?"

"Here's another twenty," MJ said. "Give it to the other delivery guy for *his* hat and you won't have to tell your boss anything. Either way, when I'm done, you'll find all your stuff in that trash can." She pointed toward the corner.

The kid took the money. MJ took the hat, the shoes, and the food. Neither looked back.

Minutes later, a paper hat pinned upon her well coiffed head, a mature "delivery girl," her slacks rolled up at the ankles, stood in an empty corner of the building's large lobby pretending to be on her cell phone. There she watched and waited.

After a short few minutes, a strikingly attractive adequately younger woman in a particularly short skirt emerged from an elevator. As she crossed the lobby and into Slick's field of view, the young beauty, accustomed to being ogled, curved her big red and white mouth into an aloof and knowing smile, knowing too, that Slick would be smiling back.

MJ seized the moment.

As the woman headed for the exit, MJ stepped toward Slick's security station deliberately blocking his view. She flashed her long-expired City Employee ID toward the otherwise occupied security guard while he tried his best to peer around this middle-aged interloper before the object of his real interest left the building.

Given Slick's attitude toward both security and mature women, MJ's ID badge was barely glanced at. She scrawled something into the visitors log and was waved through with the same indifference he'd have doubtless afforded the ghost of Osama bin Laden at that moment.

Gliding through the metal-detector, MJ rode an elevator to the top floor of the government's leased offices. Looking in, she could see yet another security guard, this one walking his evening rounds. The elevator doors closed. She saw no camera. And she rode it down again. MJ did this for ten minutes, checking each floor, watching as all but the second floor grew ever more empty of workers. She never pressed another button, but merely rode up and down at the other passengers' will, grinning dumbly at each one. If the elevator stopped somewhere with its doors closed, she simply waited inside for someone to summon it.

Finally a custodian, the fourth to ride with her so far, entered the car with his cart and pressed Three. Bingo!

Unseen, MJ pilfered a packet of rags from the man's cart. Then, stepping off and into the empty 3rd Floor reception area, she followed as he used his key card to open the glass doors. "Excuse me," she said as she held the purloined rags out to him while he held the door. "You dropped these."

He reached back, "Gracias."

MJ stepped forward. "De nada."

She was in.

MJ moved unseen as she took off down the office corridor, her oversized sneakers flapping. Moving at a trot now, her heart pounding, she headed for Peterson's office.

Reaching the row of secretarial desks, she began to tremble, wishing she'd filled her flask instead of leaving it in her briefcase with the bartender.

Forcing herself on, she came to Peterson's door. Inhaling deeply, her trembling hand tried the knob. "Dammit!" Of course it was locked. She'd watched Peterson lock it.

Not knowing what else to do, she crouched at the rear of Gretchen's desk, just outside the great man's office. *Don't forget to lock up,* the dour Gretchen had cooed to Peterson before leaving this very spot just a couple of short decreasingly-sober hours ago.

Stiffening and wide-eyed, MJ heard voices, then footsteps; two people were coming this way. She had to do something or she'd be seen. The corridor of offices was a dead-end. The only way out was toward the voices. She had to get into Peterson's office. Surely every assistant has a key to her boss's office. She pulled at Gretchen's desk drawer. Locked. *Paranoid bitch!* The footsteps stopped, the voices didn't.

The footsteps started toward her again, only one set now. MJ's breathing was deafening as she squeezed her head between her hands. Verging on panic, she reached under Gretchen's desktop blotter. A key was there! Of course, she'd seen Gretchen secret it there, but in her alcohol fog MJ had forgotten.

Too small to be a door key, it opened the desk drawer. Miraculously, another key was in the drawer. It was all or nothing: she could attempt to hide under the desk, or stand and walk to the door. If the key failed, she'd be exposed to the approaching walker, be seen in sneakers and a paper hat. She gripped the key in her sweating fist, a woman possessed, or maybe a little drunk. Going for broke, she turned for Peterson's office door. The footsteps rounded the corner, drumbeats now more than footfalls. She fiddled with the key at the lock. The deadbolt slid, the knob turned, she was inside Peterson's office.

Silently closing the door behind her, the office went dark. Using the light on her cell phone, MJ wasted no time in finding what she knew had led her here against her better judgment. She looked first toward the door, half expecting it to open, hoping that the footsteps were not Peterson's. They passed.

She turned to the file cabinet standing alone in its corner of the office. She'd seen Peterson retrieve the document from that cabinet during their meeting. She'd seen Gretchen return it. Would the file cabinet be locked?

Reaching it, she pulled on the handle of the top drawer. It moved, but not without letting off a loud squeak.

Moving recklessly now, committed, she yanked the drawer wide, leafing through the folders until she came to the one labeled *South Wind Aviation*. The same name appeared again below, this time in Spanish. She removed the file folder and walked to Peterson's desk. Opening the folder, she read by the light of her phone.

There were Customs bonds and temporary authorization forms. There was a certificate of insurance. Then she saw it. There, with a post-it note stuck to its face, was the cargo manifest: Leif Bergstrom's cargo manifest, the ostensible original. Examining the form in the lamplight, MJ looked for the dot, Garodnik's dot.

Seeing nothing, she folded back the little number-covered post-it note, and there was the dot: one dot only. But was this manifest the actual copy Customs had acquired from South Wind Aviation, Leif Bergstrom's South American employer?

She could see the typewriter strike marks. There was a signature in ink. Rendered with a flourish, it read, Guillermo P. Filho.

Her eyes went to the line labeled, Description of Goods. She read the main section: *Wright, R-3350, aircraft engines. Nothing further to appear on this line.*

Looking away from the manifest and back at the file folder spread open before her, MJ now began reading the

Certificate of Insurance. She read the description of the insured as Wright, R-3350 aircraft engines. The following line set their value as $200,000 each. All was consistent with Peterson's claims. MJ could not help but doubt herself. Perhaps she'd heard wrong after all. In her desperation to implicate Peterson, she'd been delusional.

She turned to the second page.

There was a sound outside the door.

Impossibly loud, it was Gretchen's voice. What in bloody hell was she doing back here? Standing rigid, MJ saw a button illuminate on Peterson's desk phone. She closed the file folder while simultaneously jamming the customs manifest into her pocket as she scanned Petersen's office for a hiding place. Through the door, she heard Gretchen speak, light, overly-cute girlfriend talk. Gretchen laughed, said goodbye. MJ saw the light on the phone blink out, awaited a coronary occlusion, and forced her feet to move to the door.

Finally, she heard Gretchen's footsteps retreating down the corridor.

With mixed relief and anger, MJ stared ahead allowing her heart to slow. *Damn her!*

Remembering why she was here, MJ removed the cargo manifest from her pocket. She forced her attention back to the crumpled document in her trembling hand. All that remained for her to read now was the quantity. Her eyes went to the line. It read, Quantity: THREE (3) pieces.

MJ's heart sank and she felt sick. Garodnik had started this. The detective had reiterated the importance of the original cargo manifest. Even if it was inadmissible and if the detective didn't share her suspicions about Peterson, why would he have pointed out the dot thing to begin with?

She looked at the document again, this time under the desk lamp's light.

The heart-shaped dot was there, upper left, one dot only. It proved nothing, and she'd ruined the document. She could not return it to the file in its crumpled condition. Original or copy, MJ decided to steal the crumpled cargo manifest.

Walking to the office door, she opened it with agonizing slowness, flipped the lock button, and stepped out, softly closing the door behind her. Replacing the keys, she looked toward the corner she'd have to round at the end of the row of offices. That would lead her to the long hallway and the elevator.

She was halfway to the corner when it hit her. On the second page of the Certificate of Insurance she'd glimpsed the words *Five (5) each.* The words were read out of context, and in her panic at being disturbed by Gretchen's footsteps, their significance was lost.

They meant everything. Suddenly it occurred to MJ what was wrong.

She could not risk going back in. But, there, not ten feet from where she now stood, was the 3rd floor's lone typewriter. As in her own office, the old machine was apparently kept around and used for filling out forms and documents not amenable to computer printers. The old machine could hold the answer she sought.

Summoning all of her courage, rather than continue her escape MJ crossed the ten feet of brightly-lit open space between herself and the typewriter.

She found its switch and flipped it on, placed a blank sheet of paper into its carriage, and, with a sound not unlike that of an industrial drop-forge, she typed an upper-case letter "T" and immediately switched off the humming machine.

Then, realizing that might not be adequate, she reluctantly switched the machine back on. Looking both ways and listening with heightened sense, she pressed another key. Again, with a sound that seemed to ricochet off the walls of the silent office like cannon fire, the upper case letter 'H' appeared adjacent to its companion letter 'T' on the otherwise blank parchment.

MJ withdrew the paper sheet from the machine, and headed for the corridor. Approaching the corner, she again heard footsteps. There was no turning back. Her mind raced. The footfalls, now no more than ten paces distant, were not those of a woman this time.

As the security guard came into view, MJ tipped her paper hat, smiled and said, "Good night, sir," and the elevator doors enwrapped her like a warm blanket.

- CHAPTER 11 -

Bolting upright in bed, MJ slapped at the infernal alarm clock. With her head pounding, she was suffering her first hangover in three decades. It was 7:00 a.m.

She knew that to recline would only herald a descent to the nauseated, room-spinning maelstrom from which she'd awakened. So, she summoned her will and dragged her body from the bed.

Shoeless, she shuffled toward the apartment's small kitchen, all the while holding her pounding head and wondering how a thing so demonstrably empty could hurt so very much.

Arms above her head, she stretched. *Headache be damned*, she thought, there was a great deal to be done this day. She would have to rally.

Coffee.

Something about the purloined cargo manifest nagged at her. So she planned to make a stop before going into the office. A cool shower made her feel marginally better, and by eight a taxi was wending his way up 6th Avenue to the heart of the city's diamond district. She climbed out at 6th Avenue and 47th Street.

Midway up 47th, she stopped at the familiar shop with its Omega and Rolex watches, gemstones, and engagement rings sparkling in the window. The same glossy black-and-gold sign that had identified Eisen & Sons Fine Jewels since 1959, still hung proudly above the door. Though she knew the store was not yet open for customers, she also knew the door separating the sidewalk from a king's ransom in gems would be unlocked to accommodate the early-morning trading that went on between the district's diamond dealers. Between the police—most in disguise—and private security, New York's 47th Street diamond district was among the most patrolled thoroughfares in the entire city.

As MJ entered Eisen's, she winced when the old bell above the door clanged with the perceived volume of a medieval carillon. The shopkeeper did not look up from his work.

"Good morning, Eli," she said to the top of the proprietor's bald head.

Eli Eisen: septuagenarian, journeyman jeweler-owner-heir to Eisen & Son Fine Jewels, and older cousin of MJ's lost Myron, was bent over his workbench. The jeweler was concentrating on some microscopic task and appeared for the moment to not acknowledge his departed cousin's dear widow.

MJ knew that Eli was not being rude, just cautious. If he were to look up from his intensely focused piece of work at that moment it could be extremely costly.

Standing as still as a statue, she waited.

Finally, completing whatever surgically-delicate operation he was performing, the jeweler said, "Good morning, my dear," as he stood to kiss her cheek. "Stephie and I called last night but you were not at home."

MJ raised a hand as if it were all too much, which of course it was. "As you might imagine, Eli, I had police business."

"A terrible thing," Eli offered. "My prayers are with our Jacob."

"I know that comes from the heart." MJ placed her briefcase on the long glass counter. "But, Eli," she said, "it's not your heart that I need today, but your eye."

"My eye? Are you being Biblical or cryptic?"

To MJ, there was scant distinction. The two had spoken of religion just once in all their years of kinship. That was when the Old Testament scholar asked his soon-to-be cousin-in-law if she'd ever believed in a higher power. After a moment's feigned introspection, the young iconoclast had answered, "I've never been sufficiently terrified." The topic never came up again.

However, as she stood before her oldest and in many ways dearest friend now, the possibility of Jake's being safe or even alive diminishing with each minute he remained missing, MJ was fast approaching sufficiently terrified.

"I'm being pragmatic," she finally answered. "I need your eye to peer through the magnifying loupe that's always on your head and examine something for me."

"You're here for an appraisal, then? You want to sell your jewelry? Your ring?" Eli raised his palm, "I won't let you do that, Myrna. Please, I know you're frightened, my darling, but we can't put a price on Myron's memory. If you need ransom money, we can raise money… the congregation, the relief fund, the poker boys, Stephie and me…"

"No, no," MJ demurred. "It's not come to that, not yet. I almost wish it had. At least then I'd know…"

"What then?" he said, standing. Coming closer, his brow curled as he observed her struggling to maintain control. "What can I do?"

"Look here." Sniffing, MJ opened her briefcase and removed two sheets of paper. She set them next to one another on the old glass counter. They were the purloined cargo manifest and a blank sheet containing only a pair of typed, upper case letters: a T and an H. They were the ones she'd made on the Homeland Security office typewriter.

"I need you to examine these two documents using your most critical jeweler's eye," MJ said. "I can't go to the police with this, not until I'm sure. You and your extraordinary eye can make me sure."

Eli scanned the papers. "What am I looking for? This one's almost blank."

"Yes, but as you see, not quite," MJ said, pointing to the typed letters, TH. "Take note of any irregularities in these letters, texture, anything, everything. Memorize them."

Dropping the jeweler's loupe over his right eye, Eli took a full two minutes to thoroughly examine each letter under various lights and magnifications.

"Okay," he said. "I know everything about these letters, and nothing about why I should."

"Patience is a virtue, my scholarly cousin," she teased, now calling Eli's attention to the cargo manifest. "Do the same with this form, please. There are a few upper case T's on this form. See if one of them matches the one that you just examined so carefully on the other, plain white sheet of paper, and I mean matches it exactly, every imperfection, every texture, shade, contour, everything."

Again, the jeweler dropped the loupe over his right eye, and moved his head close to the manifest, focusing on one spot. "Right away, I see a match." He pointed out the letter T in the word Three. "This first letter T in the word THREE, it's identical to the other capital T, the one on the blank sheet. Want to see?"

"Not if you're sure."

"I'm absolutely sure," Eli said, and picked up the first sheet of paper. "They're identical in every detail, strike angle, pitch, edge rise, fall, face texture, shade, geometry, everything."

MJ knew that to Eli's eye, there were too many details to detail.

"But there's more," the jeweler went on. "See the relationship between the T and the H? The H is offset in elevation–and its pitch is different. It's several micro meters higher than the T right next to it and it has a slightly gradient density, top to bottom. Same on both sheets."

MJ could discern no such minutia, few would, but she nodded her assent.

"These were typed on the same typewriter." Eli wrinkled his brow. "Who uses a typewriter anymore?"

"You've uncovered what could be the most important piece of physical evidence so far in the most publicized murder case of the year, and that's your question: 'Who uses a typewriter anymore?'" MJ cupped her cousin's face in both her hands and kissed the top of Eli's bald head. "Thank you, my sweet. You're a genius."

Laughing, the old jeweler struggled from her grip, while saying, "Go, go. Find your boy and bring him home. That will be thanks enough."

As he spoke, another jeweler entered the shop, a small paper bag in hand. As was routine here, the rumpled bag was less likely to contain a cup of coffee than it was a fortune in gems.

As MJ left the shop, she could hear Eli ask the new arrival, "So who uses a typewriter anymore?" The normal world was taking another spin.

Rather than cab it, MJ took the subway to the Battery Park office she'd maintained since retirement from City Hall. She used the place to keep herself busy mostly handling the legal affairs of the Common Sense group. Had she not been so distracted, she'd be fighting the U.S. Justice Department's push for sentencing "reform," which she'd concluded was little more than a ruse to further enrich private prison corporations.

The small, two room office in a classic limestone building was a far cry from the glistening corner suite she'd once commanded as District Attorney. But the view of New York harbor was magnificent, and the passion and wisdom she'd brought to her profession remained undiminished.

When MJ arrived, Darlene jerked a thumb toward MJ's inner office. "Lieutenant Garodnik's in there," she whispered. "He was waiting in the hall when I arrived."

"Good morning, Patrick," she called from the outer office, feigning a well-rested voice. "I'm pouring myself coffee. Be right in."

"Good morning, Counselor," the detective said. "I trust you made it home in one piece."

"Yes, mother dear," she said as she walked in and sat behind her desk. "I put myself to bed and everything."

"Have you seen this morning's *Register*?" asked the detective, whom she noticed was wearing a suit, his hair parted.

"No. I already have a headache," she said. Nonetheless, she powered up her computer and went to the tabloid's website. "PILOTS CONNECTED IN CASSANDRA MURDER: A Register Exclusive by Wendell Leitch."

"I saw Leitch on the news last night," MJ said.

"Yeah, the little parasite is everywhere now."

"Patrick, what do you know about this drug they're calling the Analog?."

"Different thing. For years there's been speculation about the drug. It's a sort of legend in the drug culture."

"What is it?" MJ asked. "The people at Common Sense don't know of it."

That's 'cause there's nothing to know," Garodnik replied. "A street version of this Analog does not exist. It's imagined to be the perfect synthetic, as good as the best primo cocaine but not natural. Supposedly there's a formula that gives dealers a way to make their own high grade alkaloid-synthetic without smuggling in Colombian or paying the cartels' high prices. Anyway, the Russian mob has shown an interest, but the Analog's never been seen on the street. Our lab guys say it's not plausible."

"Then why are the papers saying the stuff they found at Jake's is this Analog?"

"Not the papers, Counselor," the cop said, his tone gentle, "the *Register*. I think their fact-checker is Bigfoot. I'm telling you, what they found at Jake's will turn out to be just another piece-a-crap synthetic. They'll never get it right. It's like no-cal potato chips. Forget the Analog. This case is about something else."

"But just suppose it's the real thing this time. Wouldn't that explain Peterson's obsession with Jake and Tina Bergstrom?"

"It might if there we're a street analog of cocaine.

"Look," Garodnik continued, "cocaine analogs are useful in anesthesia. But as high-grade primo-narco, there's always a downside. Nothing can substitute for the real thing. Not yet."

Noticing that MJ had stopped listening the moment he'd mentioned the word *plausible,* Garodnik changed tack. "Listen, Mrs. S, after I left you yesterday, I got to thinkin', you know, about that cargo discrepancy you mentioned, how Peterson switched his facts, insisting he'd always said there were only three engines, not five?"

"Of course," MJ said, itching to share her findings.

"Well," the detective went on, "I did a little snooping. Located the insurance company that held the policy for Bergstrom's outfit, this, uh...Aveee...ento..."

"In English it's, South Wind Aviation," she assisted. "Leif's boss."

"Right. They're insured by a company in Hartford, right here in the good ol' USA. I called them before coming here. The guy there was real helpful. He said nothing like it had happened in all his years in the insurance game."

"Nothing like what?"

"South Wind had a blanket policy, adjusted for all their shipments. Bergstrom's shipment was covered for a cool million bucks, flat out, no questions asked...a real primo policy."

"So what's unusual?" asked MJ.

"Well, the insurance guy said the cargo outfit's client called him yesterday, late. Guy said someone in his organization had miscalculated the value of the materials Bergstrom was carrying. He then insisted that the potential loss settlement be reduced to only three-hundred grand. Claimed there were just some old run-out engines aboard Bergstrom's plane. The million-dollar valuation was a mistake. The shipment that Bergstrom was flying had been confused with another. That's why the Bergstrom engines were insured as new, a clerical error. Said he was real insistent that no overpayment be made."

MJ calculated. "So we've gone from a cool million, down to something over half-a-mil, and now all the way down to three hundred thousand. How commendable."

"Yeah. The insurance guy thought so too. He said the executive was a prince of a fellow."

"Get a name for his highness?"

"The executive at the cargo outfit is one Dwight Chichester. He is–or he was—Leif Bergstrom's boss. The guy who was receiving the cargo, Chichester's customer, is the one who signed the Customs papers, though." The detective paused, struggling with the pronunciation. "Guy's name is Guillermo P. Filho."

MJ looked at the copy she'd stolen from Peterson's files. Filho's signature was there, rendered with a continental flourish, but typed neatly below the line.

"Nice bit of detective work, Patrick."

"I live to serve," Garodnik cracked. "I'm gonna run it down some more. Were you saying you had something for me?"

She stood, went to where the detective was seated and showed him the apparently forged manifest. She explained, how the typed word THREE in upper-case letters was covering what was originally written on the quantity line.

After staring at the form for a long time, the detective simply uttered, "Jeezis."

When Garodnik took his leave, MJ took three aspirin from her desk drawer. She swallowed them with the second black coffee Darlene mercifully brought her.

Unable to work, she fidgeted with her pencils or paced the office. "Darlene, please hold my calls for a while. I need to think."

Darlene stepped into MJ's office. "You might want to know that two of Jake's friends from the airline phoned before you got here this morning." She held three pink phone message notes for her boss's attention. The calls had come from Bill Gance and Ed James.

"Did either of them say..?"

Darlene answered quickly. "They didn't know anything. Just checking to see if we'd heard from Jake, or if you knew anything. Captain Gance said he'd be in the air all day, but left a cell number where you could reach him tonight if there was anything he could do." Darlene handed MJ the messages, and took up the last pink note. "Mr. James left a cell number as well. Said he'd be at the airport all day. You could call him any time."

After Darlene stepped out, MJ tried to focus, to reason and deduce. She found herself drifting, her mind getting lost in thoughts of Jake. It was then she recalled a conversation she'd had with her son.

A few years ago, mother and son had been enjoying a pleasant day together, a rare treat given their busy schedules. Jake had just passed on the opportunity of an early captain's spot, opting instead to transition from medium to long haul jets. MJ had never revealed her abject, nightmare-inducing terror over his Air Force work, but had not similarly demurred when he announced that flying would be his career choice in civilian life.

Though she'd always secretly wanted her only child to follow a career in the law, and in fact, Jake had gone so far as to take the LSATs, scoring high. But opted for military flight training instead of the law.

Nonetheless, being a good son, he'd wanted to assuage the disappointment his mother thought she'd hidden from him. What better way than by introducing Mom to the magnificent Boeing 747, the very jumbo into which the younger Silver was about to transition.

As it sat in a JFK hangar, hand-in-hand, mother and son had walked around the giant craft, which appeared large beyond comprehension. MJ was awestruck. What sort of man could make such a gargantuan thing leave the ground, bring it to the stratosphere, control it, and return it to earth along with the lives of hundreds in his charge... and do it day after day, in every weather? She made Jake know how proud she was that her son had become such a man.

Now, pacing her office, and lost in such thoughts, an idea struck MJ. It was an idea born of desperation, certainly far outside the lady lawyer's area of expertise, and farther still from plausibility.

But, implausibility characterized this entire affair. Just as something so insignificant as a speck of dirt on a scanner had led to the discovery of a forgery, so too could MJ's latest and even less plausible hypotheses bear fruit.

At her desk, she picked up the phone and fell into her padded chair, spilling a dollop of coffee in the process. Ignoring the spill, she picked up the pink phone note and dialed Ed James's cell phone.

Two rings and the pilot picked up.

"Mornin', this is Ed."

MJ identified herself, and the two exchanged the requisite words of concern.

When Ed asked if there was anything he could do to help, MJ was ready. "Well, there *is* something, Mr. James."

"Let 'er rip, Mrs. Silver," Ed said. "Anything at all."

"Please, call me MJ.'

"Yes'm, and please call me Ed."

"Are you familiar, Ed, with an airplane engine called the Wright R-3350?"

"No, MJ ma'am, I'm not. But I do know that the 'R' prefix, means it's a radial engine, y'know, the old kind they used on prop planes." Ed paused a moment, then asked, "Does this have something' to do with Jake's Air Force buddy Swe… I mean Leif Bergstrom? He was flyin' one of those old prop jobs. I hope I'm not out'a line but the scuttlebutt around here is somebody's tryin' everything in creation to connect that accident to Jake."

"We're on the same page here, Ed. It *is* connected somehow: Jake, Leif Bergstrom, the plane crash. It's just not connected in the way it's being painted by the authorities."

"Hell, MJ ma'am, I figured that." Ed's tone had turned reserved. "Same goes for everyone here at North Am. Jake is an upright honest man, and he sure as hell ain't a drug runner. No way. No way in hell! Pardon my French. And, by the way," Ed continued, "Jake said the same about Bergstrom. According to Jake, they's no way Swede Bergstrom was a drug runner, either, and that's sure good enough for me."

"Thank you, Ed. That means a great deal. So, how can I learn what a Wright R-3350 radial aircraft engine might be worth? How much money might one of these things be covered for in an accident, for example? …covered by an insurance company."

"Hot dang, that's way above my rating," the pilot admitted. "But I'd bet your son Jake could've–I mean *could*—Jake could answer that question without even thinkin'. Look, Mrs. Silver, how about I have one of the A an' P boys give you a call?"

"A and P?" MJ queried, her brow furrowed as she pictured an old supermarket. "I'm sorry, Ed, I don't understand."

"Sorry, ma'am. A and P stands for airframe and power-plant. If anybody could answer that question, it'd be one'a the A and P boys, the mechanics."

"If it's not too much…"

"If your about to say the word *trouble*, please don't," Ed asserted. " Heck, I tell 'em it's for Jake Silver's mom, they'd dig up old Orville himself to find an answer."

The two exchanged contact info, said their goodbyes and MJ waited to hear from Ed James's A and P boys. Within a half-hour, the call came.

"Yeah, uh, hi, Mrs. Silver," said a nervous voice. "This is Sean Wilke from North American Airlines…"

"Ah, yes, Sean, thank you," a grateful MJ answered the young mechanic whom she'd met when Jake had introduced her around, and remembered as the youthful, cowlicked crew-chief of Jake's airliner. To the mature woman, this A and P boy, actually was a boy. "It's good to hear from you, Sean. Thank you for calling back so quickly."

A few courtesies were exchanged before MJ asked, "Tell me, Sean, do you have the information I had asked for? Did Mr. James forward my request?"

"Yes, ma'am, he did," the young voice said. "That's an old engine type you're asking about. I haven't seen one since school. We don't have any information on anything like that here at the airline so I wanted to make sure it was okay to ask my friend over at Butler Aviation. Butler is the general aviation operator over at LaGuardia. They know all this stuff."

"I'm sorry to put you to so much trouble. But, sure, ask away."

"No sweat, Mrs. Silver. I'm glad to help… we all are. First Officer Silver was… *is*, is a great guy. I'll get back to you the minute I have something."

As the two rang off, another call came in.

"G'mornin' again, Mrs. S," the pleasant voice said.

"Good morning, Patrick. Do you have something?"

"Yes, as a matter of fact. There's a new wrinkle in the Cassandra McRea case. I just got through looking over the evidence tech's report, and we got a partial print. One print, in blood. But it's not from the scene."

MJ's heart raced.

"Beat cop found it a block away on the lid of a garbage dumpster. He also found a pair of rubber gloves *inside* that dumpster. They'd been rinsed, but still had blood traces on them. The blood samples matched the victim's. There was nitrile and powder residue under Cassandra McRea's fingernails. So she must have ripped the killer's glove in her struggle. We can't get a positive match on the print yet. Smudged. But it's a fifty percent match with the latents from the apartment. We're awaiting DNA. But the good part is, the lab compared the partial to Jake's eliminations and concluded that it couldn't have come from him. It's our first lead." Pausing to check his watch, Garodnik said, "I didn't realize the time. Listen, Mrs. Silver, can you meet me at the Javits Center?"

MJ's brow wrinkled, thinking, what's with this guy and the *Mrs. Silver*? We're close in age. "The convention center?" She finally said, welcoming the prospect of activity, but still asked, "Does it have to do with the case?"

"Maybe. I'll fill you in when we get there. I'll be in the lobby."

It was just past ten when MJ's cab pulled up at the convention center's main entrance. Climbing out, she spied Garodnik, not in the lobby, but pacing out front.

A gigantic banner stretched above the center's entrances with the words, *Welcome American Petroleum Association.*

"American Petroleum Association," Garodnik said, pointing, reading as if she were illiterate. "They're having their annual convention."

He expected a response. She expected details.

"They're the guys who look for oil and gas," he said.

"Well they won't have to look far," she observed with a sweeping gesture toward the surrounding cityscape.

"They'll get more oil and gas from the restaurants in this neighborhood than they'd find in the whole Arabian Gulf."

"Forget the neighborhood," Garodnik said. "Think back a couple days, Counselor. The very first article in the *Register*. It mentioned the guy who found the wreckage of Bergstrom's airplane down in the Caribbean? In the...what was it? The... the Windward something or other."

"Of course," she acknowledged, her curiosity piqued. "He's the frogman who found wreckage floating around in the straits off Cuba. He found Leif's body, too. Sure I remember him. Funny name... Something Irish..."

"Aloysius Grogan, and guess what? He's here. He's giving a talk right now." Garodnik pulled a rumpled program from the pocket of his sport jacket. "That's why we have to hurry."

"You think he has something to add to the case?"

"He's a witness," Garodnik shrugged. "Could be he saw something. Maybe shed a little light on your cargo discrepancy theory, for example. Since we have no authority in the Bergstrom case, this is the only chance I might ever get to question him. I can't miss the opportunity."

"Lead on, Patrick."

The pair rode an escalator up, and wandered around the perimeter of the convention center's second floor, looking for Room 1A19.

Finding it, they were met by a uniformed staffer who told them the talk had been moved to 1A23 to accommodate the unexpectedly huge audience.

It turned out to be the convention center's largest room. Despite his topic, *Geo-Spectral Analytic Applications of Robotic Submersibles*, Aloysius Grogan was now a celebrity, and his nerdy talk seemed to have attracted more microphone and camera wielding rowdies than it did the cerebral types its arcane title might suggest.

Opening the door, the interloping detective and lawyer could see the auburn-haired man standing on a raised platform at the front of the big room. As they stepped in, the diver was just wrapping up his talk.

The pair took up a standing position along the rear wall where they were the only ones, except for a pretty, long-haired brunette in a short dress.

"…and so, in conclusion," Grogan was saying to a smattering of camera flashes, "if we are to truly understand the three-quarters of our own planet's surface as well as we already understand the equivalent area that forms the entire surface of Mars, then autonomous robotic submersibles, intelligent devices capable of sonar imaging and spectral analysis, deployed in the public sphere, represent an idea whose time has come." He nodded. "Thank you."

The room erupted in shouts and camera strobes, men and women standing, running up the aisles and jockeying for position. Despite that most of the din had little to do with his learned remarks, Grogan smiled broadly.

As the seminar moderator called for order, quiet, and respect for what was the intended purpose of the session, several unruly types were removed by security. The room calmed.

In the interim, Aloysius Grogan had shed his jacket. In rolled-up shirtsleeves, his big arms straddled the podium. He looked like he could easily toss it across the room. That room now held what looked like an audience of some 300 people: Grogan understood photo ops. As the applause built and faded, people began to leave or jockey for position. Most stayed put.

When Grogan called for questions, pandemonium erupted yet again. After a show of mock surprise at the sea of hands and shouts, the diver added with a smile, "Wait, please. I'm only taking questions about robotic submersibles. I'm not gonna talk about the *Queen of the Southern Skies*." Then, directing a question of his own to the sea of interlopers, "This is a big town, folks. There must be at least one Kardashian you could be out there chasing?"

With a collective mix of laughter and groans, many of the hands went back down. Several people carrying cameras stood and headed for the exits.

As MJ stepped aside to allow the river of paparazzi to pass through the doors, she leaned toward the detective and nodded at the raised hands in front of them. "This could take a while."

"I'll wave a little tin, interrupt…"

MJ grabbed the big cop's arm. "Let Aloysius do his thing. We'll wait."

They took newly empty seats near the last row.

"So what do you make of this fingerprint on the dumpster?" MJ whispered.

"I'm not sure. The computer is crunching it against IAFIS. Maybe we'll get a hit."

"I got a hit for you," MJ said, opening her briefcase. "But I'll only show it to you if you promise not to book me. Not yet, at least."

"I promise nothing."

She produced the cargo manifest she'd pilfered from Peterson's file.

"Yeah, this is…" Garodnik said, then, seeing but a single dot, looked at MJ and with a jaundiced grin and added, "Only one dot."

"Exactly, and here's the typewriter strike marks."

"This typing is first generation," Garodnik affirmed. "Mind if I keep these papers? Crime lab will determine if it's an original Customs form."

"I don't want them," MJ said, feigning shock. "That stuff is stolen property and I'm an officer of the court. I got ethics, too."

The detective looked at MJ with admiration and not a little empathy, and he noticed perhaps not for the first time how attractive she was, despite the harsh overhead lighting on her face, reflecting off her hair, still mussed form the wind outside.

"But Patrick, there's more. Since we know the manifest's been doctored, I did more snooping."

"Very ethical of you," Garodnik chided, still examining the rumpled document.

"The insurance guy you spoke with, remember?"

"Sure."

"He said Leif Bergstrom's employer contacted him personally, right?"

"Bergstrom's boss asked him to reduce the amount of the settlement. Sure."

"Well," MJ revealed, "I learned today that each of those engines couldn't be worth much more than two-hundred grand. That correlates with the reduced value of the insurance claim."

"Right," Garodnik surmised. "But that washes only if the airplane was carrying three engines, not the five we were initially led to believe. That would imply insurance fraud."

"Suppose it wasn't carrying engines at all," MJ suggested.

Garodnik curled his bushy eyebrows, thought for a moment and said, "Reducing the value of the cargo would reduce any interest salvage crews might have in pulling it up."

"It'd probably cost at least half-a-million to raise the plane and restore the engines. That would discourage salvage, and eliminate the risk of having the nefarious deed exposed."

Garodnik changed the subject. "What do you know about Christina Bergstrom?"

"Jake told me she had a drug problem, was abused as a kid, ran away. He thinks her brother intervened. That's about it."

"Well," the detective said, "she had a drug problem, past tense but real. I been doing a little checking. That's where Philippe Sinclair surfaced."

"Who's that?"

"Some dirtbag she was involved with back in the Nineties. Drug dealer, pimp, petty crook, all-around pinhead.

Nothin' special except, and here's the kicker, this Sinclair disappeared in late 2003… dropped out of sight like he fell off the Earth."

"Yes, and..?"

"At about the time Philippe Sinclair disappeared, Leif Bergstrom got released from Walter Reed. That's an Army…"

"Really," MJ said, impatient now.

"Well, we can place Leif Bergstrom, and this Philippe Sinclair, and Bergstrom's sister all in Stockton, California at around the same time. In fact, a body was found in the trunk of a car in Oakland. The car contained Sinclair's fingerprint. It'd been wiped, but the Oakland PD lifted one latent. Problem was, they had a fingerprint but no fingers…the stiff's fingers, teeth, face, even the feet, were all gone. The car was intact, but the stiff in the trunk had been mutilated and burned beyond recognition."

"So, you make this John Doe to be Sinclair?" MJ deduced.

"Fills a vacuum," Garodnik said. "And, looking into the Bergstrom woman, if appearances are any indication, she starts getting her life together at around that same time. Records show she went into rehab in '03. After that, she goes dark. But she resurfaced in 2006. Moved around a lot. Tax records show she lives in San Francisco now. Runs a dancing school." He produced a picture.

"Hmm. American beauty," MJ said.

"Smart, too, apparently," Garodnik added. "I was impressed by how she'd pulled it together. But you know as well as I do, it doesn't really wash." As he said it, a quizzical look crossed the detective's big red face.

MJ's dark eyes flashed. "What doesn't wash, Patrick?"

"We looked a little deeper," the detective said with a matter-of-fact shrug. "Or I should say Frisco PD has. They tossed her place when she went missing."

"And?" MJ asked, palms up.

"Let's see." The detective flipped out his notepad. "She lives pretty well for the owner of a little dance school. Babe lives in a $4,000 a month apartment in Pacific Heights."

"So? You live in Forest Hills on a cop's pay."

"I worked vice for a year," the detective joked while continuing to read the notepad before adding, "Beyond the dance school, Christina Bergstrom shows no visible means of support...visible being the operative word here." The cop's expression was smug as he turned the page. "Little Miss Twinkle Toes also has two numbered accounts registered to a Caribbean bank...in a place called San Cristobal. Very hush-hush."

"How did you find them if they're, y'know—*very hush hush*?"

"Frisco PD found the accounts in her computer, plus the checkbooks were right there in her desk drawer. They are joint accounts, though. That much I figured out."

"I thought the feds were cutting all the locals out of this," MJ asked.

"Chief Portlock has his own opinions about stuff like that. Plus, the San Francisco PD is all over this, and they like the Feds pissing on their opens as much as we do. So they're sharing everything they find with us, however insignificant. Besides," Garodnik added, "as long as the G-boys are tying this Bergstrom incident together with the Cassandra McRea murder, we local-yokels maintain jurisdiction as well. The fed's prob'ly figured we'd be only too happy to drop it on them. That was their mistake."

"Well," MJ waved it off, "what you found on Christina Bergstrom is interesting information to be sure, but not worth much by itself."

"The facts say it better than I can," Garodnik contended. "She showed over fifty large in the two offshore accounts, American money, and the balances have grown steadily over the past twelve months. No withdrawals, not even through her business. According to the IRS, her dance school, Bay City Barre, lost eight grand last year alone."

"So? The Feds lost a trillion. They should arrest themselves."

The cop went on. "Then, last month one of the offshore accounts was liquidated, leaving the other one at twenty-five-thou. One withdrawal of 25 grand just before all this hit the fan? What's she doing, Christmas shopping in February?"

"Maybe she invested it in the losing business, living expenses. Pacific Heights, remember? Besides, it's not that much money, Patrick."

Garodnik held up a hand to silence her. "Her dance school partner is not the other number on the joint account. I'm thinking it's drug money. Or if she's half as good-looking as that picture, she'd have no trouble accumulating fifty grand by peddling her charms up on Nob Hill."

"That's a sexist leap of imagination, Patrick. Be objective. There are plenty of ways a smart woman can make money. We're in the post-cretaceous era, you know."

"Call it cop's instinct, Counselor. Consider her background. She was a pretty heavy user. And if you don't mind my saying, she had to find some way to pay for her horse."

"Heroin?" MJ asked, considering the import of such a circumstance. "When was she last implicated in anything? Any priors?"

"Drug related?"

"Any priors at all?"

Garodnik checked his notes. "Let's see...nothing useful. Just juvie stuff, closed sheet. Probably possession, soliciting. No adult priors."

"That's what I figured," MJ assessed. "Sorry, Patrick, but I'm not convinced of her involvement beyond acting out of a genuine interest in her brother's welfare. This kid came up hard. She did whatever it took to stay alive. Trust me, I get that. Which leaves me more impressed than suspicious. Maybe she sent that money, however she made it, to Leif."

"Well, Counselor, I'm not about to lecture you on criminal behavior like you're someone who just fell off a Long Island patata truck. But I think you're a little starry-eyed. This babe's got a few warts. Add that to this fishy business with the cargo manifest, and we're onto something. I just don't know what."

"You're the big city cop, and I'm an old prosecutor," MJ noted, shrugging resignedly. "We've both seen things nobody should. We just process it in different ways, Patrick. So, getting back to Christina Bergstrom. They say there's no zealot like the newly converted. Given what she's made of herself, I do not see her getting back into that scene, not as a user, and certainly not as a dealer. Call it naiveté, but if this woman is with Jake right now, somebody's gotta take her side."

Garodnik frowned. The venerable attorney was behaving less like a former prosecutor than she was a worried parent unwilling to accept that her son was the victim of a set-up.

"Who you trying to convince, Counselor, me or yourself?"

As the pair speculated over Jake's plight and Tina Bergstrom's possible complicity, Aloysius Grogan's Q and A session showed little sign of winding down.

"I'm gonna get a cup of coffee," Garodnik said. "You want anything?"

"No. I'll stay here."

Garodnik headed for the lobby, and MJ pulled a folder from her briefcase and began leafing through its contents.

Five minutes later, Garodnik returned. "I took the liberty of sending that Customs document downtown with a patrolman I ran into in the lobby. I also called the chief and told him what's up. Chief knows you're a crook now."

"I represented Portlock when he closed on his Atlantic Beach summer house. He knew I was a crook the minute he got my bill."

"What's that?" the detective asked, seeing the folder spread open on MJ's lap.

"Some material Will Yost prepared for me on Peterson. It was for a meeting I had with our nosey G-man. Came too late."

He marveled at her casual use of the commissioner's name. "You and Commissioner Yost go back quite a ways."

"We met at Columbia Law," she said, cringing at Garodnik's inflection. "It was right after the glacier melted."

Garodnik changed the subject. "That's a pretty thick report."

"The commissioner is very thorough. This is Peterson's whole CV. Everything the federal government has on him that's not covered by the privacy act, and maybe a gem or two that is."

MJ began reading, leafing ahead. Finally, she let out a huff. "Nothing here Peterson would want to hide. He was a decorated war hero. He was even wounded."

"Peterson was in Desert Storm?"

MJ held up papers for Garodnik's interest, one by one. "Purple Heart, Soldier's Medal, couple of others I never heard of. He was somewhere nasty alright."

"But not for long," Garodnik noticed seeing his service dates. "That's a lotta fruit salad for a fifteen minute tour."

Recalling that none of these citations were evident among the awards so prevalent on Peterson's office wall, MJ looked over the official Veteran's Administration records again. The report was handwritten, probably by Peterson himself prior to being hired at the VA. "Says here he was an Army warrant officer. Flew assault helicopters. Got shot up, too."

"I was in Panama, back in eighty-nine," Garodnik interjected. "A Marine Corps M.P."

"Now this is something," said MJ. "Says here Peterson was hit by friendly fire."

"Everybody hated the MP's," Garodnik went on. "Our guys, the swabbies, even the friggin' whores all looked down their noses at us. No picnic bein' an MP in a war zone."

"Says here Peterson was pulling American troops out of an urban trap," MJ read. "The Marines were pinned down, and the Republican Guard troops were picking them off from the upper floors, while more Iraqi troops are pouring from the houses. Meanwhile, Peterson's hanging in there with his helicopter, his ordnance was spent it says here. He was getting every Marine he could on board or hanging off the skids."

"Those chopper jocks are a breed apart...all balls. What it don't say there," Garodnik pointed to the brief, "is that if this guy was an attack pilot, he didn't need to be down in the dirt hauling out grunts."

"Grunts?" MJ asked.

"Riflemen," the detective continued. "If Peterson was flying a gunship, he didn't have to come down into a landing zone that's under siege."

"I see," MJ said, reflecting. "So Peterson was being quite heroic."

"Right," said Garodnik. "He didn't have to hang around pulling out Americans once his ordnance was gone. If you're tryin' to make me dislike this guy, you're doin' a terrible job, Counselor."

"People change," MJ interjected, reading on. "It says here, he went back for a second time. That's when a wave of air cover arrives."

"You lost me," the detective said. "That seems backwards."

"Close air support. I remember my Jake trained for that. What's backwards?"

"Well, Peterson must have known a few Marines were left behind, went back to get 'em."

"I see. Well," MJ read on, "this air support, which the soldiers on the ground had called in themselves, starts dropping bombs on the buildings where the enemy was holed up. Meanwhile, Peterson's helicopter flies into the middle of it all but it gets hit by something coming off of or out of one of those buildings and he crashes. The last couple of Marines he was trying to evacuate wind up having to pull him and his crew out of the burning helicopter, hit the pavement, and start to defend themselves against the enemy soldiers who're running from the buildings. But the Iraqi's didn't engage. They just left. When it was over, Peterson had suffered serious injuries in the crash."

"Like what?"

MJ leafed ahead, then back, and ahead again. "It doesn't say exactly. I saw his face, or what was left of it, though. He'd been terribly burned. His lips..."

"His lips?"

"Yes," MJ explained, "Third-degree burns. Peterson's lips are severely scarred, as are his nose, side of his face, ear, a good bit of his hair, one eyebrow. Terrible thing."

"You never mentioned that. If he got cooked by our own air support, it might be why the government was so quick to give him a good job."

"First they mess him up, then they shut him up."

"Here's an old picture," Garodnik held out what looked like Peterson's high school yearbook photo.

"Nice looking," MJ observed. "Pity."

"Well, Counselor, this guy doesn't fit the profile you're trying to establish. If he's behind a government cover-up, we're gonna face a lot more resistance than cooperation."

"We're reading Peterson's own account, Patrick."

A final small burst of applause indicated that Grogan's Q and A session was ending at last. As the room emptied, Grogan descended the stage and walked rearward, raising a wave and a self-satisfied smile to the pretty brunette with the shapely legs who was waiting at the rear of the big room.

Smiling back at him, she continued clapping. The two were together.

Garodnik stood to intercept the diver. "Aloysius Grogan," he said, stepping into the aisle. Rather than risk a photo storm, the detective lowered his voice. "I'm Lieutenant Garodnik, New York City Police." Moving his jacket aside, he gave Grogan a peek at his badge. "I'd like to ask you a couple of questions."

"Time's up, Lieutenant," Grogan said with a smile. He, too, spoke in hushed tones, while still looking toward the woman. "You should have raised your hand." Turning back to his inquisitor, the diver paused, breathed deeply, then added, "I'm sorry, but this drug plane thing has taken over my life. You've just seen it. I came here to give a legitimate talk about the reconnaissance techniques I've developed. It took me a year to compile information and prepare this thing. Instead of a professional audience, I'm swarmed by a mob of pointy-headed imbeciles with cameras." Making exaggerated air quotes he concluded, "I'm done with this *Queen of the Southern Skies* bullshit."

"I'm afraid you're not, Mr. Grogan," Garodnik bluffed. "You can talk to me here, or you can talk to me at the station. I'm sorry, to have to put it this way, sir, but you *will* talk to me."

"This is bullshit," the diver said. "I've already answered about five-million questions from the DEA and even Homeland Security for crissakes. They know everything I know about it. Go ask them and let me get on with my life."

"This *is* your life now, Mr. Grogan… Call it the price of celebrity."

"Okay," Grogan said, throwing his arms in the air. "I found half a goddam airplane floating in the Cuban straits... a wing, the cockpit. A dead pilot was strapped into the thing, bobbing in and out of the water. I set up some floatation, and called the Haitian authorities and I sailed away. But no sooner did I put in at Port au Prince, than the goddam

American Homeland Security tied me up for another day and a half. Homeland goddam Security, for crissakes. Are terrorists using antique airplanes now? Well," he said, calming, "I finally hopped a plane here last night, had Corn Flakes for breakfast, gave this talk, answered questions, and now you're all caught up." Grogan raised his hands palms out, a gesture of resignation. "I don't mean to be a jerk, Lieutenant. I know you have a job to do, but, c'mon. I'm here to meet clients, and the goddam Feds already wasted my best day. That leaves me a few lousy hours to make my year—a few hours to round up enough work for me and my crew. Instead of that, I get all this baloney, all these bozos with the flashbulbs. I'm probably three, four months short already, and this thing is finished tonight."

"Mr. Grogan, you seem like a decent guy," Garodnik said. "So I'm gonna level with you. A young woman has been killed in my city and I think an innocent man–also from my city—is being squeezed for it. You might be able to help him. Answer a few questions and we'll be out of your hair."

"See that crowd out there?" The diver pointed toward the hall. "They're waiting for me. This is my best hour, Lieutenant. Let me have a few minutes of that hour, twenty minutes, then we can talk. How about that?"

Just then MJ's cellphone vibrated.

"Yes... Oh, hello, Sean," she said stepping away, pleased that airplane mechanic Sean Wilke was calling back so soon with the information she'd requested. "What did you come up with?" MJ nodded, smiled, nodded again. She jotted some notes. "That's wonderful, and you'll text me that as well. You've been a great help, Sean. Thank you." She hung up the phone and looked at Garodnik.

"Look, can I go?" Grogan cut in.

"Yeah, okay," Garodnik relented. "But stay where I can see you."

"Then follow me or get a warrant," Grogan said, and headed into the lobby.

"What was that phone call about?" the detective asked MJ.

"Unfortunately, nothing," she said, writing as she spoke. "Remember when Peterson first told me Bergstrom's airplane was carrying five R-3350 engines for a total worth of a million bucks?"

"Right," Garodnik thought of the altered manifest, "but he changed it to three engines and reduced the value."

"Three, five, doesn't matter," MJ contended, "the values check out."

The cop scratched his orange pate. "So, why forge the cargo manifest?"

"I don't know," MJ said, resignedly, "but it's a dead end if no laws were broken."

"Oh," a voice from behind them said, "sounds like one law could've been broken."

Both MJ and Garodnik turned with a start to see who was eavesdropping.

It was the pretty brunette in the short skirt.

"Excuse me, miss, but who..?" Garodnik began.

"It's all right here," the young woman said while looking at her smartphone. "If Leif Bergstrom was carrying five R-3350s in a Curtiss Commando, he was perhaps not breaking the law, but he was certainly challenging it."

"Young lady, this is no time..." Garodnik began to admonish when MJ cut him off.

"Let her speak," she demanded. "She's already heard everything."

"I'm so sorry," the young woman said. "I thought..."

"No, dear," MJ cut in, looking daggers at Garodnik, surprisingly resplendent and clearly quite uncomfortable in his dark suit and combed hair, "we're sorry. Bill Blass, here can be a little impatient, but he means well."

"I apologize, Mr. Blass," the younger woman said, causing MJ to wince, suddenly feeling quite old. "I, just... I couldn't help but overhear, and..."

"Please go on, dear," MJ cut in. "I'm MJ Silver and this is Detective Garodnik, NYPD."

With a slightly confused look toward Garodnik, who returned it in kind, she began. "Well, if the plane you're discussing was the Curtiss we found in the Gulf, and if Leif Bergstrom took off carrying five Wright radials in cargo, he might've been breaking the law alright, the law of gravity."

"Who are you, miss?" asked the detective.

Before she could answer, Grogan returned, looking disappointed and agitated. "Her name is Gina Ferranti, and she has nothing to do with this. So I'd appreciate it if…"

"I got this, Red." Gina said while placing a hand on Grogan's wrist before turning back to the pair of New Yorkers. "I'm Captain Grogan's lead diver," she said, "but I'm also a commercial pilot." Then, addressing Grogan, she added, "Let me help them, Skipper."

Grogan, trusting his diver's judgment, grudgingly said, "Long as it gets 'em off of me."

"Thank you, Captain" MJ said. "Please, Ms. Ferranti, you were explaining."

"I've flown that airplane, the Curtiss Commando," Gina began, her calculating smartphone in hand. "There's a few of them still flying in the tropics. Flying one in Argentina was my very first job, and I know the type by heart." With everyone's attention focused on her every word, the tech-nerdy diver punched a few buttons on her calculator. "The A-type, for example, has an empty weight of 29,500 pounds. If we subtract that from its maximum take-off weight of 50,000 pounds, minus 1800 gallons of gas—which it would need to complete the flight plan Bergstrom had filed…." She punched a few more keys on her calculator, "…and with avgas weighing about six pounds per gallon, that'd leave at the most 10,000 pounds of useful cargo load." Again she went to her calculator. "The specs for the Wright R-3350 engine give its weight at 3000 pounds. That's without…"

Her quick mind yielding to her enthusiasm, MJ cut in, "Ms. Ferranti, if the Curtiss Commando can carry only about 10,000 pounds, could one have gotten off the ground with five engines and crates weighing over 15,000 pounds in its cargo hold?"

"Maybe Bergstrom was a really good pilot?" Garodnik interjected, his patience waning. "Can we please..?"

"I'm a really good pilot, too," Gina shot back, emboldened by her findings, "but good or bad, no pilot is dumb enough to try it, at least not the ones who get to have grandkids. Lifting off with full tanks and two or three tons over maximum gross weight? That would put the plane at about 140 percent of payload. Add to that an aft center of gravity, a sweltering, damp, probably crude tropical field, and even then, presuming a runway long enough that he could lift off, he'd risk a tail-slide into hell once he was out of ground effect. Possible, maybe, but I wouldn't try it."

"So, why would Bergstrom attempt a take off if he knew his plane was overweight?"

"I'd suggest he didn't know," Gina speculated, "at least not right away. Most cargo outfits have a loadmaster, usually a ground crew guy. He'd have confirmed the weight, the placement, and CG, then given that data to the pilot on a load sheet before take off. A good pilot would look it over, go aft and check the lashings, maybe even challenge the loadmaster's calculations, but he would at some point have to trust that his loadmaster got the actual individual weights correct in the first place. It doesn't sound like you're talking about Federal Express here, and numbers don't lie. So, since Bergstrom *did* take off, and he made it into the Windward Straight before he crashed, he was either dumb-lucky, or something's off kilter. If that old Curtiss were really that much over max gross a good pilot would know it by the takeoff roll, the feel of the controls, the climb...or lack thereof."

MJ gave Gina a grateful nod, then said, "Which must mean that when it left South America, Bergstrom's plane was probably *not* weighted with five airplane engines, or maybe not even three. Maybe none at all."

"Conjecture," Grogan said. "The cargo sank with the fuselage."

"Not conjecture, Patrick, physics," MJ corrected. "Suppose Leif Bergstrom's *was* carrying five crates that looked to him like they contained engines, but in fact had something else inside, something lighter." Here the lawyer paused dramatically, before adding, "Something less dense, more diaphanous, something like…"

"Don't even say it," Garodnik interrupted, looking annoyed. "Something powdery, something like cocaine, but maybe not cocaine. Tell me you're not buying into that reporter Leitch's line about the damned Analog again."

"What the hell is *analog*?" Grogan asked. "I thought everything was digital now."

"Let's stick to the point," Garodnik interjected. "If Bergstrom was hauling this mysterious Analog—which does not exist, by the way—why would he be smuggling it in from South America? They could just make the stuff anywhere. Isn't that the point?"

"Maybe it's not easy to make," Grogan piped up, engaged now. "Maybe you need a real lab and formulas and test tubes and whatnot. That would make it uncommon, sure, but there'd be no need to smuggle it in once you had the fixings and the formulas. Formula like that'd be worth, I dunno, millions, right?"

"Billions," MJ said.

"I'll say this just one more time," Garodnik said with a sigh of frustration. "The Analog is *not* easy to make. It's impossible to make. Which is why it does not exist!"

"Last year Fentanyl didn't exist," MJ argued, "neither did W-18. Now they do. They're more addictive than anything else that's out there, and they're being peddled on every street corner in town! Tomorrow there'll be another synthetic, and next week they'll be two more with half the profits going to ISIS and the other to Bratva. The secret of cocaine is its mitigated dopamine release. Replicate that property, and you snare the big money yuppie customers. Please, Patrick, you've made your point about the Analog. You made your point as well, Captain, and it certainly explains a lot. And by the way, doesn't a captain outrank a lieutenant?"

Ignoring the jibe, Garodnik summed it up. "Let's stick to what we know, which is that Bergstrom's plane was apparently not carrying five R-whatever the hell aircraft engines the night it crashed. If what the skipper here says is true, an important piece falls into place."

"Correct," MJ exclaimed, sensing they were finally getting somewhere. "These facts support what I've been suspecting all along. Peterson and the government are less interested in Leif Bergstrom's drug digressions than they are in covering up what was really on board that airplane." Turning her attention to the divers, she said, "Look, if these two agree to what I'm about to say, then we'll know the answer to that mystery as well, and maybe, just maybe we'll get a step closer to figuring out what happened to Jake."

"Wait a minute," Grogan said. "Who's Jake? I'm not getting involved in some crazy drug thing. I'm sorry, but I've had it."

"Hear the lady out," Gina said, touching Grogan's arm.

"Captain Grogan, Ms. Ferranti," MJ said, speaking directly to them as professionals. "You say you're in New York to engage with your clients, to drum up business, make your year."

"That was the plan," Grogan said. "Not that it matters all that much anymore. Half of today's opportunities are gone, thanks to him." He nodded toward Garodnik.

"What do you figure you've lost?" MJ asked.

"More than I can afford."

"How much?"

"I dunno."

"I do," Gina said, as everyone's attention turned to the young woman. "As I said, I'm lead diver, chief cook and intrepid navigator on this crew, but I also hold a master's ticket, and I'm the outfit's business manager. Yeah, I'm an overachiever. But businesswise, things are not as bleak as the skipper makes them out. Considering all the publicity this thing has generated, to say nothing of what these knuckleheads with the cameras will generate, we've picked up about half of our losses already in new business, not counting what we'll pick up from Red's talk over the next few weeks." With that, she nodded toward the lobby currently crowded with prospective clients, most of whom were oilmen. "And this boy's club shindig is not over yet. I'll see to that." She removed the conservative cashmere blazer she'd been wearing to reveal the rest of her clingy little black dress: clingy and little suddenly its defining characteristics.

Having discretely observed MJ's red, swollen eyes and wan countenance, the kindly younger woman considered a gesture. Something normal, she thought, light-hearted, momentarily distracting. She handed the jacket to MJ. "Try it on," she urged. "With your height, it'll look killer." Then, glancing toward the lobby again, the comely diver thumbed her stack of business cards and said, "Listen to what Ms. Silver has to say, Red. Meantime, I'm going to take little walk."

As Gina turned toward the lobby, Grogan spoke up. "Hang on a second, hotshot," he said stopping the feisty diver before turning to MJ. "I've been running the numbers, too, and like Gina here said, we can make up much of what we lost."

"You might already have," MJ said as she slipped into Gina's Lenox blazer. Then turning to the young woman who was nodding approvingly, began, "Tell me, Ms. Ferranti, are... By the way, may I call you Gina?"

"Of course," Gina answered, adjusting the jacket's shoulders while admiring the appearance of this woman at least a quarter-century her senior. "Beautiful."

"Ladies, please," Garodnik said, appreciating MJ's emotional need for distraction while noticing that she really did look splendid. "We're wasting time we don't have."

Interpreting the detective's words to mean time *Jake* might not have, MJ returned Gina's jacket with a Thank you, and spoke directly to the divers, saying, "If you answer the lieutenant's questions, and your answers are what I expect, I'd like to discuss making back your two months' losses, and maybe the rest of your year as well. What do you say?"

Grogan was leery. "I told you I won't get into anything shady."

Smelling an interesting deal, Gina Ferranti turned back to MJ. "What exactly are you proposing?"

"I might be acting out of desperation, Captain Grogan. I don't know if you'll find anything, and if you do what it might or might not even mean, but I'm also proposing work, straightforward, legal as lemonade diving and documenting work."

"If you're talking about the Windward Strait," Grogan said with authority, "that's deep water, five-hundred fathoms. We left our boat in Port au Prince and our deep-water diving gear is in Florida. We were down there dragging a sonar sled. We're not equipped for a deep dive, not with what we have on board.

"But we can take deep-water optics and sonar, Red," Gina said.

"I'm not interested in…"

MJ held up her hand to forestall the captain's persistent qualms. "I won't tie you up with questions now. I know you both want to get out there on that convention floor and beat the bushes some more. But it sounds like Gina has a solution to my problem. If so, I have one for yours, Captain."

"I think I do," Gina said with confidence. "Because I heard you and the detective talking, I'm pretty sure I know what you're after. We can use the combination of sonar and the robotic submersible to find the plane and maybe even poke around inside of it. Take a bunch of hi-def video, infra-red optics, whatever." She turned to Grogan, "This is a perfect application of what you just spent a year preparing for, Skipper. It's your speech made real, empirical validation. Think of the publicity that can generate."

"Publicity? I don't ever want to hear that word again." Grogan growled, as he leered at a seedy paparazzo lurking nearby.

"Excuse us a second," Gina said, pulling Grogan aside.

"This is good business, Red," she coaxed. "A hell of an opportunity just fell in our laps. Plus, I really admire this woman. She's putting up a brave front, but, trust me, she's torn up inside, and scared to death for her son. Maybe we can help. We're talking genuine damsel in distress stuff here. Add to that a treasure hunt, and–at the risk of being keelhauled—great *publicity* for your new sled, and all you can think of is making your year. That's not the Red Grogan I know…" she stretched on tiptoes to kiss his cheek, "…and love."

"The cop is a jerk," Grogan groused. Embarrassed, he turned away, but she pulled him back. "C'mon, Red. Life is short. Let's be a little crazy?"

Grogan rolled his eyes. Turning toward his inquisitors with a sigh of resignation, the skipper said, "Okay, Mrs. Silver, spell it out for me."

With an appreciative nod toward Gina, and a requisite, Please call me MJ, she began. "Captain Grogan, I need you and your crew to locate and somehow explore the wreck of what you're calling the drug plane and try to identify its cargo. I will pay you the equivalent of six months pre-tax profit and cover your costs for what may turn out to be a couple of days' work. It's all quite legal, and any salvage not held in evidence, is yours."

"Six months' pay for a couple days' work, and if we find something and go back later, equipped for a deep water salvage, we keep the haul? What's the catch?"

"No catch," MJ said, speaking to both Grogan and Gina. "And by the way," she added, "it's more like a day of searching, two at the most, and the acceptance of whatever reasonable costs are associated with the work, documentation of, and… " MJ paused, considering the ramifications of Jake's having been killed, she added with a sigh, "…and perhaps testimony under oath on what we find. But time is of the essence." Focusing her comments to the captain alone, she asked, "Captain Grogan, did I hear you say your boat is docked at Port au Prince?"

"That's right. We were pulling a sled in the straits when we sailed into the drug plane's debris field. We're headed back tomorrow."

"That's perfect," MJ said. "What I'm proposing, then, is that we leave today, right now. I'll make one phone call and have a helicopter waiting at Waterside. It'll take us to Teterboro Airport. A private jet will get us to Haiti this afternoon. Then you get yourselves, and me to the place where Leif Bergstrom's plane went down."

"The Windward Strait," Gina said. "We're docked right there."

"Great," MJ confirmed. "We sail from Port au Prince, find the fuselage of Leif Bergstrom's plane, photograph the wreck inside and out, and if at all possible, recover a sample of that cargo. But, again, time is of the essence." Stopping there, she looked squarely at the pair of divers. "Are you up to it?"

Before Grogan could decline, Ferranti said, "We can be on station a couple of hours after your jet lands. If the captain determines that it's feasible, and the weather cooperates, damned right we're up to it." She held a palm up to Grogan, and said, "Go with me on this, Red. Please."

"And it's all above board?" Grogan asked. "Like I said, I'm not getting involved in…"

"You know the whole story," MJ said.

"I know half the story."

Seeing the crowd drifting back into the hall, Gina tossed MJ an encouraging little chin thrust.

MJ rushed her pitch. "I'll say it again. My son, Jacob, is missing and implicated in a murder he didn't commit. We don't know why, but what we do know points to whatever is still on that plane. It's not much to go on, but it's all we've got. Answer that question, and maybe, just maybe, it shifts the government's investigation to the right people and away from my son, and who knows, maybe get us all a step closer to finding my Jake alive." With that said, MJ knew she had him. "Agree, and my assistant will wire you half the money we discussed, in advance." She extended a hand. "So, Captain, do we have a deal?"

- CHAPTER 12 -

The eerie quiet of a tropical sunset descended on the Guianese jungle, casting long shadows across the aerodrome at that jungle's heart.

Pushing back against the encroaching darkness, a harsh white light streamed onto the field's cracked tarmac from the wide open doors of the hangar where Jake Silver, already in the cockpit of Major Dwight Chichester's modified Invader airplane, was hurriedly acclimating to the machine's worn controls and mechanical instrumentation.

With the major to his right, St. John and Montoya taking up positions in the airplane's rear compartment, Jake was well aware that every second Tina Bergstrom remained in the brutal hands of Emiliano Cegato, could be her last. That his own fate might be no different was a concern he'd have to address at some point. For now, though, this band of reprobates was all he had... and all Tina Bergstrom had.

Subordinating a ritual preflight procedure to time, he started one, then the second of the plane's big engines. As the massive radials coughed, sputtered, and roared to life, their smoky blast sent chairs, ladders, and tool chests tumbling backwards against the hangar's rear wall. Taking little notice, Jake taxied the old machine through the hangar's wide doors and across the broken and overgrown tarmac to the runway's threshold.

Switching on the ancient navigation/communication radio, Jake heard no sidetone or static. "What's wrong with this radio?"

"It's valves need to warm up," Chichester answered to Jake's dismay. "Give it some time. It receives well enough, but its transmitter section is intermittent. Works sometimes, other times not. No matter. The navigation head works, and we won't need a radio at Kourou."

With a headshake of incredulity, Jake made a quick verbal check of his ragtag crew, ran through the checklist, and took the runway.

"Even with the empty tip tanks, she'll be over her landing weight when we get to Kourou," Chichester advised.

"Let's ignore one law of physics at a time," Jake said, his focus on the towering wall of trees looming at the runway's end, aware that he was breaking every rule of sane airmanship in his haste to get aloft. "Say the numbers."

"Twenty-five-hundred feet of runway, another 500 to the trees and the lowest of them are about 75-feet AGL," Chichester shouted back.

Jake set the altimeter to 2,700 feet MSL, the airstrip's height above mean sea level and made a mental note of the barometer.

Both he and the airplane would have to perform perfectly to avoid flying into those treetops, or exploding against the hills beyond, presuming the old warbird rose at all.

"Flaps to fifteen and arm the ADI," Chichester advised. "Fifty inches MP," meaning manifold pressure, "then power to 50, and release the brakes," Chichester advised. "Takeoff power. The water will kick in at 44 inches. Lighten the nose wheel the moment you feel elevator and rudder authority. Fly her off at 100 indicated. Stow the gear as soon as we're up. Hold her flat until we clear the trees, then lose the flaps, and climb her at 140 knots indicated. I'll watch the fuel flow and be with you all the way."

His hand on the throttles, Jake cast an apprehensive glance at the trees.

"She's mightily overpowered," Chichester assured. "She'll speak to you if you'll listen."

Jake listened, and the big radials roared. He released the brakes, and the sinewy old plane fairly leapt forward. The airspeed indicator began bouncing off the peg at 40 knots, with the aspired-to 100 knots residing a long and sweeping arc away as ever more runway was devoured.

Jake considered aborting, but the machine continued its acceleration, its huge props gulping the wind.

"Steady on, Silver!" Chichester shouted above the din as they raced for the greenery that began to fill Jake's field of vision.

At 60, Jake lightened the nose wheel.

"Good show, old man!" Chichester shouted. "Don't waver!"

As their speed approached 80 knots and some 1500 feet of the cracked and broken runway had disappeared beneath the airplane's wheels, Jake felt the overloaded machine growing light. He felt the main landing gear begin its stretch as the long, slender wings gained lift. With the airspeed tickling 90 knots, the airplane lifted off. They were flying, but were still 65 feet below the treetops as Jake retracted the wheels mere inches from the ground.

"Steady on, old man!" Chichester barked, the whirling props fairly kissing the pavement.

As the runway vanished in their wake, through his windscreen and against the last glow of evening sky, Jake saw birds, their fluttering silhouettes rising, as they wisely departed the sea of foliage dead-ahead of the now speeding plane. As the jungle rushed the old warplane and its four occupants, Jake pulled the yoke back ever so lightly only to feel the airspeed dissipating. The wings were losing their grip on the air and the controls grew mushy. In a supreme act of will, Jake resisted pulling the yoke back, and lowered the nose to keep the machine accelerating as the jungle rushed the old warplane and its four occupants.

Still, he pushed the throttles forward, as the steamy outside air sapped the engines of power and the wings of lift. With a slight pull of the yoke, to climb away, the stall horn joined the ambient sound and fury, and the shuddering machine hung by a thread when its propellers chopped into the treetops sending leaves and woodchips flying. As Jake braced for the sickening deadfall, the airplane lurched upward and the treetops drifted silently below the portside wing.

He was flying by feel now, a pilot again, aloft in a pilot's airplane.

Clear of the obstacles, Jake lowered the nose again, watched the airspeed build to 135 knots, and he let his airplane fly.

Getting the heavy, unfamiliar machine to rise off that short, hot, broken strip, felt good. Jake sensed a growing affinity for this machine as she clawed for altitude. Responsive and powerful, this was a pilot's airplane.

"One is never more alive than when his heart stops," said an ebullient Chichester, smugly satisfied with his choice of a pilot. "What say you, laddie buck?"

"Give me a heading for Kourou."

Disappointed Chichester did as he was told. "Turn northwest, heading three-zero-zero."

As their course took them through the still, clear, tropical air, a vast sea of jungle drifted below. The converted warbird's acceleration was stunning once it left the ground. Its responsiveness reminiscent of Jake's Air Force fighter. But rather than excite, the climb to altitude brought with it thoughts of his former flight leader and steeled Jake's resolve to the task ahead.

Ten minutes into the short flight, Chichester switched on the portable GPS receiver. "When we're a mile out, I'll key the radio five times on Kourou's frequency. That will turn on the field's runway lights. You'll have 3,000 feet of paved runway 47 feet above sea level. There are no obstacles except for those at the rocket base. You should make a wide sweeping approach from the east. Piece of cake, really."

"Unpublished RNAV approach to a short field, night landing in a strange, overweight airplane through obstacles. Sure, piece of cake."

"I have boundless confidence in your abilities, old boy."

As the lights of Kourou village and its gleaming spaceport flickered through broken clouds, Chichester keyed the radio mic repeatedly, theatrically while Jake peeled his eyes for the parallel rows of lights that would indicate a runway. Nothing.

"This radio is still not transmitting," Chichester said. "A fiddly valve I'd wager."

Jake knew valve was British for vacuum tube. "A bad tube? A tube?"

"I'll keep trying, but it looks like we'll be taking her in blind." The airplane began to buffet in ground effect. "Trust the GPS," Chichester advised, pointing to the futuristic portable device stuck onto the ancient flat instrument panel. Again he tried the microphone. "Line up on centerline, and begin your descent." In the dim light, Chichester could see Jake's furrowed brow. "Don't get your knickers in a bunch, lad. I've done this approach a thousand…"

"Please shut up and get that radio transmitting," implored Jake as the ground came up to meet them. "Give me ten degrees of flaps and the descent parameters!"

The altimeter showed 800 feet AMSL. With the Kourou airport at 47 feet above that same sea level, it placed the airplane about 753 feet above its runway elevation. If the runway's approach end was exactly where the GPS indicated, they were lined up correctly for a straight-in approach to landing. To Jake's mind, it was a big if.

"Runway heading and fly her down flat," Chichester advised. "Half flaps and 170 knots."

So far, so good. Still, there was no runway anywhere in sight as both men strained their eyes against the blackness, blacker still through the fingers of fog that groped from the sea. Daylight was gone, and a bulbous moon was rising, too low on the horizon to be of any benefit.

With neither runway nor landing lights, Jake descended through complete darkness relying wholly on his futuristically out-of-place GPS and appropriately archaic altimeter.

"Runway environment!" Jake barked.

"Full flaps and slow her to one-fifteen," Chichester shouted.

"One hundred fifty feet," Jake barked. "One twenty-five, one-hundred... Dammit!" he exclaimed with the GPS squawking. "We've already crossed the threshold!"

"Blast! Not enough runway! Pull up!" Chichester was shouting as the field, suddenly visible 200 feet below them, rushed by the still speeding plane. "Pull up and go around!"

Ignoring Chichester, Jake put the airplane into a side-slip and the converted Invader fell like a stone. Pulling her into a flare just as the main wheels were about to connect with the runway's midpoint, the airplane stopped falling and settled to ground like a feather. It was an exquisite display of airmanship. In a single swift motion, Jake reversed pitch on the props, retracted the flaps, and stood on the brakes.

The machine roared and slid and its tires squealed as the runway's end loomed ever larger.

Jake instinctively kicked hard right rudder, and the machine skidded sideways, as if responding, stressing the already overloaded landing struts before bounding to a full, smoking stop, its empty port side wingtip tank extending a few feet beyond the runway's end.

Both men's eyes met across the cockpit, and in unison they declared, "Piece of cake."

Rather than a bulkhead and door, the plane's 's cockpit was isolated from the rear cabin by a stout wing spar that spanned the entire width of the fuselage just behind the pilots' positions. This unusual arrangement was a holdover from the Marksman's having been originally designed as an A-26 Invader. Open spaces above and below that spar's starboard side afforded visibility aft and the only transit between the flight deck and cabin.

As Jake shut down the engines, Chichester cast his gaze rearward, through the space above the spar and into the makeshift rear cabin, actually the plane's converted bomb-bay. "Step lively, lads," he ordered St. John and Montoya. "We've no time to lose."

Exiting the cockpit by crawling through the small starboard-side companionway beneath that spar, Jake and Chichester made their way aft to the cargo door and jumped down to the tarmac. St. John who now pulled on a huge green and black knitted wool hat into which he tucked his considerable mane, followed.

Turning back to the open hatch, St. John began receiving provisions and weapons from Montoya. Each of the four carried a sidearm, and St. John handed Jake three seventeen-cartridge magazines for his pistol, giving Jake over 50 chances to hit something if need be.

"Be ginger with that weapon, old man," Chichester cautioned Jake. "Unlike the Walthers, that Glock has no safety."

Supplies distributed, Montoya jumped down and joined the others on the tarmac. In addition to a Walther P99 holstered at the big man's side, he carried his imposing old AK-47 on his shoulder. St. John wore a Walther automatic on his hip. It appeared to outweigh him.

Peering through the still open hatch, Jake saw that the mysterious wooden crate of undelivered cargo remained undisturbed.

With provisions and weapons distributed, the major ordered a disappointed St. John to remain with the airplane and he turned to move out.

"Not much gonna happen here tonight," hinted St. John.

"The cargo should not be left unguarded," Chichester said.

"Four guns better den three, boss, an' I can be real sneaky."

"Damn him," Chichester muttered. But St. John's entreaties were sound. An extra gun *would* do more good against Cegato than it would at a deserted airfield and the slightly built Jamaican *did* have an annoying habit of coming up on Chichester silently. That quality could prove useful. The sleek machine was a familiar sight at Kourou and wouldn't be disturbed.

Without looking back, Chichester shouted over his shoulder, "Very well, St. John. Leave a note for the day crew to fill the tip tanks, secure the hatches and catch up with us at the beach."

The gesture was met with sounds of approval from both Jake and Montoya as St. John turned to his tasks.

"Poor fool doesn't know when he's well off," Chichester muttered.

"What's really in that wooden box?" Jake asked, not expecting an answer.

"We're only a half mile from the beach," Chichester responded. "There will be a boat waiting. Stay to the side of the road and step lively, lads."

The paved road wound northward before curving to a narrow unlit street. Large trees rose on both sides. Jake noticed the increasingly moist air. "Feels like weather," he said. "Something's approaching from the southeast, a squall line maybe."

"No matter, Silver."

Moving west, after some five minutes the glow of electric lights became apparent to their north. The glow highlighted an ever-thickening mist rolling in from the beach.

As they entered the village of Kourou from its southern end, white-sided dwellings lined a widening, sparsely lit road. There were neither curbs nor sidewalks. No one was about. Crickets chirped, a dog barked somewhere in the mist, their lonely emanations merely highlighting an otherwise empty silence.

As St. John ran up to rejoin them, Chichester led the small contingent off the main road and onto a path that opened upon a short sandy beach where the river met the sea. Sweeping the scene with his flashlight, its beam fell upon a small wooden boat, a tiny grayish phantom bobbing at the water's edge. The open craft appeared to be about sixteen-feet in length.

St. John and Montoya took off at a trot toward the diminutive vessel, their feet sinking in the sand as they ran.

"St. John," Chichester called just above a whisper, "free that line and heave to." Then to anyone listening, "Once she's free, put a shoulder to her prow, boys. Her draft is shallow, but let's muscle her farther off shore before boarding all the same."

Jake stepped into the shallows to help push the badly weathered craft free of her moorings before loading it. Once into deeper water, he maneuvered it seaward and climbed aboard.

Taking the tiller, Chichester turned the key. The big Evinrude outboard roared to life, its exhaust sending a roll of foam churning against the transom.

Jake felt water on his face, and assumed it to be spindrift. However, he soon realized it was coming not from sea, but sky. An off-shore flow from the south was being met by a weather system to the northeast. It was raining.

Chichester took up a heading of due north and advanced the throttle. With a roar, the round-bottomed craft rolled level, its bow lifted and they were off in a bounding, accelerating rush to open water.

Once away from land, the swells grew larger but the small craft easily powered over or through each in its turn. One wave followed another in their rhythmic and perpetual march to shore. The engine's note would change as the boat climbed a wave face, hung on its crest for an eternal second while the propeller screamed and the tiny vessel fell bow-first into the trough ready to confront the next roller rising before them. Visibility was fast becoming a memory as the rain intensified. And, but for the orange glow of the compass light and intermittent moon reflecting off the spindrift, all around them it was black as a cave.

To his credit, Chichester read the swells perfectly, anticipating their period while adjusting the engine's power. With a deft hand, he kept to their northward course.

Holding an aggressive 30 knots, the rise and fall between walls of water brought more than spray over the chipped paint of the little boat's prow and onto Jake who was seated forward.

Finally, the southernmost pair of Salut Islands, the base of a triangle with Ile du Diable at its northern apex, made its first ghostly appearance through the mist.

Chichester held his speed as he steered them into the strait between Ile St. Joseph to starboard, and Ile Royale on their port side.

Once into the strait, the pattern and frequency of the waves changed on the incoming tide. They were now in a fast-moving, erratic chop that tossed their small craft about like a cork. Short wave lengths occasionally suspended the boat between peaks, its keel completely out of the water before being slammed back down.

Aware of the strains being put on his aged wooden craft, Chichester turned 30-degrees to starboard. As the sea-bottom rose beneath her hull, water began breaking over the small boat's low sideboards, and though he couldn't feel it through the leather of his boots, Jake realized his feet were submerged. Breakers meant the sea was shallowing.

Chichester bellowed above the din for St. John to lift the lid of his and Montoya's wooden seat. Doing so with his left hand, St. John looked at Chichester and nodded.

"Man that pump," the major shouted.

Montoya reached over and took the long tube-like device from St. John. The big man fell to his knees between the benches and began pumping with long piston-like strokes, bailing what was now three inches of water. His persistence proved adequate. The water halted its rise, if not its ingress.

Jake found himself gripping the soaked and slippery gunwales as the boat rocked, rolled, yawed and lifted only to slam back down onto the churning surface. He would let go only to relieve the big man at the pump.

The rain subsided and they came out of the strait as abruptly as they'd gone in.

Behind them the two southernmost islands were consumed by the mist and the sea calmed.

As the boat stabilized to a slow northward drift, a ghostly apparition emerged. Shapeless and dark and as ominous as its name, Ile du Diable–Devil's Island–lay dead ahead.

The major cut the motor back to near idle and turned to starboard, putting them on an easterly heading, away from the island. He shut the motor and the boat drifted silently. The sea turned strangely calm. The only sound now that of ripples gently lapping the boat's sideboards as all four men stared wordlessly at the dark shape rising before them.

"Why have we turned east?" Jake whispered, breaking the ominous silence.

Chichester, handed his binoculars to Jake and pointed, whispering, "Look there on the island's southern point."

Jake took the glasses and focused to where Chichester had pointed. He could barely discern a yellow glow at a spot just about where the land sloped downward to meet the water. "I see it," he said, handing the glasses back to Chichester. "A campfire?"

"A window," Chichester ascertained, waving for St. John and Montoya to join them at the tiller. "There's a stone building on the south promontory," Chichester whispered to the group. "It was a lookout station and reception building for the old French dungeon. If Cegato's holed up in there, he'll have fortress-like protection and a broad killing field to his south. We'll drift for another 100 yards or so. Then we'll power north before coming about. We can put in along the eastern shore. Cegato will be looking south. If he's in that building, we'll come up from his blind side."

"Is a mighty big if," said a laconic St. John to no one in particular.

After ten minutes of silently drifting northward with the current, Chichester turned west toward the beach. As the fog rolled over the little boat in waves of its own, the island faded in and out between mist and darkness as the party made their hopefully clandestine approach.

"Ship oars, lads," Chichester whispered.

As Jake and Montoya raised their oars from the water, the little boat rode the tide in silence, carrying her crew of four westward toward the beach. Suddenly towering trees and rocky shoals lay before the men in bold relief. Executing what rudder authority remained, Chichester wove through the rocks and they made landfall with a scrape and sudden stop as their keel met the rugged shore of Devil's Island.

- CHAPTER 13 -

Jumping into the shallow water, St. John, rope in hand, scrambled up the fifteen feet of steep, rocky beach and made fast his line to a tree. He waved the others ashore.

All was quiet as Jake, then Chichester, disembarked. The rain had subsided for the moment, but the winds had shifted to the northeast and picked up. Montoya handed Jake an ammo case, and he too disembarked.

It was 8:00 p.m. Chalky gray moonlight shone between fast moving clouds, casting long, intermittent shadows across the rocky shore.

St. John broke the silence. "If we're goin' to surprise Cegato, we need to know his situation. Maybe I should go ahead. Check things out and report back."

"Too dangerous."

"I'm small, dark, natural born scout, boss."

St. John's reasoning was sound. Chichester acquiesced.

When St. John stood, Montoya rose as well. To Jake's surprise, the big man removed his shirt to reveal a bulletproof vest, small against his massive torso. Quickly removing it, Montoya handed it to St. John.

The smaller man took the vest, adjusted it to fit, albeit loosely over his shirt and headed off down the rocky beach. In less than a minute, the self-styled scout disappeared.

Looking at Chichester, Jake realized that the major also wore a vest beneath his shirt. It was apparent who among the small party the Englishman considered critical to his mission, and who among them was expendable.

Alone and without a radio to slow or betray him, St. John headed into the thick, sheltering vegetation some twenty feet above the waterline. Leaping from rock to rock, he advanced stealthily under a canopy of palms toward the stone building with the light in its window. After a few minutes fighting the underbrush, he stepped from the forest onto a clearing. An orange moon crested the canopy between the swiftly-moving clouds to illuminate a broad natural terrace of black rock. The terrace sloped to the water's edge some 30 feet from where he stood. Its rough surface shone wet with long shadows in the ghostly lunar pallor. Exposed, St. John stepped back, closer to the tree line.

His long hair slapped quietly against his face as he nervously looked left then right along the rocks. He took a moment to stuff his rope-like locks back up under his big hat. That's when he saw the front of the building facing southward. Its brown stone sides climbed to a pitched metal roof rising some twenty feet from his position. Its rear and western sides were hidden in the trees, while the eastern side facing St. John was protected behind a crude stone wall. He saw no sentry.

Everything to the building's east and south-facing sides was cleared of trees and vegetation, leaving only the broad rocky terrace fanning out to the sea.

St. John needed to get to the building's south, seaward façade, the side with the lighted window. It meant he'd have to traverse twenty feet of bare, slick rock. He recalled Chichester having described the broad terrace as a killing field left over from the island's dungeon period.

Girding his courage, St. John made his way across the rocks to the sheltering stone wall, turned its corner and crawled across the rough surface toward that lone, lighted window. The window was some six or seven feet above the ground. Careful to not disturb the rocks beneath his feet, St. John stood.

His heart raced. Somewhere a dog barked. It meant the island was not completely deserted. "Be quiet, dog," he whispered, and blinked in disbelief as the barking stopped.

The window was crisscrossed by stout iron bars, prison bars. Behind the bars, clear in the dim glow of a lamp or candle, hung a tattered cloth.

St. John heard muffled voices.

Breathing in rapid bursts, he crouched frozen beneath the barred opening that glowed just above his bulbous hat. The voices became clearer, louder. A raspy one, male; a second voice, possibly that of a woman, could be heard between the lapping of the waves. Both voices spoke a language St. John had never heard before.

"Go to hell!" shouted a third voice, this one clearly female, young, angry, and loud. Hearing it caused St. John to jump, momentarily thinking the words were directed at him.

St. John's fear was subordinated by his need to get better look inside. He stepped back and assessed the building's stone wall. To look through its window he needed a perch.

Examining the ground around him, there were plenty of stones. Finding a large one, he quietly rolled it to a spot directly below the window.

He found another, slightly smaller, flat bottomed. Using all his strength, he placed it atop the larger stone. Locating a rotting log, he placed that atop the two stones creating a two foot high, rather unstable, series of steps.

Very slowly, he climbed to the top of the pile. Placing his palms above him on the slippery rocks of the building's south wall, he straightened his leg and ascended. He could easily reach the barred opening with his hands. Not fully erect, his eyes were level with window's sill.

The voices inside had become raised, animated. All spoke English now.

"What are you going to do with that?" a female voice shouted in an American accent.

With both feet atop the highest of the three objects, his hands gripping the bars, St. John pulled himself erect. Moving his free hand along the flat sill, he reached through the bars and lifted a corner of the cloth window-covering. Though he could see clearly through the rusted iron bars, the sill's thickness prevented an adequately downward perspective. Using his other hand, he reached through the second tier of bars and raised the curtain higher. Orange light flickered, causing shadows to dance on the ceiling.

He needed to get higher, gain a downward perspective. Gripping a rusted iron bar with one hand, with the other St. John carefully un-holstered his Walther and gently placed it on the window's ledge.

"I've told you a thousand times," the woman shouted, freezing St. John in his place, his hand still on the gun. "My brother never stole anything from you or anyone else."

"You know he did," said an aggressive male, speaking Spanish-accented English now. "He was going to bring it to you! Where it is?"

Outside, St. John stretching on tiptoes, felt the log tremble beneath his feet. Steadying himself, he pulled the cloth covering through the bars. His big hat and his entire face were now visible to anyone who might look upward. Rolling his eyes downward, in the flickering lamplight he saw the room's occupants.

One, a black-haired, pale skinned young female wore only her undergarments. Her face was scraped and bloodied, her chest bloodstained. She stood barefoot, her back against a floor to ceiling pole. Her clothing, jeans and a sweater, lay in a heap at her feet as if they'd been searched and cast aside. Atop the pile of clothing sat a pair of white rectangles which might recently have been the front and rear halves of a cell phone.

The pale woman was not bound, and stood under her own power. She was bent forward, her backside against the pole. With both hands on her knees, her core heaving with each gasp, she appeared to have suffered a blow to the midsection.

At one side of the little room, a large woman, Mestiza by her look, held an enormous monkey spider between two sticks. Big as a toad, the spider wriggled above a bowl of burning oil. The oil-lamp splayed the spider's death dance in shadow on the walls and ceiling as the big woman cooked the creature alive.

On the floor at the pale woman's feet knelt Cegato himself. He wore only a leather thong. A blood-stained rag encircled his neck. A patch at the center of Cegato's head was scraped clean of hair. His face was painted chalk white. St. John recognized the man's ritual affectations as being a theatrical fabrication never practiced by the ancient, native peoples of Guiana, the Arawak, but instead designed to instill terror.

Kneeling before her, Cegato grabbed the pale woman's ankles and pulled her down, spreading her legs wide.

St. John saw her sinews tensing as she struggled to toss the nearly-naked Cegato off of her. Holding tight, he assessed the rest of her with snakelike eyes.

In his right hand Cegato held an evil looking, foot-long, pointed bamboo spike. He shook it in front of the woman's face while chanting what sounded to St. John like gibberish.

Eyes closed in resignation, the woman shook her head.

"Donde este el Analogo?!" Cegato shouted an inch from her face. St. John understood.

"I've told you a thousand times, I don't have it," she shouted back, her big eyes burning with equal parts terror and rage. "Poking me with your goddam stick won't change that."

With a snort of derision, Cegato gestured to the big woman who stepped forward as St. John stood spellbound, watching the malevolent ritual unfold below him. The big woman held the cooked spider in her hands and cracked it apart, feeding the head to Cegato. The legs and body she chewed herself, before spitting it onto the prisoner.

Expressionless, the big woman returned to the lamp-table.

Casting the spider's remains into the flame, she lifted the skull of what might have been a small dog or a big rat. She handed it to Cegato.

Holding the small skull high, he waved it in front of Tina's wide eyes. His other hand held the foot-long, tapered bamboo spike. Placing the spike's pointed end into the skull's mouth he began a series of stroking movements and continued chanting, louder now, his eyes lolling.

Ignoring Tina Bergstrom's pleas and epithets, Cegato sharpened the spike against the skull's teeth.

Unable to look away, Tina tried to regain her feet, but the larger woman locked her meaty arms around the pole and Bergstrom's neck, easily closing her windpipe, while forcing her smaller victim to crouch, her back against the pole, her bottom inches above the floor.

Denied breath, Tina's struggles abated. Cegato moved forward.

Stretched out and held at a tortuous angle between the pole and the floor, St. John could see the small woman's quadriceps tense visibly as her tormentor moved his painted face close to the white delta Tina's skimpy underwear formed between her upper thighs. Cegato's intentions were clear, if unexpected. This was not part of any ritual.

Sweat visible along her brow, black lines beneath her wide eyes, Tina twisted, defiant, pounding his painted face between her knees over and over again with all the strength she could muster, all the while grunting something St. John need not decipher to understand. But, despite her pounding and cursing him, Tina's captor finally managed to spread her powerful legs wide apart and his face moved closer to the white cloth and she bared her teeth and growled like a wild thing as Cegato's mouth finally touched her.

The big native woman, grating at the scene, grunted something, and again began to choke her captive, threatening to deny Cegato the only physical pleasure or sense of power she might vouchsafe grant of this skeletal creature: her slow, ritual murder. Cegato withdrew his face and glared at the Indio woman and Tina brought a knee to his chin, only to receive a fist to her own.

Watching the grotesque scene unfold, St. John knew he had to act, and quickly. Because he also knew what came next. He felt the log unsteady beneath his feet and struggled to calm his breathing. Focusing his eyes on the scene below, he watched as Cegato lifted his right hand, now clutching the foot-long, tapered, razor-sharp bamboo spike.

The small woman, blood dripping from her lower lip, thrashed about more wildly than ever, not succumbing, still trying to kick her tormentor as the larger woman leaned in maintaining her devastating chokehold, releasing the pressure only when her victim reached the edge of consciousness. As her breath left her in a long exhale, Tina stopped fighting and fell limp.

Cegato slid the spike's razor sharp point along the length of the woman's pale thigh, leaving a vivid red trail in its wake. He twisted the stick, rubbing her blood onto its tip.

"Bone ticklin'," St. John whispered, as he feared he was about to witness a rumored local torture inflicted on the half-conscious women.

In bone tickling, a spike is driven through the subject's quadriceps, and scraped back and forth against the femur—the long thigh bone. It imparts unfathomable pain, yet denies the victim the refuge of shock. It was purported to have been used by the Colombian cartels against American drug agents to extract information before killing them. Holding the spike before him as one would a trophy, Cegato admired the bloodied instrument. His arm muscles tensed as did Tina's bloody left quadriceps. In one swift motion, Cegato lifted the spike high, moving to drive its razor-sharp point home when St. John's voice yelled out, "Stop!"

The scout's voice boomed in the stony chasm of a room. His right hand released the rusted bar and groped for his pistol while continuing to shout and generally create as much of a disturbance as he could. "That's right, mon. You heard me. Let the woman go before I blow your ugly head off," he warned as he gripped his weapon. Finally, raising the gun, he maneuvered it through the bars where it could be clearly seen by those in the room, only to have the crown of his big hat push against the window's upper sill and fall over his eyes. Unable to aim, unable to lift the hat, he pointed the gun at a spot in space he hoped would more-or-less be that occupied by Cegato.

"I'm warning you, mon," he shouted. "You too, lady. Drop your weapons and come with me."

But St. John's left arm began to fatigue, just as a deafening shot rang out from the room, dislodging a large chunk of the stone window frame right next to his head. The bullet ricocheted past and into the night.

Having never fired a weapon in anger, possessed of far more courage than marksmanship, he was unwilling to return fire for fear of hitting the small woman. So he simply hurled another empty threat.

Firing at the voice, Cegato's next shot missed his target's head, but grazed St. John's hand causing him to lose his one-handed grip on the rusty bar while his wool hat fell into the room. In grabbing for the window's bars with his free hand, he was forced to drop the Walther. The gun, too, tumbled into the room. The log rolled from beneath him and St. John fell straight down the stone wall, scraping his face against its crude blocks.

Now, flat on his back on the damp hard ground, unarmed, his left cheek and right hand bleeding, St. John heard the sounds of struggle coming from the window.

Two more shots rang out from inside. St. John saw the ragged curtain flap outward as Cegato fired wildly, three, four five times, hitting only the burlap or the stones surrounding the barred opening where St. John's face had been seconds earlier. After two more shots, Tina Bergstrom screamed as she'd never screamed before

Had he not fallen and been left to his vivid imaginings, St. John would have seen the events unfolding in the room's dim interior. He would have seen Cegato point toward the single door, and shout the words, "Encantrar el!" to the big woman, ordering her to chase down the intruder as he ineffectually fired at the now empty window. Had St. John been able to remain at that window without being shot, he'd have seen the Indio woman release Tina's neck, allowing her to breathe again, as her tormentor lumbered to and through the door, taking chase of the crazy interloper. He would have seen Cegato scramble for the gun St. John had dropped. And he would have seen the pale woman hurl her body through the air as only a dancer can. He'd have seen Tina fly across the room, reaching the dropped pistol first after knocking her drugged and drunken captor aside.

But instead of witnessing those dramatic events, unable to know he'd ended the torture and prolonged the woman's life, St. John, bleeding and unarmed, had no option but to warn the others. He got to his feet and ran for their encampment.

Inside the stone hut, Tina used the time St. John had bought her.

Now, rolling onto her back, she unsteadily brandished the gun, holding it in front of her, aiming it at Cegato's shaved and painted head. Surprised by its weight, she held the weapon in both hands, freezing her captor where he stood seven feet from her. She clambered to her feet, never taking her eyes off Cegato's as she aimed the gun squarely between his own serpentine orbs. Without firing she backed toward the hut's single, open door, dragging her trousers. One shot would stop his advance. One shot and she was free. The decision was surprisingly simple. But, as her finger tensed on the trigger, it did not move. However hard she squeezed, the trigger did not move. It took less than a second. But that was long enough for Cegato to see Tina's eyes narrow in confusion, and he knew she was not going to fire. Confident now, he waved the bamboo spike close to her eyes.

"Stop right there!" she shouted. Using both hands, her fingers squeezing the immobile trigger with all her strength, until with a scream of frustration she threw the gun at his head.

As she moved backward toward the room's door, the lumbering Indio woman reappeared. Her meaty arm again encircled Tina's neck. Cegato, laughing cruelly, retrieved the pistol and stepped up and Tina kicked him.

Holding St. John's Walter before Tina's face, with a click and a flourish, Cegato released its safety and pressed the gun's muzzle hard against her left temple.

With a laugh of derision, he brought his face an inch from hers. His breath as vile as rotted flesh, he growled, "Estupida puta blanca."

She spat in his painted face, and he drove her to her knees with another merciless blow to the midsection, striking her with a force that would've buckled a man twice Tina's size.

Gasping for breath. Alone with Cegato, Tina knew that to capitulate was to die. She had to collect her wits.

But there was Cegato, bending before her, his painted face an inch from hers. Again, he brandished the bamboo spike, breathing on her, almost panting as he considered where and how to use its razor sharp, splintered tip.

She would not close her eyes as he pressed closer still. His nearly naked body was against her now, his diapered groin pressing hers. She tried to move away but the stone wall prevented it.

She felt the spike's tip at her groin and she stood stock still.

"Tell me what I want to know, puta" he growled.

Breathing in deeply, she felt helpless, and with that feeling something changed.

"I'll tell you," she said, speaking the words quickly, her teeth bared, her face an inch from his. "I'll tell you everything. But first, take that thing away from me."

Struggling at the edge of control, deprived of his pleasure, yet drunk with the power of his apparent triumph, Cegato withdrew the spike.

Not diverting her glare from Cegato's chalk-white countenance, she spoke calmly. "Yes. I know what you want, and I know where it is. But you've been found. That face in the window was only the first. Others will be coming for me, and for you."

"Estamos solos aqui. Era solo un vagabundo!" *That was just a lone vagabond*!

"A vagabond with a pistol?" she challenged. "That was a scout, and you know it."

"No scouts come for you, puta."

"Can you risk being wrong?" she asked. And with that she pointed to the pile of clothing on the floor. "Go! Look!"

Releasing Tina, he stomped over to the pile of discarded clothing. He lifted his rumpled trousers from the pile. Shaking them, Tina's cell phone fell to the floor in pieces. Its screen illuminated for a second before going dark.

In his desperate search for the microchip, Cegato had earlier opened her phone, only to find nothing inside but its circuitry. It had not occurred to him then that the device was traceable. With slow realization, an expression of rage crossed his ghoulishly painted face.

Even with its back removed, the device had been powered on all the while. He threw it across the room where it landed right back in the pile of clothing.

As an enraged Cegato again moved ominously close to her, Tina, emboldened now and bluffing like a riverboat gambler, bought herself more time. "They're coming for you," she taunted casting her gaze toward the window where the man in the colorful hat had appeared. She then added icily, "That man was only the first. You're alive now only as long as I am."

PART TWO

- CHAPTER 14 -

The maritime strait known as the Windward Passage is 50 miles of blue water extending from the large island of Cuba in the west to Haiti, Isle of Hispaniola, on its eastern shore. Named by the 16th Century mariners who were the first to traverse the waters between the two great continents of the New World, the strait has been a portal for trade, and a haven for smugglers, bootleggers, pirates, drug runners and seagoing reprobates of every stripe.

It was here, and for the fifth time in 24 hours, that Aloysius "Red" Grogan cut the twin diesels of his 85-foot dive boat, the Strait Shooter.

A day-and-a-half had passed since Captain Grogan, along with his lead diver Gina Ferranti, Garodnik the cop, and their client the lady lawyer, had left New York aboard that client's leased Learjet.

At Port au Prince, they were joined by the boat's first mate, Antonio Zervigon, and like a well-oiled machine, the crew of three had wasted no time casting off and heading west on what they knew would be a tedious and probably fruitless search for submerged wreckage of the *Queen of the Southern Sky*.

After having begun on the spot where Captain Grogan had first sailed into the airplane's debris field three eternal days ago, they'd spent a full 24 hours scanning the depths with side-scan-sonar.

Aware that time was of critical importance to their client, the crewmembers took turns at the helm, the sonar scope, and their bunks.

While the sailors worked, the cop and their client remained below.

As clouds darkened overhead, and the winds shifted northeasterly, a moderate rain began to fall. They'd now crossed the entire breadth of where Grogan calculated the sinking fuselage might have settled to the bottom.

Captain Grogan, already feeling guilty for having accepted their client's money, expected, this last, desperate sweep would also prove unsuccessful. At the helm, Grogan let the boat drift into Cuban territorial waters.

"It's good to get outta town."

The skipper, his eyes peeled for any sign of Cuba's Guarda Frontera, whose gunboats prowled this part of the smugglers' strait, turned to see Detective Garodnik stepping onto the bridge. "Could'a picked a better night," the captain answered.

Garodnik scanned the western distance to where the lights of Baracoa flickered.

"You're looking in the wrong direction," Grogan said. "There's a hurricane building in the east." He jerked a thumb rearward. "Just a Cat-two at the moment; Hurricane Mathew, they're calling it. But the sea is warm, and the weather services expect bigger things from young Mathew. We'll have to work fast and get the hell away from here." With that, Grogan's tone turned inquisitive. "Say, Lieutenant, I've been reading the papers, and well, this case... y'know, the drug plane, Mrs. Silver's son gone missing, the dead model and all."

"Yeah," Garodnik nodded. "What's on your mind?"

"Well," Grogan said, "with all this other stuff, why is that reporter at the *Register* making all this fuss about some fake cocaine? It's not like there's a shortage of the real thing."

"True enough," Garodnik said. "But our government keeps getting better about cutting off the smuggling routes. Cocaine used to come in from Colombia by air over the Gulf. Now, though, with the Aerostat balloons, satellites, Coast Guard, the radars, interdiction planes, and every other zillion-dollar gadget the feds can buy with our dough, that's become tough. So the dope's coming through Mexico now. It hasn't stemmed the flow of coke, just raised the price and expanded the market for addictive synthetics like meth and Fentanyl. Now we got politicians yakkin' about building a wall to cut even some of *that* off and screaming' about an opioid epidemic, both of which will drive the price of organic cocaine through the roof."

"Wasn't el Chapo using a tunnel? What's a wall gonna do?"

"Cast a shadow. I dunno. But anyway," the cop went on, "when the American drug dealers get scared, they look for home-grown alternatives, meth, bath salts, ivory, charge, molly, whatever. There's a new designer drug every damned day. But, like I said, they're all either weak or highly addictive shit. High-end users, your Wall Street and Silicon Valley types won't go near that crap. That's why this myth about an the Analog came to be. It's supposed to mimic high grade alkaloid cocaine to a tee."

"What's the difference?" Grogan asked.

"That's the holy grail, my nautical friend. With high-grade coke, the dopamine release—and the buzz—wear off naturally. You take a hit after dinner and you're a Greek God, your girlfriend all of a sudden looks like Ava Gardner and you can go all night. But, when morning comes— as it always does—the dopamine bond has released your brain, and you're straight as a laser beam again and back at your desk stealing your clients' money. The other shit, meth, fentanyl, whatever, the rush from that crap just keeps coming, so does the dopamine. The shit clings to your brain in a way that keeps you high way longer. I've heard about tweakers staying stoned for a week on one fentanyl hit. But when you come crashing down, you're so chemically depleted that you're deeply, clinically depressed, suicidal even. All you want is another hit, and another after that, and you'll do anything to get it. Next thing you know, your either robbing liquor stores or you're that toothless asshole selling five-dollar blowjobs behind the strip mall to pay for your next high."

"Who's Ava Gardner?"

"Jeez!" Garodnik bellowed.

Grogan just shrugged and watched the horizon.

"Look," Garodnik went on, "I'm just a homicide cop. But the narco guys tell me that this Analog is bullshit, just a dealers' wet dream. Lab techs agree. Mrs. Silver, though, is not so sure. But she does know more about this drug stuff than I do. You should ask her. Get her mind off her son for a spell."

"Maybe later," Grogan demurred, adding, "She's a good looking widow, Lieutenant. You two are about the same age. You ever consider…?"

"Five-hundred down," first-mate Antonio's voice boomed from the deck below.

Grogan retarded the throttles. "Set up the sled, we'll take a listen." With a glance toward Garodnik, the skipper leapt down and joined the others on the main deck.

"Good luck," Garodnik shouted over the rail, aware this would be their last chance to find a needle in a very big haystack.

"We're gonna need it," Grogan shouted back, aware they were searching so far west only because Gina had insisted on it. Pilot that she was, she had realized that they'd failed to take into account that the *Queen of the Southern Sky* came down in a thunderstorm. If Bergstrom was at altitude when the aircraft had broken apart, if the wings and elevators stayed on, the winds aloft might have carried the fuselage well to the west of where they'd been searching. It was a long shot, but Grogan had learned long ago to never dismiss Gina's judgment.

As Antonio swung the boom free of the deck and out over the edge, Gina, wearing the top of her wetsuit over a black bikini bottom, splashed into the dark water to help ease the sonar sled down and check its power below the surface.

Using both sonar and optics, they would begin by searching a 25 square-mile crescent-shaped section of the strait's western extreme.

MJ made her first appearance topside. In jeans and a flannel shirt, wrapped in a blanket, she'd managed a tortured catnap, and was now urging herself to concentrate. She'd determined to avoid the histrionics that might compromise her superb intellect. As a mother, her survival instincts were strongest when focused on Jake. "Where are we?" she asked.

"A long way west of the debris field," Garodnik answered pointing toward the lights flickering on the distant shore. "Oh, by the way, while you were napping, I was on the horn to the Ivory Tower." The jaded detective's reference was to One-Police-Plaza, the NYPD's Manhattan headquarters. "I used the Internet. Did you know they have Internet on this boat?"

"How about a coffee pot? They have one of those?"

Almost immediately, Antonio appeared with a steaming mug of coffee.

Between sips and yawning, MJ asked, "New York have anything new?"

Without answering, the cop gripped the ream of papers, about twenty pages that the wind prevented him from spreading out on the instrument panel. "Yeah. They got the results from the search of Christina Bergstrom's West Coast apartment. Seems Frisco PD found something."

"Like what?" MJ asked, cradling the warm coffee cup in both palms.

"For one, there were a lot of letters, emails on her computer between the Bergstrom sibs. Mostly routine brother-sister stuff, small talk. But a couple stood out."

MJ perked up. "Oh?"

Garodnik explained. "The last few letters seemed to discuss the same subject. In the first one, Leif Bergstrom says to the sister that *he* was right all along and he'd found the evidence to prove it. She should not have doubted him. He's still her older brother, blah, blah." Garodnik leafed ahead, searching as he spoke. "Here," he said, pointing to a flapping page. "Right here, Christina Bergstrom says if he really wants her to believe him, then he–big brother–needs to show her the evidence. *Bring it to me,* she writes. Reads like a demand."

"Yes," MJ agreed moving closer, their faces nearly touching as she read. "Christina wants physical evidence But of what? You say these were e-mails?"

"Yeah. But it seems like at the brother's end he didn't always have access to e-mail. Sometimes it would be weeks before he answered his sister. Leif Bergstrom's e-mails were sent from a computer the Frisco techs traced to a place called Saul. That's in French Guiana."

"The Kool-Aid place?" MJ asked, incredulous.

"No, no," Captain Grogan cut in, correcting as he returned to the bridge. "You're thinking of *Guy*ana. This is French Guiana. It's a French protectorate. Look here," he continued, pointing to the screen of the bridge's navigation computer. "This is our present position, between Cuba and Haiti." He then expanded the screen to include the northern coast of South America, scrolled down and zoomed in. "Now here's French Guiana, on the coast about 1,500 miles south of where we are now. And here's Saul," Grogan added, pointing. "Saul is way the hell deep in the rainforest, hundred miles or so inland from South America's north coast."

"Why would Leif Bergstrom be there?" asked MJ.

"There's a tiny settlement," said Grogan. "Very low rent. A few buildings, a mine, a satellite dish, and a dirt airstrip. Not much else. I know some pilots who fly stuff in there. Some Euro scientists come down from Kourou now and then to study stuff, too."

"Scientists?"

"Yeah. There's a French rocket base on the Guianese north coast. It's the European version of Cape Canaveral. But Saul, that's another story altogether. That's real heart of darkness shit, accessible only by air. No roads in or out. Remote as the moon."

"Maybe Leif flew people or supplies to and from the place," Garodnik speculated.

MJ nodded. "When Leif was at Saul, he must have used their satellite hookup to retrieve emails from his sister, and answer them before flying out."

"Makes sense," Garodnik held. "Leif was keeping this communication secret from somebody, his employer maybe. Why didn't he want them to know he was corresponding with his sister?"

"Tell me about the emails, Patrick," MJ said. "You mentioned the last few..."

"Yeah. There was one from Leif that the sister printed out, so it must have been important. Frisco PD found it on the Bergstrom girl's bedstead. It was time-stamped just before she disappeared."

"We could be looking at Leif Bergstrom's last communication. Anything relevant?"

"If by relevant you mean, does it accord with a cover-up hypothesis? Then, yeah, maybe."

"What's it say?"

"It wasn't like other letters from him," said Garodnik. "The others were routine stuff: *Hope you're feeling okay, It sucks here*, like that, simple writing, stunted."

"Sounds like the kind of stuff Jake would write home from summer camp."

"Yeah," the detective went on, "like kid writing. But one letter was different, like it was written in a hurry. See for yourself." He handed the copy to MJ. "Except for the misspellings and typos, there's nothing childlike about this one. Leif Bergstrom was deadly serious. See where he says he was leaving South America for good?"

"He'd been ordered to fly a load of airplane engines to the States," MJ said, picking up where Garodnik indicated, slowly pacing the bridge as she took in the letter's contents. "Leif writes that it would be his last job. He'd deliver the engines as planned. He'd then contact her. They could meet somewhere. Leif says he'll find her and give her the evidence she needed to stop these people. After that, he plans to disappear." MJ stopped reading, curled her eyebrows and looked seaward. "Evidence of what? Stop what?"

"Anybody, guess," said Garodnik.

"Whatever's at the bottom of this," the lawyer continued aloud, "is worth an awful lot to somebody. Look here." She held the letter up to Garodnik's face. "Leif tells Christina that if anything happens to him, he'll have the evidence in his hand. He closes by telling his sister he loves her. There's finality about that. This last email has the ring of a suicide note."

Garodnik scratched his crimson pate. "When he says evidence, he can't be talking about the bag of synthetic they found on his person when the skipper here discovered the wreck of Bergstrom's plane. For one thing, it's small potatoes, for another it wasn't in his hand, it was in his jacket. Nothing else was entered into evidence."

"No," MJ said. "Whatever someone was looking for in the Haitian morgue was small. Someone put Leif Bergstrom on that autopsy table and cut him open to look in his stomach. That person or persons must have known that whatever Leif was holding was small enough for him to swallow, maybe just before he crashed. Why else would they cut him apart?"

"So you're telling me that this butcher then snatched Jake and the Bergstrom girl, thinking maybe they'd found it first."

"Nothing else makes sense, Patrick."

"And that does?"

- CHAPTER 15 -

The rain increased as the Strait Shooter settled into the monotony of to-and-fro sonar sweeps. Leaving Gina and the captain to the elements, MJ and Garodnik headed below to the well-lit comfort of the radio room.

Antonio sat before the humming radio equipment, luminous scopes, blinking lights, and glowing computer screens that covered two of the room's bulkheads. A long console ran at waist height in front of the electronic array. Spreading their papers out, the two landlubbers pulled a pair of padded swivel chairs up to the console, which served quite well as their desk.

MJ opened her briefcase. Atop her papers and notebooks lay a two-day-old copy of the *New York Register.*

Looking at the top sheet, something clicked, and Garodnik let out a surprised, "Hey!"

MJ looked up. "What's wrong?"

"Counselor," he said, "Leitch's so-called unnamed source is quoted here as saying the dope found in Jake's apartment was of the same unusual composition as that recovered with Leif Bergstrom's body. We learned later that it was a synthetic..." The detective paused, pensive, then added, "We got caught with our pants down on that."

"We?"

"NYPD. The evidence from the scene, the bag of dope from Jake's apartment, it was put aside between the time the evidence techs did their preliminary tests at the apartment, and the time the sample made it to the crime lab."

MJ's eyes widened. "And?"

"It was locked in the CSI vehicle and the techs went on another call to another scene, and another one after that. We had an iron pipe in a backpack at Penn Station same morning. The techs spent the whole day and night on *that* false alarm while *our* stuff got put on hold. So the evidence sample from Jake's apartment didn't get field tested, catalogued or even to the crime lab for 36 hours after its discovery."

MJ moved to speak, but Garodnik anticipated the ex-DA's concern. "No worries, Counselor. We confirmed chain of custody."

"Why does it matter then?"

"Timing is everything," Garodnik answered. "Unfortunately, *we* found out through courtesy call from the damned FBI that the dope at Jake's was a synthetic. But they didn't even know that until they read the *Register* article because we had the only sample. The dope actually *was* a synthetic cathinone, just like the Bergstrom sample, which we figured out, but not for 36 hours. Not until the CSI techs brought it in and the crime lab…"

MJ cut him off. "I see where you're going with this. This is really important!"

"You got it, Counselor," the detective said, offering MJ an unreturned high-five. "That weasel Wendell Leitch knew the dope's composition before we did, before the CSI techs did, before the FBI did, before the crime lab did, before anybody except Leitch's friggin' unnamed goddam source did!"

MJ's dark eyes flashed as she spoke. "The scoop-hungry sonofabitch went ahead with the story figuring your crime lab had already done the analysis and was withholding the details from the press."

Garodnik, tight-lipped, pounded his leg with a balled fist. "Find Leitch's source and we find Cassandra McRea's killer."

"It's protected, but Leitch will probably say it was an anonymous tip and he's off the hook. But why would whoever's behind this thing call the newspapers, especially the *Register*?"

"The Register is keeping it front page while the News and Times have moved on." The detective hit it squarely, adding, "The rag is implicating Jake for a story, and unwittingly diverting attention from whatever's really going on here."

"And the awful Colombian necktie thing?" MJ asked. "Why all the grisly melodrama?"

"Makes it look like she was killed by the cartels in retribution against your son's and the Bergstroms' private drug enterprise. It's the perfect frame: it takes down Jake and by association, discredits Common Sense. Two birds, one stone. It also puts a police spotlight–intentional or otherwise—on Christina Bergstrom."

"Why implicate her?"

"Maybe she was in on it and went rogue," Garodnik, ever the suspicious cop, mused. "Wouldn't be the first time an accomplice didn't want to share the score. I'm telling you, Counselor, that's one shady lady."

MJ mulled this theory. "Something troubles me, Patrick," she said, brushing aside the Tina reference yet again. "If Leitch's source is connected to the McRea murder, how would he or she also know what kind of dope was found on Leif Bergstrom's dead body?"

"It was in the papers, day before the murder."

"No." She shook her head. "The papers only said that Bergstrom was carrying a strange new modality. How would anyone conclude from that simple account that it was the same stuff as that found at the Cassandra McRea murder scene?"

"I don't know, but if we're right, it pretty much eliminates Peterson as Leitch's source."

"Not so fast, Patrick" MJ countered. "Could just mean he's not the only source."

"Two sources?" Garodnik's knee-pounding quickened. "Both calling Leitch? Not plausible. If one's after you and the other's after Jacob or the Bergstrom woman, it doesn't wash, even before considering that Peterson's a federal exec."

"Peterson has motive to discredit me precisely because he's a border fed. They hate me. I threaten their precious Drug War and now their so-called opioid epidemic. Besides, he tripped up once already with that cargo manifest."

Leafing ahead through the report whose pages were spread before them on the radio room's console, Garodnik said to MJ, "There's more."

"Good. We're getting somewhere."

"I want to discuss Christina Bergstrom's apartment."

"Okay."

"There were messages from Jake on her answering machine."

MJ stood, felt a rush, paced the room. "What did my son say?"

"In his first message, Jacob–Jake—says he'd called her earlier. There was no such message on her machine. We checked his cell records and it confirmed; she got that message and must've erased it. His other calls came later and were still on the voicemail."

"Anything solid in the other messages?"

"Not at first. But when you compare the messages Jake left, with the information from the next caller, things become damned curious."

MJ's brow furrowed. "What next caller?"

"A second caller phoned Christina Bergstrom right after Jake. He called her Tina, and identified himself as *Me, Phil*—somebody she's cozy with. Me Phil's message said everything was coming together and he'd be there waiting for her. We don't know what it means, but have good reason to believe that caller was Philippe Sinclair."

MJ leaned back in her chair. "A man who's been dead for twenty odd years leaves a message? You buy that?"

"If I do, it implicates the Bergstrom babe."

"What makes you think it's Sinclair? Phil is a common name. Besides, if this guy wants the world to think he's dead, why use his own name?"

"It's just a crook calling his girlfriend. You think they got code names?" Garodnik held up his hand before MJ could launch another challenge. "Frisco PD had taped an interrogation they conducted with Sinclair when he was picked up on some drug charge back in the Nineties. They'll do a voiceprint. If it comes up Sinclair—and it will—that means he and the Bergstrom dame are cozy. It appears your Jake's the patsy in a smuggling operation. If he's been set up, he's been set up by a pro..."

"...or a pro's girlfriend?" MJ mused. "Is that what you're implying?"

"Yes," Garodnik insisted, "a pro, his girlfriend, or both of them. It's called a *honey trap*."

"I know what it's called," MJ countered. "But my Jake is no wide eyed schoolboy when it comes to women. Besides, why in the world would Christina Bergstrom want to implicate Jake, of all people, her beloved brother's comrade in arms, in a thing like this? It doesn't wash, Patrick. Not at all."

The pair's sleuthing was interrupted by the clatter of the ship's phone.

First Mate Antonio answered, then handed the instrument to Garodnik. "It's for you, sir."

"Garodnik here...yeah? No kidding? Thank you." He hung up and turned to MJ. "Counselor, your last argument just went down for the count. That was my commander. DNA and IFPB results just came back. The smeared latent they recovered from the garbage dumpster outside of Jacob's apartment turned out to contain Cassandra McRea's blood."

"Well, we sort of expected that, didn't we?"

"We were hopeful," the detective said. "But the big surprise is, the print itself came back as Philippe Sinclair's."

"You said it was a smudged partial," MJ challenged.

"Right. But it's a three-nines-probable match." The detective paused, seeing no response beyond a furrowed brow from MJ, he went on. "Philippe Sinclair is alive and somehow neck deep in this thing. I'm telling you, he's still cozy with Christina Bergstrom."

MJ struggled for an alternative explanation. Shifting gears nervously, her bias abdicated to her logical mind. "If Sinclair's still walking around, Patrick, then who's the stiff they found in the trunk of his car back in 2003?"

"Does it matter?"

"I think it does. A killer took great pains to make that body unidentifiable." She reached into her briefcase and again pulled out the cargo manifest. Pointing to the signature line, she said, "If Sinclair is implicated in this, where does that leave Peterson? Let's not forget, he lied about the cargo."

"Government spookiness. Where's the connection?"

Unnoticed, the mate Antonio had sidled up to where MJ and Garodnik were working. He excused himself politely and began operating the equipment.

When the mate had completed his tasks, MJ asked. "Antonio, might I make a telephone call back to New York from here?"

"Sure," he said. "Here, let me…"

"Don't worry about it, Antonio," Garodnik said. "I'll walk her through it. I've been using the phones all night."

Antonio handed MJ the radiophone and left.

Garodnik watched as MJ considered the handset. He saw that she was already fixating upon the button in its middle. As the detective expected, she pressed the button while holding the handset away from her face, the way a singer holds a microphone.

"What does this button do?"

"Mind if I try?" the detective said. "Who do you want to call?"

"Bill Yost."

Garodnik got the marine operator on the line, and MJ gave him the phone number.

Within twenty seconds, Yost's important phone was answered. "This is Yost."

"MJ Silver calling, sir." Garodnik handed her the handset. "Just press the button when you speak, release it to listen."

"Bill, last night before I fell asleep I got to looking over the reports you gave me on Sinclair and Peterson."

"And?"

"Sinclair and Peterson are both Iraq veterans. Both Army. Both injured in combat. Both medical discharged to Stockton, California in 2003."

"Where are you going with this?"

"I'm grasping at straws. Can you get me anything else that links those two?"

"I'll call you," Yost said, adding, "By the way, MJ, how's my man working out?"

She looked at Garodnik. "If you mean Pat Garodnik, he's a teddy bear."

"Oh, Jeez, no," Garodnik said, slapping his forehead. "Don't say that..."

"Okay, Bill," she concluded, "I'll sign off now." Terminating the call, she looked at Garodnik. "What? It's true."

"It's gonna be my new name now, Teddy... Jeez, woman."

"No worries. I'll tell Yost you have masculinity issues. He'll protect you." She tweaked his mustache and his cheeks turned redder still. "I still say Peterson lied about the cargo."

"The Feds do all kinds of spooky shit. I say Peterson's a dead end. Probably has security clearances as long as your arm. You're wasting time. I still like the Bergstrom dame for this."

"Well, right now it so happens that we have time, Patrick. If I work on one of these," she indicated the dossier, "and you work on the other," she tapped the companion folder, the one Bill Yost had sent her on Sinclair, "how long do you think it'll take us to read them both?"

While the two worked in the radio room, on the bridge Gina pored over the bathometric charts, while Grogan hunched over the sonar scope. As expected, the images returned were devoid of anything significant. Two hours became four, each seeming to last ever longer until finally the tropical night arrived and the equipment was hoisted onto the deck.

"Make fast that sled," Grogan ordered, "and, Antonio, set a course for two-seven-zero. There's nothing here, and we gotta stay ahead of this weather. We're going closer to shore."

As the revving engines reverberated through the boat, below deck MJ was updating her notes.

"Forget that for a second," Garodnik asked, touching her wrist. "What'd the commissioner say?"

"Told me the Oakland County coroner had concluded that the corpse on Yerba Buena Island was a male Caucasian, nothing more. His report lists the cause of death as lethal injection of heroin."

"So we've got a closed sheet, but no solid ID on the corpse."

"What does your report say about the crushed skull?"

Garodnik checked the papers before him. "The crushed skull was administered postmortem and the body was set afire after that." Garodnik turned in the swivel chair he'd taken up in front of the radio console. "Counselor, I still think you're chasing your tail."

"We have blessed little else."

"Anyway," the detective pressed, "I'm thinking we have two separate things going on. Leif Bergstrom was running something for his sister, something pure un-exotic dirt-bag felonious. And if those dumpster prints tell me anything, they tell me *she's* still hooked up with Philippe Sinclair."

"You told me she got her life together, Patrick," MJ said with unbridled cynicism. "Why would she still be with that loser... or his ghost? I'm just saying."

"Once a junkie, always a junkie, *I'm* just saying." the jaded cop mused. "She might not be a user anymore, but somewhere in some dark corner of her mind she's still considers herself a piece of worthless crap, a product of her past, flawed, dirty and not worthy of any other kind of man. If I've seen it once, I've seen it a hundred times. So have you. It even has a name. It's called the Svengali syndrome, Counselor."

She moved to speak, but stopped herself. A life a spent in the company of homicide cops investigating every kind of savagery, MJ was only too aware of why this sweet man had never yet called her MJ. Contrary to the apparent formality, it really showed that to him she was less a colleague than she was a victim's mother. To a murder cop, getting too close with a victim's family member, a mother in particular, was a one-way ticket to the bottom of a bottle—many bottles. To MJ's dismay, this realization told her more than she wanted to know of what Garodnik secretly considered the fate of her missing son. "What's the second thing, Patrick?"

"The second thing, Counselor, is a perfect cover for the drug running. Suppose Leif Bergstrom, or maybe the outfit he worked for, was picking up a few bucks doing something for Peterson and the government spooks, something that had to do with the airplane engines Bergstrom was supposed to be hauling but apparently wasn't."

"That has merit," MJ reluctantly agreed.

"Occam's razor," Garodnik said.

"First Svengali, now Occam?" She looked at the detective askance. "You really need to get out more."

"Occam's razor," he repeated with feigned impatience. "When you have more than one theory, go with the simplest first. I know you're pulling for Christina Bergstrom, but this is why trying to implicate the G-man in the McRea murder is far-fetched. We need to concentrate on this new Sinclair stuff and forget Peterson, at least for now."

"So why doesn't Peterson want anyone to know what Leif Bergstrom was carrying the night his plane went down?"

"Because we're likely to uncover some covert government bullshit that has nothing to do with Jake or Cassandra McRea. Peterson pissed you off, and you're letting it cloud your judgment."

The lawyer, wrongly interpreting the oft-jaded detective's comment to mean MJ's *female* judgement dismissed the allegation as biased. "Two problems," she countered. "Not only did Peterson put Leif Bergstrom in that job, but he also knew that when the plane crashed there'd be an investigation, if not by the government, then by insurance investigators. They would have figured out the weight and balance inequity, just like Gina did. That's why Peterson changed the cargo manifest. He used Leif Bergstrom as his pawn, or worse."

"How does that tie in with the dope, the imaginary cocaine analog?"

"It ties in with Sinclair. Do you think that Sinclair's showing up again at just this time is mere coincidence?"

"That's consistent with both arguments. What I cannot buy is that an experienced felon like him would be dumb enough to leave prints around...even a block away?"

"But he did," MJ said. "He thinks he's old news, dead and forgotten, untouchable."

"Could be." Garodnik checked his folder on Sinclair. "Yost is thorough. Here's Sinclair's military records, fingerprints, photo."

MJ looked at the old picture. "Nice looking young man."

"Not my type," the detective cracked without looking up from the notes. "Same branch as Peterson," he observed. "Army. Get this. Sinclair was on a chopper in Iraq, too...a gunner."

"Oh, really," MJ said. "Suppose he and Peterson were on the same combat helicopter crew. Both were discharged to Stockton, California. Maybe Peterson became Sinclair's VA counselor. What else does it say?"

"Stockton, California, 2003."

"Don't you see?" Becoming animated, MJ leafed frantically through Peterson's folder. "Isn't it likely Peterson would've kept in touch with his old comrade in arms? Don't you think he might've used him in a covert operation, just like you're speculating that he used Bergstrom... another wounded flyer?" MJ read on. "Peterson flew attack helicopters in Iraq." Leaning over, she leafed ahead. "Earlier we read that he'd won the Purple Heart."

"No record of decorations on Sinclair, though he was sent back with shrapnel wounds. Why would the commander get a medal and his wounded crewman get passed over? C'mon, really, what are the odds they were on the same chopper crew?"

"Better than the odds of Sinclair surviving his own murder and resurfacing twenty years later, on the same day Peterson contacts Leif's sister," said MJ. "What day was Sinclair wounded, Patrick? Does it say?"

"August 7th, 2003."

MJ leafed ahead, finding the date of Peterson's injury. "Guess what?"

"Another coincidence?" Garodnik said half-heartedly.

"Yeah," MJ countered as the radio room door opened to reveal Antonio.

She stood and pointed to the folders on the counter. "I want the autopsy report on whoever was in that car trunk." She slapped the console. "I've seen enough coincidences."

Antonio walked toward them. Holding up his hands in deference to MJ's momentary intensity. "Sorry to disturb you again."

"We're just talking," Garodnik grinned as the mate walked over.

"We're from New York," MJ added. "We talk loud because of all the horns. Do you need the space?"

"Just have to use the ship-to-shore again," said Antonio.

As the mate sat himself at the console, and moved a few of the men's papers aside, careful not to mix them. "Well, how about that!" he said, smiling broadly, touching one of the papers.

"What?" both said simultaneously.

"Sorry," the mate said. "That just came out. I don't mean to pry."

"Speak up, son," Garodnik said. "What is it?"

Antonio shrugged. "Kind 'a silly, really, it's just this name, what with all the talk about coincidences and all. It's weird." He was pointing to the name Guillermo Pedro Filho that MJ had highlighted in her notes. Filho, the client of Leif's Bergstrom's employer, the person who'd contracted for Bergstrom's to transport his cargo, had of course signed the cargo manifest.

Antonio now had Garodnik's full attention. "You know this guy?"

"No. It's just, well… strange," Antonio said, with deference. "This sentence, it reads 'Information provided by William Peterson, and confirmed by Guillermo Pedro Filho.'"

"Why is that strange?" MJ asked.

Antonio shrugged his broad shoulders. "I'm third generation American, but of Portuguese descent," he began, "world's best sailors, y'know - and in Portuguese, Guillermo Pedro Filho means...well, I mean...in Portuguese, Guillermo Pedro Filho translates to William Peter Son in English.

That's a funny coincidence, isn't it...two guys with the same sort of name?"

The mate saw the pair's stern expressions, not understanding why his clever observation would cause such a stir in the Strait Shooter's client's. "I gotta learn to mind my own business," he said, palms out. "I'm sorry if I was outta line. Really, I'm…"

As Antonio began to back away apologetically, MJ squeezed the young man's big arm firmly. "No, Antonio. In fact, you were absolutely *in* line…directly in line with what we're thinking."

She picked up the phone again, handed it to Garodnik. "Patrick, that makes three Sinclairs by my reckoning."

"Three and counting?" Garodnik speculated with apprehension.

"Let's hope not," MJ said. "Get Bill Yost for me again, if you would."

- CHAPTER 16 -

Antonio scampered up the ladder to the main deck, peacock proud at having helped the clients. MJ and Garodnik followed.

"One hundred fathoms, Tony-baloney," Gina communicated whimsically to the mate as they drifted westward toward Cuba. "Shallowing fast. Two-fifty."

"We're approaching the Nelson Bank," Captain Grogan advised from the flying bridge. "Steady as she goes."

Despite the captain's order, the Strait Shooter's engines suddenly throttled back and the boat began a gentle turn to port.

Grogan was down and onto the main bridge in three strides, "What the hell's going on? Why are we coming about?"

As he reached for the throttles, Gina, stopped him. "I want to start here, Red. It'll be getting light in two hours and I don't want to be any closer to Punta Caleta. We can't afford to be interdicted. Add to that, there's a storm bearing down from the east. Go with me on this, boss. Let's drop the sled and do something. Please."

Knowing from experience the futility of resisting Gina's will, and more than that her instincts, Antonio was already hoisting the sonar sled on the deck-crane. Grogan's check of the weather confirmed Gina's fears; if they wasted any more time moving closer or scanning the shallows along the island's coastline, they'd be boarded by the Guarda Frontera or trapped by the approaching storm or more likely, both. Mathew was now a solid Category-3 hurricane and they were in its path as it started its inevitable northwestward turn.

With the sonar and camera rig swung over the side, Antonio announced, "Ready away!"

"Lower away," Grogan reluctantly replied, and the triangular yellow platform dropped into the water.

Gina went in after it, adjusting the optical camera's lens and floodlights. She gave Grogan, who was now at the video monitor, a thumbs-up. Without a moment to spare, the routine of scanning began again.

With time's passage, anticipation waned, the crew grew weary and Grogan ordered the sonar sled raised after three fruitless hours of scanning the sloping floor.

As the sonar sled and optical camera rose above the abysmal bank, Gina alone saw an anomaly, not on the video screen, but on the waveform monitor. "Hold it! What's that?" She pointed to the ragged green line on the monitor.

Antonio stopped the camera's vertical rise, yet neither he nor Grogan could see anything.

"Go back," Gina said. "Hit the floods again. I think I saw a spike in the noise. Pan left a few degrees, about two-six-zero."

The image on the video monitor's screen jerked as Antonio abruptly stopped both the sled's ascent and rotation, panning the camera and its flood lights back to the westerly position. "What'd you see?" he asked. "We're a mile off the bottom."

"I'm not sure," said Gina. "It was just a pulse on the waveform, like lights reflecting off of something."

"Swordfish, maybe," Antonio said. "Let me see…" He checked the instrument's depth sounder. "The rig's only at 18 fathoms. Nothin' up here."

Grogan consulted the bathometric chart. "It's what I thought." He pointed to a circle on the chart, near the center of the Nelson bank. "We're near the top of an underwater hill. It's a steep, sub-surface mesa that extends from the bottom all the way up to within about 18 or 19 fathoms, 115 feet down." Turning to MJ, who had just joined them on deck, the skipper explained, "These islands are a maritime mountain range... lots of peaks and valleys, even a few mesas. This one just never popped through the surface. I've been steering clear. The Guarda Frontera gunboats own these waters."

"Guarda, shmarda," Gina said, indifferent to her captain's concerns. "We'd have seen it on the next pass if we kept going west."

"We're a mile off the top of the bank," Antonio mused. "The camera can't see that far and the sonar was giving you a side-lobe artifact, Gina."

"Negative," Grogan groused. "I know this feature. It's a massif, sloped top, maybe a quarter-mile across before it drops off, way off."

"Right." Gina pointed to the small contour line on the chart. "Suppose Bergstrom's fuselage came down right on top of it. We drift west, maybe we'll see it. Stranger things have happened."

"Numbers don't lie," the captain said. "My secondary calculations show the wreckage never drifted that far. If it had, it would have already been well below this depth."

"But, Captain my captain," Gina said, clutching Grogan's arm to keep him focused on the charts, "suppose, just suppose your calculations were... uh, like, y'know... *wrong*."

Feigning terror, Antonio gasped. "Wrong? Our captain? What madness is this?"

"Okay, you two," Grogan said. "Clown college is over for today. But before I toss your bony ass overboard, missy, tell me how I was wrong?"

Gina took Grogan's hand, and pressed his finger to the spot on the chart where Grogan had first discovered the debris from Leif Bergstrom's crash.

"Okay," she said, guiding his finger westward across the sheet. "Bergstrom's plane went down in a thunderstorm, I never heard you mention it when doing your initial calculations. All you found was the nose. Suppose its engines were still turning… remember TWA Eight-hundred? That old big-winged Curtiss could've flown for miles after it, uh… blew its nose."

"Hmm," Grogan acknowledged. "I was distracted by our New York deadline, so never considered the strong easterly winds on the front side of that low. That blow stalled over Panama. East winds prevailed all night and the whole next day in the strait following Bergstrom's crash. That surface debris could have floated ten, twenty miles to the east while subsurface currents could've taken the fuselage west. All we had was the cockpit. Add a reasonable margin of error… Hell, that changes the numbers."

"That fuselage was loaded down," Antonio observed.

"We don't know that," Gina said. "Not anymore."

"Dammit if you're not right!"

Gina struggled to speak as Grogan squeezed her cheeks and kissed her hard on the mouth, finally saying, "The wreck could be on this side of the strait. Hell, it could even be on top of the Nelson Bank."

"That top surface is pitched at about a 30 degree slope to the east," Antonio pondered. "It would stop a westward descent, but hard to believe something would settle."

"Strange things happen in these straits," Gina said. "We gotta go back down."

"If we do, we'll be in for a wild ride going home," Antonio warned, as rain pelted the decks. The seas were getting heavier by the minute. "We gotta think of the clients."

"They're exactly who I'm thinking of."

"It's a one-in-a-million shot," Grogan lamented before glimpsing MJ standing nearby, her expression hopeful.

"But, at less than 20 fathoms, it's workable," Gina asserted. "If we see something, we can dive on it. Call it a Hail Mary pass. What else we got?"

"Same money, either way?" Antonio whispered.

Fresh with renewed if improbable hope, they would go for one all-or-nothing sweep.

Once on station over the western slope of the Nelson Bank, they crowded the monitor as the Strait Shooter rocked in the building swells.

Grogan dropped the rig to 18 fathoms, or about 115 feet and panned the camera between 245 and 275 degrees. Seeing nothing, various gain and sensitivity settings were tried. They opened and closed the iris and zoomed in and out. After a few minutes, Grogan shrugged. "We're kidding ourselves. It's a dry hole..."

"Go west, Red. We're still too far away," Gina insisted.

"Even if the plane did settle on the bank, it would've slipped off with the first nudge," said Grogan. "Let's pack it in, put in at LeMole and batten down. We're in for a helluva blow."

Gina saw fatigue on the men's faces, heard it in their voices. "This is our last chance," she said. "Let's give the client a fair shake."

"Mrs. Silver isn't paying us to drown her, Gina," Antonio said.

With that, the skipper and mate moved outside. An agitated Gina followed. "What in hell are we here for?" She admonished, facing them, fists on hips, trying her damnedest to look fierce, succeeding despite her size and causing the burly sailors to curtail their nervous laughter. "I know Mrs. Silver acts real tough," she said, undeterred, nodding toward the radio room where MJ and Garodnik were still poring over evidence. "But so do you two, especially when you're scared of failing." The two groaned and protested, looking this way and that while Gina pressed. "But I can see behind the facade," she said, "and what I see is a loving mother, a woman who's terrified and desperate and who I can hear sobbing every minute she thinks she's alone. Whatever's on that wrecked airplane is all important to her, and she's counting on us to find it. Besides," the petite diver added, forcing a smile now, melting away whatever objections her boys might yet harbor, "this isn't just a contract job for some oil tycoon. You jokers are into it this time, just like I am, just like that big city cop is. He's not quitting on Mrs. Silver. So why are we?" She paused letting her words sink in. "C'mon, guys" she concluded, knowing she had them, "we're better than that. We're way better than that."

Grogan let out a sigh of resignation and rubbed his tousled hair. A very tough decision had been made both for and with him.

Antonio moved to the helm. "Got a heading, Skip?"

"Two-six-zero," Grogan barked. "Slow as she goes."

Minutes later, Gina was guiding the camera into the water again.

Its position abeam the sloping bank, was as close as they could estimate to where Gina had estimated the video pulse had ben returned.

"Gimme a sounding," Grogan yelled.

A few seconds later came Antonio's reply. "I'm showin' 100 feet, but we're rockin' like a Tilt-a-Whirl. It's hard to say."

As the camera rig began its sweep, the crew, including a dripping wet Gina, fresh from the inky water, eagerly stared at the familiar screen, waiting for an image as the rig descended. At 120 feet, the camera struck sandy bottom. The loose silt forming the top of the bank sent up a cloud of murk, obscuring the lens. When the view cleared, the screen was blank, only this time the empty frame was bright in reflected light from the camera's floods.

"Look at your white-level." Grogan lowered the luminance control.

"No, don't reduce the gain," Gina directed. "Not yet. We're not next to it. I think we're on top of it. Come up a foot or two, and widen out. You're close to something, and it's filling the field."

Grogan raised the camera a couple of feet and slowly pulled back on the zoom lens, causing the image to recede and assume a shape. He tilted the camera up and could discern an edge, an object. The thing was long, but they were too close to focus on it.

"Looks like a whale carcass." Antonio smirked.

"That's no whale," Gina said, a broad smile on her face.

"Haul up," said Grogan. "We'll move back. Might be a hull."

Knowing better, Gina remained silent as Antonio swung the boom to the far side of the boat, increasing the distance to the object.

Grogan adjusted the camera's direction. "Full-wide. Here she comes.... Stop!"

"Looks like words," Antonio thought out loud.

"Or numbers." Gina squinted.

"Whatever it is," Grogan said, "it's not been down here very long."

By adjusting the iris, the word, written with a flourish in archaic script became clear: *Curtiss*. It was an old logo, and below it the numbers, N44.

"It's a tailfin," Gina said.

"A submarine?" Antonio pondered, half in jest.

"An airplane!" Gina answered, "*the* airplane."

A slight widening of the camera angle, and the object became a rudder, a stabilizer, then a full empennage, and finally a fuselage. The wrecked aircraft lay nearly upright. Its remaining wing had been sheared-off. The cockpit section was torn-away, leaving behind a jagged main fuselage and tail section. Mere feet below them was the forlorn wreckage of the *Queen of the Southern Sky*.

"We got it," Grogan whispered, unheard.

The shape couldn't look more foreign where she lay. The crew stared, assessing the image, saying nothing more. There was no high-fiving, no self-congratulatory whoops. There was only stunned silence at how close they'd come to abandoning the search.

Grogan spoke first. "Man, oh man." He let his words trail off, then took Gina's small face in both his rough hands and kissed her hard while she grinned.

Pretending to pull away she mumbled, "Twenty fathoms. We can dive on it!"

"Aye aye," Antonio said, reenergized. "How you wanna go?"

"I'm not sure," Grogan said just as a coffee cup slid off the shelf and shattered against the deck. "We're gonna take a helluva pounding."

"I'll inform our clients," Gina said.

"Get 'em into rain gear and life jackets. They'll wanna be topside," Grogan ordered.

As Gina had speculated, the airplane had come to rest on a high rill, one of only two such features at the mid-point of the sloping Nelson Bank. When the airplane crashed, its wings snapped. The hull descended at a shallow angle, coming to rest on the first surface it encountered—an extraordinary bottom feature, and an equally extraordinary piece of luck.

With no time to waste, breathing a surface-supplied helium and oxygen mixture, Grogan and Gina started down. The Caribbean was cool as they descended like miners, light beams twitching this way and that as they all searched for any unwelcome visitors both on and below the surface.

The wreck was perched atop the sub-surface formation. Obscured by silt, the silver plane appeared specter-like, suspended. When the massive spire itself came into view, fully a third of the wreck's length could be seen extending over its edge.

"See anything not fishy?" came Antonio's first bit of banter from above, really an operational check of the intercom system linking him to the divers.

"Affirmative," Grogan replied, businesslike. "Stand by."

Gina swam around the rear of the hull and under its exposed empennage section as it dangled precariously over the abyss. Below her was only water, and she surmised that the sea floor fell away here to its regular 500 fathom (3000 ft.) depth.

At the front of the hull, Grogan noticed that the forward bulkhead was not resting on the surface but elevated about a foot. The wreck was leaning back toward the abyss, balanced but rocking fulcrum like; if disturbed, it might slide away and down into the crushing black depths. Grogan waved Gina forward and she took several photos.

"We can get inside through the sheared-off cockpit," Grogan said. "Forward of the bulkhead, the whole thing's gone but I saw a narrow companionway into the rear cabin."

"The way that thing's hanging, are you sure we should be going in at all?" Gina asked, referring to the small oval doorway still sealing the forward bulkhead. But there was no other access to the interior and the airplane's mysterious cargo. "We'd be trapped if this thing came loose and went to the bottom. Can we anchor the hull?"

"Take too long," said Grogan.

"What's the alternative?"

"No alternative," Grogan said. Then, deferring to Gina's risk assessment skills added, "It's your call."

"You and your big ideas," Gina remarked, knowing the idea was hers and hers alone. Looking at the unstable position of the wreck, she called, "Antonio."

"Go ahead," came the reply from the surface, where daybreak had brought ominous low clouds and a soaking rain.

"We're going inside."

"Good luck. You got about 35 minutes on station, ten more to the surface. We're rockin' and rollin' up here, and not in an Elvis kind 'a way."

After investing a few more precious minutes on a thorough inspection of the wreck's purchase upon the sandy slope, the pair swam toward the cockpit area. They could gain access through the bulkhead doorway where the largely glass cockpit had been torn away.

A force had bent the bulkhead inward but it had held.

Grogan pushed at the warped and blistered door. Unable to free it, he pushed his feet against it. The whole massive hull rocked before the door opened, raising a cloud of silt. When visibility returned, the rear cabin was revealed. Grogan swam through first. Assessing the space, he waved Gina in. They had 30 minutes left at depth.

The cargo area was filled with large wooden crates lashed to the sloping deck.

"It looks so peaceful, and so out of place," Gina observed.

"My guess is she glided slowly all the way down," Grogan said. "Probably kept her starboard wing 'til she hit the water. I'm sure it sank aft-end first and the wing stubs made it behave like a submarine. I'd say it spiraled slowly. That's why it settled so far from the surface debris."

"The bulkhead is buckled, but intact," Gina noted. "The crates are still lashed to the deck."

"The bulkhead absorbed the shock of an explosion." Grogan ran his hand along the stringers. "A shaped charge did this. Sabotage."

Shining her light into a one inch space between the boards of the first crate, Gina said, "I can't make it out. Murky. Maybe we ought to haul one up."

"That would take too long," Grogan said, knowing day was breaking above them and the Cuban authorities would be all over Antonio soon. "Your calculations show this plane couldn't carry any more than three engines. We gotta count 'em." He reached into the toolkit, retrieved a pry bar. "Let's see if we can get one open."

Gina, her body half in-half outside the bulkhead companionway, swam closer to get a look at the forward-most crate.

Moving into position, a bolt of fear went through her. "Grogan, we're not the first ones down here. This crate's been opened."

Seeing no sign of earlier salvors outside the hull, Grogan swam back in.

Joining her at the first crate, he saw that its top left corner had been chopped at, then crudely pried apart. The opening, too small to reveal the crate's contents did, however, provide access enough for Grogan to reach his hand inside.

"Makes no sense," he said, feeling around inside the flooded box.

Able to discern a rough edge of something large and solid, he removed the glove from his right hand and reached in again.

"Feels like a machine alright." Groping blindly, but with caution, his bare hand felt what could be ribbed cooling fins consistent with those of an air-cooled engine cylinder. He turned, gave Gina the thumbs-up sign.

'Let's try for a better angle," Gina said.

"See if you can wiggle in behind it," Grogan suggested.

Gina removed her shoulder straps and now holding her tank, worked her smaller form around to the rear of the crate. "Hey!" she cried suddenly. "The back of this crate is busted completely apart." Reaching inside, she added, "There's a screwdriver and a ratchet wrench in here." She removed the tools from where they were wedged between two of the engine's cylinders, and held the small screwdriver aloft for Grogan's benefit. "This whole side of the box was pried open. If this screwdriver was what he used, this was one powerful guy."

Unable to get his wider girth past the crate's side, Grogan had to see for himself. "Hand me that screwdriver."

He began prying at the stout boards of the wooden crate on *his* side. But the screwdriver was too small, and however hard Grogan yanked, the muscular captain could only chip away some wood.

"Accept reality, Red," Gina teased, just as the hull shifted with a sickening scrape.

"I need something bigger than this screwdriver, more leverage."

Gina swam back outside the hull, returning with the two-foot long crowbar.

Handing it to Grogan, he pried a large wooden slab from the crate, thus allowing an unobstructed view of its water flooded contents.

"Make a mental note," he said. "In the forward most crate, we have a twin-row radial engine."

With crate number one open, Grogan could explore its contents further. "Something's loose in here," he said. "Holy crap, this whole cylinder is loose." He shone his light directly onto the ribbed cylinder. "Looks like the bolts at its base were loosened. I can move the whole jug around."

"Well, the screwdriver was used to pry open this box. Now we know what the wrench was for, too." Gina said, swimming over to have a look.

Shining her light through the murky water she could better make out the crate's contents.

Even in the poor light it was plain to see that this engine was incomplete. There were no intake or exhaust manifolds. Each of the ports were sealed over with Cosmoline, and the loose jug was missing one of its two rocker box covers.

"Red," she said. "This is what's called a *pickled spare*. It's a stripped down engine intended to be stored for future use, rather than installed on an airplane."

Grogan probed at the top of the exposed cylinder sleeve. "Would this pickled spare, as you call it, have pistons?"

"Of course it would have pistons," she affirmed. "Internally it would be complete."

Reaching down, Grogan found he could not get his hand very deep into the lining to the crankcase. "There's something in here," he said, trying to extend his reach, but able to merely probe with a fingertip.

"Should be a lot of stuff in there."

"Feels soft."

"Soft?" Gina said, incredulous. "No way."

Retrieving his hand, Grogan asked, "How many of these crates you figure there are?"

"At least three," Gina estimated, peering toward the tapering tail. "Too murky to see."

"This is weird," Grogan said. "We gotta know how many boxes, and what's in 'em. I'm afraid my manly chest prevents me squeezing into that tail cone to take a look."

Gina handed the camera to Grogan. Poking his stomach, she added, "No worries, One Pack. I got this."

Moving carefully, Gina surveyed the space aft of the first crate. Knowing her surface line would be a hindrance as she wriggled among the tapering space aft of the first crate, she instructed Grogan, "I'll need the portable tank."

Outside the hull, Gina unhooked her surface feed and clamped the mask and demand regulator to the toolkit. Then with an assist from Grogan, she carried, rather than donned, the portable heliox tank. Grogan handed her the large pry bar. "This should do it. We got maybe fifteen more minutes on this hull. Go easy, babe. This old tub is hanging by a thread."

Behind her mask, Gina winked, then blew an animated heliox kiss in Grogan's direction. She took the crowbar and hooked it to her belt. With that, she turned and disappeared into the dark void of the tail-cone just as Grogan was about to call it all off as too risky.

Fully aware of the danger, Gina propelled her small body above the coarse wooden crates. Two crates, three…

As the distance between him and his black-clad companion grew, Grogan squinted, but could discern only Gina's light beam illuminating her heliox bubbles as she moved farther aft dragging her heliox bottle.

"Five boxes," she reported. "But this fuselage tapers toward the empennage. I can barely get enough leverage on this rearmost crate to pry it open."

Unseen, she hacked at box number five, but no sooner had she begun than the hull shifted, the awful sound of rending metal confirming the plane's precarious perch.

"You okay?" Grogan called nervously. "Acknowledge."

"A-Okay," she answered, her breathing labored as she chopped away.

"Forget it, Gina. Come back forward."

Using all of her arm strength, Gina worked the bar under two of crate number five's heavy planks. "Gimme a minute."

Placing her back against crate number four, Gina pressed both of her feet against the pry bar. She clenched her eyes and pushed against the pry bar with both her legs. Finally, one large plank yielded and splintered.

Head first now, she peered into crate number five. "It's another engine. Stripped down, ports Cosmolined, same as the first, except untouched."

"What's your position?" asked an increasingly worried Grogan.

"Tail cone, working forward, crate number four now," Gina said as another board yielded, this time more quickly. "Same setup. Finned cylinders, twin-row, stripped and pickled. Same, same." With her heliox tank held out in front of her, she maneuvered to the third crate. As the fuselage widened toward the fore section, the tank in her left hand,

Gina had room to leverage her arm, shoulder, and leg muscles against the crowbar.

"Number three has the same setup. One more to go." Her movement and struggles had stirred up the bottom silt. "There's like zero visibility back here."

"All right. Just try and put eyes on whatever's in that last crate, and that's confirmation. We can't hang around at this depth much longer. You're burning gas. Get the hell back forward. And go easy. We're out'a here."

Undaunted, Gina pressed on until the fifth and final radial engine was revealed.

After what seemed an eternity to Grogan, she reappeared forward. Now standing next to the number one crate, Gina said, "Opened them all. I put hands and eyes on five engines. All except this first one were still sealed." Tapping the forward most crate, she held out her left hand, saying, "Give me the camera. If I fold up the light bars, and swim while holding it out in front of me, I can fit all the way aft again. I'll go back through and get a few evidence shots."

"No way," Grogan said. "You're exerting yourself." He checked her gauges. "You're low, and this thing is really teetering. If it goes, you're not going with it."

"We not only have to count five engines, Red, but have to identify them as R-3350s...or the outer shells of same. We'll need pictures for that."

As Gina spoke, she maneuvered the bulky equipment and slid away into the hull just beyond Grogan's reach.

"Just get your shots, then get right back here, Gina. You can't..."

"Goodbye, Grogan." Her words had an ominous tone as she slipped out of sight.

The hull shifted and slid back, hanging farther over the black abyss. Seeing the flash from Gina's camera strobes, Grogan urged, "C'mon, girl, c'mon..." into his mouthpiece, all the while beating his fist against his leg, his racing heart burning heliox.

He moved toward the bulkhead in order that his own body displacement would not shift the center of buoyancy any farther aft.

"Two more engines," her voice crackled in his earpiece as her strobe flared somewhere in the dark cone of fuselage. "That's four boxes, four engines, eight photos."

"Hurry," he said hearing Gina's small grunting as she apparently struggled to pry open the last of the big crates for a better shot.

"Okay. That's number five."

In the flashing strobe light, Grogan discerned that the water was now clouded completely by silt and sandy residue from her cutting and movements.

"Five crates, all identical, radial engines in all of them."

"We're outta time, girl!"

Gina reappeared but had to jerk up short as something snagged.

"Damn, the camera's caught," she said. "Gimme a second."

Grogan moved back inside. "Cut the strap if you have to, then gimme the damned camera." He held out a hand and swam toward the snared diver.

She worked herself free of the camera, and groped for her knife to cut its strap.

With that, the hull let out a horrible scraping sound. It shifted again, this time lifting at the rear and rolling nearly upright. Grogan quickly moved back to his position near the forward bulkhead.

Beneath him, the silt supporting the wreck began falling away, and the fuselage front section contacted the surface for the first time. The hull slid forward, forcing the bulkhead door shut, clamping off Grogan's surface heliox, severing his intercom wire and trapping the divers.

Amidships and on portable air, Gina was busy cutting away at the camera's heavy strap. Her view forward, obstructed by the massive cargo crates and silt, she failed to notice the flailing Grogan. When she raised herself high enough to peer beyond the crates, she realized what had happened. Still gripping the camera, she hurried to her suffocating partner.

She couldn't reach Grogan's position without pushing herself against the forward crate. Fortunately, the hull did not slide, but rocked steeply, each movement accompanied by the hideous groan of tortured metal. After what seemed an eternity, she came free of the obstacles.

When Gina finally got to Grogan, he was suffering narcosis and grinning like a dumb drunk. She pulled away his useless mouthpiece and jammed her own into his mask. After a full minute of buddy-breathing Gina tried to free the bulkhead door, but couldn't budge it. She searched for the pry bar, only to realize that she'd left it outside and out of reach.

"Grogan, where's that screwdriver?"

He either couldn't hear her or didn't care, and he was still too stupefied to decipher her hand signals. She took a frantic drag on her heliox and again stuck it back into Grogan's mouthpiece. Letting him breathe his fill, she then left him and swam up to the opening in the first box.

The screwdriver was there. Reaching for it, she also found the missing rocker box cover. Retrieving both, she returned to Grogan, and quickly fed him her mask. After a few gasps, she retrieved it, breathed, and stuck the screwdriver into the door's crack of an opening. She pried at it to no avail, and in seconds needed to return the life giving mouthpiece to her partner. It was then that she noticed Grogan's supply hose was jammed into the door's base. She quickly decided she would attempt to pry the door just enough to release it. She did so, and to her immense relief the hose came free. Having jammed the screwdriver into the door's opening, she left it there and turned to testing Grogan's mouthpiece. Heliox was flowing on demand once again. After sticking it into his mouth, she collapsed to the floor. Fatigue struck quickly at this depth.

Exhausted, trapped, her partner useless, Gina looked at her timer and realized they had already been on the bottom for half an hour. Her exertions shortened their safe-time at depth. Though Grogan's hose was intact, the door had apparently severed his intercom wire.

Neither of them were powerful enough to free the jammed door. They were trapped.

She reported their circumstances to Antonio along with what they'd discovered.

The hull shifted again, this time with a more ominous metallic groan. It lifted violently, and as the silty bottom disappeared below its weight, the huge fuselage creaked and scraped and began its death dive to the abyss.

As the massive aluminum tube slid rearward the bulkhead came out of the sand and popped outward like an oil can. The door swung open. Gina simply grabbed Grogan's neck as would a lifeguard, and she held on tight, letting the airplane slip out from under as she and Grogan came through the moving door.

Watching the monstrous hull slide over the edge, and kick-paddling wildly, she fought the suction as the massive derelict tried its best to suck them down with it. To her horror, Gina realized the camera was still inside the plane.

Releasing Grogan, and rather than fighting the suction, she suddenly and despite her terror, allowed the sinking hull's suction to pull her with it, into it, as she frantically paddled, dragging her air tank behind.

Breathing freely, Grogan realized what was happening. He reached for her, but she was gone, sucked down with the accelerating hulk of the fuselage. As diver and wreck vanished into the black depths, he shouted an unheard, "Gina!"

Trying to follow, Grogan was pulled up short by his surface-fed heliox hose. He called for Antonio topside to pay out more hose, but his intercom was dead.

Well below, swimming frantically, Gina raced to catch up with the retreating fuselage. While at once being pulled by the diving hulk's suction and slowed by the air tank dragging behind her, she managed to gain a handhold on the jagged metal of the fuselage's forward bulkhead. The door was wide open and flapping as hulk, camera, and diver descended as one.

Maneuvering inside, Gina reached the snagged camera. Grabbing it, she quickly swam back through the open bulkhead door and was free of the descending wreck.

Struggling to maintain her composure, Gina knew she was far from safe.

In the high-pressure environment now 200 feet down, she realized with every ache in her small body that an ascent to safety would need to be very slow. She knew only too well the consequences of doing otherwise.

Affixing the heliox tank to her shoulders and clipping the camera strap to her utility belt, she began her agonizing rise back toward the distant light and an anxious Red Grogan when her heliox ran out.

Fighting back panic, Gina was seconds from asphyxiation. She could not reach Grogan and the surface supply hose without a rapid ascent. Either way, through asphyxiation or the bends, she was going to die.

Rising too slowly to cover the now 70 feet remaining between her and the surface hose, Gina realized she was sucking uselessly at the vacuum of her tank. She removed her face mask and tried not to gasp, not to inhale water. That would come soon enough. For now, every rushing second was precious.

Concentrate on a slow, timed ascent, she thought. Avoid rapid decompression; avoid the insufferable deadly writhing, blood-boiling agony of the bends. If I'm going to die anyway, she thought, I choose to die by drowning.

Finally, as the seconds ran out, her head tilted back, and as she rose Gina Ferranti accepted the coming release of stupor. She closed her eyes, opened her mouth to fill her burning lungs with water and release, and she breathed deeply.

Heliox!

Sensing the divers' distress, Antonio had fed Grogan more hose, and he had reached Gina and was holding his mouthpiece to her lips. Now, placing both hands around the mask, Red motioned his partner to breath slowly.

As her poise and muscle coordination returned, they resumed a slow ascent, buddy breathing until they regained the top of the underwater mesa.

Sitting atop the Nelson Bank, both looked warily at the trench formed when the huge hulk had slid away, the shapes in the sand being the only trace of an airplane ever having been there.

With agonizing slowness, but clearly back in control, they ascended together until first they could make out the long, slender black shadow of Strait Shooter's keel above. Finally they saw daylight, and were soon breaking free of the water and into Antonio's and Garodnik's powerful hands.

The boat was rolling 30 degrees, and the mate lifted Gina to the deck first and sat her down. Rain was falling in sheets now, driven by a vicious northeasterly wind.

Turning his attention to Grogan still in the water, Antonio did not notice Gina trying to stand unaided on the pitching deck.

As her knees buckled, it was Detective Garodnik who grabbed her shoulders and carefully placed the exhausted diver on the padded bench running the length of the boat's stern.

"Take your time, Ms. Ferranti," he said. "You're safe now."

Looking up, into the detective's face, she mumbled, "Five engines... But…"

- CHAPTER 17 -

Five-hundred miles to the southeast, an equally disappointed and far more troubled St. John Porter stood alone, unarmed and bleeding on the rugged eastern shore of Devils Island.

Hands to his bare, scraped knees, he tried to catch his breath after having run a half mile to escape the monsters holding the pale woman prisoner in Cegato's stone fortress.

Hearing muffled voices, the self-styled scout knew he was mere yards from his party's campsite. But the feeling of relief was tempered by dread at the thought of bearing bad news.

Ambivalent, he finally decided he'd face the devil he knew. Stepping into the revealing if intermittent moonlight, he ran toward the voices.

"I seen Cegato," he said to his comrades as he burst upon the campsite. The three men jumped to their feet at the sight of their man. "He's with two females, a big one, brown-skinned with a black braid. Indio by her look. And a small, white woman." St. John cupped his chin in his hands, saying, "Pale skin, black hair to here."

"That's Tina!" Jake said. "Are you certain…?

"Oh, she was dere, alright," St. John confirmed. "But, not by…"

"Enough about that," Chichester said. "What of Cegato? Was he armed?"

"I seen handguns, boss."

"A splendid bit of reconnaissance, St. John. You've done well, very well indeed." Turning to Montoya, the major said, "Distribute the munitions. We'll approach from the east. Surprise is crucial. St. John, you'll…" Chichester stopped speaking. His eyes went to St. John's belt. "St. John," he said, eyes narrowing, "where's your Walther?"

The major stepped forward, looming above the smaller man. "Tell me what you've done, St. John. If you gave us away, your next breath will be your last." As Chichester drew his knife,

Having once witnessed Chichester's loss of control, Jake leapt to his feet and put himself between the volatile Chichester and St. John. "We're not here to murder each other," he roared. "You call yourself a soldier, act like one and hear the man out." Nodding toward St. John while blocking the major's advance, he added, "Tell us what happened, St. John."

"I… I had to stop Cegato. He was gonna kill the white woman."

"So she *is* alive," Jake said, a restraining hand on Chichester's chest.

"I hope so," St. John admitted. "I fell, but I heard a lotta screamin' and gunshots." He glanced at Chichester. "After I lost my gun, I ran back here to warn you."

"I'll should kill you," Chichester growled as he ineffectually pushed against Jake's and now Montoya's restraint.

"Enough," Jake said, his eyes burning into the major's. "He did his job and confirmed that Cegato is here and he has Swede's sister. So what if he knows we're on him? He's got nowhere to go."

Jake and Montoya exchanged a look. The big man nodded, and they removed their hands from Chichester's chest.

The major shook his arms as if freeing himself of restraints, but the balance of power had clearly shifted.

Jake bent, offering St. John a hand up. "So you fell. That means you didn't actually see Cegato kill Tina Bergstrom, did you?"

"No, but so many gunshots, mon. So many…"

Saddened, Jake offered, "What you did took real courage, St. John. Thank you."

"If the Bergstrom woman is even alive," Chichester surmised, "she's a hostage. And now, with the advantage of surprise gone, Cegato can pick us off one by one."

"Bullshit," Jake contended. "Cegato's probably given up that little fortress already. That means we can catch him in the open. The initiative is ours to take."

"Easier said than done, Silver. This is an entire island of fortresses. There must be twenty abandoned dungeons inland from this beach, each one riddled with cells and catacombs, steel doors, barred windows and stone walls. Plus, the jungle has reclaimed much of the old prison. Cegato can easily move from one ruin to another. We'll be sitting ducks. He'll separate us and pick us off one by…"

Jake interrupted. "That doesn't mean we wait for the sonofabitch to do it. We have to flush him out first."

Chichester paused, stroking his chin in somber contemplation before adding in a sour tone, "Very well, Silver, let's all behave as idiotically optimistic Americans. Let's assume that we reach Cegato's fortress without being sniped. Since you and St. John are so filled with altruistic feelings for the Swede's sister, it's only right and proper that you go first."

"Better than dying of boredom sitting here."

Jake and St. John headed out side by side while Chichester and Montoya followed.

St. John led the party of four along the rocky beach, stopping where the rocks led unobstructed from the water to the stone edifice. There was no longer a light glowing in its single barred window.

"Maybe he's gone," Jake surmised.

Chichester motioned for St. John to make his way across the rocks and take another look into that window.

"I'll go with you," Jake volunteered. "You'll need a lift if you're going to see anything."

St. John nodded his appreciation and the pair made their way up the rocky slope. The bulbous moon still shone intermittently through fast-moving fingers of cloud, propelled by an increasing wind. Both men knew they were exposed to anyone watching from that darkened window.

They made their way up the 200 foot slope of rocky beach at a run. Coming at last to the building's south wall, they stood below the barred opening, trying to catch their breath. The log and rocks that had formed the makeshift platform upon which St. John had stood earlier, lay scattered at their feet.

"Ready?" Jake whispered.

With a nod, St. John stepped into Jake's clasped hands and was lifted high enough to grasp the window's rusted bars. As St. John hung there, Jake crouched to allow the smaller man to stand upon his shoulders. When Jake stood erect again, St. John need only reach in and move the bullet-shredded curtain to gain a clear field of view into the room.

Reaching down, he signaled Jake for his flashlight.

Taking a long, calming breath, St. John again moved the curtain aside. Bracing for a bullet to his face, he flipped on the flashlight. Its small beam seemed to light the world and he switched it off quickly. Calming himself, St. John lit the flashlight again and nervously swept its beam back and forth across the room. The space was empty except for St. John's colorful hat, which remained against the far wall where Cegato had kicked it.

"Nobody home," he whispered to Jake, wasting no time leaping back down.

Turning toward the beach, both men motioned for the others to join them as they made their way to the building's rear. There they found the door left ajar, signaling a hasty exit. Jake cautiously stepped into the room, his pistol and flashlight in front of him. Chichester followed.

Montoya brought up the rear and took his place in the doorway facing into the room.

Jake turned with a start as St. John scampered around him and across the room to retrieve his hat Lifting it, he found Tina's cell phone in two pieces in its folds.

Pulling the hat over his considerable mane, and holding the cell phone high, St. John turned to face the others that he might exhibit his evidence. Doing so, his expression went from one of satisfaction to that of abject horror. Pointing, speechless, he cast his trembling flashlight beam on a spot behind Jake.

Spinning around, Jake raised his own light only to see Montoya clutching his throat while blood streamed in a torrent through the giant's fingers. As the big man fell to his knees, the merest glimpse could be had of a large, barefoot woman, her black braid trailing behind her as she quickly vanished from the doorway.

Collapsing into the room, the titan was dead before his face hit the floor.

St. John instinctively leapt to his aid, while Jake hopped over the giant's prone form and took chase, with Chichester close behind. After a few horrific seconds, the pair returned only to report that the assailant had disappeared into the wall of vegetation behind the building.

"The savage bitch is gone," the Englishman said.

"So is Montoya," St. John's trembling voice replied.

Jake stepped forward and held St. John's shoulders while the smaller man cradled his dead friend's nearly-severed head against his own meager chest.

Seeing the cell phone, Jake said, "Cegato left this as a decoy." He switched it off, replaced its back, and shoved the now dead instrument in his pocket.

Chichester, looking in upon the carnage, his slender silhouette framed in the doorway with empty darkness at his back, added in a low, knowing voice, "One by one."

Using a knife and the buttstocks of Montoya's Russian-built rifle, Jake and St. John dug a shallow grave among the stand of tall palms. Laying Montoya's body into the trench, they filled it in, but one more unmarked grave among the island's countless others.

St. John handed Jake Montoya's AK-47, the only weapon with a high-capacity magazine, and the pair returned to the stone building. There they found Chichester in detached contemplation. "The main prison yard is farther inland, beyond these trees," he said. "That's where the murdering squaw ran, and that's where we'll find Cegato and the Swede's sister." Realizing Jake was holding Montoya's rifle, he said, "I'll take that rifle, Silver."

"No, Major, you won't."

"Very well. Let's get on with this."

The jungle had reclaimed much of the island, but sky and an intermittent moon could be seen by looking inland through the canopy of trees, indicating a clearing beyond the palms. After struggling and chopping through some 50 feet of thick vegetation, the men reached it.

For a long moment, they stood motionless before the crumbling, vine-covered, stone, wood, and iron ruins spread before them, crumbling vestiges of the ancient dungeon. Here was the heart of darkness: the long-abandoned penal colony aptly called Devil's Island.

Looming silently were rows of decayed, moss-covered cellblock houses, their roofs long gone, jungle vines snaking into and out of their few barred windows. At the center of it all, a walled cistern held a pungent soup of green slime. A large iguana crouched motionless upon the cistern's rim. Watching them, its devilish eyes glowed red.

Perhaps the island's many dead could feel no fear here. But for mortal men, this remained a place of abject terror.

Jake moved first but started at the feel of a restraining hand on his arm: Chichester. The major nodded in the direction of St. John.

Taking his cue before Jake could protest, the scout jumped from the three foot high bluff that marked the end of the tree line and onto the mud of the clearing. Crouching catlike, his weapon poised, his every feature absurdly visible, St. John looked up and down the narrow strip of road running before a row of cell houses. The little band would have to go this way: hunted hunters.

St. John signaled that it was clear.

Jake and Chichester jumped down and crouched beside him, exposed in the clearing.

To Jake, every shadow was a wild-eyed maniac, every frond a gun barrel. He was rightly spooked by how easily the formidable Montoya had been eliminated. Thoughts of the equally, if ostensibly invincible Swede Bergstrom flashed across his mind.

Putting such thoughts behind him, Jake saw no sign of the major. He knew the tactical sonofabitch was back there somewhere. He could almost feel the man's gun pointed at his back lest he waver. Chichester was letting Jake and St. John draw out any possible ambush.

"Petty bastard," Jake breathed.

They pressed forward until St. John held up a hand.

Jake froze as the scout pointed to a spot just off the road. A small and solitary footprint could be seen in the soft earth, its heel mark deeper than that made by the sole. It was made by a woman's boot.

The print looked too perfect, too apparent to have been made accidentally.

"Could be another decoy," St. John said. "But if Cegato was inside lookin' out, we'd already be dead."

As if to validate the scout's words, gunshots erupted, not from the blockhouse but from behind them.

Hit, St. John fell forward as Jake spun to his left and saw muzzle flashes from atop the wall surrounding the central cistern. Raising his pistol, Jake returned fire while pulling St. John up by his shirt collar.

Gaining his feet, St. John bled from the side of his neck. He waved to indicate that he was only grazed and pointed toward the cellblock entry door.

Running for the shelter of the two story cellblock house, Jake rained covering fire in the direction of the cistern wall, allowing St. John time to take shelter inside the stone building's doorway.

Ascending three concrete steps at a run, Jake followed St. John through the arched portal. Inside the cell house, they took up positions on either side of the doorway, their backs pressed against the wall.

Facing inward, a faint glow outlined a portal at the hall's end, otherwise, all was darkness.

It began to rain again.

St. John slowly stood, shining his flashlight down a long corridor.

As Jake reached up to pull St. John back down, the flashlight's glow was met by the deafening sound of automatic weapons fire. The roar was accompanied by blinding white muzzle flashes coming from the corridor's far end.

Before Jake's horrified eyes, St. John's torso was wracked by gunfire as he took the full force and fury of multiple rounds. Propelled jerkily backward, St. John was thrown against Jake in the surreal strobe of a muzzle flash. The pair tumbled back through the doorway and down the concrete steps as Jake ineffectually returned fire.

Once outside, they again began taking fire from the shooter behind the cistern wall. Jake and St. John were trapped in a crossfire.

In the mud and on his stomach Jake alternately led or dragged a limp St. John the few feet to the side of the concrete steps. Sheltered for the moment but with no escape route, Jake made an effort to control his rapid breathing.

He gently leaned St. John against the side of the steps, out of the direct lines of fire, and tried to assess the smaller man's wounds. Unable to use his flashlight, Jake extended his left hand to feel St. John's chest. What he felt was the shredded remains of Montoya's not so bulletproof vest.

St. John was trembling uncontrollably, unable to speak, but he was alive.

"Try not to move," Jake cautioned, though consumed by panic and nauseating dread himself. His newfound friend was suffering badly and Jake could do nothing to help him. St. John had been taken out of the fight as easily as had Montoya before him.

Knowing they were sitting ducks where they huddled, Jake had to act and quickly. Struggling to reconstruct the scene he'd observed, he recalled seeing the staccato movements of a solitary figure behind the gun. The shooter's head and face had been chalk white, as if painted.

That Cegato did not appear above them in the cell house doorway, where he might easily pick them off, could mean he was momentarily unable to leave Tina.

Jake used his knife to cut away St. John's shirtsleeve. Rolling the sleeve into a ball, he took his friend's left hand and helped the injured man hold the cloth against the grazing wound at his neck. It might buy him some time. "I know you're in pain, St. John, but stay conscious," Jake pleaded. Then, cutting the straps of the smaller man's decimated bulletproof vest while trying not to jostle his injured friend, he added, "I'll need to borrow what's left of this vest for a minute."

"Worthless thing…"

Jake rose to a crouch and pulled the Glock from its holster. Pressing the pistol into St. John's free hand, he stepped away.

The smaller man reached out as if to stop him, but Jake, now holding Montoya's AK-47 with some 60 remaining rounds in its magazine, moved toward the front of the building, stopping at the foot of the steps below the entry portal. As expected, gunfire erupted from the cistern, chipping the concrete step an inch above Jake's head. Before he ducked, Jake saw the shooter was Cegato's murderous female accomplice.

Sliding back down, Jake, still exposed, turned to return fire as her bullets whistled just above his head. But before he could take aim and get off a shot, a second shooter opened up from the cistern's far side. As quickly as it began, the firing stopped.

"Got her!" It was Chichester's voice. When the Indio woman had revealed her position in the cistern, Chichester pumped four bullets into her. "Bloody well cut her in two, I did. I'm coming around."

"Cegato's in the cell house," Jake warned. "He'll have a bead on you."

Not knowing Chichester's position or intentions, Jake raised the vest to his chest, holding it in front of him as he rushed the stairs, firing single shots into the empty corridor.

In the light of his muzzle flashes, Tina suddenly appeared in the corridor, stumbling directly into his line of fire. She'd been pushed out of one of the cells and into the path of Jake's bullets.

Shielding her face, Tina fell to the floor. As quickly, Jake raised his gun and stood horrified, helpless, and afraid that one of his shots had hit her.

In that second of hesitation, Cegato reappeared from the same cell, opening fire.

Diving into a cell at his end of the hallway, Jake took cover.

Unable to return fire for fear of hitting Tina, Jake crawled toward the doorway and held St. John's vest out into the corridor to draw Cegato's fire again.

Nothing.

Continuing to use the compromised vest more as a security blanket than a shield, he pulled it to his chest and burst into the hallway, his finger on the trigger. He'd kill or be killed.

But for the rain, only silence.

Tina and Cegato must have retreated into one of the cells or escaped into the rain, now a downpour. Completely exposed, Jake would have but a millisecond of advantage.

He'd spent perhaps another ten rounds. Pressing his back to the cell wall, Jake mustered his courage, desperate for a plan. Through the darkness, he noticed the front of his white shirt was bloodstained.

Frantically patting his torso with both hands, he searched for the wound. Finding none, he realized the blood had come from St. John's vest when Jake had pressed it against himself as a shield.

Examining the thing further, in the dim light Jake's finger found holes and tears, at least one of Cegato's rounds having gone through. It meant St. John had sustained at least one chest wound. The large amount of blood on the vest's back portended a serious injury.

A sudden burst of fire, followed by the sound of running footfalls retreating at the corridor's far end brought Jake back to the present. Rejecting the nearly overwhelming impulse to run, Jake breathed deeply. *The Lady or the Tiger* story flashed across his mind as he stepped into the corridor and made his way silently toward the doorway of the adjacent cell.

Only rusted hinges remained on the portals opening to each cell, the heavy doors having long since been removed.

Rifle and flashlight first, Jake thrust himself into the first narrow space and found the tiny 10x4 cell empty but for a rusted metal frame that must have once supported a mattress.

Jake repeated the action, making his way along the concrete corridor portal by portal, cell by cell. Damp moss and insects underfoot made each step precarious, slippery. He heard a muffled groan emanating from a cell at the corridor's end.

Fearing a trap, Jake forced himself on, cell-by-cell. Finally, flashlight ablaze atop his rifle, he approached the corridor's end. Rifle first, finger tense on its trigger, Jake lunged into the penultimate cell of the twelve.

Reflected in the flashlight's beam was a dirty, disheveled Tina Bergstrom.

Alone in the tiny concrete room on the floor with her legs curled beneath her, the soles of both her boots were muddied. Her jeans and shirt were unbuttoned as if they'd been hastily donned. Her wrists were bound to what remained of the cell's steel bedframe anchored to the floor and wall. Terror filled her expressive eyes and she tried to retreat from the bloodied Jake as he lowered the flashlight to better reveal his identity.

Halting her retreat, she tried to crawl toward him, but was stopped short by her bindings. Despite the gag, the expression on her small dirt-streaked face said she was aware of what was happening. But rather than look only at Jake, as he approached her, Tina's expressive eyes darted from him to the door behind him while she grunted indecipherable sounds through the gag, her chin jutting toward the door frantically, again and again. Jake's eyes followed, seeing nothing. "He's gone," Jake said. "You're safe now."

Kneeling, Jake caressed her face briefly, then checked for injuries. Her green sweater was gone. Her white shirt was grimy though not bloodied. She was trembling, frantic, trying to speak, but able only to shake her head.

"Are you hurt?" he asked while buttoning her shirt and trying to calm her frenzy.

Rather than respond, she pulled away as if frightened of him.

As he tried to release her bindings, Tina was anything but calm. Instead of cooperating, she frantically tried to get away, her struggles making Jake's task more difficult as she gyrated and gestured while grunting indecipherable sounds through the gag and shaking her head or jutting her chin forward.

Jake held out his hand, determined to calm her. "Cegato's gone, Tina. It's me, Jake."

She shook her head frantically and grunted while he struggled one-handed with the knotted gag.

Placing his flashlight on the floor face up to light the room, Jake listened for the sounds of gunfire, confident that Chichester would handle the fleeing Cegato with the same lethal skill he'd demonstrated in killing the man's female accomplice.

Not hearing the expected gunshots, he turned back to Tina.

Jake placed his rifle on the floor at her side that he might better deal with her bindings. "Here, look, I've put the gun down." Moving slowly as not to startle her further, Jake prioritized, and, loosening the gag, turned immediately to untying her wrists. As he struggled with the knots, she yanked her left hand free and quickly lowered the gag herself. With a muffled cough, she pulled a balled-up soiled rag from her mouth and gasped deeply.

Relieved, she coughed, and tried to swallow while greedily gulping the precious air.

"Are you injured?" Jake whispered as he brought his canteen to her parched lips.

Her thirst relieved, recognition slowly overcame disbelief. Tina extended her right hand toward Jake, spreading her fingers tentatively, as if touch would confirm the reality of him. He smiled and leaned in as her fingertips met his cheek.

As Jake worked at untying Tina's right wrist, her eyes flashed again. In a frenzy of sound and motion, she screamed and pointed behind him.

Jake turned with a start, but the specter was already airborne, his white-painted face hideous in the dim light.

With fist raised high, and a long bamboo spike clenched between his teeth, Cegato landed on Jake with his full body weight, driving a knee into Jake's groin while raining blows to his victim's head and face.

Cegato would punish before killing.

On his back, Jake deflected some of the blows while enduring others that he might lift the smaller man as one would press a barbell.

Cegato, his advantage yielding to the larger man's adrenaline-gorged strength, and knowing that his painted skull was about to be smashed against the concrete, grabbed the bamboo spike from his mouth. Gripping it in both his hands, he raised it high above his chalky death's head while his black eyes, mad with bloodlust, remained locked on Jake's.

With teeth bared and a savage growl, he thrust the spike downward.

As he did, a deafening roar exploded next to Jake's ear.

Cegato was thrown backward, the spike flying from his grip as his grimacing face and much of his skull flew away with it, spattering blood, brains, bone and torn flesh against the far wall. The rain of bullets continued as Tina, both hands free now, screamed while pouring fire from Jake's discarded AK-47 into the already dead Emiliano Cegato, chopping his body to pieces, and sending parts of him careening across the cell and into the corridor.

Ten shots, twenty, 30, finally pouring most of the magazine's 50 remaining rounds into Cegato's horribly mangled remains, Tina finally released the trigger to stand triumphant over the ragged vestige of her tormentor, the only sound now that of the rain as it clattered against the buildings tattered tin roof.

Clambering to his feet, Jake approached Tina through the dim propellant fog. His trembling hand gently coaxing her finger from the trigger, he removed the smoking rifle from her grip. "He's dead, Tina," he reassured her. "The woman is dead too. It's over."

Only half listening, the fight gone out of her, Tina fell trembling against Jake's chest, wrapping first one arm, then the other about his neck for support. As she began sobbing, her face to his chest, he stood rigid, awestricken and silent.

Jake dropped the empty rifle, and held Tina to him as her panic slowly ebbed.

Finally, Tina pulled back and her eyes met Jake's. Her hands moved to the sides of his face as if to verify the reality of him.

Her thumb wiped blood from Jake's mouth, her lips parted as if to speak when Chichester's voice broke the silence. "Well done, old Silver," he said, stepping around the carnage, his flashlight's beam washing over Cegato's scattered remains.

"It wasn't me," Jake answered, turning, his words apparently ignored.

"I say, you've deprived me of a long-anticipated pleasure, but it appears you enjoyed yourself a bit more than even I might have. Nonetheless, good show, old man." Turning away from the pulp with a feigned shudder, the major strode toward the disheveled Tina who now stood next to Jake, feet apart, rubbing bruised wrists. Looking her over appreciatively, the Englishman gave forth with a Stanleyesque, "Miss Bergstrom, I presume."

"Give her some space, Chichester," Jake commanded as the three huddled in the narrow Devil's Island cell. "You know what she's been through."

"I'm okay," Tina Bergstrom said, her eyes inquisitively fixed on Chichester. Touching Jake's arm, she asked, "Water… please."

Rather than drink, she poured its cool contents over her uplifted face. Lowering the canteen, she forced a weak smile, and asked, "Who are you?"

"All in good time, my dear." Chichester looked up and down the long corridor. "But right now, we need to be off, and be quick about it."

Taking Tina's arm, Jake gently turned her toward the cell's portal.

Stepping over what remained of Cegato, she winced. "And that, that thing... Who... what is...?" She kicked at what remained of her dead tormentor's head before Jake pulled her away. "No time for that. Let's get out of here."

"The weather's growing worse by the minute," Chichester said. "We'll need to make haste if we're to breach the strait tonight."

Recalling St. John's desperate condition, Jake stepped into the corridor first. "Keep her here, Major, while I check on St. John. I'll let you know when it's safe to follow."

Leaving Tina and the major in the sheltering cell, Jake ran to the corridor's end, and, rifle first, stepped out into what had built to a steady wind-whipped deluge. He leapt down the three stairs to the muddy ground.

"It's clear," he called to Chichester. "Bring me your light."

With Tina on his arm, Chichester came to Jake's position.

"Shine a light down here," Jake said.

As Chichester's light beam fell across St. John's upper body, it was clear that the scout was in a desperate way and failing.

Kneeling beside him in the mud, Jake ripped open St. John's blood-soaked shirt to reveal the sucking chest wound. Cegato's armor-piercing bullets had chipped away at the vest; one had penetrated St. John's upper torso, leaving his caramel flesh soaked in water and blood.

"No exit wound," Jake said, checking St. John's back. "A bullet's still in him."

"He's sucking air through his thorax," Chichester weighed-in, his tone smacking more of resignation than concern. "I've seen such wounds before. His lung is collapsed. He's done for. Let's be off."

Tina knelt beside St. John. "He's the face in the window!" Hurling a disdainful look at the major, she snapped, "He's not done for! How dare you!"

Tina untied the gag from her neck and used it to pat St. John's face before moving the cloth to his chest. "He's barely breathing," she added, softly kissing the dying man's cheek and allowing her face to remain against his for several seconds. Finally, looking up, she said, "He didn't let me die, I won't let him."

"Oh, very well," Chichester said with a wave of resignation. "I have morphine ampoules aboard the plane. Presuming he survives, the pounding we'll endure plying the strait will kill him. Either way, he'll die, you know. Let's be off."

"You heartless bastard," Tina shouted toward the departing major's back. "Who are you?"

"Dammit, woman. Leave him or take him, but let's be off!"

Ignoring the pointless acrimony, Jake's concerns remained with St. John. Lifting him as one would a baby, he made for the trees and the beach beyond.

Catching up, Tina ran beside him in the driving rain, pressing the rag to St. John's chest wound. Walking at a trot, Chichester followed.

When the four finally made their way back to the beach, their tiny boat could be seen bobbing like a cork on the building swells.

"The longer we wait, the worse it's gonna get," Jake said, the rain pelting his face. "I think this crap is coming in from the west. I thought you checked the weather, Chichester."

"Things change quickly in these latitudes," Chichester hedged, jerking a thumb toward St. John and a doting Tina

Bergstrom. "Those two are going to hold us up more than the weather."

"I'm not leaving him," Tina said.

"He's a dead man," Chichester complained. "And the lot of us will be joining him, if we don't get off this sodding rock."

"Everybody needs to shut the hell up, and get in the goddam boat. Now!" Jake bellowed above the wind.

With a look that demanded obedience, Jake lifted St. John aboard before helping boost Tina into place beside their wounded colleague. Chichester moved aft and started the outboard. Jake cast them off before jumping aboard himself.

As soon as they powered away from the beach, the small craft was lifted up and over the first breaking wave. Chichester wrestled its bow toward the south. The propeller raced as the stern lifted from the water and fell hard into the first trough.

"This is as good as it's likely to get," Chichester warned as they climbed the next roller, fell off, and so on. "We'll have to power through. Hold on and mind your stomachs."

Reaching the mouth of the Salut Strait, a wall of black water loomed twenty feet above and ahead of their small craft.

"We're in the surge," Chichester shouted. "Hang on!"

Faces to the driving rain, Jake and Tina each wrapped an arm around St. John's torso while gripping the boat's wooden seat with the other as the tiny runabout lifted and turned hard to port. Listing some 60 degrees on the towering wave front, they nearly capsized as the bow was tossed northward while Chichester fought to maintain a southerly heading.

Tossed hard to port by the massive wave, rather than fall back they crested the roller stern-first, spun full about to starboard, and tumbled into the next trough.

Chichester masterfully powered the craft ever-so-slowly southward. Pushing the engine to its limit, he made what headway he could before the next liquid assault pounded them over and backward yet again.

With the craft taking on more water with each monstrous wave, they were riding lower in the sea. Shouting above the roar, Jake told Tina to lay her body across St. John's and hold to the seat with both arms. Releasing the wounded man, he moved forward to begin bailing water from the bilge using the hand pump. Unable to lower the water level, at least Jake's strong and frantic pumping stemmed its rise.

After what seemed an eternity, they broke out of the straits and into open water.

Jake remained at the pump as Chichester powered them forward. Eventually the five mile reach became four. The waves diminished as they moved into more moderate seas. When finally South America's windswept north coast came into view, they knew they were going to make it.

- CHAPTER 18 -

"Pressure's down, Skipper," the Strait Shooter's first mate, Antonio announced as the dive boat pounded its way northward. "Ninety-two-hundred and falling fast."

Breaking out of the churning Caribbean, the stout craft was racing toward the Florida Straits and relatively safe harbor while all aboard shared the sting of disappointment following upon their noble, if fruitless efforts on the Nelson Bank.

"I'm not real confident we'll beat this weather to the mainland," the mate cautioned. "I say we make for Key Largo."

"Agreed," said Grogan. "And Antonio…"

"Aye, Skipper."

"She'll hold. So drive her like you stole her," Grogan ordered, knowing full well that they'd stayed on station too long. "Every mile counts now."

"No worries," Antonio shouted, aware that Red Grogan was still suffering some lingering effects of narcosis. So, as Antonio wrapped a stout leather belt about his waist and hooked its ends to the helm turret, he added, "I got her, Captain. Stay below and get right. It's gonna be all hands, soon enough."

Below deck, the skipper made his report. "I know the numbers don't lie, Mrs. Silver, but there were five engines on that wreck. Gina pried open every crate and put eyes on their contents. Radials, twin row, all the same, every crate. Five of 'em."

Garodnik piped up, "You say the first crate was already broken open when you reached it. Did that happen in the crash?"

"I don't think so," Gina said from where she sat, elbows on knees, on the bench along the radio room's wall, her fit body itself struggling to recover. "We found a screwdriver and ratchet wrench inside the open crate. There was no trace of anyone having been down on that wreck ahead of us, so it looks to me like the crate had been pried open before the crash."

Listening intently, MJ was examining the rocker box cover Gina had brought back. "Why did you bring this up?"

Grogan, gestured toward Gina. "She's OCD."

"It has a number stamp," Gina said. "That could identify it as part of a Wright R-3500, might even trace its provenance." She cast her gaze at Grogan, while directing her remarks to MJ. "When you aren't sure what you're being paid to find, you bring up whatever you *have* found."

"Thank you," MJ said. "You both did an extraordinary thing." Turning to Garodnik, she held up the little oblong rocker box cap and asked, "Patrick, can fingerprints survive a few days in salt water?"

The detective looked at the cap's glossy black surface, and said, "Hell, I've seen latents survive a week in the Gowanus Canal's salt water."

Familiar with New York City's grossly polluted waterway, Gina joked, "That brown stuff might be salty, but sure ain't water."

"I have my kit," the detective smiled. "Let's dust this thing and see what we got."

Garodnik took elimination prints from everyone, then carefully dusted the cap's surfaces. A wealth of prints emerged. Many overlapped. The cop photographed them all, then had Grogan email the digital images to the crime lab in New York. He sent an email to Commissioner Yost, hoping it might accelerate the process, even knowing he'd allowed the corruption of potentially important evidence.

"We're heading back to the Keys, folks," Grogan's deep voice announced.

Garodnik closed up his kit, and flopped down next to MJ. "If there were five engines on that wreck, and if the airplane in question wasn't built to lift that weight and Bergstrom knew that...well, then I say there weren't five R-3350 engines on that wreck."

"You heard the divers, Patrick. They have pictures."

"Right," Garodnik concurred, "but suppose they were not R-3350s. What if they were just another, lighter type of engine?"

"The rocker box cap might settle that," MJ said. Pausing then, she reconsidered. "Patrick, what are airplane engines made of?"

"Aluminum, mostly."

"Even the insides?"

"No," Grogan asserted, interrupting with a wave. He'd been sitting at the computer behind the two men, listening quietly. "Much of the insides are tempered steel. Why?"

"So the outsides would be light, but the insides heavy?"

"That could explain something that was curious," Grogan muttered, "but in my narco-fog I forgot all about it." He slapped his forehead. "Christ, how could I...?"

Both his clients faced the captain.

"Of course!" Gina added, anticipating Grogan's revelation. "I reached my hand into the cylinder bore. There was nothing to obstruct my reach, and there was no piston, rod, nothing inside the thing, just a big empty bore...a dummy."

Gina jerked a thumb toward the captain, and grinned. "Kind of like..."

"I'll toss you over, I swear I will." Grogan warned lightheartedly.

"So it was a dummy cylinder?" Garodnik noted. "That has to be where Bergstrom found the dope he was holding when they fished him outta the water. He wasn't smuggling. He was duped. He must have thought he was transporting engines, legal as lemonade."

Gina piped up, "Red, didn't you feel something soft at the bottom of the sleeve?"

"Yes, I did," Grogan answered, adding, "Each engine has eighteen cylinders. If they're all dummies…"

"Dummies filled with dope," MJ observed. "The Maltese Falcon, Madonna statuettes, oil drums, even the stomachs of blonde teenage runaways from Iowa, deceivers have been secreting illicit stuff in innocent-looking vessels since the Trojan Horse."

"If there were five hollow engines in that wreck…" Grogan mused.

"Yeah," Gina calculated, "that's 90 cylinders full of dope."

"And then some, I'll wager," Grogan added. "If you're gonna destroy an engine just so you can fill the cylinders with dope, why not fill the whole goddam engine with dope, crankcase and all? That'd be worth a helluva lot more than an old run out radial. I figure these things go for about a-hundred grand each, more or less. And that's only if they're rebuildable."

"Yeah," Antonio asked, almost rhetorically, "but why destroy valuable engines, even run-out ones? Why not just pack the dope in shipping crates?"

"Your question answers itself," MJ observed. "Because, for one thing, they probably knew Swede Bergstrom wouldn't be fooled by that. He'd refuse to fly narcotics. But more than that, they knew that any sensible US Customs agent would ask himself the same question: who'd be crazy enough to ruin a valuable engine by filling it with contraband?"

"And, conversely," Garodnik posited, "what agent would be crazy enough to risk his career by taking one apart? Even the flange caps were Cosmolined. That'd fool the sniffer dogs. And, don't forget, Bergstrom was on an FAA flight plan. He looked squeaky clean."

"Hide in plain sight," Grogan concurred.

"What would that much coke be worth?" MJ asked, judiciously avoiding any mention of the Analog, lest she send Garodnik on another rant.

Garodnik ran the figures in his head. "Uncut, we're talking tens of millions, several tens of millions."

"But, using the same logic," Grogan asked, "why would Bergstrom stop flying the plane mid-course, then leave the cockpit and go aft to open one of those crates and start taking the damned engine apart to begin with? Was he crazy?"

"Maybe Leif Bergstrom was crazy like a fox," MJ said.

His detective's instincts on full tilt, Garodnik prompted, "Where are you going with this, Counselor?"

"Leif was an experienced pilot," MJ said with a nod of appreciation. "He was also a man who'd been working around old airplanes for a long time." Turning to Gina, she asked, "Would a pilot like that know what an R-3350 weighed?"

"Perhaps," Gina added. "But that's not something a pilot would necessarily know firsthand. Like I said earlier, the loadmaster would've given him the weight of each package and the CG moment before takeoff." The diver paused a moment, before adding, "Are you thinking what I'm thinking?"

MJ, having recalled Gina's having described Bergstrom's outfit at the time as...*not exactly Federal Express.* "I'm thinking Leif Bergstrom got suspicious. Suppose he put the plane on autopilot, went back, and opened up that rocker box. Had himself a look-see. When he didn't see rocker arms, he kept digging. Yanked the jug..."

"Bergstrom's airplane was a Curtiss Commando," Gina postulated "Suppose it was powered by a pair of R-3350s?"

All heads turned.

"Good pilots have good instincts. Bergstrom might have realized his airplane was reacting as if it were lightly loaded. That would conflict with what his instincts told him about his cargo. He would have an operating manual on board, maybe even a maintenance manual for the engines. Suppose he got curious and looked in the book. It might tell him what an R-3350 weighed. Hell," she added, "if I suddenly thought I had a weight and balance discrepancy and flying into a U.S. Customs inspection, I'd start ripping those crates apart too."

MJ smiled and the women shared a fist-bump. Unnoticed, a post-it note from her pocket had stuck itself loosely to the back of the lady lawyer's hand before fluttering to the floor.

The detective retrieved the scrap of paper from the deck.

"What's that?" MJ asked, taking it.

"Fell out of your pocket."

MJ looked it over. There were numbers scribbled on it. Her brow furrowed as she tried to recall where she'd seen it. She read the scrawl: 9/15 0330Z 25.810052 -80.239695.

MJ was about to toss it when she recalled where she'd seen the scrap before; it was the post-it note that had been stuck to a corner of the bill of lading she'd swiped from Peterson's office. It had still been attached to the Customs form when she'd heard Gretchen's footsteps approaching, panicked, and jammed the papers into her pocket. "Damn it!" she uttered, reading the scribblings again. "Looks like nothing," she added, and passed the scrap around.

"I'm not so sure," Grogan said when the paper came around to him. The lone letter Z had grabbed his attention. Focusing on it seemed to put the rest into context. "If I consider 0330Z to be navigation jargon for 3:00 a.m. Zulu, or Greenwich Mean Time, the rest of this this falls into place

Excited, he moved to the whiteboard across the room and transcribed what was scribbled on the Post It note.

"Look," he began. "If 0330Z is a time hack, then the 10/15 immediately before it could mean October 15th. The numbers following are clearly geographical coordinates, precise latitude and longitude. They're describing a location in south Florida." He walked across the room. "If I punch them into this navigation computer, these numbers will yield a fix accurate to within a few feet."

Grogan leaned across MJ's shoulder to access the navigation computer's keyboard. All eyes were on the screen as the exact location of the coordinates came up.

"Miami, just like I said," Red Grogan said, pleased. Without hesitation, he typed a few more keys, correlating the coordinates with the boat's imaging software. Within seconds, a map appeared on the screen. It had a teardrop shaped marker on the location Grogan sought. "I'll zoom in," said Grogan.

Another map came up, this one a clear pictorial. Grogan zoomed in, his expression puzzled. "It's a recycling yard, y'know, a place where they crush old cars and and trucks then grind 'em up for the steel." The captain paused a moment, contemplating. "Could that mean something's going to happen at the location described by those coordinates at 10:00 o'clock tonight?"

"It's a junkyard?" a disappointed Garodnik said.

Her trained eyes ever vigilant for airports, Gina chimed in, "Maybe it's more than that. It's near Miami International Airport. They always seem to put places like that near big airports, makes for a nice view coming in. This one is stupid close, though, right off the approach end of runway Two-Six-Left. That could be significant."

"It's all grist for the mill, I guess," Grogan said, and printed the map, including the street address on Northwest South River Drive. He handed it to MJ. "Need anything else?"

"No." MJ said, disappointed. Just the same, she took the map, address, and Post It note from Grogan and thanked the captain for his troubles before returning it all to her briefcase. "A junkyard," she mused. Before closing the briefcase, MJ handed the cap over to Garodnik. "So what does it all mean, Patrick?"

Looking over the small black object, the detective said, "Put this whole cylinder ploy together with the bill of lading and it means William Peterson knew something about what was going down here."

"Don't you mean Guillermo Pedro Filho: aka William Peterson?" a slightly smug MJ said.

"Okay," the detective relented, "let's just say our chameleon."

"A reptile," MJ said, "how fitting."

"Under that alias, Peterson must have set up a phony Brazilian company," Garodnik deduced "and is using his Homeland Security office as a cover to run drugs. But, his plan began to unravel when Bergstrom crashed."

"Exactly," MJ agreed. "Since the Curtiss was an American-built aircraft, he had to change the bill of lading to say something an NTSB inquiry would believe, and worse, the insurance underwriter. He changed it from five engines to three."

Garodnik picked up MJ's file from the console, the one Will Yost had compiled on William Peterson.

Garodnik returned MJ's compliment. "And you were right about Peterson."

"I guess so. From the first time I met him I said he's so full of shit his eyes are brown."

"Are they?" Garodnik asked while looking over the file.

"I said it in jest before I'd met him," MJ said, staring idly at the glowing numbers flashing before her on the navigation computer. "But, yes, his eyes really turned out to be brown."

"Not according to his file," the detective noted, sticking the foreign service officer's description in front of MJ's surprised face. "Baby blues, it says here."

MJ grabbed the Peterson file from the detective's hand. Spreading it before her, she opened the folder Will Yost had prepared on Philippe Sinclair. Then she handed it to Garodnik. "Patrick, let's compare notes."

Garodnik nodded.

"If Peterson and Sinclair were both on the same chopper crew…"

"We have no evidence to support that."

"It'd be easy enough to confirm with DOD. Just humor me. It's a long way back to Key West."

"Okay, for argument's sake, assume they were."

MJ nodded. "We've already determined Peterson's undoing was his decision to descend into an overrun fire base so he could evacuate the ground troops. He did not have to be there. He did it voluntarily… heroically."

"Right. He flew a gunship. He could've stayed aloft."

"But he went down and it cost him dearly. He was bombed by coalition air assets, friendly-fire."

"Right. It scarred his face up. Incendiaries, fuel, who knows?"

"Suppose Sinclair was on Peterson's chopper crew." MJ held up a hand to stop Garodnik's interruption. "If Peterson got cooked, maybe his crewmen did too. Right? Maybe their whole gunship blew up."

Garodnik looked through Sinclair's file. "Yep. Sinclair was wounded too. He took multiple frag wounds to the head and upper body. Doesn't mention burns. So they were probably not on the same crew."

"Head wounds? What date?"

"Seven August, '91."

MJ looked at the date of Peterson's injury. "Bingo!"

"Keep talking," Garodnik said, leafing through the Sinclair folder.

"Suppose Philippe Sinclair was a member of Peterson's crew. Isn't it possible, even likely he'd disagree with his hot-hero commander and not want to go down into an overrun fire base just to pick up soldiers

"If they were Iraqi troops? I'd say more than likely."

"And if that action resulted in Sinclair's permanent disability and disfigurement, he'd probably be bitter toward his hot-hero commander. Don't you think?"

"I think he might hate his hot-hero commander with a burning passion."

MJ nodded. "Let's say Iraq is behind Peterson and Sinclair, and even Jake and Bergstrom too. Let's pretend it's 2003. A body's found in the trunk of Sinclair's car, and the car is stashed in the woods on Yerba Buena Island under the Bay Bridge. The body was mutilated. Right?"

"That stiff was killed about ten different ways. A regular trunk music symphony. Head crushed into fragments, fingers cut off, teeth knocked out, set afire..."

"All postmortem, if I recall."

"Right. Cause of death was listed as lethal injection of heroin."

"If we look over the autopsy report, I bet we'd find that the head damage inflicted postmortem destroyed exactly those parts of the victim's skull where the coroner would have found war wound scars..."

"But if Sinclair's still around, then who's not?"

"Ole blue eyes, the real William Peterson."

"Whoa, there..." Garodnik said. "With all due respect, Counselor, you gotta get off that. We got two separate cases here."

"Why, Patrick? We've been tiptoeing around him long enough. I made him for a crook after one meeting. The manifest confirms it." MJ paused. Her respect for the detective was boundless. She would soft-pedal her theory. "Consider this, Patrick. Back in '03, Philippe Sinclair was a man beset with problems. He was being hounded by the cops. Leif Bergstrom was back and had probably threatened to kill him if he kept sucking around Christina, or maybe even if he remained in Stockton. Sinclair had to disappear. Now just suppose his chopper commander from the war, who's now his VA counselor—a nice, naive guy by the name of William Peterson—was leaving Stockton at about the same time. He was just transferred to a new job, a job in another government agency, this one in far off Washington, D.C. Suppose Peterson had already taken all the tests, the background checks, lie detector tests, fingerprints from his VA hire. Suppose he had nothing to do but pack his car and leave Stockton for DC?"

"You expect me to buy Sinclair bumping off Peterson and taking over his life at precisely the right time?" Garodnik said, shaking his head. "He'd be recognized as a different guy the minute he showed up at the new job."

"Not so fast, Patrick," MJ deflected the assertion. "Suppose a new cop started in your precinct. If you were told before he arrived that his face had been burned in combat, would you stare at him when he finally got there? Check his eye color? Would you look in his folder, check out his old ID photo–presuming you even had such a photo in this age of employment non-discrimination? Would you then accuse him of posing as some other guy whose face was all burned up?" MJ paused while Garodnik pondered.

"Look," Garodnik cautioned, "This guy is no slouch. He's a director at Customs and Border Protection. He's been vetted to within n inch of his life. Taking on a guy like that is not gonna be a cake walk... and you, Counselor, you're already painted as a radical."

"You'd better call your boss, Patrick. Because taking the bastard on is exactly what this radical intends to do. It's time to have Mr. Director Peterson, or whatever his name, rank, and serial number is, picked up and brought in for a little unfriendly Q and A."

Garodnik was already dialing. On the other end, it was picked up on the first ring.

"This is Portlock!"

"Hello Chief, it's Lieutenant Garodnik. Sorry to bother you at home, but…"

"I been trying to get you for an hour, Garodnik! What's with this marine operator bullshit? Where are you?"

"I'm sorry, sir, I left word. It must be the circuits."

"Look, Garodnik, the lab called about a cargo manifest you sent them. You know, the one that government guy Peterson's secretary…uh, mistakenly gave to MJ Silver…the supposed original."

"Yeah," Garodnik said. "I know there was no reason to tie up a technician to check a document from a federal officer but I had a hunch. I'm sorry. I didn't think you'd care."

MJ cut in. "Put the chief on the speaker, Patrick."

Garodnik flipped a switch and Chief Portlock's booming voice filled the radio room. "Christ, Lieutenant! I'm not chewing you out," he said. "I was trying to reach you so I could tell you about the prints."

"Good morning, Sunshine," MJ chimed into the speakerphone.

"Sir, the prints?" Garodnik asked sheepishly, grimacing.

"Yes," the chief responded, "the latents on the bill of lading from William Peterson's office file. They came up funny, so we had the FBI dust his office."

"What do you mean *funny*?"

"There were no fingerprints on that document or anywhere else in Peterson's office matching his IFBB prints."

Garodnik spoke up, "Was the space wiped?"

"No," Portlock answered. "That's not what I mean. We lifted about 80 latents from Peterson's office, his personal effects. Figured most of 'em for eliminations. The only latents that matched those on the bill of lading, came up as the prints of a small-time moke who turned up as a little trunk music on some island off Oakland, California, like twenty years ago. So how is it that prints–fresh prints–of some dead shitbag are all over this G-man's office, but not a single print from the G-man, himself?"

"How'd you match the prints?" asked MJ.

"Moke was booked and cut loose way back in 1998. That, plus the burned-up face matched old Army records from Walter Reed of the same guy."

Looking squarely at MJ but directing his question to Portlock, Garodnik said, "I don't suppose that allegedly dead shitbag's name was–or maybe I should say, is—Philippe Sinclair?"

"That's right," Portlock said, surprise edging his voice. "You buried my lede. How the hell…?" Portlock paused. "Hold on, Garodnik. Are you thinking Stockton PD closed this for an easy clear?"

Rather than answer, a frantic MJ barked into the speakerphone. "Where's Peterson right now?"

"In the wind," Portlock said. "His secretary said he'd been in the office except for Tuesday and Wednesday. He'd been in DC those days. Nonetheless, since you called him a person of interest, we did a dump on the building's access control system, just to confirm."

"You haven't lost a step, you old dog," MJ said. "Keep talking."

"On the day he's supposed to be in DC, a Jersey DOT camera has his government plates at the turnpike tolls twice that day. Northbound 8:07 pm, Tuesday, and southbound again at 2:12 a.m. Wednesday…"

"Don't tell me," MJ posited, "Exit Seventeen?"

"Yeah, Lincoln Tunnel Tuesday night. Got back on the pike at two in the morning, Wednesday, off at the Delaware Bridge little past five that same morning. Couple of security cameras have his GI car headed back to DC. We're trying to locate him now, but he's not answering his cell. TSA has him boarding a flight to Miami earlier this afternoon. What's going on here, MJ?" asked Portlock.

She did not answer, a look of utter horror consuming her face, realizing this information placed Sinclair, aka Peterson, in New York City around the time of Cassandra McRea's killing.

"Look, MJ," the chief was urging, "the good news is, we have security video of what could be Jake and the female unsub we make for Tina Bergstrom. It puts them both out of the country at eleven o'clock Tuesday night. That could clear your son of the Cassandra killing and put it squarely on this Sinclair AKA Peterson."

"It's not definitive," MJ said. "The prints on the dagger are a plant. So somebody's gonna want him dead before he can prove his whereabouts. If Jake is still alive, time is running out."

Garodnik cut in. "Sir, do you have time and place for Peterson on the following morning?"

"Do you mean Wednesday, right after the Cassandra killing?"

"Yes. Wednesday morning."

"Yeah. He's back in the Homeland Security office in DC."

Garodnik's lips clenched and he tapped his fist on the counter several times.

"Is that it?" Portlock said.

"Yes, chief...and it's plenty Thank you."

"Listen," the chief said, speaking to MJ now. "I'm happy to do this blood-hounding for you but you gotta let me in on it now. What're a dead punk's prints doing in a federal executive's office? Why's that person's government automobile and key card place him in New York when his assistant says he's in DC? I'm going to have my contact at the FBI see if he can pull the GPS, but I don't want to give those Homeland assholes any encouragement. I had to call in a lotta favors just to get those keycard times but this doesn't make sense, kiddo."

"It does to me," MJ said, now certain that killing Cassandra McRea, and doing it cartel-style was economics, pure and simple. Implicating Jake in a drug-related homicide—and by association his activist mother—could only be intended to derail Common Cause, setting its legalization efforts back to square one and John Q. Public's self-righteous furor would be certain to keep cocaine's street value high, and it's import curbs tighter than ever. If the so-called Analog turned out to be real, that would be a business strategy as brilliant as it was brutal. "That's the only part of this that *does* make sense. It makes horrifically perfect sense, and it establishes motive for murder. I'll explain when I see you. Meantime, I'm going to ask you to keep this in the family for just a little while longer."

When MJ gestured toward Garodnik that the latter might terminate the call, the detective had that look on his face, a look she'd come to know only too well. "What is it, Patrick? Spill it before your head implodes."

"Well, Counselor," Garodnik began, "at the start of this thing, I interviewed Jake's colleagues..." He paused to consult his notes. "There was a captain..."

"Yeah, Bill Gance," MJ said.

"Right," Garodnik said, reading. "Captain Gance told me he'd arranged for a private jet to take Jake and Leif Bergstrom's sister to Port au Prince to ID Leif's body."

"Were they supposed to meet Peterson there?"

"No, and Homeland Security had no record of any such meeting. Besides, we have him in DC that morning."

"So somebody's lying?"

"I'm gonna go out on a limb, here, Counselor," Garodnik said, placing a hand on MJ's shoulder. "You're gonna call me paranoid, we know now that the real William Peterson is a missing person. Now, knowing that, suppose, just suppose Christina Bergstrom knew Sinclair, acting as Peterson, would be in DC that morning, and she decided to get to her brother's body without him, using Jake as her foil."

"You're still clinging to your conspiracy theory. You still think Christina and Sinclair were colluding."

"It's worth considering. Suppose she sent Peterson-Sinclair to NY to plant the dope in Jake's apartment, knowing Jake wouldn't be there, while she dragged Jake to Haiti, further implicating him while cutting Sinclair out of whatever she was looking for on Leif's body?"

"Oh," MJ said, "so Christina Bergstrom has now been promoted to criminal mastermind. How would Sinclair even know where Jake lives? It's absurd."

"A Homeland Security officer, an exec at that, would know where everybody lives," Garodnik said. "Plus, don't forget Counselor, I've been to your son's place. No doorman, nothing. With a little creativity, anybody could get in there. All an intruder would need to do is get into the lobby, get up to the apartment, knock on Jake's door, or jimmy its lock, and bingo. Maybe McRea though it was Jake coming back. He left a key, she might have thought it was his only one, something like that."

Knowing her confirmation-bias caused MJ to initially reject the detective's conspiracy theory, she stared at the Post-It note again. Reading the geographic coordinates written there, she suddenly sat upright. "Captain Grogan, get me to someplace with an airport!" she shouted, leaping from her chair, surprising everyone as she and clamored to the bridge.

"The closest one is Port au Prince," Grogan advised. "But that's already behind us. Not that it matters. With this weather, it'll be closed by the time we got there. You'll be stranded."

"Okay, then how fast will this boat go?"

"We're running full out now, ma'am," Grogan shouted, his bellow barely audible above the din of the Strait Shooter's screaming engines. "We're making 45 knots."

"Are you willing to risk a crossing with a hurricane approaching?"

"That decision's already been made. I filled our tanks last night. We're still in front of this thing, and I'm ahead of you, as well, Mrs. Silver, ma'am. We're making for Key West and home right now, have been for the past hour. It's gonna be a rough ride, but I'm not about to get you weathered in down here for three days. We'll put in at Key West by about eight o'clock tonight. There should still be time to batten down and get across the causeway."

"Too risky," MJ said. "Tell me, Captain, can you make straight for Miami instead?"

- CHAPTER 19 -

As the small boat carrying Christina Bergstrom and her rescue party made landfall on Guiana's north coast, Jake Silver lifted a badly wounded St. John up in his arms, and wasted no time leading Tina Bergstrom back toward Kourou's Airport and the waiting plane.

Dwight Chichester, however, let himself fall behind. Once out of earshot, the major pulled the satellite phone from his pack. Protecting the instrument from the elements, he waited to hear the click that confirmed the connection. "It's done, Filho. Cegato's dead, and I have Bergstrom's sister. Cegato stripped her naked, tortured her, searched her things, even opened her cell phone. She does not have the chip. So what would you have me do with her?"

"Bring her to me, Chichester," said the despised voice. "If you want to save your miserable life, you'll bring the devious bitch to me. I want her alive. And," here Filho stressed his every word, "you'll bring the sample. We'll have to give whatever's left of Franz's analog to the Russians. You do have the remaining sample aboard your airplane, do you not?"

"*Give?*" Chichester balked.

"Yes, *give*, thanks to your bumbling," Filho admonished. "The Bergstrom bitch was our last hope. It's clear now, she knows nothing. That means we give up the product. The Russians can cut it ten times and still make millions. Eventually they'll analyze it and make billions—what could have been our billions but for your incompetence. Perhaps I should have them cut you ten times while they're at it."

As he considered Filho's insane demands, Chichester knew that within hours a monster storm bearing down from the Atlantic would plunge the entire region into chaos. The winds could reach 100 knots at low altitude, propelling hail the size of oranges at anything daring to venture aloft. "We've wasted another day goose-chasing this woman, Filho. Meantime, things have changed. We're in a bloody cyclone. Do you expect me to navigate an airplane through a category-three storm while evading American coastal radars, Aerostat balloons, and the picket planes they have all along their Gulf Coast and bust the ADIZ just to satisfy your mad whim?"

"It's that or your life," said Filho. "This *cyclone,* as you call it, is a blessing. It will keep everybody grounded... everybody except you, your new pilot, that double-crossing bitch, and a crate containing what's left of our treasure. Tell me I'm correct."

"Flying into a category three, maybe four on seventy-five year old wings is madness!" Chichester said, ignoring Filho's admonitions while wiping rain from his eyes. "We'll wait out the storm in Kourou."

"And that's where you'll die, Chichester. Leave now and you'll have the entire maritime airspace to yourself. Squawk code 7600 on your radar transponder precisely as you exit the Windward Strait. Stay below 13,500 feet, and make certain altitude reporting is disabled. I've seen to everything else. You'll be identified but not interdicted. I've seen to that, as well."

"Hah. Am I to believe you have that kind of influence with American border security, too? It's madness, Filho! The risk..."

"You have a capable pilot. With him, you can handle it. If not, you'll die like a man at the controls of your airplane. Defy me, Chichester, and you'll die a thousand times at the hands of my Russians. By the way, *old boy,*" Filho said, an unsettling calm in his tone, "I've made a Good Samaritan call to the Gendarmerie Nationale in Cayenne, French Guiana. Told them of a plane crash at your aerodrome. I expect they'll be crawling all over your compound by now. Your crippled transport plane and Tretooey's pungent corpse will be hard for them to ignore…as will the bullet holes and spent shell casings lying about. You need to get yourself airborne and away from French Guiana. Trust the coordinates and the instructions I gave you. And when you land–or should I say, when your American pilot lands—at our designated drop, kill him. Shoot him in the head. Do you understand me, Chichester? If he's alive when I come aboard, I'll kill you both."

"Yes, yes," a disgusted Chichester groused.

"And I want the girl alive. She's for me." The connection went dead.

"Major!" Jake called out. "Who were you talking to?"

Without meeting Jake's eyes, Chichester nodded toward his sat phone. "Tretooey's body has been discovered back at the compound. We can't return there, not without facing an interrogation and not with St. John shot full of holes."

Tina approached from behind Jake. "We need to get him medical attention."

"We need to get out of French Guiana," Chichester declared, "or we'll all need medical attention. I say we fly north, Port au Prince perhaps. There are hospitals there. It's St. John's best hope. Listen to me, Silver. Our objectives have been realized. Cegato's dead, and you've rescued Miss Bergstrom. Let's not muck things up now. We need only to make Port au Prince. You can clear yourselves with the authorities and from there make your way to the States and home."

"And you?" Jake asked.

"Just leave me to my devices, Silver," Chichester assured. "You just get us to Port au Prince, then get yourself and that woman to the States as you'd planned from the start. I'm an old Caribbean hand, lad. I'll be fine, as will St. John."

After stopping twice to rest, at last they crossed the Kourou Airport's boundary. The plane appeared ghostlike through the driving rain. All lanky struts and oversized engines, she was rain-soaked but undisturbed.

"Flying into this weather won't be any picnic for St. John," Jake warned Tina.

St. John stirred, groaned, "Don't be talking 'bout me like I ain't here," he said, his words barely audible. "Just do what you gotta do and stop fussing."

Tina, ecstatic at St. John's revival, caressed his cheek. "We're getting you to a hospital."

"Let's get him aboard or he'll drown before the bullet kills him," Jake instructed, reaching for the entry hatch.

While Jake and Tina hoisted St. John aboard, a vastly different concern occupied Dwight Chichester. Filho had lured him into a trap, but the old airplane was tough. With the right man in the left seat she might handle this weather. Chichester knew a landing at a storm-ravaged Port au Prince would be impossible. Once denied landing clearance, he need only suggest to Silver that they should race for the States, just ahead of the storm's worst fury. Already airborne, outrunning the storm was their best option. Plus, such a gambit would ostensibly serve Silver's objective: that of finding Tina Bergstrom and returning her home. It would also cause Jake Silver to fancy himself the conquering hero, returning triumphant—a rescued Tina Bergstrom in tow—to American soil.

If Filho's assurances that he'd handled the US authorities and that they'd cross the ADIZ—the Military Identification Zone unchallenged—Chichester need only keep the two Americans unaware of Filho's plans for them when they arrived at the drop.

Retrieving a crowbar from the plane's forward hold, Chichester busted the lock on the airport's gas pump and filled the wingtip tanks.

As the Marksman accelerated down Kourou's runway, in the rear cabin Chichester prepared a morphine ampoule. With a thrust, he injected the painkiller into St. John's bare leg.

"He's drifting in and out of consciousness," Tina said.

Chichester placed a Scott Airpac on the deck next to her. "Put the oxygen mask on him when we get to altitude. I can't believe the little bloke is still alive."

"And that's how he'll stay," Tina countered.

With St. John left to Tina's tender mercies, Chichester crawled through the small companionway leading from the cabin to the flight deck, and took the seat beside Jake.

As they climbed away from Kourou, wind pelted the airplane and it lurched violently. Wrestling to maintain attitude and heading, Jake shouted across the lurching cockpit, "I can't calculate our groundspeed, Chichester. This headwind is killing me."

"This is the tropics, Silver. Storms roll through here like the tides. Try higher."

"Zero-zero with no radio, no flight plan? I'd put other traffic at risk."

"We have a working communications receiver," Chichester corrected. "We can monitor traffic. And buck up, extraordinary circumstances call for extraordinary measures. We're alone in this sky, of that I have little doubt."

"I'm gonna level off at 12,500, but that's as high as I'm willing to risk without cockpit oxygen. Gimme a heading for Port au Prince and try to get a weather report. Use your satellite phone or the ADF. I don't like this sky."

The ADF, or automatic direction finder, is a piece of electronic navigation equipment even older than the plane itself. Rarely used for navigation anymore, a cockpit crew could use it to monitor commercial A.M. radio broadcasts.

Chichester donned a headset and started searching the ADF bands for a signal.

He raised a finger. "I'm picking up a radio station in Port au Prince," he exclaimed. "The storm has gained intensity. It's now a strong category three hurricane, and bearing down on these waters from the southeast. Chichester pressed the ADF headphones tightly to his ears. "Best I can gather is we're still on its western edge. We can outrun it. Turn northwest to three-one-zed."

"A goddam hurricane and you're just telling me this now? Put that thing on speaker."

Chichester did so, but the only voice coming through the static spoke in Spanish.

As Jake took up the new heading, Tina called from the rear cabin, "I'm not sure St. John's oxygen is working."

Jake tried to hold the airplane level. "Chichester, hold her straight and level while I see what's going on back there."

From the co-pilot's seat, the major took the controls, and Jake climbed from his seat and crawled through the companionway into the rear cabin. Kneeling beside Tina, he tended to St. John's mask. Removing it to check the seal and flow, he donned it himself. As he did, he saw St. John force a smile and try to speak but his words were inaudible above the din. There was blood on his teeth.

With oxygen flowing again, Jake adjusted the regulator and returned the mask to a gasping St. John. As he did so, Jake felt the airplane slow as it entered a steep, nose-high bank. Chichester was attempting to gain a more northerly heading. His touch was heavy-handed: too little rudder, too much aileron, either not enough or too much airspeed in the wild turbulence. Suddenly, the plane rolled into a 60-degree bank with the nose pointed upward, causing Jake and Tina to grab the cargo straps holding St. John in place. Chichester's maneuver was sloppy and uncoordinated.

"Level off, goddam it!" Jake shouted to the cockpit.

As the wings maintained a tenuous grip on the rough air, another powerful updraft caught the plane's starboard wing while a downdraft pummeled her to port, rolling the machine inverted, and the aeronautically-slick Marksman fell into a tail-spinning dive for the sea.

"I cannot hold her in this turbulence!" Chichester shouted from the cockpit.

Jake was slammed against the deck as the airplane rolled. Struggling to regain his equilibrium, Jake had to get back to the cockpit before Chichester's ineptitude killed them all.

Reaching the massive main spar separating him from the flight deck, Jake grabbed its top edge, muscled his body over the thing and into the pilot's position, quickly belting himself in.

Seeing Chichester fighting the controls, Jake drove the heel of his right hand against the Englishman's left ear and roared, "Let go of that goddam yoke!"

Right hand on the throttles, left on the control yoke and both feet to the rudders, Jake ever so slowly finessed the screaming machine back to level flight. They'd lost 6,000 feet of altitude and were flying south in stronger, low-altitude winds.

Clawing to regain altitude, Jake put the airplane back on a northwesterly course.

"Is everybody okay back there?" he shouted just as the machine lurched upward, its windshield now being pelted by high-velocity hailstones.

Getting no response above the din, Jake turned to look aft and called after Tina again.

To his surprise, she stumbled up to the spar, obviously alarmed. "It's St. John. He's spitting blood. I think he's choking!"

Before Jake could react, Chichester leapt from his copilot's seat and crawled aft.

Kneeling beside the wounded man, it was plain to see that St. John was suffocating. With blood clogging his airways, the wounded man was unable to draw breath. Chichester pulled the hose from the oxygen tank and fed the gas to St. John directly. Still, he thrashed against his restraints, frantic, unable to aspirate.

Careful not to apply chest pressure, Chichester held the frantic man down and removed the oxygen hose. He instructed Tina to try mouth-to-mouth while he restrained the patient.

Their efforts, however persistent, seemed to little avail.

Tina and the major could not know that the bullet in St. John's chest had dislodged during Chichester's turbulent loss of control. It had found the wounded man's heart. The chest contractions pressed the errant projectile against his right pulmonary artery, collapsing St. John's functioning lung, slowly suffocating him.

After five minutes of frantic attempts to resuscitate, it was clear: St. John Porter was dead.

Chichester took Tina by the shoulders and tried to pull her away from her deceased benefactor, but she continued her futile effort. "Get off of me!"

"He's gone. There's nothing more you can do."

Cupping her face in both hands, Tina sobbed violently. "He saved my life!"

Ignoring what he considered female histrionics, Chichester pulled a packing blanket over St. John's body, and again muttered the ominous words, "One by one."

As its northwestward course skirted the storm's outer bands, the plane lurched in the increasingly unstable air. Approaching Cuba, Jake turned her northward, into the Windward Strait, and toward the Florida peninsula. From here, the worst of it would be on their flank.

Chichester wriggled himself back into the cockpit where Jake was using every muscle to maintain control as the tough old warplane was tossed about like a cork. Jake was also listening intently to the ADF, trying to decipher what Spanish he could through the static and pounding of hail against the aircraft.

Seeing the Englishman, Jake shouted, "Port au Prince is deluged."

Chichester fought his way into the copilot's seat and struggled with his harness. "St. John is gone, Silver. We have only ourselves to save now."

Jake considered his options. They could expect torrential rains and 80 knot north-easterly winds to greet their arrival. Given such conditions and what fuel remained in their auxiliary tank, Jake knew he had but one option. "We have the airspeed to outrun the eye wall, Chichester. But we'll need an ILS beam to get down, and plenty of upwind runway. He pointed to the GPS receiver. "I'll lose my license for this, but give me a heading for Miami. We'll intercept the ILS off runway nine." Suppressing an expression of grim satisfaction, Chichester did exactly as he was told.

- CHAPTER 20 -

Well north of the speeding Marksman's position, Red Grogan was swinging his Strait Shooter into Biscayne Bay. Ignoring the rules of maritime etiquette, Grogan blasted through the sheltered waters of Florida's all-but-abandoned South Channel and did not throttle back until he entered the marina itself.

Sensing calmer waters, his client, MJ Silver, wrapped in a too large yellow slicker, came topside with Detective Garodnik following close behind. Both were awed by the sheer number of glistening yachts rocking on their moorings in the dive boat's wake.

Red Grogan had friends here, and he'd plied one of those friends for a vehicle to be awaiting his arrival. As Gina and Red leapt onto the pier from the still moving Strait Shooter's deck, a marina employee ran toward them through the wind-whipped rain.

"Aye, Gina." The young man shouted to the comely diver while tossing Red Grogan a set of car keys. "You looking so good, *chica*."

"*Tu tambien*, Carlos," Gina replied with a wink and smile as the hood of her black rain jacket blew from her head.

"You two can flirt later," Grogan shouted above the gale. Turning over his .32 Colt in his hand, he asked, "Carlos, will you help Antonio tie-off the boat? Mathew's eye is just 100-miles southeast of here and we're in its bullseye. Is the truck ready to go?"

"Ready and waiting, Rojo," Carlos answered, indicating a red Ford pickup parked next to the office. "I topped it up." With that, the young man slapped his forehead. "Oh, damn. I forgot. It's a crew cab and I have some spear fishing gear on the back seat. Just stow it somewhere. And by the way, Rojo," he added with raised eyebrows as he watched Grogan spin the pistol's chamber before jamming it back into its holster. "I'm not going to ask why you need the pistola, but please, try to bring my truck back without any new bullet holes."

"It has *old* bullet holes?"

"No," Carlos said, making his point as he turned and headed for the boat to help Antonio lash the rocking and rolling craft to a stout cleat while Gina and Detective Garodnik helped MJ step off the pitching deck and onto the waiting dock.

Shaking off their sea legs, crouching against the deluge, MJ and the detective followed Gina as she scampered white shorts and deck shoes, through the downpour toward the red pickup which sat under a madly-flapping and banging Gulf Marine sign above the office door.

Grogan was already behind the wheel with the engine running as Garodnik helped Gina and MJ squeeze into the compact "crew" seat before taking his place next to Grogan up front.

The captain turned to the women, "You sure?"

Gina answered for both. "Forget it, Red," she said, holding Carlos's spear gun in her lap. "As much as I'd prefer to stay right here where Carlos could keep me warm, we all know you'll get lost after driving two city blocks." She turned to MJ who offered a quick validating wink. Gina reached forward. "Hand me the GPS," she said to Grogan. "I'll confirm the coordinates."

Seeing the slightest trace of a grin cross Grogan's lips as the skipper turned to hand his diver the portable GPS device, it was clear to MJ that the two were more than shipmates.

"MJ," Gina asked, "may I have that little note, the one with the coordinates?"

The lawyer opened her briefcase and handed Gina the scrap she'd pilfered from the Homeland Security office. MJ had never expected that so fruitless an encounter would lead to this night and its unlikely group of companions.

"In addition to the coordinates, the note reads *3/15 0330Z*, which is a half hour from now," Gina reported, without looking up from her task. "We got one shot—a long one. Step on it, Red, and hang a right when you pull out of here."

The pickup truck's tires rumbled across the rough boards of the dock as they left the marina for the city's empty streets.

MJ considered the three relative strangers with whom she'd shared these past strange days to be real-life heroes. "You're going above and beyond, all of you. You don't have to risk…"

"Too late," Grogan said, cutting her off while patting his holster. "My crew and I talked it over, Mrs. Silver, and figured we'd already gone too far to turn back. I practically had to chain Antonio to the mast to keep him from coming too. We gotta know how this thing ends."

"No goddam way I'm going back to New York without your son," Garodnik chimed in, checking his .38 Police Special. "Chief Portlock scares me a helluva lot more than some weasel named Peterson or Philippe or whatever else the jerk calls himself."

The detective had not yet encountered the Filho personality.

MJ touched Garodnik's hand. "Thanks, Patrick, for not bringing in the locals."

To her surprise, he squeezed her fingers ever so slightly. "If this thing goes the way I hope it will," he said, "the locals will be involved soon enough, and your Jake will be home safe."

"Only one way to be sure," Red Grogan said, pushing the accelerator down.

As the red pickup hit the rain-soaked streets, Gina added in her best smoky Bette Davis voice, "Fasten your seatbelts, boys. It's gonna be a bumpy night."

As the Strait Shooter's crew and clients followed their GPS coordinates toward they knew not what, unseen in the roiling skies a few miles south of them, Jake Silver, retarded the throttles of his own speeding craft, and descended to 1500 feet. There'd been a periodic hum coming from the ancient ADF receiver very few seconds since they'd crossed into the Coastal ADIZ — the Air Defense Identification Zone— so he suspected they were being tracked. That they were not being interdicted seemed consistent with Chichester's boast that, "it's been handled," whatever that meant.

Crossing the beach at Plantation Key, the old warbird's own GPS showed it to be a mere 60 miles south of her pilot's intended destination: the landing beam and 13,000 foot Runway-9 at MIA.

Tuning the VHF communication radio to Approach Control's frequency, it was apparent that no aircraft were operating in Miami's airport traffic area. The storm had grounded everyone operating below 18,000 feet–everyone save those aboard the lurching Marksman and whatever might be tailing them.

As the Invader descended, the ADF became overwhelmed by ground interference and noise. Unable to discern the periodic hum any longer, he turned the device off. "Tune the nav-head for Runway-Nine's localizer," he ordered. "Does this thing have a glideslope receiver?"

"It does," Chichester assured him.

"I'm getting nothing from ATC."

Both pilots were well aware that if they couldn't talk on the radio, they had only the navigation and intermittent communications receiver to safely guide them down from altitude on the east-west runway's ILS.

"You heard nothing from Approach Control, so you know it's handled." Chichester said, again recalling Filho's cryptic assurances that he'd *seen to it*. "The airspace is cleared, Silver, just like I told you. Neither will you hear anything from the tower. So, fly on."

Chichester's assurances notwithstanding, Jake's clandestine and unannounced interception of the albeit closed airport's pencil-thin ILS beam, was anathema to him as it would be to any responsible pilot.

Jake spent as much time with his eyes trying to penetrate the solid clouds and blinding rain as he did scanning his flight instruments. Sporadic position reports could be heard from other aircraft, all distant, all at high altitude, none traversing this piece of storm-ravaged airspace.

But, the eye of Hurricane Mathew was closing in on them from the south and west, leaving Jake to battle punishing crosswinds from the outer bands of the storm's cyclonic flow.

The winds had already cost them precious fuel. Jake had drained both the wing tip fuel tanks, as well as her mains of every last ounce of gas. The single remaining tank, the auxiliary tank, hadn't a fuel gauge, and it too was probably three-quarters-gone, but still held enough gas to make Miami International. Everything else within range being closed left them little choice but to opt for the long rain and windswept runway.

"The GPS says we're twenty miles out." Even as he mouthed the words, Jake knew all too well that as they descended toward the city, their piece of sky though empty of other aircraft, would soon fill with stone and steel, as towering skyscrapers and radio antennae thrust their lofty way into the ever-more-urban sky. There was only one safe way down, one way to thread the needle. "I'll join the ILS beam at 1500 and shoot a straight-in to Runway-Nine. If I timed that aux tank right, we have another 15 minutes. The winds have cost us dearly."

"Carry on," Chichester said. While Jake concentrated on pilotage, the Englishman headed aft with the radio's microphone firmly in his grip, its cable having been secretly snapped off at the jack to make doubly certain there'd be no transmissions from this rogue aircraft. With Tina watching him, Chichester offered her a reassuring smile while he reached down and, with the auxiliary fuel tank blocking her vision, he did something in the floor just forward of that tank.

In the cockpit, unaware of what was transpiring behind him, his every sense elevated, Jake descended to 1500 feet AGL and listened for the ILS localizer's identifying Morse beeps. With the airport closed, Jake was reasonably certain no other aircraft would venture into Miami's always-on ILS beam. If another—a legitimate—aircraft were to announce its presence, Jake could only gauge such a phantom's position and blindly squeeze his airplane in behind or above it. This was not unlike running across a wide road blindfolded while listening for approaching cars, but Jake had no other options, no other way down without risking a crash and additional casualties on the ground. He watched the crosshairs of his ILS indicator move toward center scale. As a precaution, he intentionally drifted high. All was quiet. At this second of this minute of this hour, he was alone in the roaring black deluge above the sleeping city.

Fighting to keep the plane under control in the punishing winds, Jake rode her throttles, flying the beam downward, blindly threading a course between the towering obstacles he knew were hidden in the raging murk beyond his cockpit's windows. Ever closer to the rain-soaked ground he drove his machine. At 200 feet, pounded by turbulence, they broke free of the dense, hanging clouds. Though the airport was closed, Jake's eyes were greeted by the welcoming flash of runway strobes.

At that jubilant moment, Chichester's face appeared in the space above the main spar.

"Get back there and strap her in, goddammit!" Jake shouted as his airplane lurched and shuddered in 70-MPH headwinds and ground effect.

His eyes glued straight ahead, Jake did not see the Englishman gripping Tina by the neck, and pressing her against the spar. "Listen to me, damn you!" Jake shouted. "We're on short final and I'm fast! You need to strap in and hang on." As the runway's VASI lights appeared through the driving rain, Jake lowered the landing gear and wing flaps. As they crossed the field's boundary, Chichester leaned into the cockpit. Pushing Tina's face into Jake's field of view, her hair clamped tightly in his clenched fist, the wild-eyed Englishman had his pistol pressed against her temple as she fought to free herself from his grip.

"What? Why you…" Jake growled as anger turned to horror. Releasing his seat belt, he turned and lunged at Chichester's gun hand, only to be thrown backwards as the airplane rolled wildly onto its side.

In that instant the wild-eyed Englishman released Tina and stretched his upper torso over the spar and well into the cockpit.

As Jake wrestled with the controls, Chichester stretched forward and to Jake's horror, the madman raised the landing gear.

Falling back behind the obstructing spar, Chichester grabbed Tina again and he pushed her head into Jake's field of view. While pressing his pistol at Tina's face, he shouted, "Stay on those controls, Silver. It's too late to be a goddam hero. Level off, and overfly the field!"

"Don't make us crash, Jake," Tina pleaded. "Please! I'm begging you."

"Listen to the wench, Silver," Chichester growled, keeping Tina's head in Jake's field of view, the gun pressed against her temple. "Straight and level, and maintain this heading. Do it and the bitch lives!" Chichester growled as he jammed the Glock into Tina's mouth. "Keep us at 200 feet and mind that GPS or I'll blow this one's lovely head clear off!"

In the dim light, Jake discerned that Tina's face was bruised and swollen.

"He's crazy, Jake," she said. "He did something in the floor back here."

Unable to release the controls without killing them all, and not yet understanding what Tina meant by *He did something in the floor back here*, Jake heard the landing gear bang into its retracted position making a landing at Miami impossible. So, he did the only thing he could: he raised the wing-flaps, and applied power to both engines.

Behind him, Chichester's face, was also bloody. His eyepatch dangled beneath the scratched and swollen orb. Tina must have fought him like a tigress before Chichester pistol-whipped her into submission.

Trapped at the controls, his wheels and flaps retracted, his fuel all but gone, Jake held a slight climb attitude while the Marksman accelerated. He reached for his gun as two miles worth of runway and what remained of his fuel were disappearing, unseen, unindicated under the speeding plane. The pistol's clip was gone!

Baring his teeth in anger and frustration, Jake threw the useless Glock to the flight deck.

"Full throttle, Silver, or she dies!" Chichester ordered through clenched teeth.

Trapped at the controls, Jake watched horrified while the plane hurtled toward MIA's perimeter fence. "Climb, goddammit!' he growled. Lightened by its lack of fuel, the old warbird did just that, and Jake realized to his horror just what Chichester had done *in the floor back there*; the sonofabitch had pulled the belly tank's emergency dump valve, and in doing so spewing the last of their precious fuel into the night air.

With the muzzle of Chichester's Glock jammed into her open mouth, Tina forced a barely discernable, "Please, Jake."

Out of options, Jake held the throttles to their stops and tried to regain some altitude. Rain propelled by the slipstream pelted the windshield, limiting visibility as he struggled in ground-effect mere feet above the runway. He watched the concrete slab disappear as his airspeed indicator stopped its rise at 200 knots, much of it headwind, and he knew the climbing machine had gulped at whatever fuel its engines could suck from its lines and sumps.

As he crossed the airport's eastern boundary, the swarm of ugly industrial buildings that rushed at his airplane one upon another, drifted past.

"Turn to zero-eight-zero," Chichester shouted. "We're close.

"Close to what?" Jake bellowed, rolling left while glancing at the GPS screen. It had updated, and now showed their destination one mile dead ahead. There was no airport a mile dead ahead! "Close to what, you crazy bastard? Close to what?"

"Steady on, Silver. You'll know soon enough."

The port-side engine fell silent and the airplane yawed and rolled to the left as Jake struggled to maintain velocity and control.

In the rear cabin, Chichester grabbed a seat cushion and placed it against the massive main spar. Pressing Tina against the cushion, the gun to her head, with his free hand he wrapped a stout cargo strap around her waist, lashing them both to that spar. "If you value what's left of your life, lass, you'll hold on and stop fighting," he said. Then, pointing toward Jake, he added, "...and his life as well."

On the flight deck, Jake watched the airspeed as he climbed his ever-lighter airplane on a single, sputtering engine. Carefully trading velocity for altitude, he held the climb.

Back in the clouds at 400 feet, the starboard side engine coughed and it, too, fell silent.

Holding an easterly course, Jake's eyes tried without success to pierce the night. Blinded by cloud and rain, and with only the sound of rushing wind and water to give any sense of forward movement, Jake felt the plane stop climbing, tip forward, and begin its death dive.

Falling through 300, 250, 200 feet, the hanging fingers of cloud retreated. With no power and unable to drop the landing gear without shortening the Invader's glide, Jake watched rooftops nearly brush his airplane's underbelly. In seconds, those rooftops would become walls and still no landing field in view. A bridge rushed Jake's windscreen and he pulled the yoke to his chest.

The nose pointed upward and the Marksman just cleared the obstacle, but the maneuver robbed the wings of critical airspeed. Storm-force headwinds slowed the groundspeed to about 65 knots, radically limiting his glide.

Sweat poured from Jake's brow and into his eyes as the aircraft rocked and lurched through the turbulent eddies of ground effect. Empty of fuel, gear up and props feathered, the sleek old machine remained controllable. He'd never flown such a plane!

"What am I looking for?" Jake shouted desperately as the altimeter wound down to 150 feet. An industrial landscape flashed by his cockpit windows. He was silently flying down a deserted industrial thoroughfare with no options left.

His gun pressed firmly against Tina's temple, Chichester roared, "Full flaps, keep her flat and don't touch that gear handle. All we need is ten feet to clear the fence."

"Fence! Fence of what?" Jake exclaimed, his question answered as the plane's nose smashed through that fence, leveling it. At 90 knots indicated airspeed, he felt the wings mush, burble, and finally stall just as the GPS announced, "You have reached your destination."

With a horrific screech of tortured metal, the Marksman's belly hit the pavement.

Jake's forward vision restored, he saw walls looming on either side of his centerline, not 500 feet directly ahead. Its engines dead, its landing gear retracted, the machine was speeding on its flattened belly into a canyon of metal. Jake's wide eyes were assaulted by the bizarre sight of crushed automobiles, trucks, and busses, their carcasses piled high one atop another rising on both sides of the out-of-control airplane. They'd come down in a sprawling wrecking yard! This was Chichester's landing field!

The ground was rain-soaked and greasy. With no ability to slow the hurtling machine or control its direction, the Marksman and its occupants hurtled toward two walls of crushed steel directly ahead and to the sides of the sliding plane. "Brace for impact!" Jake shouted as he instinctively kicked left rudder. The machine careened toward a narrow aisle between the walls of smashed cars. With a crash and scream of rending metal, his portside wing smashed against the towering wall and sheared off at the eye mounts bringing the plane to a violent, side-skidding, part-shedding stop.

The impact brought tons of crushed steel crashing down around the airplane. Her trapped occupants covered their heads and crouched against this latest terror while horrific thuds pounded and shook the airplane as manmade steel boulders crashed down all around them, crushing the plane's already slender empennage further and flattening its vertical stabilizer.

The fuselage was folding up like a stomped-on beer can, while a seemingly endless avalanche tumbled from the teetering 40 foot wall.

Jake, panting like a wild thing, released his seat belt and peered aft.

The deck rose at an unnatural angle as the tail section of the plane had been crushed and pinned beneath the carcass of a flattened delivery van. "Tina!" he called.

The only sounds he heard were of wind and rain and the whine of spinning gyros.

Looking rearward, through the dust cloud, Jake saw the wooden crate still in one piece while everything behind it, behind the ring-spar and aft of the cargo door was crushed, one of St. John's mercifully dead feet along with it.

Jake's eyes went to a wide-eyed, terrified Tina. Beyond her bruised cheek, she looked uninjured. "Get me out of here!" she moaned.

Looking to Chichester, Jake saw that the Englishman's jersey was red-soaked. He'd suffered a penetration wound to his side in the crash-landing and appeared to be losing a lot of blood. Still hanging from the cargo strap, he appeared barely conscious.

Jake, reaching across the massive forward spar, wrapped an arm about Tina and he released the strap. Chichester fell to the deck.

After remaining frozen for a moment, her arms already about Jake's neck, she leaned in and began kissing him on the face with desperation. "You did it. You saved us." Her fervor nearly caused her to fall backward on the steeply sloping deck.

Leaving Chichester writhing at her feet, Jake took hold of Tina's wrists where they squeezed his neck. Looking squarely into the big eyes he warned, "Tina, listen to me..."

"Is it going to explode?" she asked.

"No," he assured her, his voice a study in forced calm, "but we gotta get out of this thing before that whole wall out there comes down on us!"

Crawling through the small companionway leading from the cockpit, Jake made his way into the rear compartment. Rising to a crouch, he took Tina's waist and moved her toward the cargo hatch. There, they saw that the wooden crate had slipped its lashings and burst the door open. It now blocked the opening, denying them egress.

Unable to budge the thing, Jake looked forward. "We gotta climb back up toward the cockpit."

She nodded, but was thrown upon Jake again as the plane was rocked by another weighty ejection from the teetering wall of trashed vehicles looming above.

"Sonofabitch!" Jake cursed, realizing the cockpit's roof hatch was partially smashed and pinned below a teetering derelict. Strangely he recognized it as a Chevy.

On the deck behind them, a wounded Chichester let an anguished scream, then all was silent again but for the howling wind and the rain pelting the plane's metal skin.

As Chichester groaned again, Jake stepped down mercilessly on the Englishman's wrist relieving him of his pistol. "Forget the cockpit. We have to clear the main hatch," Jake said, referring to the cargo door, and again he tried to move the wooden box, this time with Tina's help. It didn't budge.

Moving toward the narrow space between the crate and the doorsill, Jake heard the sound of an approaching vehicle.

"Shut up," he shouted to the groaning Chichester. "Listen."

"Hey!" a strange and barely-discernable voice shouted from outside. "Are any of y'all alive in there?"

Unable to see the caller, Jake shouted, "Get us out of here before this whole wall comes down!"

"Move away from the hatch," the approaching voice said, its Southern drawl now clear.

Jake stepped back and Tina hugged the opposite wall. The crate shifted slightly, giving off a squeal as it scraped the floor. The man outside was apparently operating a machine.

Though neither Jake nor Tina could see it, the machine was a towering Caterpillar excavator. Its long articulated boom terminated in a massive hydraulic grappling claw.

Feeling the deck below him rock ever so slightly, Jake shouted to the man, "Easy! If this thing moves, that wall comes down on us."

"Crate's jammed," the voice said, and both Jake and Tina heard the sound of the machine's powerful engine rev up just outside the deformed cargo door. "I got an idea."

Suddenly the entire fuselage shook as the big Cat gripped the plane's starboard side wing in its enormous, claw like jaws, and clipped that wing off as easily as shears would clip a sheet of paper. Jake had seen this same thing done to an obsolete F-100 fighter at the government's Mojave bone yard.

Both wings gone, the excavator now had unobstructed access to the plane's cargo hatch.

"Whoa, hey!" Jake and Tina shouted in unison as the entire fuselage rocked.

They were being dragged to an area away from the walls of crushed automobiles. Locked in the unseen machine's massive jaws, the Marksman's occupants could do nothing now but hold on and wait.

Once clear of the crumbling wall of steel, Jake gripped a horizontal stringer, and Tina held even more tightly to him. Chichester remained prostrate forward of the crushed tail cone.

As abruptly as it had begun, the forward motion stopped.

"I'm gonna slide this crate away from the door," the man outside shouted. "Stay back."

With little choice but to comply, Jake said, "Go ahead."

Again, just audible above the wind's howl, the Cat's diesel engine roared.

Jake moved Tina back as the machine's jaws spread the hatchway wide as they slid their way around the wooden crate, pushing it against the collapsed ceiling, and maneuvering it to an angle that would allow its extraction through the torn-open cargo door.

"Stay back," the voice shouted. The box and the entire fuselage began moving.

Barely clearing the door on all sides, the operator slowly shook and slid the crate free.

The cargo now clear, Jake and Tina moved toward the opening and freedom.

Jake stepped into the doorway first. "We…"

"I said stand clear!" the man barked as he advanced the Cat, slamming into the fuselage and rolling it slightly and causing Jake to stumble backward. To his shock, the massive grappler began smashing against the airplane's skin time and again, crushing the fuselage and flattening the cargo door to a slit. For a brief instant, however, the man was visible. In that instant, Jake got a look at his face, one entire right side of which was severely scarred and burned away.

"I told you to stand back, goddammit!" and the next impact closed that slit completely.

Jake and Tina hung on as the plane moved again.

With a screech of torn metal, the wingless fuselage rolled over, sending Jake and Tina tumbling against the far side bulkhead. They could only watch, stumbling helplessly as the entire tail section was rocked and squashed in what could only be the Cat's massive jaws.

Finally being snipped off, the tail was eliminated as easily as was the starboard wing.

Recalling that which he'd witnessed in the Mojave, Jake realized to his horror that the Marksman was being cut apart, this time with Tina, the wounded Chichester, St. John's corpse, and himself trapped inside.

Next to go was the cockpit. Partly crushed and cut off immediately forward of the main spar, it left them trapped between the forward end and pinched empennage of what was the Marksman's already tapering rear compartment.

Barely able to move, they could but cower as again and again the giant grappling/cutting claw slammed against the fuselage with awesome, deafening power, crushing what remained of the cabin into a smaller and smaller tube as easily as one might crush a soda can underfoot.

Searching madly for any opening, any means of escape, Jake's every effort was stymied by the continuing distortion rendered by each blow that fell upon their soon to be tomb.

Ironically, the always-confining tiny crawlway below the main spar remained undisturbed.

Clawing for any handhold, Jake pushed Tina toward the tiny space, which now appeared cavernous to him. As she grabbed its sides with both hands, suddenly the tiny, crushed fuselage was lifted high, twisted nearly 90 degrees in the excavator's jaws and dropped aft-end first.

Landing with a metallic bang, the shock caused Tina to lose her grip on the crawlway's edge and fall rearward into Jake's arms.

Holding tight to both Tina and an exposed stringer, Jake could see that Chichester had slid rearward along the now nearly vertical deck.

Rain poured in from the crawlway below the front spar, which now lay open to the sky, and Jake realized the already very-narrow rear fuselage was closing in on them.

Then it hit him. They'd been cut and crushed small, then lifted, and dropped into the gigantic rotating steel teeth of the wrecking yard's shredding apparatus!

Chichester let a blood-curdling scream. Casting a look rearward, Jake could see the the shredder's rollers—like those of a gigantic paper-shredder—had started turning. Breaching the fuselage it had the man's legs and was about to draw him in when it stopped. The terrified Englishman rallied his strength and uttered a guttural: "Filho..."

Only three feet remained now between Jake and Tina, and the folding walls where the rotating drums' meshing steel teeth had momentarily halted their voracious consumption.

In an act of supreme irrationality, Jake crawled rearward, and while ignoring the traumatized and thrashing Chichester, he opened the cargo strap holding St. John's dead body and slid the corpse forward, away from the rollers and into the arms of Tina Bergstrom where she worked his dead arms through a dangling cargo strap.

Knives of sheared aluminum and steel protruded from the folding, splintering, and now nearly vertical tube in which they huddled.

Every trace of the once noble airplane and her trapped occupants would soon be gone, leaving but a pile of metal shards and a bit of blood-soaked bone splinters.

His movements restricted, and knowing he'd be ground to pulp the moment the steel drums began to rotate again, Chichester cried out in catharsis, "Your brother was no smuggler, lass. His only crime was trusting me. And for that, I sent him to his death."

With a scream, Tina released St. John's corpse and lunged for the dying man as the machine again jerked to a start. Chichester's feet and lower legs were drawn into the rotating steel teeth. Still, she clawed at his screaming face as would a madwoman while he slowly raised an arm, pointing above Jake to the tiny square that was the crawlway and he died.

Though distorted, and now too small for a man to traverse, Jake could see that it still remained open to the sky.

Again, the shredder ground to a halt.

Acting quickly, Jake crouched, grabbing Tina below her waist. With adrenaline-fueled might, he pulled her away from the now dead Englishman and grappled his way upward. Finally, with a single adrenaline fed motion, he thrust her small, slim upper torso through the crawlway, into the howling wind and driving rain and freedom.

"Grab the sides and push yourself up," he demanded. "Pull your legs free and run. Don't look back, just run, run away from this place! I'm finished. Save yourself, Tina. Do it for Leif."

She wriggled her body out and stood, straddling the opening. Standing inside the hopper, she was some twelve feet above the ground. Turning, she reached her hand down for Jake. "Not without you!"

"I'm done, Tina. I can't make it," he shouted. What little remained of the fuselage was poised for consumption by the shredder's interlocking jaws and teeth.

"Please, just try."

"There's no time! It's too narrow," he shouted. "Get away. Tell your brother's story."

Before her terrified eyes, Jake disappeared inside the ever-smaller space below.

"Run!" his disembodied voice shouted from the pit.

In the open air above him, the machine's operator had abandoned the controls and was climbing the ladder toward Tina as she stood at the hopper's bottom on the edge of the shredder's gaping maw.

As the man reached down, stretching for her, he shouted what sounded to Jake like, "Take my hand..." He also thought he heard the man call Tina's name, but could not be sure.

Out of Jake's sight, Tina did take the man's hand, and she pulled him to her. As he complied, she side-stepped, causing him to lose his balance and plummet into the shredder's funnel-like hopper to land atop the drums where the crushed fuselage met their steel teeth.

Though the machine was stopped, the man's coat impaled itself upon a metal shard. "You're dead, you double crossing little bitch!" he shouted, struggling to gain his footing.

Through the opening, Jake could see the man's leg. He fired four rounds from Chichester's Glock but the man wriggled free and out of sight. Jake heard him shouting to Tina, who'd apparently gotten away: "Come back! It's okay. You don't have to..." The voice was consumed by the howling wind.

Barely able to move, Jake's attention turned to the hanging body of St. John and the horrific vestige of a mangled Chichester, the Englishman's corpse having now been mostly eaten by the shredder, leaving only the man's head and shoulders visible.

Trapped between the forward spar and the shredder's teeth, bleeding from how many cuts and scratches he couldn't guess, Jake could only hope that Tina had made her escape. He also knew his pistol had at least three shots remaining. If it was humanly possible to put at least one of his bullets into the man Chichester had called Filho, Jake would find a way.

His face open to the driving rain, Jake's world was reduced to the small fissure above him as a scream followed by two, three gunshots rang out through the din above. "Tina!" Jake shouted as he withdrew in anguish.

With Tina down, he alone remained. Determined to die fighting, Jake cocked the pistol one last time. Pointing it squarely at the fissure that was once the crawlway, the gun was so close to his own bruised and bloodied face that he could barely focus as he waited his turn. "Come on, you sonofabitch, show your goddam face!"

The man grunted, so close to the opening that Jake was momentarily startled.

If the man's shadow advanced, Jake would fire before the bastard knew what hit him.

An anguished cry assaulted Jake's ears causing him to dart aside as two shots were fired outside the fissure, close enough that the muzzle flashes lighted Jake's confined space.

"Try again. You gotta look at me to shoot me, you yellow sonofabitch!" Jake growled in response. Then lower. "One more inch," he breathed, his every muscle a coiled spring, his finger tensed on the trigger poised to fire. He had time for one shot. He'd make it count. The maniac need only take Jake's bait. "C'mon, you sonofabitch! I'm right here."

Then, just as Jake knew it would, a face appeared in the fissure an inch from the muzzle of his cocked pistol.

Hesitating, Jake struggled to clear his eyes as he looked into the wide-eyed, tear-stained, beautiful face of his mother.

- CHAPTER 21 -

It's been said that Fortune favors the prepared mind, and Phillipe Sinclair, aka William Peterson, aka Guillermo Filho had prepared well.

Before the storm's eye could make landfall, a stalled high-pressure system in the Gulf had sent the storm on a northerly tack, sparing the city some of its wrath. Nonetheless, residents of the outlying region had already been ordered to shelter in place or evacuate. Most had chosen the latter option. Between the abandoned nature of the area, and the sound and fury of the storm's outer bands, the commotion unfolding at the wrecking yard was completely hidden from the eyes and ears of anyone save those involved. Thus it took a phone call from Garodnik to persuade a skeptical desk sergeant at Miami Metro to reroute a lone cruising patrol car to the scene. Within an hour of the stunned officer's arrival, however, the wind-whipped compound was awash in not only rain, but activity. Uniformed men and women ran every which way, slipping and sliding across the grease and waterlogged ground, their movements staccato in the flashing strobes atop a cadre of glistening emergency vehicles parked haphazardly amid the orderly rows of silent derelicts piled high around them and threatening to topple with each new gust.

The same gigantic excavator machine that had lifted and dropped the slender fuselage and its occupants into the jaws of the shredder, was now in the hands of a Miami

DPW operator. He'd used it to open that fuselage allowing a crew of firefighters to extract a grateful and very-much-alive Jake Silver from the wrecked aircraft, where only its nose protruded from the shredder's death grip. Those same rescuers now concentrated on extricating St. John's bullet-riddled corpse.

Nearby, a plainclothesman photographed the body of a man lying dead on his back in the grease and mud at the shredder's base were he'd fallen.

In the strobe lights' glare, it was evident that the dead man's face was scarred and badly burned. Bizarrely, what looked to be a fishing spear protruded from his shoulder.

Gathered next to that body, detectives spoke with a young woman whose white shorts were drenched and muddied as she demonstrated what appeared to be a spear *gun*.

At the center of it all, a trembling, tearful MJ hugged and kissed her son for what seemed the thousandth time, her desperate ardor nearly causing the younger Silver to not see the Miami Metro Fire and Rescue truck as it departed this particular bedlam. He'd wanted to thank his rescuers properly, as if such gratitude could be conveyed. To his dismay, he saw only their rig's receding lights. But in so turning, Jake glanced a bruised and disheveled Tina Bergstrom sitting leeside to the wind, in the back of an ambulance and being attended to. Her hands were bandaged and a paramedic was administering a shot to her arm.

Jake tried to go to her, but was restrained by not only his doting mother's embrace, but by a Miami PD detective determined to keep him from Tina while trying to ask the first of many questions both would face in the coming hours.

The coroner was next to depart the scene, taking with him the bagged body of the burn-scared man.

Major Dwight Chichester's torn and twisted torso would be identified and eventually cut from the mangled empennage.

The broken wood crate containing the purported Analog was being inspected by a small army of scruffy narcotics cops. Its contents, some 200 or so 50-pound bags of white powder, would be hauled away for cursory analysis. Its essence would be overlooked, a casualty of the storm of synthetics overwhelming every metropolitan police lab.

Eventually, the number of uniformed, helmeted police, anxious to find shelter, dwindled, leaving but a small cadre of homicide and crime scene investigators to scour every filthy inch of the slowly flooding junkyard turned landing strip/drop zone/crime scene/torture chamber/killing field/lake.

Since it was Lieutenant Garodnik who'd fired the shot that actually killed Philippe Sinclair, the Miami detectives directed their most urgent questions his way. Nonetheless, the NYPD detective managed to shuttle between Jake's and Tina's positions. He would do what he could to deflect the inquiries away from the traumatized pair, sensitive to the rigors of too-soon recollection. Garodnik's Miami Metro counterparts reluctantly accommodated their carpet bagging Yankee colleague; the apparent perpetrators were dead, after all, and as for the rest, there would be time for in-depth interrogations in the hours to come: indoors.

As the flurry subsided, Gina Ferranti made her way to where Tina Bergstrom sat.

Climbing into the ambulance, the diver removed her rain jacket and wrapped it about Tina's shoulders. The smaller woman had noticed Tina trembling, thus the kind gesture.

Tina thanked her, and while the women commiserated, the petite diver's big redheaded male companion seemed more consumed with the steaming bullet hole in the radiator of his borrowed pickup truck than he was with the many other extraordinary events transpiring.

That pickup truck, the first functioning surface vehicle to have arrived here, now stood hissing and smoking exactly where Red Grogan had driven it onto the property by rolling over the fence at the junkyard's edge. It was the same 15 foot fence that had been flattened by the airplane's having smashed through it during its silent approach to this place. It was the same fence that Tina had crawled and scampered across when escaping Philippe Sinclair's embrace at the edge of the shredder pit, her dancer's legs making short work of what remained of the collapsed chain link, this while Sinclair had been struggling to extricate himself from the shredder pit and the wreck's jagged metal.

Once on the street, her hands torn from the razor wire attached to that fence, Tina Bergstrom had waved down the red pickup truck as it cruised ever-so-slowly by, its occupants looking lost and confused as they gawked about, pointing at their GPS screen and wondering why it had led them to this, of all places.

The question was answered when Tina, her bloodied hands smearing the passenger side window and her wide eyes met MJ's through the glass.

In time, the scene cleared, the parties were released to their own recognizance and told where to report in the morning.

Unlike his civilian companions, Lieutenant Garodnik, though exhausted, had agreed to accompany his Miami homicide counterparts to their headquarters. There he'd spend the night detailing the run-up to the events at the wrecking yard more efficiently than would the others. The big detective had already surrendered his gun, as was protocol: he'd fired three shots, the first bullet was spent returning Sinclair's fire while leaping from Grogan's still-rolling, borrowed pickup truck.

He'd explain in his report that Sinclair had fired at him first from his perch atop the shredder's 10 foot high tower, the gunman's bullet grazing the detective's leg. Sinclair had missed, not due to poor marksmanship, but because no sooner had the gunman aimed his weapon, than did a fishing spear, fired up at him from the pickup truck's rear seat, slam into and through his shoulder, causing Sinclair to tumble backward while firing, his errant bullet coming to rest not in Garodnik, but in the red pickup truck's radiator. The detective would report that he'd returned fire, striking Sinclair in the chest, and causing the gunman to fall forward, tumbling 10 feet from the shredder's maw to the ground. Running up to him, Garodnik saw the supine and dying man slowly raise his gun. The detective's next two rounds, stopped Sinclair's heart before he could get off a shot.

With the others waiting inside the patrol cars lined up to take them from this place, unseen Jake quietly made his way across the muddy ground to the base of the shredder machine. There, rain-soaked, bent and broken, her long nose pointed forlornly toward a sky she'd never know again, lay a last vestige of what was first and finally the noble Invader.

A pilot to the end, Jake reached out and touched its tortured skin.

For how long he didn't know, he stood there in silent contemplation, his hand on the fallen old warbird, its meager remains—a bent and severed cockpit—uncannily similar to those of his old wingman's Curtiss and he knew it was time to leave this place and all that it recalled.

Turning, he he could see Tina Bergstrom running toward him.

Wrapping her arms and bandaged hands about his neck, he held her to him and they remained locked in a desperate embrace as she sobbed. "I'm so sorry, Jake," she said, her eyes looking deep into his. "If I'd known, if only I'd known I would never have dragged you into this. If only I'd known…" He held her head to his chest and her voice trailed off and the nightmare was over, ending as violently and abruptly as it had begun, leaving Jake Silver to quietly wonder just what it might be that the beautiful enigma he held in his arms, so desperately wished to have known.

With but a few short hours before they'd need to report for statements, MJ had arranged to put everyone up at the luxurious Delano Hotel on Miami's South Beach for what remained of the night and the fast moving storm. The invitation included not only Jake and Tina, but divers Gina Ferranti and Red Grogan as well.

Morning would bring with it clearing skies and the ordeal of a formal police interrogation. A few hours' sleep in a luxury hotel would be good medicine.

The sight, then, of the largely disheveled, mud and blood stained quintet pulling up to the swanky hotel's reception area steps in a caravan of Miami Metro patrol cars was no doubt disconcerting to the bellmen of the majestic old art deco palace

Nonetheless, the five dubious-looking guests were met with umbrellas, checked in and retired to their rooms while police sentries arrayed themselves at the hotel's exits.

Once alone in his room, Jake couldn't control his racing mind. Something he'd overheard Red Grogan say when being questioned at the wrecking yard gnawed at him. Grogan had said that when he'd come upon the wreckage of Leif Bergstrom's plane floating in the strait, it was clear to him that damage at the separation points showed the *Queen of the Southern Sky* to have been brought down by an internal explosion, an explosion from a shaped charge.

When considered along with Chichester's cryptic "I killed him," confession delivered as the crusher consumed him, Jake had a horrific realization.

Chichester had boasted to Jake that he was both a mining engineer and a military demolitions expert. Knowing this, Jake could not help but surmise how easy it would have been for the skilled Englishman to booby-trap Leif's Bergstrom's plane by fashioning a GPS or altitude-based fuse that would somehow detonate in the event their already suspicious pilot discovered the ruse into which he'd been drawn. If Jake's supposition was correct, it meant that once his old wingman, Swede Bergstrom, took action and changed course or climbed to altitude in an effort to foil his deceivers' plan, his simple honesty became his undoing.

Jake paced his room, each revelation more disturbing than its predecessor. Thoughts of Sandy McRea, whose murder Garodnik had disclosed earlier, also weighed heavily, impossibly so, on his psyche. What could he have done differently? Could he have prevented Sandy's murder? Should he not have persuaded her to stay, not left that key, or worse, not had her leave the spare key in the potted plant out in the hallway? Could he have prevented St. John's death? His racing mind made sleep an impossibility.

Unable to wash away the emotional grime, Jake decided to take a hot shower, his second since arriving. This time he'd shave his healing jaw as well. After that, he vowed to stop obsessing, and await the dawn in quiet solitude.

It was past midnight when he stepped from the shower. As he reached for a towel, there came a knock at his hotel room door.

Jake, a veteran of far too many Friday-night hotel stays uttered a muffled, "Dammit," and prepared to redirect what was doubtless a drunken guest who'd found his way to the wrong room. Dropping the towel, he pulled on a pair of trousers one of the cops had offered him and he hopped barefoot toward the door. Swinging it wide, he was greeted by the sight of an apprehensive Tina Bergstrom.

Also shoeless, fresh bandages on her cut hands, an oversized white hotel bathrobe wrapped nearly twice about her small frame and her hair wrapped in its own towel, she smiled nervously at Jake. "Oh, I woke you. I'm so sorry."

"You didn't wake me." His eyes drawn to the turban-like towel on her head. "Most swamis would of known that."

Despite Jake's attempt at levity, she took in his troubled countenance. Pulling the towel from her head, she smiled and while tossing it to him, said, "Yeah, funny, but don't quit your day job just yet." Then pausing, she added, "You do still have a day job…"

Catching the towel, he smiled and wrapped it about his neck while Tina shook her wet hair free. "I can't sleep, either. Too wound up." Anxious to be out of the hallway, she stepped into Jake's room. "Jake," she said tentatively, "there is something."

Feeling much the same as he had when the enigmatic beauty first burst upon him in the coffee shop of another hotel only days ago, Jake realized he was being sized up. He looked away and fumbled to close the brass button while gripping the waistband of his police drunk-tank jeans to prevent their falling. When he looked up, Tina stood mere inches away.

"Why didn't you tell the police what you knew about me and Philippe?"

"Because I saw no reason to dredge up all that stuff, put you through all that again. The past is prologue. It must have taken incredible strength to pull your life together after that scumbag tried to ruin it, and he would have if not for your brother. We both owe your brother a debt. Leif didn't save me just so I could finish what Philippe had started."

"But, how…?"

"Look," Jake interrupted, "I'm no fool. A million thoughts have been swirling around in my brain. But, the bottom line is Philippe tried to kill you tonight. That sealed it for me."

They remained still, awkward smiles.

"You're nothing like I expected, Jake," she finally said, locking eyes as her robe brushed his bare chest and she repeated what she'd said at the wrecking yard. "I wish I'd known."

Overcoming his reluctance to get that answer, he asked, "What is it you wish you'd known, Tina? I don't…"

Putting a finger to his lips, she boldly closed the inch separating them. There was no trace of timidity or indecision in her expression now. She wiped a trace of shaving cream from his upper lip, her face now close enough that he could feel her wisps of warm breath on his still-damp skin. Yet his question went unanswered. "You saved my life," she said. "You were willing to die just to save me. It took incredible courage, but you did it. You did it twice."

Had she thought him a coward? Did she have reason to think it? What was it she wished she'd known? Jake struggled to put such thoughts behind him, and with them the guilt that had haunted his dreams these many years. But Tina was on him, clearly seductive, their lips nearly touching. Touching. Jake, fighting his rising desire, gently but firmly cupped her shoulders. "Tina, stop. You've been through hell. You're vulnerable and you're not thinking clearly."

"But I am, Jake," she said. "I'm thinking life is precious… and it's fragile and it's short." Her hands cupped his face, her tone turning more serious, her words strangely cathartic. "I've squandered so much of my life to anger and rage and hatred, to wanting retribution." Again he moved to speak, and again she stopped him. "Jake. I need this," she went on, maintaining control. "You said I've been through hell, and I have. Much of it my own doing. But so have you. What happened to Cassandra McRea was not your fault. You'd never have left her if you'd thought for one moment…" Tina was thinking aloud, recalling what she'd learned in the interrogation. "That girl's murder was not your fault any more than what happened to Leif was…was…" She inhaled deeply.

Did she know? Was Tina's pause deliberate, a minor torture?

"I'm sorry about Leif," Jake said, his retort a catharsis of his own. "I should have…"

"You should have nothing," she snapped, cutting. "For the longest time I blamed you for what happened to Leif. I hated you for it—hated you!"

There it was. She knew! A million thoughts raced through Jake's mind. If she hated him so, why then had she sought him out? He recalled her bereaved behavior in the LAX hotel coffee shop at the very start of this thing. Was it an act? A ploy to draw him in? He needed to know. "Tina? I…"

Seeming to sense a change in Jake's demeanor, she cut him off again, holding the offensive. "But now I know better, Jake," she pressed. "I know *you* better. My brother is what happened to my brother. He told me things, things he never told the authorities. He told me about the unmarked MiG that appeared out of nowhere, how you were not supposed to engage, as he put it, so without alerting you to his intentions he chased it. He made me swear I'd never tell a soul, especially not you."

"Leif flew right up the tailpipe of that jet," she revealed. "He knew it was Russian, and he deliberately taunted its pilot because that's who my brother was, and well, you know the rest. It was war, and you both broke the rules. But the fat old cowards who made those rules were sitting in easy chairs not ejection seats, safely removed from any fight. So fuck them and their rules. My brother's plane exploded because he used their bullshit to put himself in harm's way. Fighting is all he knew, and everything he needed. Leif's fate was sealed long before he met you.

"My brother is gone," she pressed. "Cassandra, too. But we're here, Jake. We're alive!"

Overwhelmed by the albeit, ambiguous, catharsis, by the possibility that she'd forgiven his actions, Jake took Tina's wrist, gently moved her hand away from his lips, determined to speak. But her mouth was on his. Her fingers entwined his hair, pulling him to her, pressing her lips to his, her ardor consumed him and Jake's every sense responded as his resolve collapsed before Tina's assault. Her robe fell to the floor, and her slim heather-scented body melted against his while the kiss lingered, and the taste, the scent, the soapy-fresh feel of her skin against Jake's bare chest engulfed him and he swept Tina up in his arms and carried her to the bed. Placing her gently down, her big eyes watched him as he drank deeply of the perfect alabaster beauty in her every curve and shadow, and the world intruded.

His muscles tensed as elation turned to shame when he recalled having admired Sandy McRea much the same way mere hours before her life was savagely stolen, and though Tina's words rang true, the flood of relief they carried, waned before the realization that Sandy McRea would be alive today had she never met Jake Silver.

Seeing Jake's gaze grow distant, Tina reached for him, her head slowly shaking, denying him retreat. Her eyes burning into his, she repeated the words, "Life is precious…and it's fragile and it's short." And as she spoke, her arms and legs enwrapped him and she drew him to her, into her as their passion, a thing born of horror and salvation, built again, slowly this time without interruption to its crescendo, and they both cried out as the nightmare they'd endured together faded while they held each other tightly, trembling and lost in the transient joy of release.

- EPILOG -

With morning, the survivors reported to Miami Metro HQ, to face a rigorous interrogation.

Red Grogan and Gina Ferranti were first to be cleared of any wrongdoing.

MJ took Grogan's address, with a promise to have his six-figure fee couriered to his Key West office within two days. The Strait Shooter's skipper, however, anticipating the business windfall that would accrue to the media storm those same two days would no doubt generate, had other plans: after the briefest of discussions, he and Gina had decided that they'd quietly await MJ's check, only to return it to her by mail, uncashed, torn in half, and accompanied by a bill for the repair to the bullet hole in Carlos's red pickup truck.

So, with long hugs, emotional goodbyes, and promises to stay in touch the divers headed off, well prepared for their next adventure.

The interrogation of Jake and Tina, however, continued long into the afternoon. Guided by MJ's learned counsel combined with Garodnik's statement, they were unable to connect Tina to the Cassandra killing or to Phillipe Sinclair, beyond his obsessive and decades-long pursuit of her. Both she and Jake were cleared of any wrongdoing.

Depositions and statements were taken and personal belongings returned. These included Jake's map case, his iPad, and Tina's life-saving fractured cell phone.

Though free to go, and despite Tina's objections, Jake stayed behind to accompany Tina to the coroner's crypt. With Leif Bergstrom's body having arrived from Port au Prince and his name cleared of any pending charges, Tina would be allowed to finally assume custody of her brother's remains–officially and under controlled circumstances.

As for MJ, it wasn't until 6:00 p.m. that she got back to the Delano.

Having arrived first, she used the time to pick up a fresh outfit at the pricey women's shop in the lobby before meeting the others in the Alabaster Bar as planned.

Back at her room, she freshened up quickly, hiding her puffy eyes behind makeup, only to smear that makeup again when she made emotional calls of appreciation to both Will Yost and Alton Portlock.

Finally, she headed back downstairs where she took a seat at one of the tall bistro tables in the Delano's Alabaster Bar.

The lounge was empty, and she sipped a cognac while awaiting the others.

Hoping Pat Garodnik might arrive first, she found herself looking forward to personal time with the detective. He did not disappoint.

Grabbing a stool next to the lawyer, he ordered a much-needed Bass Ale. "Been talking all day," he said breathlessly. "Throat's parched."

MJ allowed the detective a moment to savor the cold brew before finally asking, "Well, Patrick, is it over?"

"I suppose," he said with little conviction.

"I know that look, Patrick. You are not gonna let this go are you?"

The grizzled detective paused, grinned and changed the subject. "I was late getting back here because I'd headed over to the coroner's branch. Thought I'd offer Christina

Bergstrom a shoulder to lean on. Identifying a loved one's remains is no picnic, even if it's just a photo."

Having suffered the experience years earlier following the murder of her husband, Jake's father Myron, it only added to the affinity MJ already felt for the resilient young woman, but she said only, "You went there to lend Christina a shoulder?" Her words dripped with cynicism. "Really, Patrick. That's what you're going with?"

"Least I could do, Counselor," Garodnik offered, poker faced. "Didn't matter, though. Jake was already with her, so I left quietly."

"Missed your chance to, uh, *comfort* the bereaved, did you?" she teased.

"A blind man could see that she was already more than comfortable hanging onto your son's arm and didn't need me—or anybody else—interrupting."

"Don't you mean, *interrogating*?" MJ challenged, adding, "My Jake was willing to die just to save her, Patrick, and from what he said in his deposition, she was quick to return the favor. Nonetheless, you still don't trust her. Admit it. You were there to take one last crack at getting her to slip up, to say something, anything that implicates her in this thing. You're like a dog with a bone."

"I'll accept bloodhound," the detective said, feigning umbrage.

"I know you think she baited Sinclair into going to NY so she could get to Leif's body in that Haitian morgue first, cut Sinclair out of whatever deal you think they had together. Meantime, she could chop her own brother to pieces for God knows what reason. You'd never prove any of that in a courtroom. And, if that were her intention, why drag Jake along? You're a dear man, Patrick, but a cop too long.

"Look," she went on, "DNA, a bunch of prints, and the Jersey Turnpike time stamps all nail Sinclair, aka Filho aka Peterson for the Cassandra McRea murder. Jake's statement indicts the morgue thug, Tretooey, for abducting Jake and

Christina and, finally, this Major Chichester character's death-bed confession in the wrecking yard crusher, buries *him,* so to speak, for the sabotage of Leif Bergstrom's plane. Period. That's it. Everything fits. Case closed. Your boss wants this in the books, and you on a plane back to New York. He went out on a limb, for me." She placed her hand on the detective's. "So did you, Patrick, and I cannot thank you enough. But now you must let it go. You're just going to anger New York and give yourself an ulcer."

Garodnik nodded, faking acquiescence while wondering why this otherwise tough, pragmatic prosecutor was failing to see the connections less as a closed case, than a closed circle in a larger system, a Venn diagram of sorts, and by no means coincidental. To his mind, MJ was giving too much slack to the younger woman, a woman his every instinct told him to distrust. More than anything else, though, the thought of that dagger found in the elevator just outside the Haitian morgue nagged at the detective. Who left it there? When? Why?

He decided to drop it...for now.

Jake arrived, ordered a Jack Daniels from the bar, shook the detective's hand, kissed his mother's cheek and took a seat.

"Are you done with the questioning?" MJ asked.

"For the moment. But sooner or later the feds will want to talk to me. I did bust the Air Defense Intercept Zone, after all. Of course I got away with it only because Sinclair acting as Peterson conned the interdicting authorities into standing down. I'll be happy to tell them whatever I can. But they'll be busy cleaning up their own mess before they get to me."

"Have you seen Tina?" MJ asked.

"She should be here soon," Jake said, checking his watch. "Once we got done with the ID session, she said she was heading over to Lincoln Avenue. She needed to buy new clothes. The Metro guys offered her a ride, but she didn't want to be seen climbing out of a black and white. Said she already looked like a vagrant and didn't need the attention. I got the sense she needed some time to herself, so I cabbed it back here." Jake finished his drink and ordered another. Then he curled his brow, thinking. "Funny thing though…" he said while looking at his glass.

With Jake's words, MJ saw Garodnik perk up, all ears. Her fingers tightened slightly on the cop's hand. "She," Jake continued, "Tina, I mean, she was choked up at the photos of her brother's body. She really broke down."

"Of course," MJ concurred. "They were close. Seeing him like…"

"I get that," Jake allowed with a shrug, "but her response didn't jibe with the way she reacted when first seeing Leif's corpse the night we broke into the morgue. She actually tried to drag the body with her that time. Pulled it right off the table, like she couldn't bear to leave her brother behind. Might've done it, too," he added," if we weren't beaten and snatched."

MJ moved to speak, but Jake continued.

"Then, this afternoon, when the coroner had her sign the custody transfer remanding her that same body, he naturally asked where she'd want Leif's remains sent."

"Nothing unusual about that, Jake," MJ advocated while Garodnik sat quietly, listening.

"Well," Jake went on, "Tina did something kind of… well, I think it was a little weird."

Garodnik locked eyes with MJ, demanding her attention and Jake said, "Tina told the coroner she didn't want the body. She asked if he'd be kind enough to see to its interment himself. All she wanted of her brother's so-called remains was his prosthetic hand!"

"Did the coroner give it to her… the hand?" Garodnik asked.

"He did. Seemed to settle her down, too."

"Hmm," MJ inhaled softly, pondering. "I guess there's no accounting for family."

"Speaking of family," Jake said, moving on. Tina Bergstrom's advice about closure, though offered in the heat of a seduction, was still fresh in his mind, "I have an early flight to Des Moines in the morning. Cedar rapids from there."

"Are you prepared for what you'll be met with, Jacob?" MJ asked, proud of her son's motivations, but protective of his feelings. "You've just come through a nightmare."

"As have you, Mom. But Sandy's parents will never come through theirs. I must do this."

"Will you and Tina continue to see each other?"

"Yes, Mother," Jake answered, good-natured cynicism coloring his inflection as he squeezed MJ's free hand, adding, "I expect we'll see each other any minute now."

Reconciled to her son's bachelor ways, MJ led her "boys" to the dining room. Before sitting, she called Tina's phone to let her know they'd left the bar.

Rather than the now-familiar, "*This is Tina...*" recording that had greeted her two previous calls, a mechanical voice informed MJ that the number was no longer active.

Standing dead-still at the restaurant table's edge, her mind racing, her pulse pounding, she never heard Garodnik when he said, "You look lovely tonight, MJ."

- END -

ACKNOWLEDGMENTS

Writing a novel is often considered a solitary pursuit. For those more capable than I, perhaps it is.

If so, then I am grateful for my shortcomings, because without them I'd not have saught the ideas, knowledge and generosity of so many others, and this scribbler would still be staring at a blank first page.

For those whose contributions enriched this work, my heartfelt appreciation goes out first to my wife, Gloria, who patiently read and made every iteration smarter; to my sister, Linda Stasi, a real writer, who encouraged me to keep at it; to brilliant New York editor, Dana Isaacson, who might call himself an editor, but is in fact a magician; to Eileen Eberhardt-Thompson, whose stage directing skills brought structure to my chaos; to Captain John Scordato of American Airlines, who gave the story its wings; to Richard Fulwiler, friend, pilot, genius, and a man whose knowledge of the Douglas A-26 Invader and its civilian variants borders on the superhuman but whose selflessness in sharing that knowledge is sublimely human; to a couple of Great Lakes divers who never gave me their names; and to the steady friends and itinerant strangers of the flying fraternity whose tales inspired this one. Finally, to Steve Jackson, Michael Cordova, Ashley Butler, Rowena Carenen, and everyone at WildBlue Press who took a chance on this writer's late in life debut effort, a great big thank you, one and all!

For More News About Dom Stasi,
Signup For Our Newsletter:

http://wbp.bz/newsletter

Word-of-mouth is critical to an author's long-
term success. If you appreciated this book please
leave a review on the Amazon sales page:

http://wbp.bz/thestraita

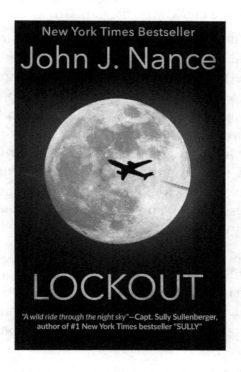

them to land - the confused pilots discover that Flight 10 is streaking back toward the hyper-volatile Middle East and there is nothing they can do about it.

With an alphabet soup of federal agencies struggling for answers and messages flying between Washington, and Tel Aviv where the flight began, the growing supposition that Flight 10 may be hijacked is fueled by the presence of a feared and hated former head of state sitting in first class, a man with an extreme Mid East agenda who may somehow be responsible for the Airbus A-330's loss of control. As frantic speculation spreads, the possibility that the unresponsive airliner could be the leading edge of a sophisticated attack on Iran designed to provoke a nuclear response drives increasingly desperate decisions.

As time and fuel runs low, flying at full throttle toward a hostile border ahead, Captain Jerry Tollefson and First Officer Dan Horneman have to put their personal animosities aside and risk everything to wrest control from the electronic ghost holding them – and perhaps the world - on a course to certain disaster.

And in the "Hole" - as the war room in Tel Aviv is called - the interim Prime Minister of Israel grapples with a horrifying choice in the balance between 300 airborne lives and the probability of nuclear war.

http://wbp.bz/lockouta

the National Transportation Safety Board's inquiry only to discover that someone is going to great lengths that include murder and kidnapping to prevent the facts from being exposed. But who? And why?

These are the questions Lindy will need to answer in order to get at the truth about what really happened to Flight 63. His task is complicated by his own personal demons, including the horrors of past airline crash investigations, as well as having to walk a diplomatic tightrope with an eccentric FBI special agent who is barely tolerating NTSB protocol, and an ambitious female NTSB investigator with eyes for Hart.

Written by a veteran airline pilot and aviation analyst, Paper Wings will keep you up in the air and on the edge of your seat in first class. You'll want to keep your belts fastened while in flight!

http://wbp.bz/paperwingsa

WILDBLUE
PRESS

Thrillers You'll Love From WildBlue Press

HARD DOG TO KILL by Craig Holt

Stan Mullens is an American mercenary in the Congo who is sent into the jungle to track and kill a former colleague. Stan discovers that his victim hasn't done anything wrong. And as he struggles to survive, he is increasingly drawn in by the man he is supposed to kill. Ultimately Stan has to choose between old loyalties and new friends.

wbp.bz/hdtka

HUNTER by James Byron Huggins

In yet another experiment to extend human life, scientists accidentally unleash a force that might well be a terrible curse. Now an infected creature is loose in the Alaskan wilderness, and the America military is forced to ask the world's greatest tracker, Nathaniel Hunter, to locate the beast and destroy it before it reaches a populated area. **wbp.bz/huntera**

16 SOULS by John Nance

On takeoff from Denver during a winter blizzard, an airliner piloted by veteran Captain Marty Mitchell overruns a commuter plane from behind. Bizarrely, the fuselage of the smaller aircraft is tenuously wedged onto the huge right wing of his Boeing 757, leading Mitchell to an impossible life-or-death choice.

wbp.bz/16soulsa

BORDERLAND by Peter Eichstaedt

When a prominent land developer is brutally murdered on the U.S.-Mexico border, it's not just another cartel killing to journalist Kyle Dawson. The dead man is his father. Dawson, a veteran war correspondent, vows to uncover the truth.

wbp.bz/borderlanda

CPSIA information can be obtained
at www.ICGtesting.com
Printed in the USA
LVHW081525021220
673222LV00043B/2120

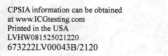